# NEVER DOUBT A VISCOUNT

## LAUREN ROYAL

August 2021 Edition
**FORMERLY TITLED "VIOLET"**

NEVER DOUBT A VISCOUNT by Lauren Royal

*Formerly titled "Violet"*
*Originally published by Penguin Putnam Inc.*

Published by Novelty Books, a division of Novelty Publishers, LLC, 205 Avenida Del Mar #275, San Clemente, CA 92674

COPYRIGHT © Lauren Royal 2002, 2012, 2017, 2021

August 2021 Edition

Cover Art Illustration by The Midnight Muse

PUBLISHER'S NOTE: This is a work of fiction. Names, characters, places, and incidents either are the product of the author's imagination or are used fictitiously. Any resemblance to actual persons, living or dead, business establishments, events, or locales is entirely coincidental.

Learn more about the author and her books at www.LaurenRoyal.com.

ISBN: 978-1-63469-154-3

# MORE CHASE FAMILY BOOKS

~

## CHASE FAMILY SERIES

*When an Earl Meets a Girl*

*How to Undress a Marquess*

*If You Dared to Love a Laird*

*A Duke's Guide to Seducing His Bride*

*Never Doubt a Viscount*

*The Scandal of Lord Randal*

*A Gentleman's Plot to Tie the Knot*

*A Secret Christmas*

*A Chase Family Christmas*

## CHASE FAMILY SERIES: THE REGENCY

*Tempt Me at Midnight*

*Tempting Juliana*

*The Art of Temptation*

*For Ken Royal*

*Mom calls you the perfect son,*
*but I think you're the perfect brother.*

*Thanks for always being there for me!*

# ONE

*England*
*July 15, 1673*

S T. SWITHIN'S DAY. Well, it was fitting.

Viscount Lakefield stared out his carriage window at the miserable, wet landscape. According to St. Swithin's legend, if it rained on the fifteenth of July, it would continue for forty days and nights. Normally not a man given to superstition, today Ford Chase found such nonsense plausible.

This was shaping up to be the worst day of his life.

The carriage rattled over the drawbridge and into the modest courtyard of Greystone, his older brother's small castle. Cold raindrops pelted Ford's head when he shoved open the door and leapt to the circular drive. Drenched gravel crunching beneath his boots, he made his way down a short, covered passageway and banged the knocker on the unassuming oak door.

Benchley cracked open the door, then slipped outside and shut it behind him. "My lord, what brings you here today?"

"I wish to speak with my brother." Ford frowned down at the small, wiry valet. What was he doing answering the door? "Will you be letting me in?"

"I think not." Benchley lifted his beak of a nose. "I'll fetch Lord Greystone." And with that, he disappeared back into the ancient castle.

Shivering, Ford stood frozen in disbelief before deciding this treatment fit in with the rest of his day. Rain dripped from his long brown hair to sprinkle on the stones at his feet. Wondering why he should need permission to enter his brother's home, he moved to reach for the latch.

The door opened, and his brother stepped out. He looked haggard, his face a pasty gray, his green eyes and black hair dull.

"Colin? What the devil's going on?"

"Illness. Measles, we think. Thank God you're here."

Ford pulled his surcoat tighter around himself. "Come again?"

"Amy is ill, along with little Hugh and the baby. And half of the servants. One of them died yesterday," Colin added grimly.

"Died?" Ford's gut twisted as he thought of Amy—Colin's beautiful, raven-haired wife—and their bright four-year-old son, Hugh, and the baby, Aidan...all dead.

"It's not so bad as all that," Colin rushed to assure him, evidently reading the concern on his face. "The poor maid was eighty if she were a day, and the disease went straight to her lungs. I'm not expecting my family to perish."

"At least you won't be getting it. If you'll remember, all four of us had it while in exile on the Continent."

"I could hardly forget." Appearing as though he could barely hold himself up, Colin leaned against the doorpost. "But what does that have to do with now?"

"At a Royal Society lecture, I learned one cannot fall ill with the same disease twice," Ford explained.

"I've had measles more than once."

"Not true measles, the one with the high fever. Spotted skin is a symptom of many different conditions."

"Trust you to know something like that." Although Colin looked relieved, his smile was bleak. "Still, the fever is savage, and Jewel has yet to suffer measles. True measles, as you put it. Will you take her from here before she succumbs as well? It would relieve my mind, and Amy's too, I'm sure. The worry is doing her recovery no good."

Alarm bells went off in Ford's head. Take his niece? Where? What would he do with a young girl? "Well, I only stopped by to let you know I've left London and will be at Lakefield for the foreseeable future—"

"Perfect."

"—working on my new watch design. I...I just wanted to be alone for a while. Lady Tabitha has eloped."

"With the rest of the family off in Scotland, I was at my wit's end deciding what to do. I was about to settle Jewel in the village. But this will be much better—"

"Tabitha *eloped*," Ford repeated, wondering why his brother hadn't reacted to this astonishing news. After all, Tabitha had just upset his entire life plan.

"She eloped?" Colin blinked, then shook his head. "Come now, Ford. What did you expect? After six years of suffering your attentions whenever you deigned to show up in London, and sharing your bed, I assume—"

She had. So what of it? No one in King Charles II's circle was virtuous. Colin hadn't been a monk before meeting his wife, and neither had their oldest brother Jason. The three Chase brothers were all titled and intimates of the king, which naturally meant they were popular with the ladies at court—and none of them had hesitated to take advantage in their day.

"—a lady," Colin continued, "would expect a proposal."

"I *told* her we'd marry someday. In two or three years." Tabitha had seemed the ideal woman for Ford—stunningly beautiful, always ready to attend a ball or an evening at court. They matched well in bed, and when they weren't together she busied herself with whatever women liked to do, leaving him plenty of time for his work. "For heaven's sake, she's only twenty-one, and I'm just twenty-eight. Jason married at thirty-two, and no one was on his back."

"I married at twenty-eight."

"*You* were in a hurry to have children."

"While I'm sure *you* would as soon do without them altogether." Colin rubbed his eyes. "You really have no idea why Tabitha gave up on you, do you? I hate to tell you this, little brother, but it's time you grew up and realized there's more to life than science and seduction. As the baby of the family, maybe Jason and I coddled you too much."

From beyond the passageway, the patter of rain filled their sudden silence. Colin was obviously weary, so Ford thought it best not to argue. Doubtless Colin had spent sleepless nights watching over his wife and sons—exactly why Ford wasn't ready for a family of his own.

"You look tired," he said. "You'd best get some rest."

His brother heaved a sigh. "I'd rest easier if I knew you had Jewel. You'll take her, won't you?"

What the devil would he do with a girl who wasn't yet six? He loved her, of course. She shared his blood. But that didn't mean he had a clue how to care for her. Bouncing her on his knee or playing a simple card game with her was one thing. A few minutes of fun before returning her to her parents. But to be responsible for a child...

He shoved a hand through his wet hair. "For how long?"

"A week or two. Maybe three. Until the illness has run its course." Colin twisted the signet ring on his finger, narrowing his gaze. "Why are you hesitating? I need you."

"I'm not hesitating," Ford protested. "I just..."

His brother's eyes opened wide. "Did you think I'd expect you to care for her on your own? Heaven forbid." His lips quirked as though he might laugh, but he coughed instead. On purpose, Ford was sure. "I'll send Lydia along with her."

Despite his annoyance at being read so easily—not to mention distrusted—the tension left Ford's shoulders. With

Lydia, Jewel's very competent nurse, on the premises, he wouldn't have to care for the girl, wouldn't have to struggle to interpret her mystifying female language and needs. He could just poke his head into her room and say hello every once in a while.

"You won't have to do a thing," Colin added, his tight expression easing into a wry half-smile. "You might try talking with your niece, though. It's time you learned to communicate with the lesser species. You know, those of us of insufficient age or intelligence to grasp the deepest secrets of the universe."

"I don't—"

"Maybe *that* was your problem with Tabitha."

Ford gritted his teeth. He'd never fooled himself into thinking he understood the opposite sex. His science was what drove him. But he'd had no problems with Tabitha, and he was finished with this discussion.

"Of course I'll take Jewel," he said, consciously relaxing his jaw. "Bring her out—I'll be waiting in my carriage."

# TWO

"*L*ISTEN TO THIS." Sitting with her two sisters while their mother worked nearby, Violet Ashcroft cleared her throat. "'To say that a blind custom of obedience should be a surer obligation than duty taught and understood...is to affirm that a blind man may tread surer by a guide than a seeing man by a light.'"

"What is that supposed to mean?" her youngest sister, Lily, asked. Busily stitching her tapestry in the grayish light from the large picture window, Lily probably had little real desire to know what the quote meant. But she was unfailingly kind, and Violet would never turn away from anyone willing to listen.

She hitched herself forward on the green brocade chair. "Well, now—"

"Why do you care?" their middle sister, Rose, interrupted. Rose cared little for anything that didn't have to do with dancing, clothes, or men. Looking up from the vase of flowers she was arranging, she tossed her gleaming ringlets. "It's nothing but a bunch of gibberish, if you ask me."

"Nobody asked." Violet pointedly looked to Lily. "Did you hear anyone ask?"

"Girls." Clucking her tongue, their mother poured a

dipperful of water into the kettle over the fire. "I used to comfort myself that when you all grew up, this bickering would cease. Yet it never has."

Lily's blue eyes were all innocence, despite having reached the advanced age of sixteen. "But Mum," she said sweetly. Their mother's proper name was Chrystabel, but as their flower-obsessed father called her Chrysanthemum, they'd taken to calling her Mum. "It's loving bickering."

"And a bad example for your young brother." With a sigh, Mum resumed plucking petals from a bunch of lush pink roses. "What *does* it mean?" she asked Violet. "And who said it?"

"It means we should understand why we are doing things instead of blindly following orders. Rather like our Ashcroft family motto: *Interroga Conformationem*, Question Convention. But said much more eloquently, don't you think? By Francis Bacon."

Violet snapped the book closed, its title, *Advancement of Learning*, winking gold from the spine in her lap. "But I'm wondering," she teased. "When did *my* Mum become interested in philosophy?"

"I'm interested in all my children's hobbies."

"Philosophy is more than a hobby," Violet protested. "It's a way of looking at life."

"Of course it is." The kettle was bubbling merrily, spewing steam into the dim room. The fire and a few candles were no match for this gloomy, rainy afternoon. "Will you come and hold this for me, dear?"

Violet set down the book and wandered over to the large, utilitarian table she always thought looked somewhat out of place in what used to be a formal drawing room. "Did Father cut more roses for you this morning?"

"Doesn't he always?" Mum's musical laughter warmed Violet to her toes. "Sweet man, he is, rising early to gather them between dawn and sunrise, when their scent is at its peak."

Violet's laughter joined her mother's. "Insane man, you

mean." *Sweet* wasn't a word she'd use to describe the Earl of Trentingham—*eccentric* fit her father much better. But her parents both seemed to be blind where the other's oddities were concerned.

Not that that was a bad thing. For certain, if Violet were ever to wed—an event she considered unlikely indeed—her husband would have to be more than a little bit blind. She didn't have rich chestnut hair like her sisters—hers was a blander, lighter brown. And her eyes were plain brown as well, not the mysterious almost-black of Rose's or the fathomless deep-blue of Lily's. Just brown.

Average, she decided. Neither fat nor thin. Not tall like Rose nor petite like Lily, but medium height. Average.

But, happily, she didn't mind being average. Because average was rarely noticed, and the truth was, she'd never liked being the center of attention.

Rose thrived on it, though. "Let me help, Mum," she squealed, dropping the stem of blue sweet peas she'd been about to add to her floral arrangement. "Violet probably won't get the top on straight."

Tactless, at best, but at seventeen, Rose still had some time to grow up. With an indulgent sigh, Violet stuck a wooden block upright in the big bowl. She held it in place while her mother sprinkled in all the rose petals, then turned to lift the kettle.

In a slow, careful stream, Mum poured just enough water over the fragrant flowers to cover them. Quickly Rose popped another, larger bowl upside down on top of the wooden block, using it as a pedestal. The steam would collect beneath and drip down the edges to the tray below. As it cooled, it would separate into rosewater and essential rose oil.

Distillation, Mum called it.

A rich, floral scent wafted up, and Violet inhaled deeply. As hobbies went, she did appreciate her mother's unusual one of perfume-making.

"Thank you, girls," Mum said when Violet released the bowl. "Would you hand me that vial of lavender essence?"

Violet turned and squinted at the labels, then reached for the proper glass tube. "I read in the news sheet this morning that Christopher Wren is going to be knighted later this year. And he was just elected to the Council of the Royal Society."

Mum took the vial. "That odd group of scientists?"

Violet smiled inside, thinking Chrystabel Ashcroft a bit odd herself. "There are philosophers as members, too. And statesmen and physicians. I'd love to hear one of their lectures someday."

"The Royal Society doesn't allow women at their meetings." Mum pulled the cork stopper and waved the lavender under her nose. "Besides, most of the men are married."

"I don't want them to court me, Mum." On the whole, she didn't want anyone to court her, much to her mother's distress. "I only wish to cudgel their brains."

Frowning, Mum lowered a dropper into the vial. "Cudgel their—"

"Talk to them, I mean. Share some ideas. They're so brilliant."

"Men aren't interested in *talking* to women," Rose told her, "and the sooner you learn that, the sooner you'll find one of your own."

"Faith, Rose. I'm only twenty. You'd think I was in my dotage, the way you've become set on marrying me off."

"You're expected to wed before I do."

The words were uttered so innocently, Violet couldn't find it in her to hold a grudge. Of course Rose wanted to marry, and convention dictated the girls wed in order.

But Violet was nothing if not realistic. She knew her plain looks, together with her unusual interests, were likely to make it difficult—if not impossible—for her to find a compatible husband. But that didn't really bother her, and she would never want her own dim prospects to keep her lovely sisters from finding happiness.

Besides, when had the Ashcrofts been conventional? They could marry in any order they chose. Or in her case, not at all.

She watched her mother add three drops of lavender to the bottle of fragrance she was creating, then swirl it carefully.

"Is that a new blend?" Violet asked.

"For Lady Cunningham." Mum sniffed deeply and passed the bottle to her oldest daughter. "What do you think?"

Violet smelled it and considered. "Too sweet. Lady Cunningham is anything but sweet." The woman's voice could curdle milk. Violet handed back the mixture, hunting for the vial of petitgrain she knew would soften it.

Nodding approvingly, her mother added two drops, then made a note on the little recipe card she kept for each of her friends.

"Look," Lily said, her embroidery forgotten. She rose and settled herself in the large, green-padded window seat. "There's a carriage about to pass by."

Mum and Rose hurried to join her at window, while Violet returned to her chair and opened her book. "So?"

"So..." Lily brushed her fingers over one of the flower arrangements that Rose left all over the house, sending a burst of scent into the air. "We get so little traffic here, I'm just wondering who it might be."

"The three of you are too curious for your own good." Violet flipped a page, hoping to find another sage insight. Not that she'd bother sharing it this time.

"It's our occasional neighbor," her mother said. "The viscount."

Violet's attention strayed from Bacon's brilliance. "How do you know?"

"I recognize his carriage. A hand-me-down from his brother, the marquess."

"How is it you know everyone's business?" Violet wondered aloud.

"It's not so very difficult, my dear. One need only take an

interest, open her eyes and ears, and use her head. I believe the viscount is in tight straits. Not only because of the second-hand carriage, but heavens, the state of his gardens. Your father nearly chokes every time we ride past."

"I'm surprised Father hasn't made his way over to set the garden to rights," Lily said.

"Don't think he hasn't considered it." Mum leaned her palms on the windowsill, studying the passing coach. "Why, I do believe Lord Lakefield isn't alone."

Despite herself, Violet rose, one finger holding her place in the book. "And how do you know that?"

"The vehicle's curtains aren't drawn." Mum gave a happy gasp of discovery. "There's a child inside! And a woman!"

Her interest finally piqued, Violet wandered to the window to see, but of course the carriage was only a blur.

Everything more than a few feet from Violet's eyes always looked like a blur. It was the reason she preferred staying at home with her books and news sheets, rather than going about to socialize with her mother and two younger sisters. She was afraid she'd embarrass herself by failing to recognize a friend across the room.

"Well, well, well," Mum said. "I must take the lady a gift of perfume and welcome her to the neighborhood."

"You mean find out who she is," Violet said.

Her mother's second hobby was delivering perfume and receiving gossip in exchange. Not that anyone begrudged her the information. To the contrary, Chrystabel Ashcroft never needed to pry a word out of anyone. Warm and well-loved, she barely walked in the door before women began spilling their secrets.

On the rare occasions her mother had succeeded in dragging her along, Violet had seen it happen, her bad eyes notwithstanding.

"I wonder if the viscount has married?" Rose asked.

"I expect not," Mum said. "He's much too intellectual for anyone I know." As the carriage disappeared into the distance, she turned from the window. "Why, he's a member of that Royal Society, isn't he?"

"I believe so." Violet watched her mother wander back to the table, wishing she'd never mentioned wanting to attend a Royal Society lecture. The last thing she needed was Mum plotting her marriage. "Perhaps he would suit Rose or Lily."

"I think not." Mum sniffed the perfume in progress, then chose another vial. "I cannot imagine whom he would suit, but certainly not your sisters."

"It's just as well," Rose said, "since you know we three have a pact to save one another from your matchmaking schemes."

It was one thing—perhaps the only thing—the sisters agreed on.

"Heavens, girls. It's not as though I arrange marriages behind the backs of my friends." *Everyone* Mum knew was her friend. Literally. And they all adored her. "All of my brides and grooms are willing—"

"Victims?" Violet broke in to supply.

"Participants," Mum countered.

Lily sat and retrieved her handiwork. "How many weddings have you arranged this year, Mum? Three? Four?"

"Five," their mother said with not a little pride. She tapped her fingernails on the vial. "Only seven months in, and a banner year already. But none, I assure you, against the participants' will."

Rose plopped back onto her own chair. "You're not matching me up, Mum. I can find my own husband."

"Me, too," Lily said.

"Me three," Violet added.

"Of course you all can." Mum's graceful fingers stilled. "I wouldn't dream of meddling in my own daughters' lives."

# THREE

"**N**URSE LYDIA SAID if it rains today, it will rain for forty days more." In the dim cabin of the carriage, Jewel cocked her raven head. "Do you believe that, Uncle Ford?"

"Of course not. It has no scientific basis in fact."

"I know a poem about it, though."

"Do you, now?"

A smile gracing her heart-shaped face, Jewel nodded. "Nurse Lydia taught it to me last year. And I still remember."

Ford threw a glance at the woman sitting across from them, but she was leaning against the window, sound asleep. "Will you quote it for me, then?" he asked Jewel.

She cleared her little throat.

> *"St. Swithin's Day if thou dost rain*
> *For forty days it will remain*
> *St. Swithin's Day if thou be fair*
> *For forty days 'twill rain nae mair."*

"That sounds more like something your Aunt Caithren would have taught you," Ford observed, thinking of his brother

Jason's pretty Scottish wife with all her stories, superstitions, and verses.

"Maybe she did." Jewel turned to her caregiver. "Nurse Lydia, did you teach me the poem, or did Aunty Cait?" When Lydia didn't answer, the girl rose and reached across to poke her shoulder. "Nurse Lydia?" A frown creasing her forehead, Jewel sat down and looked at Ford. "She's sleeping."

"I can see that." Frowning himself, he put a finger to his lips. "Perhaps we should be quieter, then."

His niece surprised him by obediently settling back. He smiled. Maybe having her stay with him wouldn't be as bad as he'd thought. She was adorable, after all. Most females were adorable. And on the whole, he adored them.

But they were baffling. He was really better off without them, he decided, thinking of Tabitha's abrupt change of heart.

Rain pounded on the roof and streamed down the windows, an oddly comforting tattoo. Lulled by sound and motion, Ford's lids slid closed—then flew open when the carriage bumped into a rut. The nurse pitched forward, and he leapt to set her aright.

He jerked his hands away. She was burning up.

Her eyes opened, looking glazed, the pupils huge black voids.

"Nurse Lydia?" Ford raked his fingers back through his hair, his mind racing. If she was ill, what the devil would he do with Jewel? The nurse *couldn't* be ill. "Are you feeling unwell?"

"Hot," she mumbled. "Tired." Her eyes shut again.

Bloody hell, she *was* ill. An all too fitting development for an all too dastardly day.

He had to get Jewel away from her.

Trying not to panic, he reached to shake the woman awake. "Where are you from?"

She blinked, swayed, then managed to hold herself up by planting both hands on the bench seat. "G-Greystone, my lord."

"No, before that. Have you family, miss? Parents? Brothers or sisters?"

"Mama," she murmured. "In Woodlands Green." A soft, prolonged snore followed, nearly drowned out by the relentless rain.

She hadn't gone far from home to find employment, then— Woodlands Green wasn't more than half an hour south. Ford knocked on the roof, barely pausing for the carriage to stop before throwing open the door.

Without waiting for the steps to be lowered, he lifted Jewel and jumped down.

She let out a little squeal. "What are you doing, Uncle Ford?"

"Lakefield isn't far." He balanced her on a hip. "We're going to walk from here."

"In the rain? Mama says not to get cold and wet. You could fall ill." Her little forehead furrowed. "We could get measles."

"Staying with Nurse Lydia could give you measles. Besides, it's not cold. It's summer." Never mind that Jewel's teeth were chattering. Surprised to find himself feeling protective, he held her closer. "Can you tell me Nurse Lydia's surname?"

"Her what?"

"The part of her name that comes after Lydia." Huge drops splotched his brown surcoat and dripped from the brim of his hat. He shifted the girl on his hip. "Like in your name, Chase comes after Jewel."

She only cocked her small head, which was rapidly becoming soaked.

Taking a deep breath for patience, he tried again. "Your name is Jewel Chase. Nurse Lydia's name is...?"

"Nurse Lydia. Two names, just like mine."

He rolled his eyes heavenward before looking to his coachman. "Spalding, take the nursemaid to Woodlands Green and find her mother." Woodlands Green was tiny—even without a surname, it probably wasn't an onerous request. "Lady Jewel and I have decided to walk home in this fine weather."

Setting his niece on her feet—where she promptly slipped in the mud—he wondered if things could get any worse.

# FOUR

*G*ENERALLY, FORD didn't mind sleeping with females. But this one had wiggled the entire night. When not snuggled up against him, she'd been smacking him with an outflung arm. Her little toenails had left scratches in the vicinity of his knees.

"Hey!" he growled as she managed to elbow him in the ribs for the dozenth time. He wondered what tool she used to hone the bone to such a point. "Lie still."

He heard a whimper and suppressed a groan. Not the tears again!

Tears were what had landed Jewel in his bed in the first place. He'd breathed a sigh of relief after tucking her in last night, only to find himself awakened by her heartfelt sobs.

No wonder he'd decided to swear off women.

Of course, he couldn't blame the girl. Between her hiccups and gulps, he'd gathered that last night had been the first she'd ever spent away from her parents or nursemaid. But if he'd had any doubts he wasn't ready for marriage and fatherhood, they were gone now.

When she sniffled, he turned his head to see her heart-shaped face snuggled on the pillow beside him, her rosy cheeks damp with tears. More tears threatened to spill from her emerald eyes.

He pushed the shiny black hair off her face and felt her forehead. No fever, for which he was insanely thankful. Illness was the last thing either of them needed.

"Ah, Jewel, baby. Come on. It's morning, can you see?" He waved a hand toward the window, where yellow light shone through spaces between the crooked shutters. One more thing on his repair list.

At least the rain had stopped. So much for St. Swithin's prophecy.

"We'll have a pleasant day, you'll see." He'd send a message to his brother, informing him Jewel's nurse had come down with the measles. Colin would send a replacement. Someone who knew the girl. Someone who knew what to do.

*Did you think I'd expect you to care for her on your own? Heaven forbid.*

No. Damned if he'd give his brother the satisfaction of seeing he was right not to trust him with his precious daughter. Somehow he and Jewel would manage. And next time, Ford's family wouldn't underestimate his abilities.

He turned back to her sad little face. "Come on, baby."

"I'm not a baby."

"Of course you're not." He hadn't consciously used the endearment; it had simply slipped out of his mouth. "If you stop crying, I'll give you a shilling."

That did the trick. The tears ended, and she struggled to sit in his rumpled bed, apparently more clever than he'd given her credit for.

Thank heavens. A girl bright enough to be reasoned with. Never mind that his estate was in sad shape and he could ill afford to throw around bribes—he'd give Jewel his entire meager savings if it would ensure her cooperation for the days they'd be together.

He stared at the canopy above him, wondering when his

blue bed-hangings had faded to gray. And if the old ropes that supported the mattress would hold, since his niece was jumping up and down on it now, giving him an instant headache.

"A shilling," she chanted in a sing-song voice, timing her words to her bounces. "A shilling. Will you take me shopping?" she asked breathlessly.

Not yet six years old and already eager to shop, he thought with an inward smile. Where did females learn this behavior? Was it in their chemical composition? "There aren't any shops nearby, but if you're good, after breakfast I'll show you my sundial."

She bounced once again to land on her bottom, then sat there in her twisted white nightgown, looking dubious.

"And later this week, I'll take you to the village."

"To shop?"

"Yes, to shop." The way things were going, she ought to have amassed a small fortune by then. He rolled over and swung his legs off the side of the bed, rubbing his face.

"Gads, Uncle Ford! I can see your knees!"

Blinking, he cast a glance over his shoulder. "Have you not seen your father's knees? And your brothers'?"

"Yes." She giggled. "But they're my family."

"I'm your uncle, which is family, too." He stood, grateful the shirt he was wearing covered him to midthigh, wondering if he should have left his breeches on as well. It had been years since he'd worn anything to sleep, but he supposed, for her sake, he'd have to keep himself clothed while she was here.

He held little hope that she'd stay in her own bed at night, so he'd best steel himself for more long hours of nocturnal pummeling.

What had he done to deserve this?

As the youngest of four, he'd never had to deal with children before, save as a loving uncle who bestowed the occasional coin or pat on the head. Whatever compelled people to desire these strange creatures—and the responsibility that went with them—was beyond him.

His clocks struck noon before he managed to coax some breakfast into her and get her dressed in a little pink confection of a gown whose fastenings he found confusing. He was itching to work on his watch design, but she hadn't forgotten about the sundial.

Would that he had such a memory.

Although St. Swithin's clouds and rain would have better matched his mood, the day was warm and sunny when they finally stepped outdoors. A fluffy white rabbit blinked at Jewel, then took off toward the Thames. She bounded after it, but Ford followed more slowly, feeling the effects of the sleepless night.

He would have to hire some servants. Although he'd been granted Lakefield House twelve years ago, shortly after King Charles's restoration, he'd never really lived here. Naturally he'd visited on occasion, but the sheer work involved in renovating the manor house had always seemed overwhelming. So he'd lived in the family's London town house, or at Cainewood Castle with his older brother Jason, the Marquess of Cainewood, and poured what income the estate produced into his scientific pursuits. He'd known that someday he would fix up the place, most likely when he decided to marry. But "someday" always seemed far, far in the future.

He hadn't left Lakefield unoccupied, of course, but the elderly couple who cared for the house—and cooked for him on the rare occasions he was in residence—was no match for a six-year-old's energy. If he wanted help, he was going to have to hire it. Perhaps the "shopping" trip to the village would come sooner rather than later. He could shop for a nursemaid and household help while Jewel shopped for whatever little girls bought with their shillings. Ribbons, he imagined, already dreading the daunting task of fixing her hair.

"Uncle Ford! Where is it?"

He looked up, noticing Jewel had wandered back while he

wasn't watching. He hadn't been watching at all, as a matter of fact. She could have fallen into the river.

He heaved an internal sigh. He would have to be more vigilant.

"Have you lost the rabbit?" he asked.

"No." She giggled. "Well, yes, but I meant the sundial. I cannot find it."

Damnation, where had it gone to?

He paced the garden, shocked to find it totally overgrown, although by all appearances it must have been that way for years. Green and wild, plants and vines intertwined with weeds, all semblance of order gone. Jewel ran after him, her short legs no match for his long strides. The sundial had been in the middle of a neat circle of hedges and wooden benches…

"Here it is." He pushed his way through a ring of bushes that seemed to have grown together. His niece followed. The benches he'd remembered were covered with vines. In the center of the mess, he yanked at some greenery and brushed dirt off the carved stone surface of the sundial. "Under here."

She beamed up at him as though he were a genius, melting his heart. "How does it work, Uncle Ford?"

He lifted her into his arms, remembering why he loved women. But from now on, he'd be sticking to ones under six. "Well, you see—"

"Good afternoon, my lord."

A warm, melodic voice. He turned and frowned at its owner, who had followed them into the hedge circle. Although he had a feeling the comely, middle-aged matron wasn't quite a stranger, he couldn't for the life of him place her.

She plucked two stray twigs off her bright yellow skirts, then raised a groomed brow. "So nice to have you in residence. Trentingham Manor can seem lonely when all our neighbors are away in the City."

Mystery solved. Trentingham. As in *Earl of*. The neighboring estate.

His niece still in his arms, Ford executed an awkward bow. "Pleased to be here, Lady Trentingham."

When her wide mouth curved up, her brown eyes smiled to match. Plainly curious, her gaze flicked to Jewel before focusing again on him. "Will you be staying long?"

"Just while I finish a project." And until he felt up to facing his family and friends. He set Jewel on her feet and leaned a hand against the sundial, grimacing at the crusted dirt.

The countess shot a glance down the side of the house—he noticed the paint was peeling—to where her carriage waited, a coachman sitting up top. The door was open, and someone waited inside as well, enjoying the sunny day. A lady's maid, if he could judge by the woman's starched white cap.

"Pretty lady," Jewel said, staring up at his neighbor.

"Why, thank you, Miss…"

"Jewel," the girl supplied.

"Lady Jewel," Ford clarified. "My brother's daughter. I'm looking after her while her family recovers from measles."

"Ah," Lady Trentingham murmured. Some of the confusion cleared from her face. "I'm glad of your acquaintance," she said with a graceful curtsy, for all the world like they were meeting in Whitehall Palace.

Jewel mimicked the motion. "I'm glad of your ac-ac—"

"Acquaintance," Ford said helpfully.

But apparently Jewel didn't take it that way. She fixed him with a malevolent green glare. "I can say it."

"Of course you can." Palms forward, he took a small step back. "Forgive me, will you?"

"All right." She turned to the woman, focusing on something in her hand. "What's that?"

"Don't point, baby," Ford said. His twin sister might routinely accuse him of being oblivious, but he did know his manners.

Lady Trentingham knelt by Jewel's side. "It's a bottle of

perfume. I brought it for the lady of the house. And I suppose"—
she looked to Ford for confirmation—"that's you?"

He nodded his agreement as Jewel squealed. "For me?"

"For you, young lady. Would you like to smell it?"

"Oh, yes," his niece breathed. She waited, dancing from foot
to foot while the woman removed the stopper and handed her
the bottle.

Jewel waved it under her nose. "It's lovely, my lady!"
Tipping the bottle, she wet her fingers and dabbed the potion on
her neck, wetting some of the overgrown greenery in the
process.

"You must use only a little," Lady Trentingham warned her,
"or you'll smell like a field of flowers."

"I like flowers."

"Then you must come and visit Trentingham Manor." She
rose to her feet, smiling at Ford. "My husband enjoys
gardening."

"I've heard that of the earl." Everyone had heard that of the
earl. And standing in his own shambles of a garden, knowing
what Lady Trentingham and her husband must think every time
they saw it, made Ford want to squirm.

"Who is caring for Lady Jewel?" the countess asked.

"I am, now. Her nursemaid fell ill, so I sent her home."

"Alone?"

"No, with my coachman and two outriders."

Amusement flickered on her face. "I meant, are you caring
for Lady Jewel on your own?"

"Oh." Feeling thickheaded, he cleared his throat. "I suppose
I am."

"And how are you getting along?"

His neighbor had a straightforward way about her that
Ford found refreshing. Lord knew Lady Tabitha hadn't
been so.

"Well, I've had Jewel for…" He twisted around to see the
sundial. "…it's going on eighteen hours. And no disaster has

befallen her yet, so although I haven't managed to find time for anything else, I reckon I'm doing all right."

Lady Trentingham's laughter tinkled through the riotous vegetation. Her gaze turned contemplative. "I have a son."

"Yes?" he prompted, feeling more thickheaded still.

"Rowan. He's seven years of age. A bit older than Lady Jewel, but his favorite playmate is away from home for the month—perhaps I'll bring him over to play. That might give you a bit of a respite."

"A *boy*?" Jewel interjected.

"A kind one," the woman assured her. "He doesn't have maggots."

Jewel looked dubious. But she also looked lonely. And as far as Ford was concerned, Lady Trentingham could be his savior. An angel sent from heaven. A fairy come to wave her wand and sprinkle magic dust.

Her miraculous solution to his problem was almost enough to make him believe in such ludicrous things.

"I shall bring Rowan tomorrow," she decided. "He has lessons in the morning, but perhaps after dinner."

"He's welcome for dinner," Ford offered. Breakfast and supper, too. Anything to keep his niece occupied so he could work on his watch. He was sure his new design had promise, if only he could find the time to test his ideas.

He must have looked as desperate as he felt, because his neighbor released a tiny, unladylike snort.

"After dinner," she confirmed, hiding a smile as she pushed through the bushes and made her way back to her carriage.

∼

"*H*OW DID IT GO, milady?" Anne asked Chrystabel as she climbed inside.

"Fine," she assured her maid.

*Perfect*, she added silently.

Now she just had to make plans to keep both Rose and Lily busy tomorrow. As well as herself. Violet—her wonderful, willful, bookish daughter Violet—would be the one to take Rowan to visit Lady Jewel.

Picking dead vegetation off her skirts, Chrystabel smiled. She'd met Ford Chase before, but this visit had confirmed it. If ever a perfect man existed for Violet, it was the charming, slightly preoccupied but brilliant Lord Lakefield. These two needed each other.

Her daughters were dead set against her arranging their marriages, and well Chrystabel knew it.

But a resourceful mother could always find a way.

## FIVE

"**P**LEASE WAIT,** Margaret," Violet told her lady's maid the next afternoon. "If all goes well, I'm going to leave Rowan here and come back for him later."

She stepped down from the carriage and grumbled all the way to the front door of the large, if somewhat shabby, Lakefield House. She couldn't fathom how she'd ended up here, escorting her reluctant young brother to play with a strange little girl.

Mum's convoluted explanation had made sense at the time, but how was it that suddenly Rose and Lily both needed to be measured for gowns, and she didn't? True, she hadn't been clamoring for new clothes like they had—she'd never really cared about such things—but Mum had always been careful to treat her three girls evenly.

At the bottom of the chipped stone stairs that led to the entry, she pulled Rowan out of the bushes where he was hiding. He promptly scurried to hide behind *her* instead. With a sigh, she mounted the steps and raised the knocker.

Before she had a chance to bang it down, the door swung open, and she stumbled forward and nearly fell into the house. She was saved from that indignity when a man's hands clasped her shoulders. Warm hands, keeping her upright.

He held on to her a bit longer than necessary before pulling away. Impertinent, this footman, but she was only inches from his face, and oh my, he was handsome up close. She'd rarely seen a man up close—close enough to clearly *see* with her poor vision—and this one looked divine. She felt herself sinking into brilliant blue eyes.

"I—I'm—" Backing away a little, she cleared her throat and tried again. "I'm here to see Lord Lakefield—"

"At your service." He bowed. "Ford Chase," he added in a deep voice. The sound of it made butterflies dance in her middle. "And you are...?"

*This* was the viscount?

He couldn't be. "You're not wearing a periwig," she said nonsensically.

"Pardon?" He blinked. "None of the men in my family ever wear wigs."

It was true her father often went wigless out here in the countryside, but ever? Although, come to think of it, this man wasn't wearing a footman's livery either. The last time she'd seen him, she'd been a girl of only fifteen, and all she'd really remembered was long, untidy brown hair and a harried expression.

He looked rather harried today, too. He raked his fingers through his still-long hair, but it didn't seem to help.

And those eyes. She hadn't noticed his eyes all those years ago...well, she'd probably never been close enough to properly see them. Aristotle had said that beauty was the gift of God. She wondered what this man could have done to be so deserving of the Lord's favor.

"And you are...?" he repeated.

She shook her head to clear it. "Violet Ashcroft."

"The Earl of Trentingham's daughter?" He looked somewhat perplexed. "I expected your mother."

"Well, you have *me*." She was regaining her equilibrium. She was, after all, a very levelheaded woman. "And this is my brother, Rowan, who has come to claim the pleasure of meeting young Lady Jewel."

*The pleasure of meeting young Lady Jewel?* Why was she babbling like a featherbrained courtier? She drew a deep breath and pulled her brother from behind her skirts.

"Pleased to meet you, young man." The viscount gave him a proper, grave nod.

Much more stoically than normal, Rowan bowed.

"Uncle Ford!" A little girl came bounding up to the door, skidding to a stop on the dull wood floor. "Who is here?" The moment her gaze fastened on Rowan, Violet knew he was in trouble. "You must be that boy the pretty lady told me about." She glanced up at her uncle, appearing both surprised and pleased. "He looks like *me!* I like him!"

While it was true Rowan was a handsome lad and shared Jewel's coloring—jet-black hair and deep green eyes—the girl's enthusiasm was enough to send him skittering behind Violet again.

Following him, Jewel poked him on the shoulder. "What're you hiding for, huh? Don't you want to play?"

"No," Rowan muttered. His fingers clawed at Violet's skirts. Sensing his panic, she figured it would be only a matter of seconds before he found his way underneath.

Lord Lakefield also looked panicked, though she couldn't fathom why. "Do come in," he urged, grabbing Violet quite improperly by the arm. Before the door shut behind her, she shot a helpless look back at the blur that was her maid Margaret in the carriage.

She hadn't intended to go inside.

But here she was. Still gripping her arm, the viscount fairly pulled her down a hallway whose paneling was so worn that even with her bad eyes she could tell it needed refinishing. Behind her, Rowan held on like a drowning man clutching a life preserver. He was literally dragging his heels.

Evidently undeterred, Jewel chattered cheerfully as she

walked along beside him. "How old are you? Your mother said you were seven. Are you seven? I'm almost six. When's your birthday? Mine's next week. Mama said we would have a cele-bration. But now she's ill."

"I'm sorry to hear that," Violet said to Jewel, since it was clear Rowan wouldn't. Her heels clicked on the wood-planked floor. She could feel the warmth of the viscount's fingers through her indigo broadcloth sleeve.

"Papa promised me she'd get well," Jewel said. "And he always keeps his promises."

They turned into a drawing room decorated in various shades of red and pink. Or perhaps they'd once all been matching crimson, but some pieces had faded.

Lord Lakefield dropped Violet's arm and waved her toward a couch. She pried Rowan's hands from her skirts in order to sit, and he dropped cross-legged to the floor, his gaze on his lap.

What were they doing here? Violet wondered. Rowan was clearly miserable, and she hadn't planned on staying in the first place.

"Make yourself comfortable," Lord Lakefield told her. "I'll go ask for some refreshments. I rigged up a bell"—he gestured toward the wall where she assumed it was placed—"but I'm afraid my staff is getting on in years. They're a bit hard of hearing."

Dazed, Violet nodded. "So is my father."

"Pardon?"

"He's half deaf. Although my sister sometimes claims he just doesn't want to listen to whatever philosophy I'm spouting at the moment."

Egad, she was babbling more than Jewel.

"Philosophy?" He blinked, or maybe he grimaced. She wasn't close enough to tell which. "I'm certain whatever you have to say must be fascinating. If you'll excuse me." And with that, he took his long, lanky form out the door.

She rose and wandered over to see where he'd pointed. A

pull cord disappeared cleverly into a hole, attached, she assumed, to a bell. Her ears were still ringing with his words.

"Fascinating..." she murmured to no one in particular. Apparently the man was trying to flatter her. No man ever thought a woman discussing philosophy was fascinating.

"Well," she said aloud, glad she had the common sense to recognize an empty compliment, "Jean de La Fontaine has written that all flatterers live at the expense of those who listen to them."

Jewel blinked. "Huh?" She blinked again, then knelt on the floor next to Rowan. "Do you think I'm pretty?" she asked.

# SIX

*F*ORD HURRIED to the kitchen, not least because he had a feeling Violet Ashcroft was poised to bolt. And he couldn't allow that to happen.

Philosophy. Truth be told, he abhorred the subject—he wasn't drawn to anything that couldn't be proven. But it seemed the woman might have a keen brain in her head, which was uncommon, in his experience. He'd always gravitated toward the fun and frilly in female companionship—he depended on male colleagues for intellectual stimulation. When it came to women, he was looking for diversion, not meaningful conversation.

Lady Tabitha had been quite a gorgeous diversion. Yet not particularly useful, and he'd decided practicality would dictate his interest in women from now on. Hilda, for instance—his housekeeper—was a useful woman to have around.

And as for Lady Violet...

With her shiny light brown hair and eyes the color of his favorite brandy, Violet was pleasant looking, although not the sort of beauty who would turn men's heads. Which was fine with him, since the last thing he wanted was his head turned. He wanted it right here, thank you, square on his shoulders, where he could use it to concentrate on his experiments and inventions.

He'd sworn off women in a romantic sense, but if he could convince this Violet to stay a while—and maybe even come back with Rowan tomorrow—perhaps he could finally find time for his work.

Now, *that* was his idea of a useful female.

As he barged into the kitchen, his housekeeper looked up from polishing the silver, one gray eyebrow raised in query. "Yes, my lord?"

"Are the refreshments ready?"

Hilda never answered a question—she always had one of her own. "Is Lady Trentingham here?"

"No," he said, wondering where Harry, Hilda's husband, had gone off to this time. The two of them might be servants, but their marriage mimicked most of the aristocracy's—which was to say they stayed as far from each other as possible.

"Lady Trentingham is at home," he told her. "The woman's daughter came instead. Lady Violet Ashcroft."

"The practical one?"

"Come again?" Spotting a tray of biscuits on the kitchen's scarred wooden worktable, he inched his way over.

"The oldest, yes? Lady Trentingham calls her 'the practical one.' The middle girl—Rose, I believe—is 'the wild one,' and the youngest, dear Lily, 'the sweet one.'"

"She has three daughters? All named for bloody flowers?" What sentimental frivolity.

"Are you not aware that her husband enjoys gardening?"

"Yes. I am." He slid one of the small, round biscuits off the tray and popped it into his mouth. "How do you come to know all this?"

Hilda frowned. "Why shouldn't I know my neighbors?" She shoved at the gray hair that had escaped her cap, then went back to polishing the silver. "Lady Trentingham, she's a perfumer, you know. Every once in a while, she drops by with a new bottle. Spiced Rosewater, I prefer."

"Spiced Rosewater?" He reached for another biscuit.

She slapped at his hand. "Leave it, will you? I laid them out in a pattern."

He scrutinized the tray, but his mathematical mind could discern no regular design.

"Do you not like Spiced Rosewater?" she asked.

He leaned close to a wrinkled cheek and sniffed. "It's lovely." In truth, she smelled like a cinnamon bun. But whatever made her happy.

"When Lady Trentingham brings it by, she likes to sit a spell and chat. I've heard all the stories of her girls as they've grown."

"Lady Trentingham sits and talks to the household help?" Now he was the one asking questions.

"And why not? We're people too, you know."

Of course they were—he just didn't think about it much. And he was woefully ill informed about his neighbors. Apparently Lady Trentingham was well-nigh as eccentric as the earl.

"Here comes Harry," Hilda said, watching out the window. "Don't you think it's time to serve these refreshments?" She shoved a steaming pitcher into Ford's hands and, taking the tray of biscuits, hurried out of the kitchen before her husband could make his way in.

Hilda came up to Ford's shoulder and seemed as wide as she was tall. Obediently carrying the hot beverage she'd prepared, he followed her ample behind down the corridor to the drawing room. They stepped inside to see Violet Ashcroft on her hands and knees, her backside jutting into the air.

A very nice backside, Ford observed, most especially compared to his housekeeper's. He could tell that, even through her layers of petticoats and sturdy, serviceable skirts. Which weren't frilly in the least. It was a fitting gown for The Practical One.

Her brother was under the low, square table that sat before the couch. "Rowan," she said. "You come out here this minute."

"No." The boy crossed his arms, not a simple feat given he was lying on his belly. "Not until *she* leaves."

Rowan pronounced *she* much like Jewel had pronounced *boy* yesterday in the garden.

"C'mon, Rowan," Jewel cooed, getting down on her knees herself. "Come out and play. I've always wanted to play with a boy."

Considering Jewel had two brothers at home, Ford had to choke back laughter. And she wasn't pronouncing *boy* that way now.

His niece was clearly in love.

And Rowan was having none of it.

"We've brought biscuits," Ford declared, announcing his presence. Lady Violet gave a little embarrassed squeal and jumped to her feet. Her pinkened cheeks matched his faded upholstery.

"Biscuits?" Rowan asked. "What kind?"

The way to a Chase male's heart was through his stomach, and Ford was gratified to see Rowan was no different. "Cinnamon," he said.

"I'm still not coming out," Rowan said.

"Would you like a drink of chocolate?" Hilda coaxed, taking the warm pitcher from Ford's hands.

"Chocolate?" The boy inched forward. "Real chocolate?"

"He cannot have it," his sister said firmly. "Chocolate gives him hives."

Rowan crawled closer and bumped his head on the apron of the table. "Ah, Violet…"

She reached to grab him by the wrist. "Got you, you little monster." She dragged him out. "Now, I cannot blame you for being intimidated, but you must mind your manners. Guests don't hide under tables."

"I want to go home."

"Guests don't say things like that, either. It's very rude."

Jewel rose and brushed off the mint green skirts that Ford had spent half an hour struggling her into. He was really much better at removing female clothing than putting it on.

"Here." Jewel handed Rowan a biscuit, and he reluctantly climbed to his feet. "Eat this, and then I'll show you Uncle Ford's laboratory."

"No you won't," Ford said. Not again. He'd taken her to his laboratory yesterday afternoon, hoping she'd sit quietly while he worked. Ten minutes later he'd hauled her out—just before she'd managed to destroy the place.

"Please, Uncle Ford?"

"No."

"Puleeeeeze?" The look in Jewel's green eyes bordered on pathetic. Chase eyes, like Ford's twin sister's. Just what he needed...another Chase female who could wrap him around her little finger.

Evidently she realized her feminine wiles were working, because she turned her lavish charm on Rowan. "You must stay," she told him. "Uncle Ford has magnets, and bottles of smelly stuff, and a pen-pen—"

"Pendulum," Ford supplied, remembering too late that she didn't like to be helped.

But she was so intent on convincing Rowan, she failed to take notice. "Yes, a pen-du-lum. And lots of clocks and a telescope. That's a thing to see the stars."

"Is it?" Lady Violet asked, interest lighting her eyes. "I've never really seen the stars."

Scant moments ago, she'd looked like she was ready to haul Rowan home. Not that Ford could blame her, but his own sanity depended on Jewel's ability to befriend the boy. He had to keep the Ashcrofts here. Whatever it took.

He wouldn't go crawling back to his brother for help.

"I think Rowan might find my laboratory interesting," he said with an inward grimace. "And although the telescope cannot help you see stars in the daytime, if you stay until dark—"

"I cannot stay until dark!" Violet exclaimed with a horrified gasp.

Bloody hell. If she was stuck on propriety, he would invite her maid in to chaperone. No wonder he preferred the loose-moraled ladies at King Charles's court. These sheltered country lasses must be damned difficult to seduce.

Good thing he'd sworn off women.

"I wasn't planning to stay at all," she added. "I had thought to introduce Rowan and then leave—"

"Leave me?" Rowan interrupted, looking even more horrified than she did. "I told Mum I didn't want to come here!" He turned to his sister, burying his face in her dark blue skirts. "Would you really leave me, Violet?"

She patted him on the head. "Of course not. You must have misunderstood me." She glared at Ford as though to say, *This is all your fault*. And he knew, then and there, that his happy visions of working while she and her brother entertained his niece were just that—visions. As ethereal as a dream.

Lady Trentingham's fairy dust wasn't working, after all. Violet's mother wasn't his savior, and her suggestion that the children play together wasn't the answer to his prayers. As a man of science, he should have known better than to imagine such flights of fancy, even for a moment.

His plans were spinning out of control. No, make that his life...his life was spinning out of control. And unlike the centrifuge in his laboratory, this wasn't a spin he seemed equipped to stop.

# SEVEN

*T*HE NEXT MORNING, Ford managed to get Jewel up and dressed by nine o'clock, at a cost of only two shillings. He was getting much better at this child care business. A good thing, because his dreams of hiring additional help had been dashed last night.

A letter from his solicitor had arrived, hinting at financial concerns and asking for a meeting in London at Ford's earliest convenience.

Bloody hell, he thought—it certainly wasn't convenient now. Maybe after his niece went home. In the meantime, the two of them were getting along famously this morning. Having learned what she preferred for breakfast—bread and cheese, with warm chocolate to drink—he no longer had to pay her to eat at all.

Now, if only he could bribe that Rowan boy to play with the girl, life would be rosy. True, after he'd suggested they stay into the evening, Lady Violet had hurried her brother home so fast she'd tripped over his threshold on her way out. But today was a new day, and he'd awakened with a new determination.

Desperation bred courage and ingenuity.

Getting the children together hadn't been Violet's idea, he reasoned, but Lady Trentingham's. Perhaps the mother would be willing to try again. That goal in mind, he settled Jewel in front of him on his horse and began riding toward Trentingham Manor.

"What do you call her?" she asked.

"Well, my lady, of course. I would have to be much more familiar with her to use her given name."

Jewel's little hands tightened on his where he held her around the waist. "You're not fa-mil-i-ar with your horse? That's sad. Papa is friends with *his* horse."

"My horse?" He was feeling thickheaded again. Women seemed to do that to him, to his constant irritation. "Of course I know my horse. But he's not a her. He's a boy."

"Oh." His niece was silent a moment as they reached the Thames and turned to ride alongside it. "What do you call him, then?"

"Galileo."

"Gali-who?"

"Galileo. Have you never heard of him? He was born in the last century, though he lived into this one."

"Was he a horse?"

"No." Ford choked back a laugh. "He was an astronomer and a physicist and a mathematician."

"That sounds boring."

"Oh, but it isn't." Sunlight glimmered off the water, a beautiful morning to visit. Ford was sure this encounter would end better than yesterday's. "Galileo invented a horse-driven water pump, and a military compass, and something called a thermometer that measures hot and cold. And a much better telescope than the one invented before it."

"Like the one in your laboratory?"

"Well, that one is called a reflecting telescope. It's a newer one, invented by another man named Isaac Newton, only about five years ago. But he wouldn't have invented it if Galileo hadn't invented *his* telescope first. That's the way science works. And with his telescope, Galileo discovered moons around Jupiter—"

"Aunty Kendra told me about Jupiter. But not moons."

"She was talking about the Roman god." Knowing his twin's love of mythology, she'd likely regaled the innocent girl with bloody tales of Jupiter slaying poor souls with thunderbolts. "I'm talking about the planet."

"Like Earth?"

"But much bigger. I can show you with my telescope. And I can show you Saturn, too, which has rings around it. Galileo was the first to notice those."

"That doesn't sound boring."

Behind her, he smiled. "It's wonderful, I assure you. Did you know all the planets go around the sun?"

"Mama told me that."

"Well, another man named Nicolas Copernicus thought so first, but Galileo wrote a book to explain it."

"Galileo is lucky," she said. "Your horse, I mean. To be named after a special man." She leaned forward to stroke the animal's jet-black mane, which matched her own dark, wavy tresses. "Rowan is named for a tree."

"Did he tell you so?"

"No. He wouldn't talk to me." Ford could hear the pout in her voice. "But when you were out of the room, his sister told me that in her family, the girls are named for flowers and the boy is named for a tree."

"That's because their father loves to garden," he told her as Trentingham Manor came into view.

A wide lawn studded with shade trees sat between the river and the sprawling, red-brick mansion, its uneven skyline and irregular patterned brickwork the result of a century of alterations. In the extensive gardens set around it, Ford spotted a well-dressed man fiddling with a rose bush.

"In fact," he said, "I'd wager that's Lord Trentingham there now."

Ford hadn't seen the Earl of Trentingham in quite a few years, but as they rode nearer, he could see where Rowan had inherited his looks. The earl's dark hair glistened in the warm summer sun. He looked up, raising a hand to swipe his sweat-slicked brow.

"Who goes there?" he asked when Ford reined in beside him.

"Viscount Lakefield, my lord. Ford Chase." Ford slid off Galileo, taking Jewel with him. "And my niece, Lady Jewel Chase." The moment he set her on her feet, she raced to a nearby fountain and thrust her hands into the spurting water.

The earl narrowed his emerald green eyes. "Eh?"

"A long time since we've met, my lord." Smiling, Ford held out a hand.

Though the man shook it warmly, he still looked perplexed. "What? What did you say?"

Too late Ford remembered Violet had mentioned her father was hard of hearing. "Ford Chase!" he fairly yelled. "I'm glad to see you!"

Jewel splashed herself in the face as her eyes popped open wide. Then she giggled, and her lips parted in a grin. "Jewel Chase!" she shouted, clearly thinking it was a game.

The earl bowed. "I'm glad of your acquaintance, young lady!" he hollered back.

"Joseph!" Lady Trentingham rounded the corner of the mansion. "How many times must I remind you the rest of us can hear just fine?" Laughing softly, she came close and kissed him on the cheek. "You forgot your hat," she added, plopping a wide-brimmed specimen on his head.

"My thanks, love." Apparently grateful for the shade, the earl clipped a blood-red bloom and presented it to his wife with a flourish.

"Just what I needed," she murmured. But the smile she sent her husband was genuine.

"I'm wearing your perfume," Jewel piped up.

The woman turned to her. "Well, then, come closer, and let me see if it's the right scent for such a lovely girl."

Jewel ran right over, wiping her wet palms on her dress. "Do I smell good?"

Lady Trentingham leaned down and sniffed. "You smell glorious."

A radiant smile transformed Jewel's face. "Will Rowan like it, do you think?"

"She's rather fond of your son," Ford said.

"So my daughter told me." Lady Trentingham's eyes danced as she looked up at him. "She also told me the feeling was less than mutual."

"I'm afraid she was right," he lamented. "And I was so hoping the children would get along."

"I'd wager you were." She looked contemplative. "Men, you know, they sometimes take a while to come around." Her husband had resumed puttering around, but her gaze on him was unmistakably affectionate. "My Rowan takes after his father, I'm afraid, but I'm sure, given time, he'll come to appreciate this delightful young lady."

Ford watched as Jewel went back to the fountain, sighing when she splashed her dress. Another change of clothing in his future. He could already imagine Hilda complaining about the additional laundry and ironing. And him having nothing to do but listen, because he couldn't work with a child running loose.

"Lady Trentingham..." Desperation setting in, he favored her with one of his famous seductive smiles. "Do you suppose your son might give Jewel another chance?"

# EIGHT

*P*ERCHING A KNEE on one of the window seats in the gold-and-cream-toned drawing room, Violet peered out the window at the blur she knew was the viscount and her parents.

"What do you think they're saying?" she asked her sisters.

Rose pressed closer to the panes, fussing with a floral arrangement she'd set in the window niche. "They seem to be discussing that little girl who's playing in the fountain."

"Jewel," Violet said. "The one I told you about who fancies herself in love with Rowan."

Lily's fingers glided over the harpsichord, producing a lyrical tune. "How sweet."

"How absurd," Rose countered. "She's too young to be in love." She patted her deep chestnut curls. "Unlike me. I do declare, that man out there looks mighty fine."

"He's too intellectual for you," Violet snapped, then wondered why she should suddenly be so short tempered. "Does Mum look like she's pleased to see them?"

Lily didn't miss a beat as she looked up and out the window. "Very."

Rose leaned her hands on the sill. "Now Lord Lakefield has

lifted the girl, and Mum is running a finger down her cheek." She turned to Violet. "I think she must like her...do you suppose Mum's already matchmaking for *Rowan*?"

Rose sounded genuinely worried that their little brother might beat his older sisters to the altar. Which was absolutely ridiculous.

"Well," Violet said, "she's not going to get me to take Rowan to Lakefield again. He was miserable." The blurred figures were getting bigger. "Egad. They're coming inside. All of them. Even Father."

The music stopped as Lily stood, looking puzzled. "Why shouldn't they come inside?"

"I...no reason." The sudden quiet was unsettling. Violet drew a deep breath and found herself smoothing her russet skirts, which wasn't like her. She pulled some of her hair forward to drape over one shoulder, then dropped her hand as Jewel bounded into the room ahead of the adults.

The girl skidded to a stop on the carpeted floor, backing Violet against the wall in her enthusiasm. "Lady Violet!" Throwing her arms wide, she hugged her around the knees. "Where's Rowan?"

"Having his lessons." Looking down into the child's face, Violet couldn't help but be charmed. "Would you care to meet my sisters? This is Lady Rose and Lady Lily."

"I'm pleased to make your ac-quain-tance," Jewel said quite properly. Violet's sisters exchanged an amused glance as the girl bobbed a curtsy. "This room is very fancy," she said.

It was, Violet supposed, though having lived here most of her life, she didn't think about it much. They stood on a lovely gold-and-cream-toned Oriental carpet. The room's dark oak paneling was studded with gold rosettes, the ceiling's cornice heavily carved and gilded, the furniture upholstered in gold-and-cream silk damask. From where she stood, the details looked fuzzy, but she'd seen it all up close.

"Why, thank you," Mum said.

Jewel rocked up on her toes. "When will Rowan be finished with his schooling?"

"Later today, I'm afraid. He has another lesson after dinner."

"Arithmetic," Rose informed them. "He hates it."

"A rhythmic tic?" Her father nodded sagely. "I would hate a rhythmic tic as well. Quite annoying."

"Arithmetic," Mum repeated loudly, laying a hand on Father's arm. "We were talking about Rowan, and how he hates mathematics." An amused smile on her face, she turned back to their guests. "Poor boy. I've promised him a sweet after the lesson."

Jewel tugged on her uncle's sleeve. "Can Rowan come to *our* house for a sweet? Oh, puleeeeeze?"

Lord Lakefield grinned down at his niece, a grin Violet suddenly wished were aimed at her instead. It was broad and white and just a bit devilish, extending all the way to his brilliant blue eyes. "Excellent idea, baby," he said.

When Mum smiled, Violet could see it coming.

Oh, no.

Trying to look casual, she leaned against the dark paneling, then shot straight when one of the gold rosette studs jabbed her in the posterior. "I don't believe Rowan will be interested," she blurted out, not nearly as composed as she'd planned.

Mum's smile only widened. "I'm sure Rowan would love to visit for a sweet," she said to Lord Lakefield, as though Violet's words had never been spoken. "Will three o'clock suit you? Madame is due here this afternoon for another fitting for Lily and Rose, but Violet will be happy to bring him."

Jewel jumped up and down.

Violet shook her head, but no one took heed.

"What?" Violet's father asked his wife. "What did you say, my love?"

# NINE

*I*N THE THREE hours since Ford and Jewel had arrived back at Lakefield, his niece had suddenly become very thick with Harry, Ford's elderly houseman. Although Ford held no illusions that the man and girl would become fast friends, he'd jumped at the opportunity for freedom. Now, sitting in his attic laboratory, he paused to listen to little giggles floating through the open window.

"Mud," he heard Harry say. "Clay. It's the exact color of the upholstery."

What could mud possibly have to do with anything?

"Oh, good!" The sound of clapping hands accompanied Jewel's childish voice. "We must hurry, then, so there will be time for it to start drying. And we need something fun to put at his place, so he won't be looking."

"Brilliant, Lady Jewel. I've just the thing…"

Their voices faded around a corner of the house. Shaking his head, Ford focused on the gears held in his hand. His thoughts returned to his current project, which was much more interesting than mud.

Watches were so inefficient—the single hand only approximated the hour. Within the last few years, another hand had been added to clocks, one that ticked off the minutes and made time-keeping much more precise. But since watches weren't pendulum-driven, the mechanism that drove a clock's minute hand wouldn't work inside them.

Yet it should be possible to add a minute hand to a watch. A more accurate personal timepiece would be practical, functional —a true benefit to mankind. And after years of thought and experimentation, he was so close to making it work...

"Your guests have arrived, my lord." Bustling in, Hilda started flicking a dust rag at his various instruments. "Don't you think you should be downstairs?"

~

*R*OWAN CLINGING to her skirts, Violet followed Jewel toward Lord Lakefield's dining room, wondering how it was that Mum had talked her into dragging the poor boy here again.

And her maid Margaret hadn't even come along this time! Mum had given the woman half a day off. Margaret was being courted, and Mum—who had introduced her to the "nice footman" from a neighboring estate—thought this a perfect chance for the maid to spend some time with her beau.

How very like Mum to risk her own daughter's reputation for the sake of someone else's romance. *Question Convention.* Sometimes, Violet thought, the Ashcrofts took their motto a bit too seriously.

Most of Lakefield had seen better days, but the dining room struck Violet as particularly dreary. The paneling was so dark it appeared nearly black, and although the built-in cupboards boasted glass in the doors, very few dishes were displayed inside. The room's color scheme was an uninspiring mélange of browns. Everything was clean, though—the viscount had a decent housekeeper in Hilda.

"Here, Rowan," Jewel said brightly as they entered. "Sit

here." She pulled out one of the faded tan chairs. "Right here. I put a toy here for you."

"At the table?" Violet asked.

"Uncle Ford lets me play at the table. As long as I leave him to his thoughts."

Violet would lay odds Jewel's parents didn't feel the same way. But she smiled as she watched her brother race to the chair and claim the toy, a cup and ball.

"Rowan..." she prompted.

"My thanks," he murmured absently, making the ball fly up and catching it in the cup with a satisfying—to him, anyway—*bang*. He grinned and did it again. Well, his mood was improved, at least. Perhaps this visit wouldn't go as badly as the first one.

"Oooh, you're very good at that," Jewel all but purred, sidling up to Rowan.

He smiled, making Violet think perhaps she could learn a thing or two from Jewel about flirting.

Jewel touched him on the arm. When he looked up at her, she fluttered her lashes. "Rowan, will you show me how to do that? I'm just a butterfingers. I miss the cup every time."

Faith. *Rose* could learn a thing or two from her about flirting.

But then Jewel reached for the toy, and Rowan jerked away, his frown back in place. "Mine."

"Rowan," Violet scolded, silently cursing her mother for sending her here again. "Behave yourself."

Jewel looked crestfallen. Knowing what it was like to feel awkward with boys, Violet studied the girl. The sash on her powder blue dress was tied very crookedly in back—the viscount's work, no doubt.

Perhaps some female companionship would ease the sting of male rejection. "Here, let me fix your bow," Violet offered brightly, stepping up to retie it.

"Good afternoon," came a low voice from beside her.

She turned, blinking when she saw Lord Lakefield. Silver

braid gleamed on his deep gray velvet suit, rather fancy for an afternoon at home. But she had to admit he looked divine.

Feeling underdressed in her plain russet gown, she licked her suddenly dry lips. "Good afternoon, my lord."

"Please, just call me Ford," he said with a smile.

That was so improper, she wasn't sure what to say in return. Should she ask him to call her Violet? Would doing so invite too much familiarity? The oldest of four, she knew how to deal with children, but men remained a mystery. Especially eligible, handsome men—and Viscount Lakefield was by far the handsomest man she'd ever seen.

His smile faded. "Violet?"

Egad, he was calling her Violet already. Perhaps she should just try his name in her head. *Ford.* It seemed to fit. But when she opened her mouth, it felt entirely too scandalous to say aloud. She seemed to have lost her tongue.

This was ridiculous.

Evidently her silence had stretched long enough. "I'm just going to call you Violet," he said blithely. "We're neighbors, after all. Rowan, my man, what have you there?"

"A cup and ball." *Bang, bang.* "Lady Jewel gave it to me."

"Did she? I wonder where she got that old thing?"

Violet tore her gaze from the viscount—Ford—and glanced at the toy. "It *does* look rather used," she said, finally finding her voice. "Ancient, actually."

"Harry gave it to me," Jewel said.

Ford nodded. "My equally ancient houseman."

His housekeeper walked in and set a pitcher of ale on the table. "Is that what my husband was doing with you? I was wondering what you two were up to this morning. That toy once belonged to our son—did Harry tell you that?"

Jewel nodded, then her voice took on that flirting quality. "Isn't Rowan good at it?"

"Very," Ford said, sharing a smile with Violet that caught her by surprise. Clearly he was on to his niece's ploys. He waved Violet toward a chair. "Won't you sit down?"

"I'll be back," Hilda said, "after I get my tart out of the oven."

Seating himself beside Violet, Ford reached for the ale and her cup. At Trentingham Manor, servants did the serving. For a nobleman, he didn't seem to have very many. "How was your afternoon?" he asked.

"Fine," she said, watching him pour. He had very nice hands, long fingers and square nails. She wracked her brain for a topic of conversation. "I'm reading a book by Francis Bacon."

He filled the children's cups, adding water to both. "Philosophy?" he asked, his tone cool but courteous.

"Yes."

"Of course. You did mention you study philosophy." He poured himself some ale, then drank like he needed it. "And what does Francis Bacon have to say?"

She sipped while she thought of a reply, wondering why she cared so much that he liked her. "He believes in liberty of speech."

"That's admirable." He drained his cup.

"He thinks knowledge and human power are synonymous."

He smiled vaguely as he refilled it.

"Do you agree?" she asked, feeling more awkward by the moment.

"Oh, yes. Yes, I do."

She sighed with relief when Hilda waddled in with four plates and started setting one in front of each of them. A welcome distraction. Steam from the plain apple tart wafted to Violet's nose, smelling delicious. She lifted her spoon.

"I don't like apples," Rowan said. "Do you have cherry tart?"

"Do you have manners?" Hilda retorted with a glare. Muttering to herself, she left the room.

Violet wanted to slip beneath the table. "Francis Bacon says," she rushed out, "that if a man will begin with certainties, he will end in doubts, but if he will be content to begin with doubts, he will end in certainties."

Ford finally looked interested. "That sounds very much like the new science. One puts forth an assumption and then endeavors to prove it."

"So then," she said, warming to the subject, "perhaps philosophy and science are compatible."

"Perhaps they are."

He looked surprised or dubious; she wasn't sure which. She wished she could see him clearer.

"You know," he said, "some philosophers belong to the Royal Society."

*Bang, bang.*

"Rowan," she said quietly. "We're trying to talk."

For once in her life, she was enjoying a conversation with a man.

*Bang.*

"Rowan!" Her voice was sharper than she'd intended, and her brother looked up in midtoss, the toy flying out of his hand. It hit the wall with a *thwack*, and she grimaced.

"Sorry," Rowan muttered.

"What was that?" Hilda asked, hurrying in to investigate the noise.

"A mistake." Rowan rose to go fetch the toy—or rather, he attempted to. How odd. From where Violet sat, her brother seemed unable to rise. His feet didn't reach the floor, but he put his hands on the seat and pushed, his face turning red with strain.

Jewel burst out laughing.

"Jewel," Ford murmured. "You didn't."

"Oh-oh-oh, yes, I did," she chortled. "D-don't you th-think he deserved it?"

"Deserved what?" Violet asked. "What did you do to him?"

"She stuck me," Rowan said, and for a moment, Violet thought he meant with a pin. But he wasn't crying—in fact, he didn't even look cross. He didn't look happy, either. He just looked blank. "She stuck me to the chair."

"With what?" she asked, aghast.

"Harry," Hilda muttered dangerously, bustling from the room. "I'll kill the man."

"I stuck him with glue," Jewel explained proudly between giggles. "And mud to make it brown so he wouldn't see it on the chair. And the toy was to make him sit down without noticing."

Violet felt as blank as Rowan looked. Her mouth hung open. When Ford reached over and pushed up on her chin to close it, she hadn't enough wits about her to even chide him for touching her. "What—how—why—" she stammered.

"It was a jest," he clarified. "A prank."

"A jest," she murmured.

"A Chase family tradition." He turned to his niece with a grin. "Most especially Jewel's father's tradition."

Jewel hiccupped. "Tell me again about Papa's pranks. One from long ago."

His eyes narrowed for a moment, deep in memory. "Once, when I was young, Colin tied me to a chair while I was sitting there reading a book." He leaned back, lifting his ale. "In some way or other—to this day I haven't figured out how—he managed to get the rope around my body but not my arms or hands, so I didn't notice."

For some reason, Violet found it all too easy to picture him not noticing.

Rowan stopped kicking. "What happened?"

"He left." Ford paused for a sip. "The knots were behind the chair, so even after I did notice, I couldn't reach them. I yelled for help, but the only response was the sound of his laughter."

Envisioning that, too, Violet's lips twitched. "Did he rescue you?"

"Hours later. I'd nearly finished the book."

"You just kept reading?" she asked with a barely suppressed smile. Faith, even *she* wouldn't read under those circumstances.

"What else could I do?" he said dismissively. "At least Rowan here won't have to wait so long." Setting down his ale, he rose. "Let me free you, my man," he said, lifting Rowan into his arms, chair and all.

Suddenly, seeing her brother hanging in midair stuck to a chair, and visualizing a bookish young Ford the same way, the smile that had been threatening broke free on Violet's face. Jewel was right. Given Rowan's petulance, he deserved the jest, and a rollicking good one it was, too.

"More stories," Jewel said.

"Later, baby." Carrying Rowan out the door, Ford flashed his niece a grin. "Colin will be proud of you when he hears this one."

And Violet had thought the Ashcrofts were eccentric.

# TEN

"**ALL RIGHT, ROWAN.** Let's see what we can do here." Ford set the chair down in his laboratory and turned away to locate a beaker.

"Holy Hades," Rowan said.

Shocked at the youngster's language, Ford swiveled back and stared.

"Pardon." But the lad didn't look sorry. "What *are* all these things?"

Ford let his gaze wander the chamber's contents, trying to see it through the boy's eyes. A full quarter of the huge attic space was filled with ovens and bellows, a furnace, cistern, and a still. Mismatched shelves held scales, drills, and funnels. Magnets, air pumps, dissecting knives, a pendulum, and numerous bottles of chemicals sat haphazardly on several tables. More things were shoved into half-opened chests of drawers. A larger table beneath the window—Ford's workbench—was littered with the inner workings of several dismantled watches.

It was Ford's playroom, and he was happier here than anywhere else. "Scientific instruments, mostly." He grabbed a beaker. "That's a microscope," he added, waving behind him.

"What does it do?"

"It magnifies. You can put something beneath the lens and see it up close." Forgetting the task at hand, Ford reached to a table for a book. "Here, look at this. *Micrographia*. It was written by a man named Robert Hooke." Opening the red leather cover, he set the book in Rowan's lap.

Rowan looked down at the title page. "'Some Phys-phys—'"

"Physiological," Ford said.

"That's a big word." The boy read the next words slowly and carefully. "'...Descriptions of Minute Bodies made by Mag—'"

"Magnifying."

"'Magnifying Glasses with...'"

"'Observations and Inquiries Thereupon,'" Ford finished for him. "The book is drawings of things seen under a microscope."

Unlike Jewel, Rowan apparently didn't mind help. Nodding, he turned to a random page and gawked. "Whatever is this?"

"One of the pictures Hooke drew. Of a feather. That's what it looks like very close up."

"Zounds." Rowan stared for a moment, then flipped the page. "What is this?"

"A louse." Ford unfolded the large illustration, revealing the insect in all its horrible glory. The creature was oddly shaped, with a conical head and big goggling eyes.

Goggling himself, Rowan lifted a hand to his hair. "*That's* what lice look like?"

"Up close, bigger than the eye can see alone." Pleased that Rowan was interested, Ford teased him with an expression of horror. "You don't have any lice, do you?"

"I hope not. I don't think so. Not now." Tugging his fingers from his hair, the boy turned to another drawing. "This is a spider?"

Filling the beaker from the cistern, he glanced over. "A shepherd spider."

"It's particularly ugly," Rowan said, his tone one of fascinated glee.

Remembering the glue, and his guest waiting downstairs, Ford rescued the book. "This is in the way."

As he set *Micrographia* on a table, Rowan's eyes followed it covetously. "May I take it home?"

"No." Ford sensed an opportunity. "But you can look at it whenever you're here."

"When may I come back?"

"To play with Jewel?" He knelt by the lad's chair and, after removing his shoes, poured the water over his lap.

"Zounds, that's cold!"

"It'll dissolve the glue." Standing, he attempted to pull the boy off the chair by gripping him under the armpits. "I thought you didn't like Jewel."

At that, Rowan squirmed.

"Hold still, will you?" Ford put a foot on the chair's lower rung to keep it on the floor. "You've certainly seemed to do your best to avoid her so far. And after this trick—"

"It was clever," the boy admitted.

"Yes, it was."

"Lady Jewel is...different," Rowan said. "I've never met a girl who would plan what she did. My sisters sure would never. Lily cares only for her animals, and Rose only wants to go to balls. And Violet...Violet always has to learn new things. Can you imagine a girl liking to study?"

Yes, Ford agreed silently, Violet was the oddest of the bunch. Certainly nothing like the type of woman he'd be looking for if he hadn't sworn off women altogether.

While he mused on that, Rowan's breeches finally came unstuck with an impressive sucking sound. Ford knelt to unlace them and began to pull them down.

"No!" The lad's hands clenched on Ford's shoulders. "I'll be arse-naked."

"Well, you can't sit or lean on anything wearing those." Ford sighed. "I'll go find you some clean breeches. Stay where you are," he added before taking himself off. "And don't touch anything."

When he returned a few minutes later, Rowan waved a hand at some bottles of chemicals. "What are those for?"

"Alchemy." Ford made a show of shutting the door behind him. "There. You're safe from prying eyes."

The boy pulled off his breeches and hurried to put Ford's on. "What's alchemy?" he asked, gazing down at the gaping waist-band with dismay.

"Alchemy is a science." Ford leaned to tug the laces tighter, but it was hopeless. He scanned the tables and shelves, searching for twine, silently cursing himself for the room's usual state of disarray. "We alchemists—King Charles is one, too—are working to find the Philosopher's Stone."

Rowan clutched the brown breeches with both hands. "Violet likes philosophy."

"Well, the Philosopher's Stone has little to do with philosophy. It's a name for a secret—a way to turn other metals into pure gold."

"Holy Ha—" The boy caught himself this time. "I mean...can you do that?"

"No. Or not yet—no one can. But many are trying. It's said that in days past, men have accomplished it more than once, but the secret has always been lost." Finally spotting the twine, he walked over to fetch it.

"Why didn't the men write it down?"

"At least one did, in a book—a very ancient book called *Secrets of the Emerald Tablet*. But the book is lost, too."

"Are you looking for it?"

"No. It's been lost for a very long time. Nearly three centuries." He knelt by the boy. "After all that time, perhaps *lost* isn't the right word. I suspect it was probably destroyed."

"Maybe in a fire," Rowan suggested, sounding fascinated at the prospect.

"Maybe." Making a mental note to keep the lad far from

combustibles, Ford bunched the breeches around his waist and circled it with the twine. "But if the secret has been figured out before, it stands to reason we should be able to repeat that success, doesn't it? That's what half of this equipment is for," he concluded, knotting the twine tightly. "Alchemy."

The crotch of the breeches hung to the boy's knees, and the kneebands to his ankles, but he didn't seem to notice. Evidently relieved to be decently covered at last, he smiled happily and lifted a bottle of bright yellow fluid.

His eyes gleamed when he looked back to Ford. "Can I help you find the philosophy rock?"

"Philosopher's Stone." Ford considered. He could turn this interest to his advantage. "Maybe. Maybe you and Jewel together can help me."

Rowan set down the bottle. "Maybe she'll teach me some pranks."

"I'm sure your mother would love that," Ford said dryly. But his heart took flight. Finally, Lady Trentingham's plan seemed to be working—thanks to Jewel's prank.

Whoever would have thought?

"Let's go down," he said. "Hilda will be mighty vexed if we don't finish her tart."

As Ford led him from the room, Rowan gave a wistful sigh. "What other science do you do?"

"Astronomy, mathematics, physics, physiology…"

The boy jumped down the staircase one step at a time. *Clunk.* A step. "I hate mathematics." *Clunk.* Another step.

"But mathematics can be fascinating. Like a puzzle."

*Clunk.* "Not when Mr. Baxter teaches it."

"Mr. Baxter?"

"My tutor." *Clunk. Clunk.* "He's boring." Around they went, past the middle level to the ground floor, Rowan clunking all the long way. "Jewel said you can show me the stars."

"Indeed. If you're here of an evening."

"Really?" At the bottom, Rowan pushed past him and ran straight into the dining room. "Violet!"

Arriving in the chamber, Ford saw her gaze sweep the boy from head to toe. She bit her lip—to keep from laughing, he was sure—but her eyes danced with humor as she looked pointedly to Jewel.

"I'm sorry about your clothes," Jewel told Rowan obediently, if not quite sincerely. Clearly Violet had had a talk with her in the men's absence.

Rowan shrugged. "That's all right." Hitching up Ford's too-long breeches, he turned to his sister. "Lord Lakefield says if I play with Jewel, he'll show me science. And the stars."

"You're willing to play with Jewel?" A note of incredulity tinged Violet's voice. "After what she did?"

"She's not like other girls. Will you take me again tonight? To see the stars?"

She looked hesitant, but perhaps intrigued as well.

"You're certainly welcome," Ford rushed to tell her. "It looks to be a clear night."

"Maybe," she said. "I'll think about it."

Ford mentally crossed his fingers. If Rowan could persuade her to bring him back, surely he'd tire of seeing "science" after a short while. Then Violet could take the children elsewhere, and he would be left to work in peace.

At this point, even a couple of hours sounded like heaven.

## ELEVEN

"**S**HE WRECKED his breeches, Mum!" Violet paced her mother's perfumery, skimming a finger along the neatly labeled vials. "It was amusing, I'll admit, but I don't think all that glue and mud will wash out."

"It was a harmless prank, dear." Mum calmly plucked violet petals and tossed them into her distillation bowl. "And you did say Rowan wants to return."

"Yes, but I cannot understand why." Pacing to one of the window niches, Violet perched a knee on the bench seat and leaned to look out. "How can he like her after this? Especially when he didn't like her before?"

"I've never understood how men's minds work. Does your philosophy give you no clue to that?"

Everything below was a blur. "'It may be said of men in general that they are ungrateful and fickle,'" she quoted.

"And who said that?"

"Machiavelli." She turned from the window. "Now Rowan wants to return tonight to see the stars. And I fear he'll want to go back again tomorrow."

"Isn't that what we've been hoping would happen all along?" Mum's fingers flew as she pulled purple petals, more graceful than Violet could ever hope to be. "What, pray tell, is your problem with this development?"

Violet seated herself at the table and grabbed a bunch of flowers. "He doesn't want to go alone. And I don't want to go with him."

"Now, Violet. Who said that thing about being charitable? You read it to me last week."

"Francis Bacon again," she said with a sigh. "'In charity there is no excess.'"

"A wise man. It would be a charity, for certain, for you to take Rowan to play. He's bored here in the countryside with Benjamin away." The only boy Rowan's age within walking distance, Benjamin was his favorite playmate. "And a charity to Jewel as well, stuck in that house with no other children. And you'd be giving Lord Lakefield some respite. Surely he has better things to do than watch that girl."

Agitated, Violet started plucking petals. "So I should do it instead? Am *I* not allowed to have better things to do?" The scent of her namesake flower failed to soothe her. "Can't Rose go?"

Mum frowned at Violet's busy hands. "Rose is too young, I've told you." She tossed a bare stem into a basket. "Besides, she has no sense where men are concerned, and we've all heard her jabbering about the 'handsome viscount.'"

"And he'd take advantage of her, but not me. That's what you're thinking, isn't it?"

"Violet—"

"It's true, Mum, and we both know it." She plucked faster. "I'm plain next to Rose and Lily. And men pretend to be deaf rather than listen to me prattle about my interests."

Mum touched her arm. "Violet, your father really *is* hard of—"

"No male will ever show interest in me unless it's for my inheritance." Ten thousand pounds. Added to her dowry of three thousand, it would tempt many men to wed a mule.

"Violet—"

"I'm not a featherbrain, Mum." Her hand fisted, crushing a flower. "I know I don't turn men's heads."

Because Violet had seen her parents' own successful marriage —because she would settle for nothing less than their true love for herself—she was sure she wouldn't ever wed. But Mum would never stand to hear such a thing. And as Violet had said, she wasn't a featherbrain, so she knew better than to say it aloud.

She sighed, knowing that mere weeks from now, when she turned one-and-twenty and came into the money her grandfather had left her, the offers could very well begin to come fast and furious. She'd have a harder time putting Mum off then.

But she would persevere. And someday—many years from now when she was a content, aged spinster—she would use her inheritance to fund her dream.

"Violet." Her brown eyes filled with concern, Mum gently pulled the bruised bloom from Violet's hand. "You may not look like your sisters, but you're a very pretty girl. Especially to those who love you. Which philosopher said that beauty is brought by judgment of the eye?"

"That wasn't a philosopher. It was Shakespeare in *Love's Labour's Lost*."

"Oh."

"But he was paraphrasing Plato. 'Beholding beauty with the eye of the mind.'"

Mum grinned. "See, dear? Listen to Plato."

Rose and Lily burst into the room. "Look, Mum!" Lily waved a letter. "A messenger just delivered this from Lakefield. And he said he was instructed to wait for an answer."

"The oldest messenger I've ever seen," Rose added. "He's *bald*." She said it as though that were the most disgusting physical trait she could imagine.

"That's not a messenger," Violet said. "That's Harry, Lord Lakefield's houseman." As she'd hurried Rowan out the door, she'd seen Hilda's husband cowering in a corner while his wife scolded him for his part in Jewel's prank. The man was quite definitely bald, although Violet hadn't found that at all off-putting.

Maybe beauty *was* in the eye of the beholder.

She rose and went to her sisters. "Let me see the letter." She snatched it from Lily's hand.

"It's not for you," Rose said, grabbing it from Violet. "It's addressed to Rowan." So saying, she slipped a fingernail beneath the sloppy red wax seal and snapped it off.

"Rose!" Mum chided.

"You wouldn't want to give him a letter without reading it first, Mum, would you? It could be improper for one so young." Without waiting for her mother's answer, Rose scanned the page. "The handwriting is rather messy," she commented, then began reading. "'Dear Rowan.'" She looked up. "Rather familiar salute, don't you think?"

"Goodness, Rose," Lily said, uncharacteristically impatient. "Must you criticize every word?" She snatched the letter back from her sister. "'Dear Rowan,'" she repeated. "'I am sorry about your clothes. But it was funny. I hope you will come see the stars. Love, Jewel.'"

"'Love, Jewel?' *Love?*" Violet rolled her eyes toward the elaborate plastered ceiling. The blurry curlicues up there seemed in keeping with the little girl's intricate seduction.

Lily smiled dreamily. "Yesterday when you brought Rowan back, you said Jewel was in love."

"I was exaggerating. And to write it…" She couldn't imagine declaring herself so casually on a piece of paper. Writing was permanent, important. Once something was in writing, it was there forever.

That was one of the reasons she burned to publish a book.

"I'm in love, too," Rose declared.

Violet blinked. "With whom?"

"With Lord Lakefield, you goose. He's so handsome. And to

instruct his niece to write a letter to Rowan...well, it just goes to show he's a true romantic." Looking rather theatrical, she laid a graceful hand on the cleavage exposed in the low neckline of her periwinkle gown. "Why, it's almost enough to make me over-look the fact that he's poor as a church mouse."

"What a thing to say, Rose!"

Her hand dropped. "Well, lucky for me, it doesn't matter, does it? Thanks to Grandpapa, when I turn twenty-one I'll have enough money to nab whomever I like, rich or destitute."

Violet usually tried to be patient, but she couldn't help grit-ting her teeth. "Thanks to providence, that won't be for four years, by which time we can hope you will have grown up."

"Girls," Mum warned. "That's enough." She turned to Violet. "Lord Lakefield's houseman is waiting. Will you be taking Rowan to see the stars?"

"I'll take him," Rose offered.

Taking a cue from her husband, Mum pretended not to hear. "Violet?"

"Yes, I'll do it, Mum," Violet said with an elaborate sigh.

But it was mostly for show. She had to admit, she was curious to see the stars. And for some odd reason, she felt a need to save Ford from a frivolous girl like her sister. Not that she didn't love Rose, but a man of his intellect deserved someone whose beauty was more than skin-deep.

And it *was* very well done of him to have made Jewel write an apology, though she wondered how he could have neglected to supervise its contents before sending the letter.

Love, indeed.

# TWELVE

*H*ITCHING HERSELF forward on one of the drawing room's faded red chairs, Jewel jumped one of Ford's checkers with hers and palmed her new captive. "Your turn. Will Rowan come tonight, do you think?"

"I have no idea what he'll decide. I don't understand children."

"But Uncle Ford, you like children, don't you?"

He'd never thought he had. But as he looked at his charming niece, he didn't have the heart to say so. "I like *you*." Studying his position on the black-and-white board, he lifted one of his dark-stained counters. "And I'd wager Rowan does, too," he added to put a smile on her face. "He seemed much more fond of you after your jest. That was brilliant, baby. You certainly know your way to a young man's heart."

*Click-click-click.* Three diagonal jumps over her natural wood pieces, and his darker man was at her end of the board. "King me," he said with a self-satisfied smile.

Draughts. He was reduced to playing draughts. And she'd beaten him three times already. He couldn't remember the last time someone had beaten him at draughts; he must have been seven years old.

For all his intentions to come home to Lakefield and bury himself in his projects, the opposite seemed to be happening. He was concentrating on children and fretting over his shabby estate. Rather than unlocking the secrets of the universe, his efforts were focused on persuading a lady named Violet to spend as much time here as possible.

Jewel crowned his piece with one of the hostages she'd taken. "Do you like Rowan?"

"I do. He's very interested in my laboratory." Too interested. But at least the boy had a good brain and a healthy curiosity.

"Do you think Rowan's big sister is pretty?"

Did he? He'd initially thought Violet was pleasant looking at best. But he'd come to realize she had a fresh and wholesome look about her that he found surprisingly appealing.

"She's attractive," he said.

They both looked up as Hilda came in. "Harry seems to have disappeared," the housekeeper said. "Where is he?"

Ford shrugged. "I don't know." There didn't seem to be much he knew these days.

"He went to Rowan's house," Jewel said nonchalantly, jumping two more of Ford's men.

Hilda smoothed her wide white apron. "And why is that?"

"I asked him to take a letter there."

"A letter?" Ford frowned at the board, where his pieces seemed to be disappearing at an alarming rate.

"A letter to Rowan," his niece clarified. "An ap-ap—" She glared at him, as though daring him to help her. "An a-pol-o-gy."

"You wrote a letter?" Hilda asked.

"You wrote a letter?" Ford echoed. "All by yourself?"

"Well, I know how to write, you know. Mama taught me. What's so hard about that?"

Ford took his turn, removing none of Jewel's pieces. "It's not the writing of it, baby, it's thinking to do so in the first place. I'm quite impressed."

"Mama says even a tomboy should have good manners."

"I like the way your mother thinks," Hilda said.

"Besides, I like getting letters. Nobody ever sends me letters."

Melting at her pout, Ford made a mental note to send her a letter after she went home.

Jewel perused the board. "I thought a letter might make Rowan like me."

"He likes you," came a voice from the doorway. Harry walked in, his florid face split by a big smile.

Suddenly Hilda's face wore a frown. "You could tell me when you leave," she scolded, then immediately bustled out past him.

"Women," Harry muttered. "Always so demanding." He turned to Jewel with a courtly bow. "Present company excepted, of course."

Ford stared. Clearly the girl had won him over. Just as she had Rowan. She looked so innocent in her powder blue gown. So young and vulnerable. Which sat at odds with her fully developed feminine wiles and ingenuity.

Jewel bounced on the ancient chair so hard he feared it might break. "What did Rowan say?"

"Well, I didn't talk to him, you understand." Harry related the information as seriously as if he were a hired spy. "But his oldest sister came out and said she would bring him after the sunset to see the stars."

Jewel squealed and wriggled in her chair, so excited she botched her next few moves. As a consequence, Ford won the game. And Violet was coming with Rowan.

Things were looking up.

# THIRTEEN

*R*OWAN CLIMBED into the carriage and motioned his sister after him. "Hurry, Violet. It's dark already."

"The sky isn't going away." Still amazed his attitude had reversed so quickly, Violet took her cloak from her mother and settled the forest green velvet over her shoulders. "Where's Margaret?"

"I gave her the evening off, dear. Hilda and Harry will be there. And Lord Lakefield is a gentleman. I'm sure we can trust him to behave."

Especially with the likes of her, Violet imagined, wondering why she found that familiar truth suddenly distressing.

"I've instructed Willets to come back for you at ten," Mum added, referring to their coachman. "Two hours ought to be plenty long enough to stare at the sky."

Violet looked up. Except for a milky blur, she'd never seen the stars. "I wonder what I might see there?"

"The stars are beautiful," her mother said. "Like diamonds sparkling on a black velvet gown."

Smiling at the fanciful description, Violet gazed at the heavens. She wondered if the stars really twinkled, and if she might be able to wish on one. Excitement fluttered in her stomach.

"I'll see you later, then, Mum." She kissed her mother's floral-scented cheek and followed Rowan into the carriage.

A short while later they mounted Lakefield House's steps. Rowan didn't hide behind Violet this time. Jewel opened the door before Violet could lift the knocker, but Violet had anticipated that and didn't fall into the house.

Which was a pity, since Ford was there to catch her.

He was still wearing the nice suit, making her feel underdressed in her simple cotton gown. But that was absurd—she'd only come to look at the sky.

Instead of ushering her in, he stepped outside, a bit too close for her comfort. "I have the telescope set up in the garden," he said. "Follow me."

For such a tall man, he moved gracefully. As he headed down the steps, she realized she'd been holding her breath.

*Breathe*, she commanded herself. This was ridiculous.

He was just a man. She couldn't remember ever being this nervous around one, but that was probably because she'd done an admirable job of avoiding them altogether. Surely these feelings would disappear once she got to know him better. Which she seemed destined to do should Rowan have his way.

Holding a torch, Ford led her around the side of the house and down a path toward an area so overgrown she'd be loath to call it a garden. More like a jungle, she thought, hiding a smile.

The children tagged along behind, their voices coming out of the darkness. "Are you cross with me?" Jewel asked Rowan.

He seemed to consider for a moment. "Will you help me plan a jest on my sisters?"

"Of course I will."

"Then I'm not cross."

Listening to the exchange, Violet made a mental note to be on the alert for "jests." If Rowan thought gluing someone to a chair was acceptable, only God knew what he and Jewel would come up with together.

In the midst of a tangle of vines sat a ring of scraggly hedges.

They all followed Ford through an opening in the greenery. A new one, from the looks of it.

"Uncle Ford hacked at the plants with an ax today," Jewel proudly informed them. "After Harry came back and said you would come. Wasn't that nice?"

Violet thought she heard Ford groan.

A circle of wooden benches looked newly uncovered as well. Apparently he'd been busy. In the center, atop a stone sundial, a long tube sat balanced on three spindly legs.

Ford gestured at it with a flourish. "The telescope."

"How nice," she replied, hoping she sounded suitably impressed. But the telescope wasn't exactly awe-inspiring. It was just a skinny, thin thing. Her hopes plummeted. This hardly looked like an object that could work magic.

He set the torch in a nearby stand. "Quarter moon tonight," he said, grasping the tube and maneuvering it to point in the moon's direction.

Curious, Violet moved closer. Over the fresh scent of recently cut plant life, she could smell his fragrance, something spicy. And a trace of scented soap. Patchouli, she decided, recalling the aroma from one of her mother's vials. Some years ago, Father had arranged for a number of the minty shrubs to be brought from India. He'd planted them in his magnificent garden so Mum could distill the leaves.

"A partial moon is fortunate for viewing." Ford had closed one eye and focused the other through the tube. "A full moon can be too bright and make the stars around it fade." He made a final adjustment. "Would you like to see?"

"Me first!" Jewel said.

Rowan jumped up and down. "No, me!"

Jewel stepped in front of him. "Me!"

"Well, normally I'd say ladies first," Ford said, "but seeing as how Rowan suffered this afternoon, I think he should have the first peek. Hurry, though, or you won't be able to see it."

Since Rowan was so short, Ford lifted him to the eyepiece. "Zounds," Rowan breathed. "There are big, dark spots on it."

"They're called craters." Ford raised a foot to the pedestal of the sundial and settled Rowan on his knee, looking more comfortable with the boy than Violet would have expected. "What do you think of it?"

"I wish to fly up there and visit."

"Me, too." Ford laughed. "But I expect neither of us will get our wish."

Now Jewel was jumping up and down. "I want to see. Oh, please let me see!"

"Very well." Ford set Rowan down, then readjusted the telescope before lifting his niece. "Hurry, so Lady Violet can have a turn."

"Oooh," Jewel said.

"Why must she hurry?" Violet wondered. "The moon stays out all night."

"Yes, but the Earth moves, you see—it spins. That's why we have night and then day. And because of the spinning, we're moving relative to the moon, so it doesn't stay in the telescope's sight for very long." He set his niece on her feet and waved Violet toward the instrument. "Your turn."

She stepped forward and put one eye to the end, closing her other eye like he had. "Oh," she breathed. "Stars. Just look at all those stars."

"Can you see the moon, too?"

"No, we must have spun out of range like you said." Against black velvet, lights winked at her. White, and faint yellow, and the palest, most beautiful pink. A wonderland of stars.

"Let me adjust it for you."

"Wait." She was looking at a whole new world. Or a universe, to be more precise. "I've seen the moon," she told him. "Not up close, but at least I've seen it. I want to look at the stars."

"But they don't look much different through the telescope.

They're entirely too far away for the magnification to make a significant difference."

"But they're beautiful," she said. "Miraculous. What are they, really?"

"Other suns. And some people think there are other planets around them, the same way our planet circles our sun."

The children were chattering behind her, probably planning a jest, but she couldn't stop staring. She nudged the telescope a bit, and another group of stars burst into view. "'There is an infinite number of worlds,'" she murmured softly under her breath, "'some like this world, others unlike it.'"

"A lovely way to put it."

Startled, she jerked back from the eyepiece. She hadn't meant for him to hear that. "I didn't put it that way myself. I was quoting Epicurus."

"Who?"

"A Greek philosopher."

She felt, rather than saw, him nodding beside her. "A forward-thinking man."

A smile twitched on her lips. "Very. He lived about three hundred years before Christ." She leaned close again, peering through the telescope. "Do you believe that? That there are other planets?"

He laid a hand on her back. A warm hand that made a warmer shiver ripple through her. "I do."

Giggles erupted behind them.

"My uncle thinks your sister is pretty," Jewel told Rowan in a loud, confidential whisper.

Rowan's response was a disgusted groan.

Violet stiffened, and Ford's hand dropped from her back. "So," he said a bit formally. "Should I adjust it on the moon?"

"In a minute." Of course he hadn't meant anything by touching her, Violet told herself—he was a flirt, just like his niece. The awkward moment passed as she refocused on the sky. "For now, I'm enjoying the stars."

Just then, one of them streaked across her field of vision, and she made a silent wish.

*Give me the wisdom to write a book worth reading...and the tenacity to publish it.*

Her first wish on a star.

"Oh," she breathed, "it's awe-inspiring."

Hearing the wonder in Violet's voice, Ford relaxed and decided to ignore his niece's careless comment. Violet's velvet cloak had slipped to the ground, but she hadn't bothered to reach for it. He stared at her shapely back, encased in a snug dark green bodice. Simple and practical, but it certainly didn't hide the curves underneath. Had she been wearing the same gown earlier today? He hadn't paid any attention.

Pretty or not, Lady Violet was even odder than he'd thought. She was still gazing at the sky, slowly shifting the telescope. "Wouldn't you like to see the moon now?" he asked. After all, the stars looked much the same through the telescope as without it.

"Lord Lakefield." Rowan tugged on his breeches. "Lord Lakefield."

"You may have another turn in a minute. For now, your sister's looking."

"I know." When Ford looked down, the boy's smile looked as wide as the telescope was long. "Violet's never seen the stars before."

"Never?" Baffled, he ran a hand through his hair. "What do you mean?"

"She cannot see very well. She says they all just blur together."

She straightened and turned to face them, her eyes glittering with joy in the torchlight. "Thank you," she whispered. "Thank you for showing me a whole new world."

The way she said it made Ford feel like he had *given* her the world, not just shown it to her.

It was a feeling he rather enjoyed.

He eased her aside to adjust the telescope. "Here, now look at the moon."

When she leaned to peer through the lens, he was rewarded with a gasp of discovery. "It's a sphere," she said. "I can see the outline. Even though it looks like a crescent."

"Depending on our position, the Earth blocks part of the sun, so only a portion of the moon is illuminated. But it's always a sphere, no matter how it appears to us."

"Of course. I've just never thought of it before."

When the moon disappeared from view, he pointed out some constellations—Libra down near the horizon and Pegasus up higher.

"My turn!" Rowan said, and Jewel chimed in. "Let us have a turn!"

Clearly reluctant to relinquish the instrument, Violet stepped back, and the children rushed to see.

"Can you show us a planet?" Jewel asked.

Ford scanned the dark sky. "None are visible at the moment. Another night." But he showed them more constellations, and while they waited to take turns, he entertained them with the Greek and Roman myths that went with each configuration.

All too soon they heard the crunch of wheels on gravel announcing Violet's carriage had arrived. She let out a little unladylike groan. "Is it ten o'clock already?"

"May we come back tomorrow?" Rowan asked. "Can I go into the laboratory?"

Ford gazed at Violet, thinking about how the telescope had helped her to see, wondering if there might be a way to help her more permanently. "I've something that will keep me busy the next few days," he said slowly.

"In your laboratory?" Rowan asked.

"Yes." He turned to the boy. "If you'll come to play with Jewel until I'm done, I'll take you into the laboratory after I finish. We can do an experiment together."

"An experiment?" Rowan's eyes widened, and he did a funny little dance. "Can we really?"

"Will you be working on the watch?" Jewel asked.

"No, not the watch." That could wait—it had waited years already. Suddenly this new idea seemed much more important.

"Uncle Ford is making a special watch," Jewel told her new friends. "One that tells the minutes." She looked to Violet. "My Uncle Ford is very clever."

"I'm sure he is." Violet smiled at Ford, a smile that managed to transform her whole face. "Thank you for a fine evening."

"You're very welcome. I hope we can do this again." Surprised by just how true that statement was, he smiled in return as he retrieved her cloak and settled it over her shoulders.

If she'd noticed she'd dropped it, or that she'd almost forgotten it altogether, her behavior gave nary a clue. "I hope we can do it again, too," she said with a last, lingering glance at the telescope. When she took her brother's hand and began tugging him toward the carriage, that infectious smile still curved her lips.

It made a man feel good, being the cause of that. Wishing to coax a similar smile again, Ford hoped he would prove as clever as his niece thought.

As he watched the Ashcrofts' carriage roll away into the night, he lifted the girl into his arms and pecked her on the cheek.

"What was that for?" she squealed.

"Nothing, baby." It mystified him as much as her, but he would analyze the emotions later. "You just make me feel happy."

"I'm not a baby," she said. "Put me down."

But she planted a big, sloppy kiss on his cheek before he did so.

# FOURTEEN

"**HY AREN'T WE** going today?" Rowan demanded.

When Violet looked up from the notes she was making at her delicate desk in the library, it took everything she had not to laugh at her little brother. She hadn't seen a pout like that on him since he was three years old.

But he wasn't going to change her mind. "I told you—we've been there every day since we looked at the stars. Four days in a row, each afternoon we arrive like clockwork. We're wearing out our welcome."

The pout turned into a glare. "That's not true."

Of course it wasn't. To the contrary, Violet was sure Ford was pacing the floors waiting for their arrival. Waiting for them to come entertain his niece so he could work on his blasted secret project.

Well, much as she liked children, she wasn't a nursemaid, and she didn't intend to take up the career now—never mind that it was a spinsterish thing to do. She hadn't seen hide nor hair of Ford since the night he'd shown her the stars. If he couldn't even make the effort to stick his head out of that mysterious laboratory to say hello and thank her for occupying his niece, she was finished making the effort to help him.

Rose glanced up from her desk at the opposite end of the room, where she'd been conjugating Spanish words aloud, much to Violet's aggravation. "Since you don't like him," Rose said, "I can take Rowan instead."

"I like Rowan fine."

"I meant the viscount. I was giving you leave to take a fancy to the man and get yourself married, but since you haven't, well, he's mighty handsome, and—"

"You're too young to take Rowan over there unchaperoned," Violet said pointedly. She was sick of Rose always trying to marry her off. And though she knew she should feel relieved that Ford was ignoring her, she was peeved to find herself vexed instead.

But she shouldn't take that out on her sister. She looked up, contemplating the fuzzy pattern the dark molding made on the ceiling as she searched for her missing patience. "I'm sorry, Rose." She sighed, wondering what was getting into her these days. Ford Chase's effect on her was ridiculous. "If Mum says you may go, you have my blessing."

Rose snapped the Spanish book shut and ran off to ask their mother, Rowan galloping after her. Leaving *Advancement of Learning* and her notes on the desk, Violet stood and turned to peruse the library's well-stocked shelves. But nothing new caught her interest. All she could think about was Ford's irritating lack of manners.

"Lady Violet."

She swiveled at the sound of the majordomo's voice, noting he held a silver tray. "A letter, milady."

"Father is out in the garden."

"It's for you."

She couldn't remember the last time she'd received a letter. "Are you certain?"

Raising the parchment, Parkinson cleared his throat. "'Lady

Violet Ashcroft,'" he read off the back. "I believe that is you." Handing it to her, he turned on his heel and left.

Peeved all over again, she broke the seal and scanned the childish handwriting. *Dear Lady Violet,* she read, *Why have you not brought Rowan today? Uncle Ford has something for you. Please come. Your friend, Jewel.*

Astonished, she plopped back onto her chair. The nerve of the man, asking a six-year-old to coax her into a visit. *Uncle Ford has something for you.* She could just imagine what—probably a nursemaid's uniform.

"Violet, dear." Mum swept into the library. "Why won't you take your brother to play with his friend?" In a show of checking for dust, she ran a finger along the carved marble mantelpiece, then down one of the two supporting columns that looked like palm trees. Her voice took on the prying tone that mothers must practice behind closed doors. "Did something happen yesterday?"

"Oh, Mum, nothing happened." Which was precisely the problem. And she was getting tired of Mum grilling her every time she came home from Lakefield. She couldn't imagine what her mother expected to happen there that she would find noteworthy. Nothing ever did.

"I would just like a day for myself," she said. "Is that too much to ask?"

"Of course not, dear." Mum focused on the letter still clutched in Violet's hand. "What's that?"

"A note from Jewel." Violet tossed it onto the dark wood desk. Stark white in contrast, the paper looked entirely too important.

"How sweet. What did the girl have to say?"

She wouldn't tell Mum that Ford had something for her— news like that would escalate her motherly prying to record levels. An awkward silence stretched between them while Violet stared at the note, wishing it would disappear.

"Jewel was just asking me to bring Rowan," she finally

admitted. When she looked back up, a tilt of her mother's head was all it took. "I guess I'll go after all," she said with a sigh.

"That's my Violet," Mum said.

And if her cheerful smile set Violet's teeth on edge, she was determined not to show it.

# FIFTEEN

*J*EWEL WAS WAITING on the steps when they
arrived.

"Lady Violet!" she squealed, running down the
long walk to meet the carriage outside the gate. "Just wait till
you see what Uncle Ford has for you! He had to find rocks to
make it."

*Rocks?* Violet couldn't imagine. What sort of man made
things from rocks and had a child write his letters?

A strange one with few manners.

"Perfect rocks," Jewel clarified. "They had to be perfect."
She turned her attention to Rowan. "Tomorrow is my birthday,"
she said, "and Uncle Ford promised he would take me to the
village to spend my money. He said I could invite you and
Violet."

"What money?" Rowan asked.

"He pays me to be good. And not to cry. And other things."

Rowan's jaw dropped open. He turned to Violet.

"Don't even think about it," she said.

Jewel looked toward him sympathetically. "Will you come
with us tomorrow? I have enough coins for us both."

Violet wasn't surprised. If Ford was willing to pay bribes, she had little doubt a girl as bright as Jewel could manipulate her way to a fortune.

"Rowan can bring his own money," she said.

He tugged on her hand. "Does that mean we can go?"

"I suppose. Since it's Jewel's birthday." She couldn't imagine turning six years old and being away from home for her birthday. Birthdays were major events for a child. In the Ashcroft home, they were major events into adulthood. Her family was odd that way.

She wasn't looking forward to the birthday she had coming up.

"Oh, good!" The girl's face lit. Violet was having second thoughts already, but she couldn't deny that smile. Although she still wasn't thrilled with this nursemaid arrangement, at least it would be something different to do. She wouldn't just be sitting here. And Ford wouldn't be able to totally ignore her.

She hated being the center of attention, but a *little* attention would be nice.

"Come inside," Jewel said, turning to head up the walk. She looped her arm through Rowan's and leaned close. "I have an idea for a jest."

Violet might have been half-blind, but there was nothing wrong with her ears. "I heard that," she said.

Jewel started up the steps. "Heard what?"

"You're planning a jest."

Opening the door, the girl batted her long black lashes. "Who, me? You must have mis-mis—" She paused for a breath. "Mis-un-der-stood."

Jewel's tone was so innocent, Violet would have believed her had she not known her better. My, she was going to miss the sprite when she left. And she knew Rowan would, too. But Ford would be relieved. She imagined he thought of the girl as little more than a bother.

Until he came down the corridor and swept the girl into his arms. Then, despite his preoccupation with his laboratory, his love for his niece was obvious. There for all to see, shining in his incredible brilliant blue eyes.

"Have you found our friends after all, baby?"

"I knew they would come if I sent them a letter."

He kissed her on the nose. "Did you think of that yourself?"

When Jewel nodded, Violet hid a gasp of surprise. The sprite was even more resourceful than she'd thought.

"That's my clever girl." Ford hugged her tighter. "And I suppose you got Harry to deliver it?"

"He always does what I ask."

"Doesn't everyone?" With a wry grin, he turned to their guests. "Welcome," he said, sounding like he meant it. "Please come in."

"As you wish," Violet murmured. Maybe she'd been too quick to judge him. Thinking he was even better looking than she remembered from a few days ago, she tripped over the threshold.

And once again found herself in his arms.

She couldn't imagine how he'd managed to set Jewel on her feet before catching her, but he'd done so quite handily. He steadied her, then grinned. "This is getting to be quite a habit."

"I'm sorry." Blast her poor vision, anyway. His hands felt warm on her shoulders, and she swayed in his grip. "I know I should be more careful."

"Nonsense. I enjoy catching you."

His charming smile almost succeeded in making her believe him. But of course he didn't enjoy catching her, or even being with her, for that matter—the fact that he'd ignored her four days running certainly proved that.

She not-so-subtly wrenched free of his hands. "Lady Jewel said you have something for me?"

"Did she?" He looked disappointed—as though he'd wanted to tell her himself. He turned to his niece. "What did you tell her?"

"Just that you made something from rocks. And I invited

them to come with us tomorrow." She grabbed Rowan's hand. "Let's go play in the garden."

"Wait." With an outstretched arm, Violet stopped her brother's headlong rush. She looked to Ford. "Do you think we should let them go alone?"

Ford shrugged. "I'll send Harry after them," he said. "And if you'll wait for me in the drawing room, I'll bring the surprise."

She watched the children leave in one direction and Ford go the other. The moment they were all out of sight, a little flutter erupted in her stomach. A surprise. When was the last time a man had given her a surprise?

Never.

Unless she counted her father, and most of *his* surprises involved flowers.

Trying not to get her hopes up, Violet made her way through Lakefield's now familiar corridor to the drawing room. She seated herself on the faded couch. She crossed her ankles. She uncrossed them. For the hundredth time since she'd met Ford, she told herself not to be ridiculous.

It was becoming a litany.

Although it seemed like an eternity, she didn't wait long before he entered, breathing heavily, as though he'd run from one end of the house to the other. Which she supposed he must have.

He wasn't holding anything, though. Disappointment welled up inside her—which was ridiculous. Then he drew something from his pocket—something small—and held it out, almost shyly.

"I made this for you," he said.

She took it from him, turning it in her hands. Hardly a thing of beauty, it was two round, clear pieces of glass framed by some sort of wire. A little bridge connected them, and there were metal sticks on both sides.

Puzzled, she looked up.

"Spectacles," he said. He slid onto the couch beside her, acting friendly, familiar.

What little composure she had left completely fled.

At her lack of response, his brow furrowed. "Have you not heard of spectacles? They're sometimes called eyeglasses."

That jarred her out of her haze. *Spectacles.* Her mouth dropped open, and her breath caught in her chest. "I—of course I've heard of them, but…"

More words wouldn't come.

"Would you like to try them on?"

"I…thank you," she breathed.

She truly *was* thankful. This was the most thoughtful thing anyone had ever done for her. But the sad truth was, she knew the spectacles were useless.

She bit her lip. "I…I can read just fine. I know Rowan told you I cannot see very well, but it's the distance that's a blur. Printed pages look clear as water. But I sincerely appreciate—"

"No." She'd expected him to look disappointed, but instead he grinned. "These aren't for reading, Violet."

"They're not?" Thrilled as she was at his unexpected thoughtfulness, her brain seemed to be muddled, not half because of his close proximity. "What are they for, then?"

"Spectacles for reading have convex lenses—they get fatter in the middle. These are concave, the opposite. The edges are thicker than the center. They'll help you see in the distance."

As she digested what he was saying, her hands began shaking. "What is all this metal?"

"Silver. To hold the lenses on your face. For reading, when a body is still, it's fine to hold a lens or balance a pair on your nose. But after I made these, it occurred to me that you may want to wear them and move around. So I devised the sidepieces to rest on your ears and hold them in place."

He scooted even closer, so close she could smell his clean spicy scent. It made her light-headed. Gently he took the spectacles from her hands, narrowing his eyes as he gauged them compared to her features. "I'll probably need to adjust them. You've a smaller face than I thought."

She'd never thought of herself as small—any part of her. Lily was the small one.

And she'd never, ever thought she might be able to see like a normal person. "May I try them on?" she asked, struggling to steady her voice.

"Please do. I suspect I may have to play with the lenses as well, to give you optimal vision. The degree of concavity affects the amount of correction."

She hardly understood what he was talking about, but she didn't care. Her head was buzzing. This man had made her spectacles. He was handsome and generous and warm.

He lifted her chin with a finger, and she obediently raised her face, holding her breath while he fit the contraption in place. It felt strange there, perched precariously. She closed her eyes against the sensation.

When she opened them, Ford rose and stepped back—and he was still in focus.

"Oh, my," she breathed, unable to tear her gaze from his face.

He stepped yet farther away...and she could still see him. He smiled that devilish smile of his, and she could see it all the way from where she sat.

"Oh, my." Suddenly she was looking everywhere. "I can see the bellpull!" she exclaimed. "And the clock across the room." He had clocks all over his house, and this chamber was no exception. "I can read the time! On that clock, and that one, too!"

It seemed a miracle. She stood, walking on shaky legs to the window. With the spectacles on, she felt taller than before and nearly tripped.

Nothing had changed there, but it only made her laugh.

"Look." She leaned her palms on the windowsill, aghast at the beauty of the world. "I can see it—I can see everything! The clouds and the flowers and the leaves on the trees. Each individual leaf."

"They're working for you, then," his voice came from behind her. "But odds are I can make them even better. We'll have to figure out whether more or less concavity will be optimal, and then, with a day or two to remake them, I can—"

"No." She whirled to face him. "You're not taking these away from me." She put her hands to the frame, tilting the spectacles crazily.

He laughed, a deep sound of pleasure. "Let me at least make them fit."

"No."

"A minute, that's all it will take." His lips curved with amusement. "I left the sidepieces straight, you see? If I bend them around your ears, they'll stay in place better."

"A minute?"

His eyes met hers, that brilliant, compelling blue. Something flip-flopped in her stomach. "One minute," he promised.

Reluctantly she released the spectacles, and he slid them off her face. The world immediately blurred.

She hugged herself, a little thrill running through her as she watched him manipulate the metal. "Faith, what a difference they make. Jewel said something about you needing to find rocks. Perfect rocks. What did she mean by that?"

"I took her up into the hills, hunting for quartz for the lenses. Rock crystal." He glanced up briefly, and she wished she could see his eyes better, see the heart-stopping glint she suspected was there. He refocused on his task. "Perfectly clear quartz is difficult, but not impossible, to find."

"They're not glass? They're called eyeglasses."

"True." He smiled as he worked. "But plain glass doesn't have the properties needed for optical lenses."

"How did you know that?"

Making a final adjustment, he shrugged, an almost elegant tilt of his shoulders. "My brothers would tell you I've wasted countless hours filling my brain with useless facts, when I could have been doing something productive."

Her heart lurched at that thought. "Oh, but it wasn't useless at all. Look what you've done with that knowledge!"

"My family wouldn't agree with you." Finished, he stepped closer to put the spectacles back on her face. "They would much rather see me improve this estate, instead of sinking all my income into research and experiments."

"They just don't understand you, then." She could relate to that, since her family rarely understood her.

"You're generous to say so. Especially since I'm beginning to see they're right. I should have renovated Lakefield a decade ago. I've been living with my oldest brother entirely too long."

He ran his fingers around her ears, making sure the side-pieces curved to fit. A little thrill rippled through her at the contact.

"Comfortable?" he asked.

The way he looked at her made her breath catch. She swallowed hard and nodded.

His hands still rested on her face. Warm fingertips danced beneath her jaw. "Can you see well now?"

She nodded again, gazing into his eyes, his beautiful eyes, realizing she was close enough to see them without the lenses. So close she could feel the heat radiating from his skin. "Thank you," she whispered. "You've changed my life."

With all her heart, she meant it. This incredible man had given her the most amazing gift. And now he was looking at her, really looking at her.

She was the center of his attention.

Blinking at that thought, she dropped her gaze to his mouth.

He had a beautiful mouth, too. Suddenly, inexplicably, she wanted it on hers.

And suddenly it was.

His lips were warm and soft, much softer than she'd imagined a man's lips would be. They brushed hers once, twice, then settled more firmly, caressing her mouth with a skill that sent a shiver of delight coursing through her. His hands were still cupping her face, and they threaded into her hair.

She had no idea what madness had possessed him to kiss her, but she didn't want him to stop. Instinctively, her arms came up to loop around his neck, and she pressed herself closer. He felt hard and strong against her, her body on fire wherever they touched.

Faith, she wanted to melt right into him.

The pleasure was so unexpected, a mind-numbing, delicious sensation. A little whimper escaped her throat, and suddenly, thrillingly, his mouth slanted more hungrily over hers. His fingers tightened in her hair, and her pulse raced in response.

Then he pulled away, a dazed half-smile curving his lips, his vivid eyes a little hazy. He looked as stunned as she felt.

She shook herself, an ineffective attempt to clear her head. Of course he was stunned. A man would have to be daft to kiss a woman like her. Especially when she was wearing spectacles.

But that didn't stop her from wishing he'd do it again.

"That was...amazing," he murmured.

"Yes. Well." She looked down at the unvarnished floorboards. *Amazing.* What had he meant by that? Her hands went to the sides of her face, feeling the metal that hugged her ears. "I suppose I must look a fright."

"No, Violet." His voice was a husky rasp. "You look lovely." When she glanced back up, he appeared as surprised to have said the words as she was to hear them. "Your eyes shine like bronze behind the lenses."

She was still feeling dizzy, still wishing she could lean against him again and feel his mouth on hers once more...

But she knew it wouldn't happen. Whatever had driven him to do such a ludicrous thing—such a *ridiculous* thing—was unlikely to ever recur.

"My eyes are brown," she said bluntly. She wasn't lovely, and she didn't like being lied to. If she'd been average-looking before, now, with the spectacles, she was sure she looked hideous.

"Your eyes look bronze to me," he repeated, "though I've also thought they look like brandy. My favorite brandy. And you look fine. Better than fine, in fact."

Better than he'd thought, Ford realized with a start.

Enchanted by her delight with the spectacles, he'd acted without thinking. The kiss had been impulsive. And enjoyable... much more enjoyable than he'd ever have imagined.

Now, seeing her flushed with happiness, from his gift or his kiss—he wasn't sure which, but he hoped it was both—he wondered how he'd ever thought she was plain. His sister often accused him of being oblivious, and for once he agreed. Violet's unique beauty sent the blood pumping through his veins.

He wanted to kiss her again.

Never a man to deny himself pleasure, he began to reach for her—but the children came bounding into the drawing room.

"Uncle Ford!"

"What is it?" he grumbled, then cursed himself silently when his niece's eyes turned troubled.

He had to learn to be more patient. Jewel hadn't meant to keep him from enjoying another kiss. Children and romance simply didn't mesh—another one of the many reasons he was in no hurry to have any of his own.

He sucked in a breath. "What is it?" he repeated, forcing his lips to curve in a smile.

She smiled back. "There was a spi—"

"*What* is on your face?" Rowan interrupted, staring at his sister.

"Spectacles. Ford made them for me."

Behind them, Violet's brandy eyes glowed with wonder, and Ford didn't miss the fact that she'd finally called him by his given name. The single word made him glow inside to match.

"What for?" Rowan asked.

"So I can see better." The glow spread to encompass her entire face. "I can see things all the way across the room."

"Oh." Hands behind his back, the boy rocked up on his toes. "That's good. But they look odd."

"They look better on her than on me," Jewel said. "Uncle Ford used my face to test different ideas. I think we tested about eleventy of them."

Violet grinned. "Eleventy, hmm?"

"Jewel." Rowan made a funny sound in his throat. "Remember? Remember what we were going to tell them?"

"Gads, I forgot!" She paused for effect. "You won't believe what happened!"

"What?" Ford and Violet said together.

"We found a spider in the garden. A big, fat, hairy one. Rowan saved me from it," she added, beaming at said savior.

"Did he?" Violet said very solemnly.

"Mmm-hmm." Struggling to keep a smile from his face, Rowan whipped his hand out from behind his back. "Look."

Violet screamed. And screamed some more. Then she turned to Ford and buried her face against his cravat, so hard he could feel the metal frame of the spectacles biting into the skin beneath his shirt.

She was a nice, warm armful, but he wished she would stop trembling.

The spider really was quite impressively enormous. "Get that out of here," he told her brother.

"But it's dead. It cannot hurt anyone."

Jewel erupted in giggles. "Yes, Uncle Ford, it's dead." She turned to her accomplice. "I told you it would work. I could tell your sister is lily-livered."

"I am not," Violet said, her voice muffled against Ford's front. As if to prove her bravery, she turned to look, then promptly reburied her face.

Knowing his niece well—or rather, assuming she was like her

prank-playing father—Ford sent her a warning glance. "Just get it out of here, will you?"

"Oh, very well." Still giggling, Jewel went to open a window and motioned Rowan over to toss the creature outside. "But it really cannot hurt anyone."

"It wouldn't hurt anyone were it alive, either," Ford said. "It's not a deadly sort." Somewhat reluctantly, he coaxed Violet out of his arms. "But that isn't the point."

"It was ugly," Violet said with a nervous giggle of her own.

She walked to the window and peered at the dead spider dangling ungracefully from an overgrown bush. A delicate shudder rippled through her.

"I can see very well," she declared, "and that is quite the ugliest thing I've ever laid eyes on. Perhaps these spectacles aren't such a good idea, after all."

# SIXTEEN

$\mathcal{W}$HILE ROWAN RAN for the house, anxious to tell their mother all about Lady Jewel and the spider, Violet alighted from the carriage, still looking about in wonder.

The world was magnificent. She wandered around the side of the mansion, stunned by the splendor of her father's exquisite flowers. Such brilliant colors, such delicate petals. She'd seen them before, of course, but only in her own hands or leaning down close. The gardens overall had been blurs of color, never this entire panorama of perfect shapes and rainbow hues stretching into the distance. And, oh, the subtle details were wondrous.

Oblivious to her approach, her father knelt by some roses, patting mulch into place. She touched him on the shoulder. "You've done a spectacular job here, Father."

"Eh?" Engrossed, he didn't look up. "What did you say?"

Sighing, she raised her voice a notch. "Your flowers are beautiful."

"So are you, dear," he said automatically, rising from his knees. At the sight of her, he froze. "Violet. What have you done to your face?"

She grinned. "They're spectacles, Father. Lord Lakefield made them for me."

He blinked. "What do they do?"

"Besides make me ugly?" Despite that fact, a smile bloomed on her face. Throwing her arms out wide, she spun in a circle, looking at everything at once. "I can see, Father! I can really see!"

In her exuberance, she'd yelled it, and he'd certainly heard. When she stopped twirling, he gathered her into his arms—something he hadn't done in quite a while.

He hugged her hard before pulling back, then searched her eyes with his. "Can you see everything? Just like me?"

"Everything." She knelt by his flowers. "This red rose, and that yellow one in the distance. And the hedges over there, and the rowan tree by the river." She rose, turning slowly this time, savoring the incredible view. "I cannot wait for tonight to look at the stars." Facing the house, she stopped. "I can see Lily smiling behind the window." She waved merrily, grinning when her sister waved back.

"Violet!" Rowan came running out, their mother trailing behind. "I told Mum about your spectacles, and she wants to see them!"

"Chrysanthemum!" her father said enthusiastically, going to kiss the woman as though they hadn't seen each other for a week. Normally Violet rolled her eyes at her parents' uninhibited affection, not to mention Father's absurd habit of calling Mum Chrysanthemum instead of Chrystabel. It was so sickly sweet it made her stomach turn.

Usually. But today, watching them kiss, Violet could only think of her own kiss a little while ago. Her first kiss. A tingling weakness spread through her body.

What was happening to her?

"Let me see these spectacles," her mother said, taking Violet's face in her hands and turning it this way and that. "Do they really help you see?"

"Immeasurably. It's quite a miracle. And worth looking hideous, I can assure you."

"You look fine, dear."

Now Violet did roll her eyes.

Her sisters stepped outside, both wearing new gowns they'd had fitted the past week while Violet had been at Lakefield House. Rose's was a midnight blue brocade, the skirt looped up and caught on the sides with ice blue bows to show off the matching satin underskirt beneath. Embroidered lace trimmed her chemise, peeking from the scooped neckline and the cuffs of the fitted sleeves.

If not exactly practical, it was quite a lovely dress, and Violet could see every detail before her sister even came near. Absolutely a miracle.

"What is that dreadful contraption on your face?" Rose asked. Lady Tact.

"See, Mum?"

"You look fine," Lily said. Her gown was a sunny yellow and quite lovely, too. It had a square neckline and a nutmeg-colored underskirt embroidered with yellow daisies.

"I don't care how I look," Violet told them all. "Only that I can see." She turned to her mother. "When will my own new gowns be fitted?"

"Since when do you care about clothes?" Rose asked.

But Mum just beamed. "Tomorrow. I shall send a note to the seamstress forthwith."

"Excellent," Rose said. "And I'll take Rowan to Lakefield tomorrow, since Violet will be busy."

Last week, Violet would have been relieved to hear that. But now she was just annoyed.

"That won't be necessary," Mum said. "Violet can be fitted in the morning while Rowan has his lessons. She'll be free by afternoon."

Rose's pout was so well done, it could earn her a part in a play at the Theatre Royal.

"Lord Lakefield said he would take us to the village for Jewel's birthday tomorrow," Rowan informed them. "Jewel has a lot of coins. May I try the spectacles?"

"If you're careful." When Violet gingerly removed them, her world went blurry. She handed them to her brother, and he slipped them on.

"I cannot see," he said, scrunching up his nose and squinting through the lenses.

"Well, of course not. They're for bad eyes, and your eyes are good."

"Let me see," Lily said. Rowan handed over the spectacles, and she held them up to her face. "Goodness, Violet, your eyes must be really bad."

"Let *me* see," Rose said, grabbing for them.

"Careful!" The metal frames were thin, and Violet didn't want her new treasure broken.

"I won't hurt them." Rose slid them onto her face, then gasped. "Is this what things look like to you?"

"Probably. But not anymore." She took the eyeglasses from Rose and happily settled them back in place, sighing as her view of the family cleared. "I don't care what I look like," she said again. "It's just so wonderful to *see*."

"Truly, you look fine," Lily said kindly. "The spectacles suit your face somehow."

Violet didn't believe her, but she really didn't care.

"Truly," Lily repeated, and when she smiled, her teeth looked whiter and straighter than Violet remembered. "It was thoughtful of Lord Lakefield to make them, wasn't it? He must be a very nice man."

"And handsome," Rose added.

"Yes," Violet said. "We all know you think he's handsome."

"May Jewel come for supper?" Rowan asked.

Mum patted her son on the head. "A grand idea. We'll send an invitation immediately. We all owe Lord Lakefield thanks for restoring Violet's vision."

"Eh?" her husband asked. "Did you say something about a decision?"

Mum set her hand on his arm. "I said vision, darling."

"Hmmph," he muttered half to himself as he plucked a dead head off a hollyhock plant. "The man of the house is traditionally involved in decisions."

# SEVENTEEN

ORD LEANED AWAY from the Ashcrofts' polished mahogany table, barely resisting patting his stomach. The supper had been absolutely delicious, especially compared to the unimaginative fare Hilda prepared and served.

"Thank you kindly for the invitation," he told Lord Trentingham.

"Imitation?" The earl cocked his head quizzically. "It wasn't common chicken," he said, not unkindly. "The partridges in that fricassee were hunted today."

"Darling," Lady Trentingham said loudly, laying graceful fingers on her husband's arm. Eschewing convention, she sat right beside her husband rather than at the other end of the table. "Lord Lakefield was thanking you for inviting him to dine."

"Yes," Ford all but bellowed, since *he* was at the other end of the table, "it was quite a treat to spend an evening in the company of all of your beautiful ladies."

He couldn't help but notice that Rose practically purred. "You're quite welcome—" she began.

"Thank *you* for making my spectacles," Violet interrupted. Her mother had seated her next to him. "This is the most wonderful thing anyone's ever done for me," she added, the words clearly from her heart.

Candlelight from the silver branches on the table glinted off the lenses shielding her eyes. "It was nothing," he told her, meaning it. He'd made the eyeglasses as an experiment—to see if he could devise a lens to help her see her daily world as the telescope had helped her see the stars. He was pleased his idea had proven workable, and her delight was an unexpected bonus.

Unexpected and more pleasing than he ever would have imagined.

As another experiment, he offered her a lazy, seductive smile, dropping his gaze to her lips. When her cheeks flushed fetchingly pink, he was certain she was remembering their kiss.

Hmm…he would have to continue this line of investigation. It could very well lead somewhere interesting.

"Are you finished, milord?"

"Oh. Yes." He cleared his throat and shifted to allow the maid to remove his plate. Was she Daphne or Dolly? He liked the way Lady Trentingham addressed servants like they mattered to her, and talked to them instead of just ordering them around, and listened to what they had to say. It was both unusual and admirable, and he was attempting to do the same. But the Ashcrofts seemed to have so many. He couldn't remember this one's name.

"Would you care for tea now, milord?"

"Um, yes. Please," he said, feeling more and more like a halfwit. Darla? Was she Darla?

Some impression he must be making on Violet's family. And devil take it, he hadn't yet analyzed why, but he did want to make a good impression.

They were neighbors, after all.

"Everything tasted so good," Jewel said as another maid whisked away her empty Delftware plate.

Lady Trentingham smiled at his niece. "We're glad you enjoyed it, sweetheart."

In fact, Jewel had all but licked her plate clean. Though Hilda's cooking left much to be desired, Ford hadn't realized he was starving his niece. It was humiliating.

She beamed at their hostess. "Your house is so pretty."

"You've said that," Ford told her. Six times.

Her gaze swept the exquisite molded ceiling, the gilt cornice, the heavily carved fireplace, the enormous flower arrangements set on every flat surface. "Well, it *is* pretty."

Ford felt his shoulders tense. While Trentingham Manor was opulent beyond anything the Chases owned, Jewel didn't have to keep saying it. She was making him out a pauper. Between the two of them, any hopes he had of impressing the earl and his wife were sinking fast.

"Milk, milord?" the maid asked. "Sugar?"

"Both, if you please."

Dorothy? he wondered. Daisy? She set a small silver pitcher on the table.

"I have the sugar," Rowan announced. As the boy passed the bowl along with a tiny silver spoon, Ford looked at him and wondered if he'd have been called Daisy were he born a girl.

Probably. Or Daffodil. Or Peony, perhaps.

Jewel pulled on the maid's sleeve. "Dinah, can I have tea?"

"May I please have some tea," Ford corrected her automatically. *Dinah*, he thought with relief.

"May I please have some tea?" his niece repeated obediently. "I love tea, but Uncle Ford doesn't have any."

Tea was still somewhat of a novelty and frightfully expensive; Lord knew he didn't stock it at Lakefield House. Apparently Violet's family could afford anything they wanted. And now, thanks to Jewel, they knew he couldn't.

Violet leaned close. "Children rarely think before they speak," she whispered sympathetically. "Rowan is no different."

He knew that was true. But bloody hell, was his discomfort that obvious? Avoiding her gaze, he focused across the room on the Tudor linenfold paneling—painted white in the latest fashion —while he waited for his tea.

"Heavens," Lady Trentingham said. "I almost forgot to tell everyone the news. My maid Anne is getting married."

"Goodness, that's wonderful, Mum." Lily actually clapped her hands. "Is she wedding that coachman you introduced her to?"

"Of course. I knew they would suit."

Rose sipped from her wineglass. "Her betrothed is from the Liddington estate, isn't he? Where will they live?"

"Here, naturally. We'll hire him on." The countess laced her fingers together atop the mahogany table. "Anyone can replace a coachman, but I cannot do without Anne."

"How many matches does that make for you this year, Mum?" Lily asked. "Six?"

"Just so. But I introduced Lord Almhurst to Lady Mary Spencer last week, so I expect I'll be up to seven soon."

The maid arrived with the tea and poured. "Thank you, Dinah," Ford said, hoping the Ashcrofts noticed how respectful he was of their servants. He lifted the ridiculously small spoon and began using it to shovel sugar into his tea. Though he didn't share his twin sister's habit of eating dessert before the meal, he did share her sweet tooth.

"Seven weddings," Rose said with an impressive sigh. "In case you haven't heard, my lord, Mum is the unofficial matchmaker for all of Southern England."

"I've introduced people from the North as well," Lady Trentingham said a bit huffily.

This talk of marriages was making Ford nervous, so he decided to change the subject. "What time shall I fetch you to go to the village tomorrow?" he asked Violet.

Her hands went to the frames of her spectacles. "Oh, I…well—"

"She cannot go," Rose put in from across the table. "Mum has arranged for her to have new gowns fitted."

Rose graced him with a wide smile, but although she had fetching dimples, he didn't find himself attracted. Odd, considering her tall, willowy beauty was very attractive, indeed.

"Perhaps I can accompany Rowan instead," she added. "I know how much he's looking forward to the outing."

"It won't take the entire day," Ford said. "The village is hardly a metropolis." An understatement—Jewel would likely finish her shopping in twenty minutes. He spooned in more sugar—pure white sugar, he noticed, imported from the West Indies, no doubt. Another sign of the Ashcroft wealth. He turned back to Violet. "I can come by for you and Rowan in the afternoon, following your fitting."

Behind her new lenses, her eyes clouded. "I—I..." She shifted on her petit point seat cover. "I'm not certain I'm ready to be seen in public," she blurted. "With the spectacles, I mean. I know everyone will stare and ask questions. Perhaps after I'm more used to them—"

"You goose," Rose interrupted. "Just take them off."

Violet's hands went protectively to the sides of her face, as though she were afraid her sister might grab them off herself. "I like to *see*," she said. "I don't want to take them off."

"If you're going to insist on walking around with glass and metal on your head, then you'll have to get used to people staring at you."

"Rose." Lady Trentingham's tone was soft, but a warning nonetheless. "Our Violet prefers not to be the center of attention," she explained to Ford.

"Please pass the sugar," Lily asked sweetly.

"I'd like some, too," Rose said. "Put it between us."

Ford sent the sugar across the table. "How about if we go to Windsor, then?" he suggested to Violet. "It's much bigger than the village. You're unlikely to run into anyone you know there, and Jewel will find a larger shopping selection."

Violet looked unconvinced, but Jewel's eyes lit like green beacons. "Good idea, Uncle Ford."

"But—" Violet started.

"Yes, it is," Rose interrupted. "Except that will take all day, so Violet won't be able to go. But as I said, I'll be happy to go instead."

"Rose." Now her mother's voice sounded more exasperated. "That won't be necessary. I can send a note to Madame and reschedule the fitting for another day."

"But—" Violet tried again.

"A perfect plan," Lady Trentingham concluded.

## EIGHTEEN

"*H*OLY HADES," Rowan whispered. "Look at that thing."

As they headed toward the river, Violet glanced at Harry walking in front of them, his bald head shining in the sun. Thankfully he hadn't seemed to hear.

"Hush," she told Rowan. "You don't want me to tell Mum you're talking like that, do you?"

Having expected Ford, she'd been surprised when Harry had come to the door instead. Not that she was sure she wanted to go to Windsor at all. She did want to see the town, really see it, but...

She touched the metal frame of her spectacles—egad, people were going to stare and ask questions.

"Father says holy Hades all the time," Rowan muttered.

"And you can, too," she said, keeping her voice low, "as soon as you're grown and have children of your own."

"But just *look* at that thing!" he exclaimed.

Harry definitely heard that. He slowed so they could catch up, a crooked smile on his face. "I'd wager you've never seen anything like it," he said, gesturing toward the dock.

"I haven't," Violet agreed.

On the river, Ford and his niece were waving from the deck of a barge so old, she half expected it to sink before her eyes. Flecks of gold on its woodwork glistened, the last vestiges of gilding that must have once graced the heavily carved boat. Once upon a time, she imagined, it had been a ceremonial vessel for someone very important—if not the king himself.

But now it must be more than a hundred years old.

At least the sails still looked serviceable, if tattered and gray. She waved back, and her brother did, too. Then she stopped and turned him to face her.

"Don't say anything bad about it in front of them. Please." She still remembered him asking Hilda for cherry tart, and she never knew what would come out of his mouth next to embarrass her. "Please," she repeated.

"Bad?" Rowan's green eyes looked incredulous. "It's the most wondrous thing I've ever seen!" With that, he broke into a run and didn't stop until he'd crossed the dock and leapt onto the ancient craft.

Violet was glad Harry's old legs gave her an excuse to approach more slowly, since her fashionable high heels hampered her ability to run. She wasn't used to wearing them. But at least, with her new spectacles, she was confident she wouldn't trip over the uneven ground.

A crew waited aboard, three men she recognized as Ford's coachman and outriders. As she lifted her peach satin skirts, Ford reached a hand to help her up. She smiled and put hers in it. "Good day, my lord."

He grinned, his free hand gesturing at the blue, cloudless sky. "It is, my lady." He dropped his voice as she stepped aboard. "You look lovely today, Violet."

Her own free hand went reflexively to her spectacles. Though her new gowns weren't ready, she was wearing her fanciest day dress and knew it was pretty. But she also knew she was not.

He held onto her fingers a few moments more than necessary. "I hope you'll enjoy the day."

If the fluttering in her stomach was any indication, she was sure she would. When he released her hand, she felt a distinct loss.

"I'm surprised you came by river," she said, "rather than by road." An understatement if ever she'd uttered one, though suddenly the barge seemed like the most delightful mode of transportation.

"It's a beautiful day," he said, "and Windsor just a pleasant sail down the Thames. I thought the children would enjoy it."

"They are already." With whoops of joy, the two of them were chasing around the cabin perched in the barge's center, jumping over ropes and racing around rigging as though the entire vessel had been designed as their playground.

Like Lakefield House, the boxy cabin could have used a coat of paint, but it was obvious the boat had once been elegant and impressive. "Wherever did you find this?" Violet asked.

"It came with the estate. Though a bit the worse for wear, she's seaworthy, I assure you. Or riverworthy, in any case."

"She's magnificent." Twirling slowly in a circle, Violet noted the rich details. Although spotless, the barge was old to the point of antiquity. Just the thought of riding such a silly thing made her want to laugh. But in its own way, it was beautiful, too. "Are you going to fix her up?"

"Perhaps. I haven't thought about it, really." The boat started down river, and he led her to two chairs on the deck. "Sit, will you?" She did, and he sat down beside her. "What do you fancy shopping for today?"

"There's nothing I want. This is Jewel's day." They were a long way from Windsor yet, so she settled back, delighting in the light breeze on her face and the warm sun dancing on her skin. And the company. She'd never thought she'd enjoy a man's company much, but Ford Chase was changing her mind.

The barge rocked gently as they made their way down the Thames. Father waved from the garden as they passed, and she waved in return, then stiffened.

Father had seen her. That meant other people could see her. Including neighbors.

Her gaze went wistfully to the cabin. "Can we go inside?"

"It's a sleeping cabin—there's nothing in there but a bed, so it's not really suited for the two of us." He raised a brow, a gleam in his eye, and she felt her cheeks grow hot. "Do you not enjoy the sun?" he asked.

"I worry for my complexion," she fibbed. Her mother and Rose both worried about their complexions, but Violet had never cared a fig. "I much prefer rain."

"Rain?" He looked at her as though she were a half-wit, which accurately described how she was feeling at the moment. Then a smile tipped the corners of his mouth, and she knew he had caught her in the lie. "You really prefer rain to sunshine?" he asked, much too politely.

Seeing a man wander the riverbank, she rose and turned her back. "Well, I love rainbows," she said, only digging herself in deeper. "And since rain is needed for rainbows, I do prefer it."

He grinned up at her. "I can make you a rainbow without rain."

"Can you?" He was the most extraordinary man!

"Absolutely. I will do so tomorrow. In the meantime..." With great exaggeration and a flourish, he gestured to her empty chair.

She sat back down, and Ford began talking about this and that. She was soon so engrossed in their conversation that she forgot all about her eyeglasses or being spotted wearing them. The warm sun felt good on her skin, and though their journey was a leisurely one that covered several miles, the time passed quickly.

Too quickly. Before she knew it, they were docking at Windsor. Where she suddenly got cold feet.

It was a busy town. Windsor Castle had suffered much damage during the Cromwell years, and King Charles was now enthusiastically refurbishing and expanding it, which meant many laborers crowded the streets along with the town's usual inhabitants. Wearing her spectacles here would be worse than just being the center of attention—more like being the center of the universe. At the last moment, she pleaded a headache and retired to the shady safety of the cabin.

Two hours later, the others returned to find her there.

# NINETEEN

"*I*'M STARVING." Followed by the children, Ford stepped inside to drop off their latest purchases. "If you're feeling better, can I tempt you with a meal? I promise to take you into a nice, dark deserted inn."

Violet heard the teasing in his voice and knew he knew she was a coward. He'd accompanied the children around town, where Jewel had purchased ribbons and a hat and a doll. For her birthday, Ford had bought her a lovely silver heart pendant. He'd also kindly bought Rowan some marbles fashioned from pretty stones, and they'd stopped at vegetable stands and a butcher, loading the barge with staples for Lakefield's kitchen.

They'd made three trips back and forth, and in all that time, Violet hadn't set foot out of the cabin.

Now the three of them crowded into the small space, their expectant gazes practically pinning her to the bed where she sat.

She bit her lip. Ford had been more than patient. The least she could do was be honest. "I'm sorry, my lord. But I just know people will stare."

"Will you stop my-lording me?" He swept off his hat and, in a gesture that was beginning to become familiar to her, raked his fingers through his long brown hair. "After what happened yesterday"—his voice deepened an octave, and he raised a brow as he met her eyes—"you should certainly have leave to call me Ford."

"Ford, then," she said. He was right. And she was miserable.

Jewel tugged on her uncle's sleeve. "What happened yesterday?"

"He gave me these marvelous spectacles," Violet said before he could answer, although she knew he'd been referring to their kiss.

She'd been thinking about that kiss the whole time she waited on the barge, replaying every little detail in her mind, over and over, until her lips tingled and she found herself short of breath. She'd alternated between wondering if he'd kiss her again and telling herself not to be ridiculous.

Of course, she knew the truth: He'd been carried away by the success of his spectacles, and it wasn't going to happen another time. But that didn't seem to keep her from hoping and dreaming.

And another truth she knew was that she'd never get another kiss from anybody if she hid herself the rest of her life. If she was going to wear the spectacles, she needed to get over this fear of appearing in public.

Not all at once, however. "Can we dine on the way back?" she offered as a compromise. "An inn along the river. Where I won't have to walk a street teeming with people."

He measured her for a moment. "If I cannot tempt you with food," he drawled, "I suppose a bookshop wouldn't work, either?"

"A bookshop?" she murmured.

He jammed the hat back on his head. "Right there on Thames Street. You can see it from here." Without asking for permission, he grabbed her arm and drew her off the bed and out of the cabin. She blinked in the sunlight. "There, see?" he said.

In the distance, a sign swung in the slight breeze. The cracked wood looked a century old, but the lettering was newly painted and visible from the barge: JOHN YOUNG, BOOKSELLER.

There weren't too many people on the street. "Maybe just the bookshop," she conceded.

Though his grin told her he knew he'd won, he didn't lord it over her with words.

"I'd like to choose a foreign language book for Rose," she added in a paltry attempt to save face.

"And maybe a philosophy book for yourself?" It seemed he knew her all too well. Jewel and Rowan had followed them out, and he waved them off the barge. "Hurry, before she changes her mind."

As Violet stepped onto the dock, she took a deep breath and lifted her chin. Let people stare. She had to get used to it, and she might as well start now.

"Why a foreign language book for Rose?" Ford asked as they walked.

"A peace offering. I've been entirely too short-tempered with my sister lately."

"Having met her, I suspect she probably deserved it." The street was rutted and uneven, and he took her elbow to steady her in her heels. "But I meant why a foreign language?"

"Oh." She was feeling like a half-wit again, distracted by his hand on her arm, warm through her peach satin sleeve. She caught a glimpse of herself in the mullioned glass windows of the Swan, a reflection of her walking with a man. It was difficult to think straight. "My grandfather was a scholar and spoke many tongues. Of all of us, Rose spent the most time with him before he passed on—"

"She doesn't seem the type."

"She'd be pleased to hear you say that." As they passed Bel and the Dragon, music pumped out the tavern's open door. "Although Grandpapa is no longer with us, Rose has kept her interest in languages. She teaches herself now, and she loves new books to puzzle out for practice."

"I would never have guessed it. Rose seems…"

"Rather empty-headed?" Violet supplied helpfully.

"No. Well, yes, I suppose, but I don't mean it in a bad way."

"She's constructed a good facade, our Rose." She pressed closer to him, avoiding a horse and carriage. "Rose is of the opinion, you see, that men aren't interested in intelligent women."

"I wasn't," he murmured.

"Pardon?"

Switching sides to shield her from the traffic, he cleared his throat. "I wasn't at all aware of Rose's scholarly tendencies. Philosophy, languages…you Ashcroft girls are surely not the usual sort."

"The Ashcroft motto is *Interroga Conformationem.*"

"Question Convention?" Judging from his expression, that seemed to amuse him. "What talent is Lily hiding?"

"Only a gentle heart. She cannot stand to see any being in pain, human or animal." She stopped before the bookshop, which looked blessedly deserted, and suddenly realized that with all the conversation, she'd forgotten to worry about strangers staring at her.

In fact, she'd forgotten about everything but Ford, including her unsightly spectacles—and her little brother. Amazing that a man could have such an effect on her!

Ford looked to the children. "Do you two think you can behave? No pranks in there, you hear?"

"Gads, Uncle Ford, of course we wouldn't." Jewel pulled open the door. "Pretty," she said, looking up. "Like Rowan's house, and Aunty Kendra's."

Walking in behind her, Violet bit back a smile. Although the ceiling Jewel was gazing at was heavily carved and gilded, the rest of the shop had seen better days. Row upon row of narrow aisles were crammed with books on plain wooden shelves. More books sat piled haphazardly on the floor, apparently waiting to be sorted. Dark and well-worn, the place smelled like leather, paper, and ink.

Exactly the way a bookshop should.

A man appeared, looking well-worn like the shop. "John Young, at your service." His hair was salt-and-pepper, his blue eyes lively though faded with age. "If you'll follow me, I'll show you a secret about that ceiling."

He wove through the tall shelves and stopped in the middle of the shop. "Look up," he said.

They all did. A carved molding divided the elaborate ceiling, and although the sides were decorated in an identical fashion, the front half was dated 1576 and the back 1577.

"Why are there two dates?" Rowan asked.

"That's the secret." Mr. Young smiled, revealing a mouthful of teeth with only one missing. "Tell me," he asked the children, "what happened between those two dates?" He waited a beat. "I'll give you a hint. It wasn't the first time it happened, nor will it be the last. It happened again about fifty years later, and yet again in 1665."

"I wasn't born yet," Jewel said. "How should I know?"

Rowan puffed out his chest. "I wasn't born yet, either, but I know anyway. The Black Death."

"Bright boy." The bookseller ruffled Rowan's hair. "The workmen were from Italy and sailed for home when the plague took hold. But they promised to come back and finish, and so they did, a year later. Hence the two dates."

"That's funny." Jewel stared at the ceiling a moment longer, then her gaze dropped to a table against the wall. "A draughts board!" She batted her lashes at the bookseller. "May we play?"

"Of course."

"Mr. Young said I'm bright," Rowan told her. "I wager I can beat you."

Ford laughed. "I wouldn't recommend you bet money. She's the type that goes for the throat."

"I can beat any old girl."

Jewel narrowed her eyes and set her hands on her hips. "We'll see about that."

She made a beeline for the table, waving Rowan into the chair opposite as she settled herself with a fluff of her pale yellow skirts. Her face was all business as she made her first move.

Mr. Young turned to Violet, peering curiously at her spectacles. "May I help you find something, milady?"

"They allow me to see at a distance," she explained, although he politely hadn't asked.

"How very fascinating."

He didn't seem repulsed by her appearance, just honestly interested. "Would you like to try them?" she offered.

"I can see at a distance fine. It's up close where I have trouble. My arms need to be longer." His smile reappeared. "It's a brilliant invention, though, isn't it?"

"Quite." She smiled in return. Perhaps people wouldn't stare at her, after all.

"Have you any books in foreign languages?" Ford asked. "And my lady would like to see some philosophy titles."

"Philosophy I have. This way, if you please." After directing her around the corner to a tall shelf full of books, he scratched his graying head. "Now, as for foreign languages, I'm afraid... ah, yes, perhaps I do have something in the back. If you'll excuse me for a moment."

The instant he disappeared, Ford moved close, so close Violet could smell the warm scent of his skin. Patchouli and soap and fresh air.

He backed her gently against the shelves. "How does it feel to be off the barge?" he whispered.

"Liberating." She gave a nervous laugh. "Will you look for books, too?"

"I'll look for Rose's."

"Would you? I'm hopeless at languages."

"I don't know many. French, having grown up on the Continent during the years of Cromwell's Protectorate." He skimmed his knuckles along her jaw. "And Dutch, since the English court spent time at The Hague as well. And Latin, of course." Wrapping a curl around his finger, he gave it a gentle tug. "But that's all."

"It's three more than I can claim." With his fingers teasing her hair, her scalp felt all tingly. She struggled to keep a clear head. "If you'll choose some subjects Rose might find interesting, I'd be forever grateful."

"Forever grateful. I like the sound of that." He grinned, and her insides flip-flopped. "Though I'm tempted to just stand here and enjoy the lovely view of you in your spectacles."

The proprietor ambled back, dragging a crate of books behind him, and Ford moved away. The old man nodded toward him. "I don't know what sort of foreign book you're looking for, milord, but you may have anything in here for a shilling."

"Anything?" Violet asked.

"Take your pick. My son Thomas found these in the attic— never been up there myself. Must've been there since before I bought the shop—from the looks of them, before that curious ceiling even went in," he added, his old grin quite fetching even with the missing tooth. "Tom wanted to toss them, seeing as we don't deal in foreign titles, but I cannot seem to find it in me to get rid of books." He dusted off his hands. "If you're not wanting anything else, then, I shall leave you to look."

With a nod, he walked off. They heard him stop and talk to the children, a soft murmur followed by youthful giggles. Apparently the shop had no other customers, which suited Violet perfectly. She turned to the shelves, her heart singing as it always did when she was in the presence of books.

Ford crouched on the floor and began absently sifting through the crate. "What would Rose like?"

"Anything, really, except perhaps philosophy or science." The two subjects she and Ford would want for themselves. She smiled at that thought as she peered at the titles on the shelf.

Choosing a slim brown volume, she slipped off her spectacles, the better to see up close. She set them on a ledge and began to flip pages without really reading. She could still feel Ford's fingers on her jaw, his warm breath on her face, the slight tickle of him playing with her hair.

"What is that called?" he asked without looking up.

"*Aristotle's Master-piece.*" It looked promising, though she was surprised to find a book about or by Aristotle that she'd never heard of before. "I think I shall inquire about the price."

"Here, I'll hold it for you while you look some more."

She handed it to him, and he set it on the floor, on top of two volumes he'd apparently chosen for Rose. She could understand why the bookseller would let them go for a shilling. Even without her eyeglasses, the foreign editions looked like they hadn't been opened in decades.

Still crouching by the crate, Ford began humming a soft tune as he searched. A lullaby, if she didn't miss her guess; she wondered if he sang to Jewel. She slipped another title off the shelf. The clicks of checkers told her the children were miraculously staying put. Though their voices were a bit louder than she would have liked, they didn't seem to be bothering the proprietor, so she decided not to let it bother her, either.

She'd added two more likely books to the growing pile when Ford sat down with a thud, clutching a book in both hands.

He looked like he'd seen a ghost.

# TWENTY

"**C**HAT?" VIOLET ASKED. Sitting on the floor, Ford looked as pale as her father's prized lilies. "What's wrong?"

"Nothing." He glanced around uneasily, as though he expected someone to pop up and steal the book out of his white-knuckled hands.

She couldn't help but notice those hands were shaking. The book was small and looked old. No, make that ancient, she decided after she'd reached for her spectacles and slipped them back on. It was handwritten, and the pages sounded brittle, crackling when he gingerly turned them.

"Another foreign title, is it?" Even with the eyeglasses, she couldn't read a word. "Do you expect Rose would like it?"

"No." Still trembling, he stood abruptly. "Not this one."

"Can you read it? Is it French or Dutch?"

"It's no language I've ever seen. Will you get those?" he added distractedly, gesturing to the books on the floor.

As she knelt to collect the volumes they'd chosen, he hurried away to talk to the proprietor.

"Yes, only a shilling," Mr. Young was saying when she joined them a minute later. Gazing down at the book, he lazily flipped a few pages. "It's not English or Latin, though, and difficult to decipher, handwritten as it is. Can you even read it?"

"Well, no." Ford raked his fingers through his hair—not the smooth, thoughtful gesture Violet had become used to seeing, or even the quicker one that indicated frustration. This motion was jerky and convulsive instead.

What was wrong with him?

"I have a friend, an expert in languages," he said. "I thought he might enjoy the challenge." He held out his hand, and she could almost hear him willing the shopkeeper to give him back the book.

The man handed it over, gesturing dismissively. "A shilling will do, then. Truth be told, I feel guilty taking money for the thing at all."

"Appreciate it." Ford turned to Violet, taking the books from her arms. "Add these to the total, will you?" He passed them over to Mr. Young and started digging out his pouch.

"I brought money," she protested. "I cannot accept a gift from you. It wouldn't look right."

"Rubbish. You've already accepted the spectacles, haven't you?"

Her hands went to her face protectively. "These were different. You made them."

"They're just books, Violet."

Mr. Young looked at each book, scribbling their prices on a scrap of paper, preparatory to adding them up. He paused when he came to Violet's first choice. "Are you certain you want this, my lady?"

"*Aristotle's Master-piece*? Yes. Unless…is it very expensive?"

Frowning, he blinked his pale blue eyes. "No, not particularly."

"We'll take it." Ford selected a few coins and pressed them into the bookseller's hand. "Jewel? Rowan? Are you done with your game?" He looked to be in a terrible rush.

"One more minute, Uncle Ford."

He shifted from foot to foot while they finished playing, then took Jewel by the hand to pull her from her seat. With a distracted "Thank you" called over his shoulder to Mr. Young, he waved Violet and Rowan through the door and followed them out with his niece.

"Is something amiss?" the little girl asked.

"No. No, not at all. I'm hoping something is very right." He hastened them down the street, his gaze focused straight ahead to where the barge sat waiting. "Hurry. Quickly."

In her fashionable high heels, Violet had a hard time keeping up, and she completely forgot to worry about who might see her wearing the spectacles. In no time at all, he was ushering them aboard.

"Straight home, Harry." Ford hesitated, though for barely an instant. "No, stop at the first decent inn—but not until we've cleared the town."

The children joined Harry at the helm while Ford hurried Violet into the cabin, apparently forgetting it was unsuitable. He pulled the door shut behind them. When the barge began moving, he let out a long, audible breath and dropped heavily onto the bed.

Since there wasn't any other furniture, Violet seated herself gingerly beside him. "What's going on?" she asked, concerned by this odd behavior.

"I just...I suppose I feared Mr. Young would come running out and take the book back." It was still clenched in his fingers. "It's foolish, I know," he said, offering her a sheepish smile.

"Is it that important, then?"

"If it turns out to be what I'm hoping it is, yes, it's important." He relaxed his grip and, opening the book, turned a page and then another. If she could judge from his smile, the crackle of old paper sounded like music to his ears. "Very important."

"I imagine your friend will be pleased."

In the midst of turning another page, he looked up. "My friend?"

"Your friend who is good with languages."

"Oh." She'd never seen a man blush before. "That wasn't the whole truth, I'm afraid. I just didn't know quite what to say. If the bookseller realized what he had…well, what it might be…"

Meeting her gaze, he sucked in a breath and blew it out. "This book could be extremely valuable, Violet."

Just the way he'd said her name, deep, like he cared, made her warm to her toes.

Rowan opened the door and poked his head in. His gaze sought out the book. "It looks very old," he said soberly. "Is it the emerald secrets book?"

"I'm not sure," Ford said. "Everyone thought it was gone. I'm not certain I quite believed it had ever really existed." Light streamed through the cabin's two windows, illuminating the old pages, but they didn't glow nearly as brightly as his eyes. "The book was supposed to have been small and bound in brown leather, and of course it would have been handwritten. And here, look." He flipped to the first page. "The alchemical symbol for gold. And five words in the title. But I cannot be sure. I wish I could read the thing."

If Violet had never seen a man blush before, she'd never seen one so excited, either. About anything. "The emerald secrets book?" she asked. "What's that?"

Her brother smiled importantly. "It tells the lost secret of the Philosopher's Rock. I'm going to tell Jewel." He slammed the door, and she heard his footsteps pound across the wooden deck.

"The Philosopher's Stone," Ford corrected the empty space where Rowan had stood.

Violet gasped. "The formula to turn metals into gold?"

"The very same. *Secrets of the Emerald Tablet* has been missing for three hundred years, and if this is it…"

"Do you think it really is?"

"I don't know. It could be. Everyone assumed it had been destroyed." He turned a few pages and stared down at the ancient text. "I'm crossing my fingers—and I'm probably the least superstitious man you'll ever meet."

Suspecting he was right, she smiled at that. "What is the Emerald Tablet?"

He shut the book. "It's a long story."

"It's a long way down the river," she pointed out.

"Very well, then," he said, looking pleased. He shifted to lean against the headboard, settling back against some pillows and appearing altogether at home there on the bed.

Her heart sped up at the thought, and she felt her face flush, but he didn't seem to notice.

"It all started," he said, "back in Egypt, some twenty-five hundred years before Christ. Where the Divine Art first had its birth."

"The Divine Art?"

"Alchemy. A priest named Hermes Trismegistus was known to have great intellectual powers. The Art was kept secret and exclusive to the priesthood, but more than two thousand years later, when the tomb of Hermes was discovered by Alexander the Great in a cave near Hebron, they found a tablet of emerald stone. On it was inscribed, in Phoenician characters, the wisdom of the Great Master concerning the art of making gold."

He paused, looking at her where she still sat perched at the foot of the bed. "You look uncomfortable there," he said, reaching a hand behind him to pull out one of the pillows. "Lean back against the wall." He tossed it to her.

He'd told her it was a long story, so she scooted over to the wall and tucked the pillow behind her back, her legs lying cross-wise on the bed. Noticing their outlines were visible beneath the drape of her peach gown, she fluffed her skirts a little. "Where is the Emerald Tablet now?"

"We don't know. But years later, in the thirteenth century, a man named Raymond Lully was born to a noble family in Majorca. He took up the study of alchemy and wandered the Continent to learn more of the science. Many stories have been told of Lully's abilities to make gold, which he claimed to have learned from studying the Emerald Tablet."

"What sorts of stories?"

His mouth curved in a faint smile. "You're really listening, aren't you?"

She cocked her head at him, baffled. "Why wouldn't I be?"

"No reason." Still smiling, he turned the book over in his hands, then opened it again absently. "It's said that the Abbot of Westminster found Lully in Italy and persuaded him to come to London, where he worked in Westminster Abbey. A long time afterwards, a quantity of gold dust was discovered in the cell where he'd lived. Another story has it that Lully was assigned lodgings in the Tower of London. People claimed to see golden pieces he'd made, and they called them nobles of Raymond, or Rose nobles. It was during this period that he is said to have written *Secrets of the Emerald Tablet,* I believe around the year 1275."

"Almost four hundred years ago." Looking at the pages Ford was carefully turning, she could believe the book was that old. "What happened then?"

"Lully eventually left England to resume his travels, but it was thought he left the book behind. It was supposed to have been written in language that's difficult to read."

She held out a hand, and wordlessly, he passed her the open book. She removed her spectacles and peered at the spiky writing. She couldn't read a word. Some of it didn't even look like words, but more like symbols.

"Do you suppose it's Phoenician, like the Tablet?" she asked.

"I have no idea. Legend has it that the book changed hands a few times and then disappeared in the fourteenth century, never to be seen again."

"Until now."

"Maybe." His eyes appeared wistful. "It looks old enough, doesn't it?"

"It would be priceless, wouldn't it?" Imagine being able to

produce gold. Caught up in his excitement, she handed back the book. "You could sell that for a fortune. An unbelievable fortune."

"I'd never sell it." He clutched the book to his chest. "If it's the missing volume, I'll never, ever sell it. Even should it turn out not to divulge a working formula."

"You'd feel the same even if it doesn't reveal how to make gold?" Surprised, and yet somehow not, she slipped her spectacles back on to study his face. "I wouldn't have taken you for a romantic," she said softly.

"A romantic?" he murmured, holding her gaze for a long, breathless moment.

He remained silent while he pulled off his boots and stretched out his legs. And crossed his stockinged feet. And set them on her lap.

Speechless, she looked down. Completely without her permission, her eyes wandered the length of his legs. They looked strong and well-turned, and his knees looked loose, like he was comfortable.

Suddenly wondering what those legs might look like without breeches and hose, *she* wasn't comfortable at all. Tucked behind her back, the pillow he'd thrown to aid her comfort didn't seem to be helping a bit.

"Raymond Lully is the stuff of legends," he continued blithely, apparently oblivious to their shockingly intimate position. "Any book he'd written would hold an immeasurable amount of historic and sentimental value. It would be an honor to own it, no matter what it said."

When he fell silent again, she raised her gaze to his face, and the expression there told her he wasn't oblivious at all.

He knew *exactly* how uncomfortable he was making her.

This was ridiculous.

The barge slowed and bumped against a dock, but it didn't jar her from the spell he'd so expertly woven around them.

"A romantic?" he repeated, clearly not expecting an answer.

His lips curved in a lazy smile, and he leaned forward, reaching one long arm to brush her cheek with two fingers. Her skin grew warm, and her body felt heavy on the bed.

Harry pulled open the door, and the spell was broken.

"Will this do, my lord?" He gestured toward a respectable old riverside inn that boasted tables along the bank of the Thames.

To his credit, he didn't blink when he saw Ford's feet in her lap. And, thank the heavens above, Ford managed to swing them off the bed and pull his boots back on before the children arrived in the doorway.

"It will do very well," he said. "Thank you."

## TWENTY-ONE

"*L*OOK!" JEWEL pointed to an enormous oak by the river. "There are swings!"

The children bounded off the barge and ran shrieking along the grassy bank. Violet walked more carefully behind with Ford beside her, the book still in one hand. She teetered a bit on the unaccustomed high heels—and perhaps, she had to admit, because she felt drunk with new sensations.

Ford had put his feet in her lap. Why on earth had she found herself so affected? Although they'd been sitting on a bed, nothing scandalous had happened. They'd both been fully dressed, and they hadn't even kissed.

The whole thing had been silly, really...as silly as a grown man physically attached to an old leather book. Wondering if he might sleep with it tonight, she smiled to herself.

He put a casual hand at her back. "What do you find so amusing?"

"Nothing." His fingers felt warm through her thin satin gown. She chanced a look at him, feeling flushed and happy at the innocent contact.

That was silly, too. "Nothing at all," she repeated, trying to hide another grin. When his hand dropped from her back, she could swear she still felt its imprint.

By the time the two of them caught up, the young ones had claimed the pair of rope-and-board swings that shared a heavy branch on the old tree's right. They were pumping into the air, racing to see who could get the highest, their laughing taunts floating out over the water.

"That looks like fun," Violet said wistfully. Oh, to be six, flying into the sky on your birthday, instead of almost twenty-one and dreading it.

One-and-twenty. According to Rose, that was the day Violet would become an official spinster. Not that she minded her fate. She'd been resigned to it for years—planning happily for it, in fact. A spinster enjoyed freedoms a wife never would.

But the word "spinster" sounded so very old and *final*.

Ford took her by the arm and marched her around the giant tree. A third swing there hung empty. "Sit," he said.

She giggled, feeling sillier still. "You take it."

"Sit."

With a shrug, she did. It had been years since she'd been on a swing—since the last time her family had stayed at Tremayne Castle. The board felt flat and hard beneath her skirts. She wrapped her fingers around the thick, scratchy ropes on either side of her head. When she felt a hand at her back, she gave a little shriek, then laughed as Ford pushed her swinging into the air.

He came around the side to watch her, holding up the book to shade his eyes. "It's nice to hear you laugh."

She laughed again. "I feel like a child."

"Is that bad?" he wondered.

Pumping her legs to go higher still, she considered. The wind rushed by, tangling her hair in the frame of her spectacles. When her peach skirts billowed, she clamped them between her legs. The sun sparkled on the water. Through her miraculous eyeglasses, the landscape looked clear and brightly beautiful all the way to the horizon.

"No," she said at last. "Feeling like a child isn't bad." At nearly twenty-one, feeling like a child was wonderful.

Setting the book on the grass, Ford stepped behind her and gave her a shove. She leaned back, feeling her hair flow and flutter as she went soaring over the river.

"I can go faster than you!" Jewel cried.

"No, I can go faster!" Rowan yelled, and the two of them pumped their hearts out, racing toward the sky.

Ford's hands on Violet's back felt strong and warm, the pushes rhythmic and reliable. Her lids slid closed. She didn't want to go faster than anyone; she just wanted to blank her mind and enjoy the motion.

With her eyes shut, she imagined she was flying. She imagined she was young and beautiful, and Ford was her lover, not just a flirtatious, overwhelmed uncle who wanted her help caring for his niece.

"Holy Hades," Rowan complained, jarring her back into the real world.

Her eyes popped open. "I've told you not to say that."

"No matter how high I get," he panted, "I cannot seem to go faster than her. She swings three times and I swing only two."

Jewel snorted. "Because you're heavier, you goose."

"I'm not a goose," Rowan said, and Violet cringed, suspecting the girl had learned that insult from Rose. But Rowan seemed to consider Jewel's analysis. "Anyway, you're a girl, so you'll get tired," he decided smugly. "And then I'll go faster."

"No," Ford said, giving Violet another push, "you won't."

"He won't?" Violet asked. Rowan's theory made sense to her. Well, perhaps not the part about Jewel tiring—the girl was a bundle of energy if ever she'd seen one. "If Rowan pumps harder, he won't go faster?"

"He won't," Ford repeated. "The swing is a pendulum—"

"Like in your laboratory?" Jewel interrupted loudly.

"Just like that." He pushed again. "Only you are the weight at the bottom."

Jewel's dark hair streamed behind her, then flew forward to hide her face. "And he's a heavier weight, so…"

"No, the amount of weight doesn't matter." When Violet swung back, Ford wasn't there to push. She slowed down to listen. "The time a pendulum takes to go back and forth is called the period," he said, walking over to push Jewel instead. "And the period depends on the length of the string. Or in a swing's case, the ropes." He reached to give Rowan a shove. "Jewel's ropes are quite a bit shorter, so Jewel swings faster."

"Are you sure?" Rowan asked dubiously.

"Positive. But test it yourself. Switch swings with Jewel. That's what an experiment is all about."

The children dragged their feet on the ground to stop the swings, and Ford came back to Violet.

Soon Rowan and Jewel had switched sides and were pumping again. And Rowan was going faster. "You're right!" he yelled.

"Of course I'm right." Ford gave Violet another little push. "But I didn't figure it out myself. Galileo first made the observation."

"I know all about Galileo," Jewel told Rowan importantly. "Uncle Ford named his horse after him." She swung back and forth, back and forth. "I want to go faster again!"

"I'll swing a hundred times and then you can," Rowan offered.

"Fifty times."

"As you wish. But we'll switch back after another fifty." In his loud, young voice, he began counting.

Ford gave Violet a huge shove, and she soared out over the river, swinging back so hard one of her shoes flew off and landed on the grass with a *plop*.

"Oh!" she exclaimed, the word sounding breathless and giddy. "Stop!"

"Why?" He pushed her again, and when she rushed back, he plucked off her other shoe. She heard that one, too, plop somewhere behind her back. "There," he called as she swung away again, "now you'll really feel like a child."

Laughing, she wiggled her toes, feeling free in only stockings. And he pushed her higher. And higher. And higher. "Stop!" she screamed, meaning it this time. "Or I think I might get sick!"

He grabbed the ropes and jerked her to a halt. "Better?"

"Much." Still holding on tight, she gave a shaky laugh. "I guess I'm too old for this, after all."

"No one's too old for this," she heard him say from behind her. And then an arm curved around her waist and fingers cupped her chin.

Warm lips nuzzled her neck.

Her hands clenched the ropes as a delicious shiver rippled through her. "The children..." she murmured, attempting to turn her head. But his mouth trailed her throat, making her entire body weaken and blocking her from looking.

She heard the children's chatter and hoped that meant they weren't watching, and then it didn't matter, because Ford was tilting her back, back, until his face was hovering above hers, only upside down.

And he was all she could see. All she could care about.

Slowly he drew off her spectacles and lowered his mouth to meet hers.

The kiss was gentle yet demanding, like the one yesterday, only more so. And different, like they were kissing each other's bottom lip. Something ached deep inside her, and her hands clenched the ropes. Then, unlike yesterday, his tongue slipped out and traced the seam of her mouth. It was shocking and wild and wonderful. That single caress stole her breath, her thoughts...

And it was over all too quickly.

Slanting a furtive glance to the children, he reluctantly pulled away. She shifted upright. Walking around to face her, he handed her the spectacles with a smile. A secretive smile. A smile she hadn't the experience to comprehend.

Her hands shaking, she took the eyeglasses and fitted them back on her face. Leaving her stunned, he moved from her sight. She struggled to catch her breath, listening to him collect the book and her shoes.

"Thirty-seven, thirty-eight," Rowan chanted.

Ford paused for a breath behind Violet, collecting his wits. Why the devil had he risked that in front of his niece?

Someone had left one of the inn's benches near the tree—to sit and watch their children, no doubt—and he dragged it over by Violet's swing and sat. He set her shoes on the grass and the book on his lap.

"Forty-eight, forty-nine..." On the opposite side of the tree, Rowan reached fifty, and the children traded places.

"You're very good with them," Violet said quietly from her swing.

Never, in ten lifetimes, had Ford thought anyone would tell him that. Of course, he'd never thought he'd kiss a woman like Violet Ashcroft, either. An innocent country miss who spouted philosophy.

"It was only physics," he said dismissively, gazing at her profile. Her lips were parted. They looked kissable. They *were* kissable. "Science. I'm good at science."

Still motionless on the swing, she turned her head to look at him. "You're good with your niece. And Rowan."

He felt totally inept with them, but he didn't want to argue. "Perhaps that's because I never grew up myself," he suggested instead. "My family would tell you that."

"You've said something like that before," she recalled, looking flushed and flustered and beautiful. The spectacles had slipped down her nose, and she pushed them back up. "What are they like, your family?"

"Loud," he answered with a grin. "I have a twin sister, Kendra, and two older brothers, Jason and Colin. All married.

Among the three of them, they have seven children already, and I suspect more to come. Jewel is the oldest."

"No wonder you're good with children, then."

He shook his head. "It's not like that. I've played with them, of course, and when I'm not in London, I live with Jason and his family at Cainewood. Two boys, he and Cait have. But before now, I'd never taken care of my nephews or nieces." They all had nursemaids to see to that. "I've never taken care of *anyone* before."

He'd been the baby of the family. Everyone had always taken care of *him*.

"Well, you're doing a proper job." She shifted to look over at Jewel, who was shrieking with laughter as she soared through the air beside Rowan.

His niece looked happy. Perhaps Violet was right, and he wasn't doing such a bad job after all.

"And your parents?" she asked, turning back. "What are they like?"

"Dead."

"Faith," she muttered, her face going white. "I'm so sor—"

"No need to be sorry." He turned the book over in his hands. "I was all of one year old when they left to fight for King Charles, seven when they died at Worcester. I barely even remember them. My oldest brother more or less raised me, with the help of the exiled court. It was an interesting life."

Her fingers trailed up and down the ropes. "And a rough life, I'd wager."

He shrugged. "Not really. Although my parents sold most everything to help finance the war, I was too young to worry about where my next meal would come from. Someone else always took care of that. The court moved from Paris, to Brussels, to Bruges and back...the world was my playground. I suppose things were tight, but a child doesn't need much."

When she met his gaze, something twisted in his gut. "A child needs love," she said softly.

Soft or not, he heard a challenge in her voice.

"I had love." Uncomfortable under that gaze, he looked at the sun sparkling off the river instead. "From my sister and two older brothers. I never wanted for anything."

A short silence stretched between them before he finally looked back. One of her stockinged feet reached for the grass and pushed off. "And when you were no longer a child?" she asked, swaying back and forth. "A youth has more needs than a boy."

"Mine were met." How to explain a life in a few short sentences? Why did he care that she understood? "By the time Charles regained the throne, Jason and Colin were grown. Men with responsibilities. Cromwell had stolen their youth, and neither of them were ever afforded a chance for formal study. As a younger son, I should never have owned land. But a year following the Restoration, Charles granted all of us titles and estates...and I left mine behind and went off to university."

"How old were you then?"

"Seventeen. And spoiled rotten."

He'd never thought of it that way before, but it was nevertheless true. After completing his studies at Oxford, he'd returned to live with Jason. He'd never had to fend for himself. Never worried for anyone else. Never even had to chase after a female, since they always seemed to come after him.

He grinned. "I've led a charmed life."

"I'm sure you haven't," she said quickly, and he remembered Tabitha. That part of his life wouldn't fall under the heading *charmed*...but for some odd reason, it didn't seem to matter anymore. And it certainly didn't hurt.

Leaning back, Violet stuck her legs out straight and stared at her stockinged feet. "Nothing is that simple."

But it had been. It had been for him.

They fell quiet, and he smiled at the charming picture she made on the swing, wearing his spectacles. He'd never talked with a female like he talked with Violet Ashcroft—never met one who seemed interested in discussing much beyond fashion and gossip. Never talked with *anyone* who made him reveal parts of himself he hadn't even known.

And though he'd never suffered for lack of bed sport, he'd never wanted a woman like he suddenly wanted this one right here.

Right now.

He wanted to kiss her again.

And more.

But she was the Earl of Trentingham's daughter. A sheltered country lass. "What was *your* childhood like?" he asked.

"Boring in comparison." Still looking down, she turned her toes this way and that. "Grandpapa sent money for the cause, but he never went off to fight. He put family before the monarchy. We never went into exile, either. I've never been outside of Britain."

"But he did support King Charles?"

She looked up. "Oh, yes. Of course he did. My family was never anything but Royalist."

"I'm surprised Trentingham wasn't attacked by Cromwell's forces, then. Cainewood was." And had the cannonball marks to prove it.

"They confiscated Trentingham and occupied it, but we weren't there. Grandpapa had a secondary title and property that went along with it. Tremayne Castle, very near Wales. Not helpful for the Roundheads strategically, and I suspect too far away for them to bother with." She glanced over at the children. "Rowan is Viscount Tremayne now."

"So your family stayed there for all the years of the war?"

"And after. All through the Commonwealth, until the Restoration. Besides having an odd penchant for studying languages, Grandpapa was a stickler for family security." She pushed off again, gliding up and then down, slowing immediately when she did nothing to sustain the momentum. "My parents were wed at Tremayne, and I was born there. As were

Rose and Lily. I was eight before I ever stepped foot on Trent-ingham soil."

"Eight?" he said, surprised. "How old are you now?"

"Twenty."

From the tone of her voice one would guess she thought twenty was a doddering old maid. But he'd thought she was older. Not that she *looked* older, but Tabitha was twenty-one, and except in matters of the bedchamber, Violet seemed so much more mature.

"I'm twenty-eight," he told her.

"I figured that," she said, "when I heard you went off to university at seventeen, a year after Charles returned from the Continent."

"Unlike Rowan, you're good at mathematics." He grinned, thinking she was good at a lot of things. Especially heating his blood. "Does your family sometimes live at Tremayne Castle now?"

"Not anymore. We retreated there to wait out the Great Plague—Rowan was born there during that time. But then Grandpapa died, and we haven't been back since." Seeming deep in thought, she gazed out over the Thames, swaying gently to and fro in the swing. "The castle was only ever half built. Mum says it's too far from London, and Father prefers Trenting-ham's gardens. It's a quiet sort of place, Tremayne..." She met his gaze again with a smile. "See, I told you my childhood was boring."

To his great embarrassment, his stomach growled. Loudly.

"Oh!" she said. "It's been at least two hours since you said you were starving! Before we even bought the books!"

"I haven't perished." He stood and handed her the shoes. "But I wouldn't mind wandering over and taking a table."

While she put them on, he went to fetch the children.

"Not yet!" Jewel yelled, swinging higher. "Another minute!"

"Two minutes!" Rowan countered.

"Three!"

"Five!"

"Ten!"

"Ten," Ford agreed, giving Jewel one final push. "But only because it's your birthday, mind you."

Violet followed Ford to an empty table. As she slid onto the bench, she aimed a concerned look to where the two young ones were still swinging, facing away as they soared over the picturesque river.

"Sit," he told her. "They'll be safe. If they fail to come over and join us, they can eat their portions on the barge on our way home. And the two of us can dine in peace."

A nice thought, Violet decided. Even more nice after he went inside to order a light dinner, then returned to sit beside her.

Could he actually be interested in her as a woman? Every idea she'd ever held told her no, but his actions told her yes. It was confusing, to say the least. Especially when her hands drifted up to her face and she remembered her ugly spectacles. For a while there, she'd forgotten all about them.

"No one's staring," he said gently. He lowered her hands and laced his fingers with one of them. It felt intimate, and her heart skipped a beat. "You look fine, Violet. You look lovely."

Through the lenses, he looked sincere. She surveyed the few patrons seated at the other tables. The buzz of their conversation sounded pleasant to her ears, and he was right: no one was staring.

Besides Ford, no one was looking at her at all.

His gaze dropped to the book, his face brightening at the sight. "I still cannot believe I may have found *Secrets of the Emerald Tablet*."

"I'm so happy for you."

"It might not be the right book," he reminded her, although she suspected he was actually reminding himself. He squeezed her hand. "But I thank you for sharing my excitement."

"It's contagious," she told him. Her fingers tingled every place they touched his; she'd never realized her hand had so much sensitivity. And when he leaned forward and grazed his lips over hers, they tingled, too.

Almost unbearably.

It hadn't been enough. Even the kiss on the swing hadn't been enough, and it had been so much more. If the two of them were someplace more private, she would have wrapped her arms around his neck and held him close. As it was, the brush of mouths happened so fast, she wondered if she'd imagined it.

But if so, her imagination was very powerful indeed, because her breath was coming shallow. "Ford," she breathed, unsure whether it was a protest or an entreaty.

"Hmm?" He raised one brow.

She touched her free hand to her suddenly hot cheek. "We're in a public place."

"I must endeavor to get you alone, then."

Her laugh was embarrassingly shaky. "I think not."

He only smiled. A serving maid came out and put two tankards on the table, along with a pewter platter piled with fat slices of cream toast. She set down two empty plates, and Ford dropped Violet's hand to take one of them.

Her spectacles seemed to be fogging. She pulled them off, polished them on her skirt, and put them back on. "Thank you for sharing your dream," she said, lifting a tankard. A bracing swallow of ale seemed just the thing. "I truly hope it comes true."

"It would be amazing, wouldn't it?" He also sipped, regarding her over his tankard's rim. "And what are *your* dreams, Violet?"

"You'd laugh." She'd never told anyone outside her own family. Ever. Avoiding his eyes, she busied herself sprinkling sweet brown sugar on a slice of the egg-battered bread.

"I won't laugh. I promise." He sprinkled extra cinnamon on his. "Tell me," he said, cutting a piece.

"Well, one day..." As a delaying tactic, she swallowed a bite of cream toast, then washed it down with some ale.

"Yes?" he prompted, looking amused.

"I'd like to publish a philosophy book," she blurted out. "Not now, of course, but when I'm older. I still have much to learn first."

"A lady authoring a philosophy tome." Chewing, he considered. "It's quite an ambitious dream."

He was listening, and he wasn't laughing. "I would publish it under a man's name. Else no one would read it."

"Do you think so?"

"I know so." She sipped, then rushed on. "I have an inheritance coming, you see, enough to print and distribute the book far and wide."

He finished his slice and took another. "What is it you're so burning to say?"

"I don't know yet." Perhaps that sounded rather foolish, but it felt so good to finally tell someone—someone who really listened. "I'm still researching, still changing my opinions. But I believe these things are important. Ideas can change the world. And...I dream of leaving my mark."

"So do I."

"But with science, yes?" Ford was different, like her. She'd never expected to find a man like her. "You want to leave your mark with science. Science can change the world, too."

"Exactly."

He smiled, reaching across to trail his finger on the back of her hand. She thrilled at the contact—until she heard his next words.

"You know, most ladies would think they have better things to do with their money."

The sentence cut her to the core, robbed her of breath.

She'd thought he understood.

Disappointment swamped her earlier giddiness. Raising her tankard to hide her face, she ordered herself to shrug it off. She focused on Rowan and Jewel still swinging in the distance, their lighthearted laughter floating to her on the breeze. Of course a man would think like that, she reasoned—she should expect nothing else.

Ford was different, but not as different as she'd hoped. A man that different didn't exist.

With a sigh, she lowered the tankard. "I realize most men marry for money." And Ford would be no exception, especially given his obvious lack of the same. "But as far as I'm concerned, that isn't a good reason to shackle oneself for life."

She watched him rake his fingers through his hair. "Did I say anything about marriage?"

"You didn't have to say it—I knew what you were thinking."

"I think not." He lifted his own tankard, looking puzzled, as though he had no clue he'd said anything that could possibly upset her. "Are you never planning to marry, then?"

Perhaps she'd dreamed of it for a minute—one short, self-delusional minute. "My family isn't a conventional one."

"Question Convention."

"Yes. I feel no compulsion to lead a typical female's life."

He just gazed at her for a while. A long while, while she tried and failed to figure out what he was thinking.

"No," he said at last, and paused for a sip. "Nobody would ever call Violet Ashcroft typical."

That hurt, but she only stiffened her spine. "I'm aware that I'm an odd woman, my lord. It's why I'm certain no man would want me except for my inheritance."

He bristled. "Bloody hell, is it that much money?"

She couldn't tell whether he was sarcastic or serious, and she didn't get a chance to find out. Because in the next moment, two voices rang out from the riverbank.

"I dare you!"

"I dare *you!*"

And a moment after that, both children flew from their swings into the water.

## TWENTY-TWO

*V*IOLET JUMPED up from where they were eating. "The children!"

Splashes and screams followed.

Icy fear gripped Ford's heart. Boots and all, he made a running dive into the river.

But the splashes were playful ones—on Rowan's part, at least. And if Jewel's shrieks weren't exactly in fun, they weren't a harbinger of death, either. It was immediately apparent both children knew how to swim.

The shock of cold water helped Ford regain his equilibrium as he gathered them close, one in each arm. He should have given his niece more credit. She was much too bright to jump to her death. And if she was less than happy with the outcome of her prank, perhaps it would be a lesson learned.

Mere moments later he'd hauled them ashore, no harm done. Back on the barge and sailing for home, he couldn't imagine why Violet was so hysterical.

"We shouldn't have left them!" she lamented, wringing her hands. He'd never seen a woman wring her hands. Not in real life. He'd thought people only wrung their hands in plays.

And they hadn't left the children—they'd been watching

them the entire time. There had never been a true risk of drowning, he told himself, struggling to hold on to his logic in the face of hysteria. He'd been there within seconds. His racing heart was beating only double-time now. He knew how to deal with an emergency.

"All's well that ends well," he told Violet philosophically, wondering if a philosopher had actually said that. But if she knew, she was in no state to inform him.

Jewel was hysterical, too. "There were *fish* in there!" Her entire body shuddered, and not from the wet and cold. "Fish! Slimy fish!"

Rowan was hysterically laughing at Jewel, and Ford...well, if he'd thought hysterics would have mitigated matters, he'd have been hysterical along with the rest of them.

"Of course there were fish," Rowan crowed between snorts. "You *goose*," he added with undisguised glee.

Ford suspected he'd been waiting to call Jewel a goose since she'd called him one on the swings. Pouring water from one of his boots, he rather sympathized with the boy.

Women could be so irrational. They puzzled him in general, and Violet was no exception. Take their conversation at the inn, for example. They'd been discussing their dreams, nice as anything, then suddenly she was declaring she'd never get married. Or at least not to anyone who had the nerve to be interested in her money.

Where the devil had all *that* come from?

As they neared Trentingham's dock, he sighed and tipped his second boot. Water ran out, along with a tiny sliver of silver.

"Another fish!" Jewel screamed.

Rowan snickered.

Violet moaned.

And Ford knew he wasn't going to get an answer to his question.

# TWENTY-THREE

*T*HE NEXT DAY, Ford paced Trentingham's library. He still had no idea where he stood with Violet following that confusing, interrupted discussion. He'd tried to talk to her before coming upstairs, but here at the Manor there always seemed to be a sister or two around.

Turning the old book in his hands, he sighed, supposing the conversation probably hadn't meant all that much, anyway. Violet seemed to have recovered from yesterday's hysteria, at least, and her family had allowed him in the house, so apparently they didn't hold him responsible for the young heir's soaking.

A good sign. He'd hate to think Jewel might lose her playmate.

"Lord Lakefield?" Jarring him out of his thoughts, Rose sauntered into the room with Violet, fluttering her seventeen-year-old lashes. "My sister said you wanted to see me?"

He stifled a laugh, then fastened his gaze on those bold dark eyes and tried his famous smile on her—the one that seduced all the ladies. "Violet tells me you've a special expertise in languages."

Looking a bit off her stride, she leaned a hand on one of the library's two impressive globes, then jumped when it spun beneath her fingers. "Not truly," she said, glaring at Violet as she brushed the front of her magenta skirts. "I know only a little."

"More than a little," Violet argued. "You know French and Spanish, German, Welsh, some Gaelic—"

"Would you know this one?" Ford interrupted, struggling for patience. So far as he could tell, the book was none of the tongues Violet had mentioned or anything related. He walked to a round wooden table and opened the book on its surface. "Does this language look familiar?"

When Rose didn't make a move, he sent a pleading look to her sister.

"Rose…" Violet said. It was a single word, but uttered in a tone he hoped never to hear directed at himself.

"Oh, very well." Rose unriveted herself from the floor and came to lean over the table. She frowned at the book, reaching to gingerly turn a page, then another. The brittle paper crackled in the silence of the richly paneled library.

"No," she said at last. "I've never seen this language. It may be obsolete." When she looked up, her dark eyes were apologetic. "I know only modern languages, my lord." Her false pretense of empty-headedness gone, she closed the book respectfully and slid it across the table.

Disappointment formed a weight in his gut. Reaching for the book, he sat himself on one of the table's four straight-backed chairs. Violet surprised him by sitting beside him. After yesterday, he didn't know what to expect from her.

"How about the title?" he asked, not quite ready to give up. He reopened the book. No author had signed it, but there, right on the first page, was the alchemical symbol for gold. Of course, the symbol was just a plain circle with a dot in the center, so it could mean something else. Or nothing at all—in a handwritten book, such a mark could be a decoration or a doodle. But the sight of that symbol had set Ford's heart to pounding in John Young's shop.

The title alone could confirm whether or not he'd found the right book. He pushed it back toward Rose. "Can you puzzle out a single word of the title, even?"

"I can try." Rose's reluctance disappeared as she took a seat on his other side and drew the book closer. Clearly warming to the challenge, she ran a tapered finger across the handwritten text. "There are five words."

"Yes." But were they the right words? "Can you read any of them?"

"No." She shook her head. "I think not." She flipped back to the center of the book. "Some pages are stuck together."

"It's old," he said with a shrug. He'd peeled a couple of them apart and found nothing of interest, just more of the same. And he'd ripped one of the pages in the process. "I hesitate to start tearing at it, when I don't even know—"

"This is strange."

"What?" Violet asked.

"Well, I can read this one word here. *Argento.* It means silver in Italian."

Silver. Ford's hopes took an incautious leap. A book that mentioned silver might also mention gold. And Raymond Lully had lived in Italy for years.

Violet reached across Ford to lay a hand over her sister's. "Are you sure? I never knew you could read Italian."

"I'm sure." A hot blush touched the girl's lovely cheeks.

Rose resembled Violet, but her features had a glossy perfection that was missing from her sister's. Tabitha had been like that, too. They were *too* perfect, Ford thought. Violet's looks were friendlier, more comfortable.

He could touch her without worrying about messing her up.

"I found an Italian book," Rose explained, gesturing to the shelves that stretched to the high, geometric-patterned ceiling. "It wasn't too difficult to teach myself. The language shares much with Spanish."

Nodding, Violet sat back. A pity—he'd rather enjoyed having

her hang over his lap. She'd smelled like flowers. Probably violets, he imagined.

Rose looked back down to his book. "Of course, some languages share the same words with different meanings. For example, in French *four* means oven, but in English it's a number. So just because *argento* means silver in Italian doesn't mean it couldn't mean something else in another tongue." Carefully, she flipped another page. Scanning it, she hummed under her breath.

"What is it?" Violet asked.

"It's odd, that's all. That one word appeared to be Italian, but others aren't. There are letters here that are foreign to me, and here"—she looked up—"look at this line, here."

Both Ford and Violet scooted closer, their chair legs rasping on the carpet. "Yes?" Ford prompted.

"This line is written backwards. Even the letters are backwards, like in a mirror. And then this line here"—she drew a graceful finger along some text—"has no strange letters at all." In her enthusiasm, her voice had lost its deliberate seductive quality. "The writing is a bit faded and more than a bit smeared, but all readable, you see?"

Violet shook her head. "I cannot read it."

"You cannot comprehend it," Rose corrected. "But you recognize the letters, don't you?"

"It may be a code," Ford realized suddenly.

"Different languages and patterns. You may be right." She looked up at him, her dark eyes excited rather than coquettish. "Violet said this could be an important book. Was the book you're looking for written in code?"

"I never considered it before, but it could have been." The book had been rumored to be difficult to read. If he were recording priceless secrets, he'd be tempted to do so in code.

And he knew someone who was *very* good at cracking codes.

"If it's a code," Violet asked her sister, "do you think you could puzzle it out?"

Rose shook her head regretfully. "I'm afraid not. There are too few words I recognize."

"And none in the title?" Violet pushed.

"None." Rose looked to Ford. "I'm sorry."

She looked sincere and intelligent, and although she didn't interest him like her sister did, he liked her much more than he'd thought. "That's quite all right," he told her, offering her a smile. "You've actually helped a lot—"

"Where is Jewel?" Rowan interrupted, running into the room.

"At home," Ford said. "With her new friend Harry."

"*I'm* her new friend." Jewel would positively preen if she saw Rowan's pout. "Is she in your laboratory?"

"She'd better not be."

"You said we could go into the laboratory today. You promised."

"Rowan—" Violet started.

"He's right," Ford cut in.

He *had* promised. And at Lakefield, he might find an opportunity to get Violet alone.

He wondered if she'd let him kiss her again.

Rising, he closed the small leather book. "I did promise," he reminded her. "And a Chase promise is not given lightly. You'll come along, won't you?"

Her hesitation wasn't heartening.

"Lord Lakefield..." Rose's voice was back to its practiced purr. "What is your laboratory like?"

"Messy," he said shortly. He knew she was angling for an invitation, but he wasn't at all tempted to offer one. Then he noticed Violet was scowling at her sister.

That was much more heartening.

He graced Rose with his famous smile, adding, "Perhaps sometime I'll show you."

"I'll come along," Violet blurted.

Very heartening, indeed.

# TWENTY-FOUR

"*J*T'S UP HERE, Violet."

"I'm coming." Violet followed her brother up the dark, square staircase and then up some more, the old wood creaking all the way to the attic.

They walked through a corridor lined with books—not the handsome leather-bound volumes that filled the Ashcrofts' impressive library, but books that were clearly well read, jumbled haphazardly on plain shelves. Science books, she assumed.

From what she had seen, which granted was only part of the ground floor and now this attic, it seemed Lakefield didn't boast a proper library. If she were mistress here, she would remedy that.

But of course that was never to be. Just being in this place reminded her of how much money Ford needed to fix it. He was going to have to marry for money, and she would never let that happen to her.

At the end of the corridor, Rowan stepped into a room. As Jewel scampered in past him, he waved an expansive arm in a very grown-up way. "Look."

The single word was uttered in an awed tone. Entering the laboratory, Violet could see why.

Housed in a gigantic open space, Ford's workroom was a boy's dream come true. Beneath a steeply pitched ceiling of raw beams that exposed the stone-tiled roof above, a profusion of paraphernalia lived in charming confusion. Under the single shuttered window, a jumble of gears and other parts sat among an army of watches and clocks. Their ill-timed ticks filled the air, sounding like hundreds of scampering mice.

"Incredible," she said. There was no other word to describe it.

Ford opened a drawer and took out a shallow pan. "It's nothing compared to my laboratory at Cainewood. Or Charles's laboratory—the man has at least six of everything."

She didn't doubt it. King Charles was known to take his scientific pursuits very seriously and indeed had chartered the Royal Society. She'd heard he attended the regular meetings.

Just then, the clocks started chiming, as badly timed as their ticks, and she burst out laughing at the absurdity of it all. How anyone could accomplish anything in this chaos was beyond her comprehension.

"Look at this," Rowan said, pulling a heavy red book off a shelf. He shoved aside a mortar and pestle to set the book on a table, then opened it with great ceremony. Flipping several pages, he stopped on one and unfolded a large diagram.

She blinked. "What is that?"

"A spider," he said gleefully. "Like the one we scared you with."

Jewel snickered and moved close.

Violet slanted her brother a dubious glance. "That doesn't look like any spider I've ever seen."

"It's as seen under a microscope." He pointed to an instrument across the room, a handsome specimen of chased brass. "The book is called *Micrographia*." Pronouncing the word carefully, he turned to a random page, and the children leaned over the sketches.

They all stared at the patterns of tiny squares and holes. Jewel scratched her head. "What is it?"

"'Cork and other such frothy bodies,'" Violet read. "Fascinating, isn't it?" Even more fascinating than the pictures was her brother's animated face. He treated lessons as a chore; she'd never seen him so interested in anything academic.

"Look at this," he said, unfolding another large drawing. "Snowflakes."

"No, they're not," she said, hiding a grin. "Read it."

He focused on the page. "'Several observables,'" he enunciated slowly, "'in the six-branched figures form'd on the surface of urine by freezing.'"

"Ewww." Jewel made a face.

But Rowan was unruffled. "Can we buy one of these books, Violet? Please?"

"I have no idea where to get one."

"London," Ford said, polishing a small rectangle of mirror on his breeches. "Check the title page."

She turned to it and read. "'Printed by Joseph Martyn and James Allestry, Printers to the Royal Society, and sold at their shop at the Bell in St. Paul's Churchyard.' Hmm." She looked up at Rowan. "I'll talk to Father about it when next we go to the City."

Ford ripped a piece of white paper from a page of scribbled notes. "When will that be?"

"When Parliament is in session."

"I'll see if we can get one for him sooner." He turned to his niece. "Would you and Rowan do me a favor? Run downstairs, will you, and ask Hilda for a pitcher of water."

While Jewel hurried Rowan from the room, sending a pendulum swinging as they went, Ford walked to the single window and threw the wooden shutters open wide. "Three o'clock on a clear and sunny day," he said. "The sun should be just about right."

"For what?"

"Our experiment. I promised you a rainbow, remember?"

Baffled, she decided to take a wait-and-see attitude. "I'm sorry Rose couldn't help you," she said.

"But she did. Without her observations, I may never have realized the book might be in code. Or in a language so old it's obsolete." He set the paper by the mirror and pan. "I have a friend from my Oxford days, now an expert in ancient linguistics. And codes." He laughed at some age-old memory. "Rand used to infuriate his brother by deciphering his secret journals. I'm going to send for him tomorrow."

"So you do have a friend."

A faint glint of humor lit his eyes. "I have many friends."

"I'm sure you do." More than she had, she'd wager. "I just meant I'd thought you'd invented that friend as a story to tell Mr. Young. The bookseller."

"Well, I didn't buy the book for Rand, so that much was a falsity. But he does exist. And I'd trust him with my life, although I'll admit I hesitate to let that book out of my sight." His half-smile was one of self-amusement. "I expect that's why I didn't think to call on Rand in the first place. Foolish of me—if I'd summoned him yesterday, I might know what I have already. But it never even occurred to me until Rose brought up the inconsistencies."

"You're just focused," she said. "On other things."

"You're right, you know." He moved closer. Very close. "I've always had that annoying trait. When I concentrate on one thing, I cannot think of another."

Finding herself backed into a table, she put her hands behind her and knocked over a flask. She whirled to right it. "My father is like that," she said while still turned away. "He focuses on his flowers."

"My problem is," Ford said softly, "I've been focusing on *you*." Settling his hands on her shoulders, he gently maneuvered her to face him. "Thank you," he said, more softly still.

"F-for what?" Even through her gown, her skin tingled under

his fingers. Her senses whirled and skidded—she couldn't think straight when he was so close. When he was touching her, when she could smell him, when she could feel his warm breath on her face.

This wasn't right. It wasn't fair. He wanted her for all the wrong reasons, but she wanted him anyway.

His voice deepened as his eyes burned into hers. "Thank you for forgiving me for whatever thickheaded thing I said yesterday."

Yesterday rushed back, those heady moments by the river when she'd thought he'd understood, and then his words: *You know, most ladies would think they have better things to do with their money.*

Most ladies would use their money to buy a highly ranked husband.

She swallowed hard, hurt anew at the reminder that she wasn't like most ladies. That she wasn't pretty enough—or normal enough—for a man to want her only for herself.

But his hands smoothed up her neck until they cupped the sides of her face, and those doubts fled her head. Her heartbeat suddenly seemed louder than the dozens of ticking clocks.

She wondered if he could hear it.

With his index fingers, he drew her spectacles forward and off. A little *click* sounded when he set them on the table behind her. Then he lowered his head, capturing her lips with his, and she was no longer wondering anything at all.

Her thoughts were lost in the rush of feeling. The blood seemed to heat in her veins, her knees weakened, and when his lips parted hers, the tip of his tongue hot and carnal and exciting in her mouth, she felt as though she'd been waiting for this all of her life. Without thought, she raised her arms and twined them around his neck, pressing against him, savoring his warmth.

His arms tightened around her, pulling her even closer, until every curve of her body felt like it had been formed to match his.

She'd thought she was finished with this, finished with him. But nothing could be further from the truth.

Loud, childish voices came drifting down the corridor. Ford and Violet pulled away simultaneously. Her cheeks burning, Violet smoothed her skirts as the youngsters came in, chatting happily. She blinked at their blurry faces, then spun around to the table and grabbed her spectacles, shoving them back onto her face.

"Here, Uncle Ford." Jewel held out the pitcher.

Ford took it and filled the pan with water. Nonchalantly. Like nothing had ever happened.

Well, she told herself sternly, to him a kiss probably *was* nothing. Especially a kiss with her. He was obviously proceeding with the experiment perfectly calmly. She shook her head to clear it, determined to pay attention.

With a forearm, he swept aside springs and gears to set the pan on his work surface. Bright sunlight streamed through the window and glinted off the water.

He handed Jewel the small rectangle of mirror. "Put this in," he instructed, "so one end is in the water and the other end is resting on the side of the pan."

"May I do something?" Rowan asked.

"In a moment." They all watched as Jewel, looking very self-important, placed the mirror. Then Ford turned to Violet's brother. "You get to do the crucial part."

Rowan's green eyes danced. "What's that?"

"Move the pan around, and the mirror if necessary, until the sunlight reflecting off the mirror makes a patch of light on the wall."

The walls in the attic were unvarnished wood. Rowan did as he was told, gasping when a bright rectangle appeared like magic.

"What, you didn't believe it was possible?" Ford ruffled the boy's dark hair.

Rowan gave him a crooked smile. "I just wasn't sure I could do it."

"You can do anything you put your mind to," Ford told him. "Always remember that." He handed Violet the piece of paper. "Now, hold this so the patch of light shines directly on it."

Enjoying the game, she did as he asked…and watched a brilliant range of colors bathe the white sheet.

"Holy Hades," Rowan said.

Ford's eyes met Violet's. "Do you like it?"

"A rainbow," she murmured.

"Yesterday I told you I would make you one."

Thrilled, she stared at the beautiful hues. "I thought you meant figuratively."

"Now you can have rainbows without needing to prefer rain."

She felt herself blush. "I never did really prefer rain."

"I figured that," he said and laughed, and any embarrassment she might have felt was lost in the shared moment.

"Why does it work?" Rowan asked.

Ford turned to him, all scientist now. "The water sitting on top of the slanted glass is a wedge shape. When the sunlight bounces off the mirror, that wedge of water does the same thing a glass prism would. It's called refraction. The prism refracts the sunlight and breaks it down into all the different colors of light."

"May I try?" Jewel took the paper and held it away, then slipped it back in the beam of light.

The colors burst forth again.

"My turn." Rowan tried it himself, smiling at the results. "What do you mean by colors of light? Isn't all light white?"

"No. White light, like sunlight, is actually a combination of all the colors of light." Ford's language was simple although the concepts weren't; he didn't talk down to the children. "Isaac Newton presented this experiment at the Royal Society last year."

Violet sighed. "I wish women were allowed."

"One was, once. Margaret Cavendish, Duchess of Newcastle. But not as a member. She had written a book called *Observations upon Experimental Philosophy*, and she was allowed as a guest to observe some of our own fine experiments."

She gave him a wan smile. "I don't expect the Royal Society would be interested in any book I could write."

He looked contemplative. "Not as a group, perhaps. They can be a snobbish lot. But individual members would certainly take an interest." Rowan and Jewel began playing in the water, but he didn't seem to notice. "Have you heard of John Locke?"

"No." She pulled her brother's hand from the pan. "Who is he?"

"A brilliant philosopher, although he has yet to publish any significant papers. You should meet him. Perhaps he could help you achieve your dream. His ideas are quite thought-provoking." He rolled his eyes, then grinned. "I cannot believe I said that."

"I cannot believe you said that, either." Though he'd never voiced it in so many words, she suspected he was much too logical and concrete a scientist to be drawn to philosophical musings.

When Rowan flicked droplets in Jewel's face, she shrieked, but Ford only smiled at them absently. "The Royal Society is holding an event next week. A celebration, if you will."

"What are they celebrating?" Violet asked, watching the girl pull a beaker off a shelf as Rowan turned away and became preoccupied by something on the cluttered table.

"Ever since the Great Fire when the City offices were temporarily set up at Gresham College, the Royal Society has been meeting at Arundel House instead."

Only half her mind on Ford's words, Violet saw Jewel scoop water from the pan, partially filling the beaker. He was oblivious, she thought. He could truly pay attention to only one thing at a time.

"But now that the Royal Exchange has reopened and the

government moved out," he continued, "we've been invited back. The college is throwing a grand entertainment to welcome us."

With a victorious shout, the girl dumped the water on Rowan's head.

"Jewel!" Ford gasped, finally responding at the sound of Rowan's howl. He whirled to face her. "You must ask before you touch anything in here. That beaker could have had chemicals in it."

He didn't care that his niece had drenched Rowan's hair and shoulders, Violet thought. Only that she might have ruined an experiment.

"It was empty, Uncle Ford," Jewel said.

Clearly struggling for calm, Ford dragged a hand through his hair. "Chemicals can dry and become invisible. And some can burn skin. Worse than fire."

"Oh." Jewel looked chagrined.

And Violet felt the same way, knowing she'd underestimated him. Again.

"Are you burned?" Jewel asked Rowan. "You don't look black."

"He'd be red," Ford said.

"I'm fine." His hair still dripping wet, Rowan poked her in the stomach.

Violet opened her mouth to chide him, then decided the girl deserved it.

"I'm going to plan a prank on *you*," he promised Jewel, ruining the threat with a mischievous grin.

"You'd best hurry." Ford tossed him a towel. "She's going home next week."

"Home?" Rowan's grin faded. "Can't she just live here from now on?"

"I think her parents would have something to say about that." Ford took the pan and leaned out the window to dump the remaining water. "I heard from my brother this morning. There have been no new measles cases the past week, so if matters there continue to improve, I'll be taking Jewel home on my way to London for the Royal Society celebration."

He paused for a moment, then turned to Violet. "John Locke should be there. Would you like to come as my guest?"

# TWENTY-FIVE

"**O**F COURSE you'll go with him."

"Mum!" Violet paced the perfumery. "The celebration is in *London*."

Chrystabel looked up from the vial in her hand. "So?"

"So we're not in London, in case you haven't noticed. Parliament isn't in session, and you know Father prefers the countryside and his gardens. You don't mean for me to travel to London alone with Lord Lakefield, do you?"

Knowing Violet expected it, Chrystabel did her best to look shocked. "Of course not. But I won't have you miss this opportunity, either." It was a perfect excuse to get Violet and Ford together without the children—just what they needed to make their budding romance bloom. But Chrystabel knew better than to reveal her strategy. "I know that you've dreamed of attending a Royal Society meeting, and I mean to see you go."

"It's not a meeting, Mum. Only a social event."

"And as close as you'll ever get to your dream, unless you disguise yourself as a man." She set down the vial, meeting her daughter's gaze. "Don't even think of it."

"Disguising myself? I wouldn't."

No, her daughter wouldn't try that, Chrystabel supposed—even Violet knew she could never pull off such a prank. Her face might pass for a pretty lad, but her body was very womanly.

If only a man—the right man—got his hands on that body, he would never let go. And Chrystabel wasn't averse to arranging for that to happen. Desperate mothers were sometimes drawn to desperate measures, and she knew for a fact that all would turn out right in the end.

Chrystabel's instincts were as dependable as dew sweetening a rose. And if sometimes it made her a bit uneasy to trust her intuition where her own daughter was concerned, she reminded herself how accurate her feelings invariably were.

Mothering wasn't always a comfortable job.

"Father won't want to leave his flowers," Violet insisted. Thanks to her agitated pacing, her spectacles had slipped down her nose. She pushed them back up. "He grumbles enough about spending the wintertime in London, although he won't shirk his duties to the House of Lords. He won't go in summer."

Wondering if her daughter was going to wear a hole in the carpet, Chrystabel chose another vial. "Then we'll go without him."

"Mum! We've never!"

"There's a first time for everything, Violet." She added a drop to the bottle she was working with, swirling to mix the fragrances. "Your sisters would love a few days in the City—"

"But we cannot travel without Father—"

"Nonsense. We'll take a brace of footmen, and I am certain we'll arrive safe and sound. With Jewel leaving, Rowan will appreciate the distractions London has to offer. And your sisters have been dying to pay a visit to Madame Beaumont's establishment, to see the newest fashions. It will be a lovely holiday for all." She made a notation on Mrs. Applebee's card, then smiled up at her daughter. "Now, have you a suitable gown for this event?"

A nice, low neckline would be suitable indeed.

~

O F COURSE Violet didn't have a gown. With all the delays, she had yet to be fitted for new clothing, and a ball gown wouldn't have been included in the order in any case.

But suddenly it seemed paramount to Mum—and to Violet, though she only admitted it silently—that she look as presentable as possible for the Royal Society celebration.

So the seamstress and her assistant were fetched immediately, and Violet found herself subjected to an hour of measuring and prodding, accompanied by much babbling in incomprehensible French. This was followed by a second hour, during which Madame presented her with a mind-boggling array of fabrics, along with fashion dolls from Paris, all dressed in miniature versions of the latest gowns.

As though she could be fooled into thinking she'd ever look like one of those dolls.

They ended up deciding on a gown in two shades of purple embroidered with gold thread and pearls. The dress would be started today, and tomorrow the women would be back for what promised to be a day full of tucking and pinning. Madame said she would have to "accomplish zee impossible" to have it ready in time for them to take it to London.

By the time the seamstress left, a headache was throbbing in Violet's temples. She wanted nothing more than to get off by herself for some thoughtful reading.

In the peaceful sanctuary of her lilac-hued room, the pile of new books beckoned. Between Ford's visit to talk to Rose and the afternoon in the laboratory, she hadn't found a minute to peruse the titles.

She sat on the bed and ran a finger down the stacked spines. Thomas Hobbes, *Human Nature*; René Descartes, *Discourse on*

*Method; Aristotle's Master-piece.* That was the one. "'Plato is dear to me, but dearer still is truth,'" she quoted under her breath, smiling at Aristotle's words, the perfect expression of her own feelings. She couldn't imagine why she'd never heard of this book, but she was glad she'd found it.

Leaning back against a plump velvet pillow, she sighed and opened the cover. And gasped.

# TWENTY-SIX

"*N*ESBITT!" The next afternoon, Ford hurried down the gravel path to meet his friend. "It's been entirely too long."

Three years, he realized suddenly. Sad, how friendships suffered when men's lives took them separate directions. But Rand's smile convinced him that things hadn't changed between them.

Lord Randal Nesbitt swung off his black horse, his dark blond hair glinting in the sun. "This had better be important, Lakefield." The words sounded serious, but he strode forward to give his old friend an affectionate clap on the shoulder. "So this is the place, is it?" He squinted up at Ford's house.

"Well, yes." His gaze following Rand's, Ford shifted on his feet. "I'm planning some renovations."

He hadn't been, not really, since his stay here wasn't permanent and he couldn't afford renovations in any case—not without changing his lifestyle. But seeing his home through Rand's eyes made him wonder how Violet must see it.

The paint had worn entirely off the front, leaving bare beige stone. He'd never noticed before that it was a darker color on the left half, which had been added early this century, and a lighter color on the older half. The windows were different, too—four modern ones on the new side, five mullioned ones on the Tudor portion.

The building was sound, but its aesthetics left much to be desired.

"Rand." In an effort to draw his friend's attention from the dismal architecture, Ford touched him on the arm. "I may have found *Secrets of the Emerald Tablet*."

Startled, Rand's steel gray eyes met Ford's. "That fabled book you used to babble on about? You're jesting."

"I'm not. At least I hope not." He guided Rand up the steps. "I found this book in a shop in Windsor—looked like it'd been there for ages. It has five words in the title and the alchemical symbol for gold on the first page, and it looks exactly as the book has been described. But I cannot read it. Not a word." He led his friend through the entrance hall and around the corner into his study. "Violet's sister—"

"Violet?"

"A neighbor."

Rand plopped onto a faded green chair. "What happened to Tabitha?"

"She eloped with the Earl of Berrescliffe." Incredibly, it no longer seemed important. "What does that have to do with anything?"

"The way you said 'Violet'…"

Wishing not to alienate his friend by sitting behind his massive oak desk, Ford dropped heavily to an iron chest that sat against one wall. "I didn't say 'Violet' any special way."

"Come on, man," Rand said. "I've known you since we were lads. We were at school together, remember?" His quick grin emerged. "I can tell when you're interested in a woman."

Ford leaned back against the dark, Tudor oak paneling. "You don't know me so well anymore."

A tense moment passed while Rand considered that statement and Ford mentally kicked himself for offending an old friend.

"The hell I don't," Rand finally said. When his smile grew even wider, Ford wavered between feeling relieved and annoyed. "What did you want to tell me about Lady Violet's sister?" Rand asked. "Violet *is* a lady?"

"She is." Guessing where his friend was leading, Ford sighed. "And her sister is a linguist of sorts. Her *younger* sister," he stressed, noting the interest that lit Rand's eyes.

He knew Rand every bit as well as Rand knew him.

"How young?" Rand asked, clearly not considering that an impediment. He was younger than Ford by four years—a brilliant student who had entered Oxford early, while, due to his family's exile, Ford had started a little late.

"Seventeen," Ford said. "And a sheltered country miss." Though accurate, the description somehow didn't fit Rose.

Rand ran his tongue across his teeth, a sign of contemplation Ford remembered from their days at Wadham College. "A woman can marry at twelve with her father's consent."

Ford thought of Jewel just six years hence. "A female of twelve is not a woman."

"Point taken." Rand cleared his throat. "So what of this sister?"

"She knows a language or three, you see, and she examined the book." Ford rose, crossing to the desk to retrieve it. "She noticed a word she thought was Italian. For silver," he added significantly as he opened the bottom drawer.

"And that was enough to make you decide it was *Secrets of the Emerald Tablet*?"

"You think me so simple-minded?" He handed the book to Rand, then sat again on the iron chest. "The moment I saw this book, I suspected it might be the one. Besides the book's appearance and the clues on the title page, it includes diagrams that are clearly scientific. Other than that, though, I couldn't really say why I think this is it. It just…feels right," he added, suddenly feeling foolish.

He'd always trusted facts over feelings. Until now, at least.

"It does look quite ancient." Rand turned the book in his hands, then opened it gingerly, reverently, as such an old book deserved. "You know, Old English is so different from what we speak today, it might as well be a foreign language."

"But I would still recognize a word here or there, wouldn't I? Rose—Violet's sister—thought it might be several different languages. And patterns." His fingers worried the decorative metal strips on the chest. "I'm thinking it might be a code."

Rand looked up. "What is in there?" he asked suddenly, indicating the old iron chest.

"I don't know. It belonged to the previous owners." Ford looked ruefully at the heavy lock. The key was missing, so it would have to be hacked off with an ax. One of the many things he had yet to get around to doing here at Lakefield.

"Don't you wonder if it holds something valuable?"

"They wouldn't have left it had it contained anything valuable. Do you see anything else they left around here that was worth keeping?"

Scanning the shabby room, Rand laughed. "You have a point."

Ford wasn't at all handy with an ax, and the book was much more important. "Rose said some of the lines are written backwards. And the letters are mirror images."

"Etruscan," Rand said, glancing back down.

"Pardon?"

"Etruscan. A dead language. The people who spoke it lived in what eventually became Italy."

"Raymond Lully, the author, lived in Italy for some time."

Rand nodded thoughtfully. "The Etruscans wrote left to right and then right to left on successive lines, with the letters facing backwards and forwards." He kept turning pages as he talked.

"Etruscan is phonetic and easy to read aloud, but no one's ever managed to puzzle out the words' meanings."

Ford's spirits plummeted. "Does that mean you won't be able to identify the book?"

"Not at all." Rand looked up with a grin. "Your ladylove's sister was right."

Violet wasn't Ford's ladylove, but in his rising excitement, he decided to let his friend's annoying ribbing slide. "Right about what?"

"About it being many languages. I've noticed two or three ancient words here—ones I can read. But not together. I believe you're correct that it may be a code."

"And we both know how good you are at cracking those, to Alban's constant aggravation." Alban, Rand's older brother, had been a cruel boy, Ford remembered. Rand had retaliated by constantly outwitting him. "How is Alban these days?"

"I don't know, actually," Rand said, his eyes still on the book. "I haven't been home in four years."

"I see." Reluctant to subject himself to his father and brother, Rand had often spent school holidays with Ford's family instead. Apparently matters hadn't improved. Ford hesitated to pry, though, as he knew it was a sensitive subject.

He rose and moved to stand over Rand, leaning down to turn back to the first page. "Can you read the title?"

Rand stared at the words for a moment, then frowned. "If this is a code, it's a tough one." He looked up, shutting the book. "Give me some time, man. Can you not feed a fellow before taxing his brain?"

As if on cue, Hilda walked in, holding a folded piece of paper.

"We've another for supper," Ford told her.

"And what makes you think I can provide on short notice?" She walked closer, scrutinizing Rand's healthy physique. "I suppose you eat as heartily as this one?" she asked, indicating Ford.

"Doubtless," Rand said with a smile.

With an exaggerated sniff, she held out the paper to Ford. "Here, I came to give you this." When he took it, she added, "I'll bring your guest some refreshments. For heaven's sake, milord, you haven't offered him so much as a drink."

"Why do you put up with her?" Rand asked when she had left.

Ford shrugged. "She came with the house. Besides, she's a kitten under the gruff exterior. Read this, will you?" He handed Rand the paper and went to the cabinet where he kept brandy.

While he poured, Rand unfolded the paper. "'Dear Lord Lakefield, The Ashcroft family would be honored to have you and Lady Jewel as our guests for supper this evening. If we do not receive your regrets, we shall expect you at seven o'clock. Yours sincerely, Lady Trentingham.'"

Ford handed Rand his drink. "You'll come along, of course. I'll have Harry carry a note to warn them of the extra guest. Hilda will be relieved."

"Lady Jewel?" Rand sipped, his glance speculative over the cup's rim. "Another woman? Lady Violet isn't enough?"

"Violet isn't my woman," Ford said irritably. "And Jewel is my niece. Long story."

Rand settled back. "I'm waiting to hear it."

## TWENTY-SEVEN

*A* KNOCK CAME at Violet's door. "Don't you want to come riding?" Lily called through the oak.

"No, thank you." Seated at her dressing table, Violet flipped a page of her book.

"You've been hiding in there for two days." Rose sounded typically impatient. "Are your fittings that exhausting?"

"Yes," Violet called, just as impatiently.

"Violet..."

When Lily pushed open the door, Violet hurried to stuff the book under her bedcovers.

Her eyes narrowed, Rose fisted her hands on her hips. "What were you reading?"

"Nothing."

"I saw it. It was a little brown book." She stalked over to the bed. "Let me see."

Violet pulled it out before Rose could. "*Aristotle's Master-piece*. Philosophy. Nothing you'd find interesting."

"*Aristotle's Master-piece*?" Lily breathed. Her blue eyes were round as the moon through Ford's telescope. "Where did you get *that*?"

Violet's heart pounded. "Why? Have you heard of it?"

"Have we *heard* of it?" Rose all but snorted. "The ladies whisper behind their fans about all its secrets. I vow and swear, Violet, you need to get out of the house. If you came visiting more often—"

"Does Mum know you have it?" Lily interrupted.

"No." Perish the thought. "You won't tell her, will you?"

Rose's lips curved in a slow smile. "We won't if you share."

"You're too young for a book about..." Violet peeked inside at the title page. "'The Secrets of Generation in All the Parts Thereof.'" She slammed it shut, her fingers clenching on the leather cover.

"I'm not so certain Mum would want you reading it, either." Rose walked closer, and Violet held on tighter. "I think she'd be *very* interested," Rose taunted, "to hear where you got that book."

There was nothing for it. "Come to the summerhouse," Violet said with a sigh. "We can all read it together."

~

"$\mathcal{H}$OW DID YOU get it?" Rose asked when they were safely outdoors in the garden.

Violet knew her father was in the study—they had walked right by him on their way from the house—but she was so used to seeing him out here that she glanced around, half expecting to find him lurking behind a bush.

"Ford bought it for me in Windsor," she admitted finally.

Lily's mouth gaped open.

"It wasn't like that!" Violet rushed to add. "He thought it was a philosophy book. We both did."

"Of course," Rose said with a smirk.

Violet clutched the book to her bodice. "It's called *Aristotle's Master-piece*. What was I supposed to think?"

Rose looked unconvinced.

"Never mind." Lily's shorter legs hurried to keep up with her older sisters' quick pace. "Is it really that shocking?"

"Well, yes and no," Violet said. "Mostly it's educational."

Rose grabbed for the book. "I need an education."

"Just wait," Violet snapped, snatching it back. She rushed past Father's blue and yellow flower beds, breathing a sigh of relief when they reached the circular red-brick summerhouse. She yanked open one of the small garden building's four doors, and the girls scurried inside, shutting it behind them.

They huddled together on a section of the benches that ran along the wall, Rose and Lily on either side of Violet. She placed the book on her lap. Large, arched windows over each of the doors illuminated the brown leather binding, but they were placed too high for anyone to see in.

A perfect place for illicit reading.

Violet drew a deep breath. "This was my first clue that it wasn't the sort of book I'd thought," she said and opened the cover.

"Oh, my God," Lily breathed. The frontispiece plate depicted a seated Aristotle with a nude woman standing beside him. "Is the book really by Aristotle?"

"I'm sure not!" Rose stared at the title page opposite. "There's no author listed, no printer's name or date or even place of publication." She gave a delicious shiver. "It must be truly scandalous. What does it say, Violet?"

"Well, the beginning is only advice to parents."

"To parents?"

"Of young girls. Listen." She flipped a page, then cleared her throat. "'It behooves parents to look after their children, and when they find them inclinable to marriage, not violently to restrain their affections, but rather provide such suitable matches for them, lest the crossing of their inclinations should precipitate them to commit those follies that may bring an indelible stain upon their families.'"

"What does that mean?" Lily asked.

Rose grinned. "It means Father and Mum should make certain I marry before I get myself with child."

"Rose!" Lily's mouth hung open in shock.

"Hush," Violet said. "There's more." She swallowed and turned the page. "'For when they arrive at puberty, which is about the fourteenth or fifteenth year of their age, then the natural purgations begin to flow—'"

"They have already," Rose said. "For all of us."

"Rose!" Lily's cheeks stained red as the "purgations."

"Just listen," Violet said. "'...and the blood stirs up their minds to venery: for their spirits being brisk and inflamed when they arrive at this age, if they eat hard salt things and spices, the body becomes more and more heated, whereby the desire to carnal embraces is very great, sometimes insuperable.'"

"Insuperable." Rose nodded. "That's what I am. Insuperable."

Lily huffed, a rare show of impatience. "What does it say after that, Violet?"

"'And the use of this so much desired enjoyment being denied to virgins, many times is followed by dismal consequences—'"

"Dismal," Rose emphasized.

Lily and Violet glared at her.

"'...by dismal consequences, as a green weasel color, short breathings, trembling of the heart, etcetera. Also their eager staring at men, and affecting their company, shows that nature pushes them upon coition, and their parents neglecting to get them husbands, they break through modesty to satisfy themselves in unlawful embraces—'"

"But I want to choose my own husband," Lily broke in. "I don't want my parents—Mum most especially—to get one for me."

"Either way, it must be done." Rose stood and paced the small, round building. "Else can you see the consequences? Your spirits will become brisk and inflamed. The desire to carnal embraces is very great—"

"Sometimes insuperable." Violet could hardly keep from laughing.

"Insuperable, yes." Rose pulled the book from Violet's hands, scanning the words. "Nature will push you upon coition, Lily, and you'll break through your modesty to satisfy yourself in unlawful embraces." She looked up. "We *must* get Violet married so we can find husbands ourselves."

"Oh, no," Violet said.

"Oh, yes. Otherwise, we cannot be responsible for the consequences—"

"Girls, are you in there?" Father knocked on one of the doors. "Willets said he saw you heading this way—"

Rose quickly sat on the book, folding her hands angelically on her lap while Violet went to open the door. "We're just talking, Father. Do you need us?"

"Do I need what?" Looking perplexed, he scratched his head. "Your mother sent me to find you."

"Why?" Violet asked.

"Lord Lakefield has arrived for supper. With a guest. Lord something-or-other. I failed to catch the name."

"A man? A titled man?" Rose stood and slipped the book to Violet behind her back. "Gemini! We'd better go change our gowns!"

## TWENTY-EIGHT

*A*N HOUR LATER, Mum set down her goblet. "Violet tells me Jewel is going home tomorrow."

"Yes." Ford sprinkled salt on his spinach tanzy and returned the spoon to its little dish. "I hope she also told you I've invited her to an event at Gresham College."

"She has," Mum said, "and she'll be delighted to attend. Monday evening, is it?"

A tiny gasp escaped Violet's lips. She'd never given Ford an answer, and she'd wanted to do that for herself.

She nudged her mother's foot beneath the table, but Mum pretended not to notice.

"Yes, Monday." Ford took an experimental bite of the rich spinach omelette, then smiled. "I trust you'll be in London by then? I'll need the direction of your town house."

"We're in St. James's Square," Mum answered again for Violet. "In the northeast corner, the house of light gray stone."

"Excellent. The celebration begins at ten, so I'll be by at half past nine."

"Half pastime?" Father murmured.

Nobody paid him any attention.

Violet stabbed a stewed prawn with her fork, a bit more

forcefully than necessary. If her mother and Ford kept planning her life as though she weren't around to hear it, she feared she might scream.

Seated between her sisters across the table, Lord Randal Nesbitt gave her a sympathetic smile—a smile nearly as charming as Ford's. It just lacked that hint of the devil that lit Ford's eyes.

Apparently noticing the glance that passed between Violet and his friend, Ford reached for her hand beneath the table.

Faith, what if someone noticed? But it felt good. It reminded her of their stolen kisses.

Feigning nonchalance, she smiled back at Rand. He was nice. He hadn't even mentioned her spectacles. She wondered if that was because Ford had already told him about them, or if he was just very polite.

"Pastime?" Violet's father repeated. He turned to his wife. "What's this all about?"

She flicked a grain of brown rice off his cravat. "Darling, I told you we're going to London, remember?"

"I thought that was to order more gowns for Violet, since she's finally taking interest." Father stirred some of the butter sauce from the prawns into his rice. "From that Madame Blowfont woman."

"Beaumont," Rose clarified loudly, sprinkling cinnamon on her own rice.

Egad, Violet thought, did Ford have to know that she'd never cared for clothes? *Nobody would ever call Violet Ashcroft typical*, she heard him say in her head—and her family was only confirming it.

She wished she could slide beneath the table. And then melt into the floor. Especially when she caught Ford stifling a grin, indicating he was enjoying this discussion.

"Gowns?" Mum said, trying to come to Violet's rescue. "Of course she needs new gowns, but that's not the focus of our holiday. Everyone knows my eldest daughter's main interest is philosophy, not fashion." She looked to Ford's friend. "You must forgive my husband. He's a bit hard of hearing and often misunderstands."

"What?" Father asked, proving her point.

"Nothing, my love." Mum's musical laughter tinkled through the room, a sound of relief. "See what I mean?"

"Violet did have a new ball gown made," Rowan said in defense of his father.

Ford squeezed Violet's hand.

Rose flashed her dimples at Ford's guest. "What brings you to visit, Lord Randal?" she asked, even though he'd told them all to call him just Rand.

She'd been gazing at the man all evening. Not that Violet blamed her. Like Ford, Rand wore no wig, and he had the most gorgeous mane of long, dark blond hair. Besides that devastating smile, he was tall and lean, with a poet's face and eyes of steely gray—the most intense eyes Violet had ever seen. When he looked at a person, he really *looked* at her, as though he could see right into her soul.

In response to Rose's question, he was looking at her now, and she seemed to all but swoon beneath his gaze.

Eating single-handed, Ford used his fork to cut a bite of the tanzy rather awkwardly. "I've asked Rand to translate that old book for me, Rose. He's Professor of Linguistics at Oxford—a renowned specialist in ancient languages."

"Languages?" Visibly perking up, Rose batted her long eyelashes, reminding Violet of Jewel.

When Ford squeezed her hand again, she stifled a laugh and stuffed a prawn in her mouth to hide it.

"I'm conversant in a few languages myself," Rose announced. It was the first time Violet had ever heard her sister voluntarily admit her linguistic skills to a man. Still gazing at Ford's friend, Rose spooned some salt from the cellar and began blindly sprinkling her roast chicken. "Perhaps we can work on the translation together?"

Rand lifted his goblet. "Perhaps." His voice matched his looks, smooth and rich. "Ford tells me you've already examined the book."

"Well, yes. But not for very long." Rose was still spooning salt. "Perhaps together—"

"Rose," Lily interrupted. "Do you not think you're overdoing the seasoning?"

Rose looked down and froze, the tiny spoon halfway between the cellar and her food.

Licking orange-flavored butter sauce off her lips, Violet gave her a brittle smile. "You wouldn't want to eat too much *hard salt things and spices.*"

"What?" Father asked.

Mum just looked perplexed.

"I'm afraid you're right." Dumping the salt back into its little dish, Rose released a languid sigh. "I'm experiencing short breathings, my heart is trembling...am I turning green as a weasel?"

"Has anyone ever seen a green weasel?" Rand asked no one in particular.

The children both giggled.

Ford shifted his hidden hand to lace his fingers with Violet's. "I cannot say that I have."

Lily looked down and smiled. "Beatrix, how did you get in here?" Leaning to scoop up a small striped cat, she settled it on her lap.

"Lily," Mum said. "Not when we have company."

"She's lonely." Lily stroked the animal's fur before reluctantly setting her back on the carpet. "She had a bad day."

Rand cocked his head at her. "Pray tell, how does a cat have a bad day?"

On his other side, Rose touched him on the arm, a clear bid for his attention. "Our Lily claims she can feel her animals' emotions. She collects injured creatures. Cats, birds, rabbits, the odd squirrel. She's turned an old barn into a menagerie, or rather an infirmary for damaged beasts. She even has a mouse."

Lily nodded. "His little leg was broken, poor thing."

When Ford scooted his chair closer to Violet's, she felt her blood stirring up to venery. But a quick scan of the table assured her no one was paying attention. To the contrary, the others were all looking at Rand, who in turn was focused on Lily.

Violet noticed a distinct softening in that intense gray gaze. "Cats and mice together?" he asked.

Lily, bless her, seemed unaffected by his charms. "I have but three cats at the moment, and they've been with me since they were kittens. When creatures are raised side by side, they can learn to be brothers and sisters. Even cats and mice."

"Fascinating," Rand said.

"Lily dreams of building an animal home," Rose announced.

"A what?"

"An animal home," Lily repeated softly. Like Violet, she'd never shared her dream outside the family. Reaching a hand beneath the table, she slipped the cat a bit of chicken while measuring Rand's reaction with her steady blue gaze. "A nice clean building where hurt or abandoned creatures can be brought to live. People who work there will care for them until they are healthy enough to return to the wild or they find a home with a family."

Rather than disapproving, Rand nodded slowly. "That's a very nice idea. And innovative, too."

Along with her youngest sister, Violet breathed a sigh of relief. She rather liked Ford's friend. "Our grandfather encouraged us to be innovative," she told him, trying to ignore Ford's thumb tracing circles on her palm. "Or rather to follow our dreams. And, as he put it, leave our marks on the world."

"And what is your dream, my lady?"

"Please call me Violet," she reminded him, stalling for time. Although she'd told Ford her dream and he hadn't laughed, it remained difficult to share with another.

Then Ford moved their joined hands to rest on his thigh, and the shock of that loosened her tongue. "I wish to write a book about philosophy," she blurted, shoving her spectacles higher on her nose. "My own ideas. And use my inheritance to publish it some day and distribute it far and wide. Of course," she hastened to add, "I have a lot of studying and thinking to do before then."

Rand didn't laugh. "Of course. An admirable dream, Violet." He turned to Rose. "And your dream, my lady?"

Rose didn't tell him to drop the *my lady*. "I...I dream of falling in love," she said, and prettily lowered her lashes.

Rand looked surprised, but Violet wasn't. Rose had never shared a dream with the family, unless one counted dreams of balls and gowns and jewelry.

"Oops!" Jewel dropped her spoon and dove to the floor to go after it. "Pretty kitty," came her voice from beneath the table.

"Jewel..." Ford warned. But she didn't come up. Instead, Rowan slipped off his chair to join her.

An alarmed *meow* came from somewhere below.

"Poor Beatrix. What are they doing to you?" Leaning down, Lily swept the cat back to her lap. She rubbed its small, furry head with a finger. "Go out now, Beatrix," she said, setting her down again. "I shall come to you later."

Beatrix did go out, stepping gracefully, her striped tail high in the air.

"She obeyed." Admiration lit Rand's eyes. "A *cat* complied with your command."

Ford played with Violet's hand where it rested on his leg, and she felt herself turning red.

"Holy Hades," came Rowan's voice muffled from below. "Look, Jewel."

The girl's head popped up. "Uncle Ford, are you holding hands with Lady Violet under the table?"

"No!" Ford yelped, yanking up his hands, fingers spread to prove his point.

It was the second time Violet had seen him blush. Knowing her own hue must be scarlet, she was sure the truth was obvious.

Lily gasped. Rose smirked. Mum's mouth curved into a smile.

"What's that?" Father mumbled.

It was a long supper.

# TWENTY-NINE

*L*ATER, SEATED beside Violet at the round table in Trentingham's library, Ford spread his knees farther apart so one rested against hers. Then he leaned near to whisper in her ear. "I'm looking forward to Monday."

She turned her head slightly, her cheeks prettily flushed, and he hoped that meant she was looking forward to Monday, too. But her eyes suddenly narrowed. "I just want you to know," she whispered back, "that I am nearly one-and-twenty, and my mother doesn't run my life."

He wouldn't challenge that statement for all the gold in England. "I'm certain the decision was yours alone," he assured her. Shifting closer, he held her gaze. "I'm just glad you decided to come."

"Oh," she said, and then, "Oh!" when his arm curled around to rest on her shoulder. Her hands fluttered up to touch her spectacles, which he'd noticed she sometimes did when she was flustered.

Not that she had cause for worry. It was clear as the lenses over her eyes that nobody else in this room was going to take note of their closeness or conversation.

Candles burned, warding off the late-night darkness. Reluctant to say goodbye to each other, Rowan and Jewel had fallen asleep on a corner of the patterned carpet, half twined where they'd dropped in their play. Across the table, Rand and Rose huddled together over Ford's ancient book.

The girl was plainly smitten.

"I'm not sure," she crooned to Rand now, "but do you think this might mean 'mystery'? It's awfully similar to the same word in German."

"Possible." Rand flipped a couple of pages, peering at them critically. "But I don't see much else that looks to be Germanic."

Ford traced geometric figures on Violet's shoulder, smiling to himself when he felt her shiver.

Playing with the ends of his long hair, Rand flipped back to the original page. "Do you suppose the five words might be from five different languages? I've been assuming it's only one."

"That could be." Hero worship flashed in Rose's eyes. "I hadn't considered the possibility."

"Five words?" Ford's attention was finally wrested from Violet. "What five words?"

"The five words of the title," Rose said as though he'd lost his head.

Clearly he had.

Rand frowned at the page, running a finger over the text. "What if this were German, like you were saying, but an older version?" A tinge of excitement crept into his voice. "And this looks Hellenic, perhaps meaning 'emerald,' and this maybe Slavic—"

"Mystery and emerald?" Ford breathed, his heart threatening to hammer right out of his chest.

"Yes, Slavic," Rand murmured, nodding to himself. "And this one..." Quite suddenly he straightened in his chair. "Five words, five different languages. Translating to 'Mysteries of the Emerald Slab.'"

Ford blinked, feeling blank.

His friend leaned across the table to punch him on the arm.

"*Secrets of the Emerald Tablet*, you fool." A grin spread on his face. "You found the book, Lakefield. It's a bloody miracle."

All the air seemed sucked from Ford's lungs. It *was* a bloody miracle. And a marvel, and a wonder, and—

He leapt from the chair and swept the four of them into a fierce hug. Then he kissed Violet smack on the lips, right in front of her gasping sister.

He was still grinning the next day when he showed up at his brother's castle.

# THIRTY

$\mathcal{C}$OLIN WASN'T grinning when Ford delivered his daughter, along with a still-weak Nurse Lydia they'd fetched along the way.

While Lydia crept off to her bed, Colin's wife, Amy, knelt in the entry and hugged Jewel close. "How did it go?"

"The two of us got along famously." Pleased that Amy seemed fully recovered, Ford turned to his scowling brother. Holding their tiny son in his arms, Colin looked very parental. "What's your problem?" Ford asked.

Colin swayed back and forth in the age-old motion that soothed and rocked an infant to sleep. "You mean to tell me you were alone all this time with my Jewel?"

"Of course not. Hilda and Harry were there, too."

"Those old barnacles?"

"Colin!" Amy set their daughter on her feet and took her hand, leading her from the square entrance hall. "Jewel seems no worse for the wear."

The rest of them followed. "How is Hugh?" Ford asked, referring to their four-year-old son.

Her raven hair shining with health, Amy smiled over her shoulder. "Much better. He's napping now."

He looked to the child in his brother's arms. "And Aidan?"

"Had a very light case," Colin said, patting the baby's back.

"I had fun, Mama." Jewel twirled in a circle, around and around under Amy's arm as they went down the corridor. "Uncle Ford bought me this necklace on my birthday!" Still twirling, she toyed with the silver filigree heart she wore on a black ribbon around her neck. "And he let me sleep in his bed. And he paid me to be good!" Reaching the sitting room, she dropped cross-legged to the floor and began digging in her pockets. Shillings fell to the stone slabs with a merry sound.

Amy seated herself in a blue upholstered chair and picked up a small knife. "You're rich, poppet."

"I'm saving up to buy a mi-mi"—Jewel looked at Ford, but he knew better than to help her now—"mi-cro-scope. Uncle Ford showed me a book with pictures. Written by Mr. Heck."

"Hooke," Ford corrected, leaning an elbow against the mantel. "And the book is called *Micrographia*."

"Mr. Hooke drew pictures of big, icky things. Close-up things." Jewel collected her coins, making a neat stack. "When I buy the mi-cro-scope, I'm going to share it with Rowan."

Settling Aidan in a wooden cradle, Colin raised a brow. "Who's Rowan?"

"My friend from Uncle Ford's house. Violet's brother. I'm going to marry him."

Amy's father had been a jeweler in London, and she'd been raised in the trade. Whittling away on a piece of wax that looked like it might someday become a ring, she appeared to be stifling a laugh. "Does Rowan know you're going to marry him?"

"Of course. I told him. And Uncle Ford is going to marry Violet."

"I am not." Ford's elbow slipped off the stone ledge. "Why, why—"

"Problem, Ford?" Colin drawled, taking the chair beside his wife's.

Ford ignored him, focusing on his niece instead. "What the devil made you say that?"

All innocence, she looked up from her spot on the floor. "I saw you kissing her."

"You did not."

"Did so."

"Did not."

Colin rolled his eyes. "No wonder you two got along. You're as childish as she is. I take it you're over Tabitha, then?"

"Did you think I was upset about her elopement?" Ford vaguely remembered being so, but couldn't fathom why. "She meant nothing to me. No more than a convenient diversion."

"Mm-hmm." Colin crossed his arms, looking less than convinced. "Tell me about this Violet."

"There's nothing to tell." Ford wandered over to gaze at a portrait of some long-dead ancestor. He didn't have anything like it in his house—nothing to personalize his living space, nothing to make it a home.

Jason, his oldest brother, had plenty of paintings at Cainewood Castle. He would ask him if he could spare one or two for Lakefield.

"Lady Violet is simply a neighbor," he told the woman in the picture. She stared back at him blankly, her head poking out of a huge, starched ruffle that looked damned uncomfortable. "Violet brought her little brother over to play with Jewel sometimes, that's all."

"And Uncle Ford is taking her to a ball tomorrow night," Jewel piped up. "In London."

"What ball?" Amy asked.

"Gresham College is throwing a party to welcome back the Royal Society. Lady Violet would like to meet John Locke. He'll be there." Ford turned from the painting. "End of story. It's not a ball."

"Will there be dancing?"

He walked to a chair and plopped onto it. "Yes, I suppose there will be dancing."

"It's a ball, then," Amy said blithely. "I'm sure you'll have a lovely time."

"Do you not think," Colin asked, drumming his fingers against his thigh, "that if you're considering wedding a woman, you ought to introduce her to the family?"

"I'm not wedding her." Ford's hands clenched on the chair's arms. "I'm not wedding anyone. I'm not ready to get married."

"Jason is back from Scotland." Colin's eyes looked contemplative. They were emerald green like Jewel's, and he was just as single-minded as his daughter. "I'm sure he'll be fascinated to hear about this."

"There's nothing for Jason to hear," Ford said. "Are you deaf?"

"And Cait," Amy added, apparently deaf as well. "And Kendra and Trick." Her amethyst eyes sparkling, she smiled down at the wax ring. "They've all just arrived home last week. We'll have to arrange a family visit to Lakefield."

As there seemed to be an abundance of deaf people in his life lately, Ford raised his voice. "I'm busy working on my watch," he ground out. "There will be no visits."

## THIRTY-ONE

*O*ORE **LIGHTHEARTED** than ever in her memory, Violet twirled in her new ball gown, a veritable confection of patterned lilac satin.

Monday night had finally arrived. One of her dreams was coming true. She was going to Gresham College to meet members of the Royal Society.

Feeling dizzy, she stopped and held out her skirts. "What do you think?" she asked her sisters. "Will it do for an event here in London?"

Lily smiled. "I've never seen you in anything so fancy."

Rose crossed the bedchamber to tweak one of Violet's triple-ruffled sleeves, then shot Lily a grin. "She's finally coming around."

"What do you mean?" Frowning, Violet tugged up on her bodice. The square neckline hadn't seemed this low on the French fashion doll. She didn't remember it being so daring during the fittings, either. Wondering what had happened, she smoothed her underskirt, deep purple velvet embroidered with gold thread in a diamond pattern. "Coming around to what?"

"Dressing to impress." Rose's grin turned wicked. "I'd wager he'll be very, very impressed."

"John Locke?" Violet walked to the pier glass and straightened one of the fat brown curls that rested on her shoulders. Most of her hair was pulled up in the back, twisted with strands of pearls to match the ones on her underskirt and tasseled stomacher. "I cannot wait to hear his ideas. But Locke is a philosopher. I doubt he cares what I look like."

"Not Locke, you goose. Viscount Lakefield."

"I'm not trying to impress him," Violet said. But, blushing from her hairline to her toes, she feared she must match the deep pink gown Lily was wearing.

Those pink skirts rustled as her sister wandered to the window. "He's here, Violet. The viscount. He's climbing down from his carriage. And oooh, he looks so handsome in the torchlight."

Violet's stomach fluttered. "Let me see," she said, thrilled that with her spectacles she'd be able to. But by the time she hurried over to look, Ford had already mounted the town house steps and disappeared from view.

"I'll go meet him at the door," Rose said. "Wait here, so you can make an entrance." With a swish of her blood-red skirts, she swept out of the room.

"An entrance, Violet," Lily repeated softly. "An entrance!"

*An entrance.* Contemplating her youngest, most innocent sister, Violet's heart jumped into her throat as it suddenly dawned on her that she was going out alone with Ford.

Until now, she'd focused on the excitement of meeting members of the Royal Society. Yet, for part of the evening at least, she and Ford would be alone. Really alone, not just sort of alone for a minute while the children's backs were turned.

She could hardly believe Mum had condoned it. More than condoned it—pushed it, in fact. But of course that was only because Mum knew how much she wanted to attend a Royal Society function.

Mum would never expect anything untoward to happen. Not

to Violet. Plain Violet. Violet, who would just as soon remain invisible.

If only Mum knew that Ford had already kissed her. Five times. Five glorious times.

As she'd done hundreds of times already, Violet couldn't help but replay those kisses now in her memory. And even though she hadn't eaten any hard salt things or spices today—hadn't eaten much of anything, as a matter of fact—her desire to carnal embraces seemed almost insuperable.

This promised to be a marvelous night.

For just this night, she wouldn't care that Ford showed interest in her for all the wrong reasons. For just this night, she'd put her heart into living each moment. For just this night, she'd allow herself to revel in this dream come true of mingling with England's most eminent intellectuals...in the company of a man who made her heart flutter with the merest touch or look.

Rose barged back in. "He's waiting, Violet. I think you should keep him waiting a little bit longer."

"No." She wasn't calculating like her sister. "I'm ready." As ready as she'd ever be.

Although the Ashcrofts' town house in St. James's Square wasn't nearly as massive as Trentingham, it was richly decorated and boasted a grand marble staircase. Violet's new red-heeled shoes clicked as she walked down it.

When Ford glanced up, a thunderstruck expression froze his features. His jaw went slack; his eyes widened. "You look..." he began, then seemed at a loss for words.

Moving closer, she smiled to herself. "Different?" she supplied, gliding to a stop in front of him.

"Um...yes." As that incredible blue gaze raked her from head to toe, a devilish grin slowly spread on his face. "And beautiful."

It had taken him too long to add that last bit, and she wouldn't have believed it, in any case. But it was nice to hear, even if it was only a polite fib. For just this night, she would pretend it was true. She'd never expected to hear a compliment like that from a man.

And most especially from such an attractive one. Judging from his normal attire, she'd suspected Ford enjoyed dressing up a bit. She hadn't been wrong.

He looked magnificent. His brilliant blue suit made his eyes appear even bluer. Yards of lace dripped from the cuffs. A diamond pin winked from the folds of a snow-white cravat. The buttons on his velvet surcoat looked to be of real gold, and when he swept off his wide-brimmed hat to make her a solemn bow, a jeweled hatband sparkled in the light of the entry's chandelier.

Mum had loaned her the Trentingham diamonds, but she still felt dull and unadorned in comparison.

"Shall we?" he asked.

From out of nowhere, it seemed, her mother appeared and kissed her on the cheek. "Have a lovely time, dear."

"I will, Mum." As Violet took Ford's arm, she decided it might well be the loveliest evening of her life.

After he'd handed her into his carriage, she was no longer so sure.

Egad, she was alone with a man.

She settled herself across from him, fluffing her skirts and offering him a stiff smile. "Thank you for inviting me."

"The pleasure is mine." His own smile looked amused. As the carriage began moving, he patted the seat beside him. "Come here, Violet."

"I'm comfortable over here, thank you."

"I promise I won't bite you. At least, not until later." At her gasp, he laughed. "I was only fooling. I won't even kiss you, I promise. Just come and sit by me. Please."

She did, and he kept his promise not to kiss her, which she found rather disappointing. Especially after he wrapped an arm around her shoulders and swept aside her curls to nuzzle her neck.

"You smell good," he murmured. "Your hair, your skin..."

"So do you," she said breathlessly. He did. There was that hint of patchouli soap again, tonight overlaid by some exotic, very masculine perfume. She wondered if her mother could match the scent, so she could inhale it and remember this evening.

Although the way it seemed to make her senses swirl, perhaps that wouldn't be such a good idea.

As the carriage lurched through the streets, his lips teased the sensitive hollow behind her ear, and his fingers traced a light, shivery pattern on her shoulder. Her flesh prickled, and a hot ache began to spread in her middle.

Like the *Master-piece* had promised, her body was becoming more and more heated.

"Oh my," she said—the only words she could manage at the moment.

"Shall I stop?" he asked, his breath warm against her throat. The carriage bounced in and out of a rut, his mouth bouncing along with it, landing damp against her skin. "Tell me if you want me to stop."

Rough and raspy, his voice gave her another little thrill. She didn't tell him to stop. Scandalously, his fingers trailed down, brushing the bareness revealed by her low neckline.

He might have kissed her five times, but he'd never touched her there. No man had touched her there.

Feeling weak, she slumped on the brown leather seat. The carriage's wheels bumped over the cobblestones, the springs squeaked through the traffic-clogged streets—and her labored breathing sounded louder than all of it.

They jarred to a stop, and through her thin satin bodice, Ford's hand grazed her breast.

Then returned and stayed there, lightly caressing.

"Faith," she breathed, feeling the crest swell and tighten in response. Her eyes drifted shut as a corresponding response shot through her body.

Her desire to carnal embraces was very, very great.

The carriage door was jerked open, and she bolted upright, her eyes wide. They'd arrived, and she'd learned that Ford was a man of his word.

He hadn't kissed her.

He'd done something more scandalous—and far more dangerous.

## THIRTY-TWO

*V*IOLET HAD always thought of scientific men as serious and staid, but there was an air of giddy excitement at Gresham College tonight.

Not to mention she was still excited from what had happened in the carriage.

Following Ford through the narrow gatehouse off Bishopsgate Street, she carefully tugged up on her bodice. Surreptitiously, she hoped. She wasn't sure which was worse: being seen in such an immodest gown, or having someone see her adjust it.

"This was once the home of Sir Thomas Gresham," Ford said as proudly as if the mansion belonged to him. "Founder of the college."

Hand in hand, they crossed a simple courtyard toward the house, Violet's knees feeling embarrassingly weak. Wishing she could switch off her feelings as easily as he apparently could, she tried to concentrate on what he was telling her. After all, this was a place she'd always wanted to visit.

"When did the college open?" she asked.

"At the end of the last century, following Gresham's death and that of his wife. He had no living heirs, you see, so he gifted his home to the people of London. He wished to make scholarship available free to every adult citizen." Pushing open a heavy oak door, he guided her into a large chamber that looked medieval. "Here is the Reading Hall, where the lectures are given."

"Oh, I wish I knew Latin so I could attend them." Beneath a lofty scissor-beam ceiling painted in dazzling hues of red and gold, rows of wooden benches faced a lectern, behind which rose an exquisite oriel window. "What a lovely place to learn."

"I imagine when the Greshams lived here, this would have been their great hall." Ford walked her through the soaring chamber, their footsteps echoing on the well-worn stone floor. "The college's seven professors have lodgings here at Gresham and are each required to give one public lecture a week."

Whom might she meet here tonight? Breathless with anticipation, she peeked into some adjoining rooms, a bit disappointed when she found them unoccupied. "It just looks like a big, old house."

"It was, remember. But you will see in a moment that although his family lived here for years, and his widow afterwards, Gresham had a college in mind when he built it."

Another small courtyard lay outside the Reading Hall, leading to an arched passage that opened into a massive, grassy square with colonnaded buildings on all four sides.

"See?" Ford said. "It's essentially a college quadrangle."

Flaming torches bathed the space in a warm glow. Musicians were tuning up in one corner. Talking animatedly in small groups, guests dressed in every color of the rainbow crowded the enclosure, their chatter filling the air.

She was here. Finally, she was here. A serving maid handed her a goblet of canary, and she sipped the sweet wine, turning in a slow circle, imagining the area solemn, shut off from the hubbub of London by the buildings all around.

"I can picture it quiet," she said, "students leisurely crossing the grass, or perhaps hurrying if they're late."

"Can you picture it paved over and crammed with shopping stalls?"

She looked down at the fresh green grass beneath her feet. "Was it?"

"Until recently. After the Great Fire, the whole administration of the City moved into the buildings, and the tenants of the Royal Exchange set up here in the quadrangle until it was rebuilt. A hundred small shops."

People strolled by, men alone and some couples, nodding acknowledgments without interrupting their conversation. "How long has the Royal Society been meeting here?" she asked.

"Since 1660, save during the past seven years. We were incorporated under Royal charter in 1662. On the fifteenth of July. So something good happened that particular St. Swithin's Day," he mused. "It must not have rained."

She shot him a sidelong glance. "What do you mean?"

"Never mind." A faint smile curved his lips as he began walking her around the perimeter, pointing out all the professors' lodgings. There were professors of music, physics, geometry, divinity, rhetoric, astronomy, and law—and by the time she heard about all of them, she was feeling dizzy with new information.

Or maybe dizzy with something else. She tugged up on her bodice again, then dropped her hand when a spark of humor lit his eyes.

"Do you like to dance?" he suddenly asked. The musicians had commenced playing. A lilting tune wafted over the quadrangle. A temporary floor of wood had been constructed over a patch of the new grass.

Although she'd had lessons along with her sisters, Violet had never danced much. At the many balls her family had dragged her to, she'd always done her best to fade into the background.

But this was a magical night—a night that called for her to rise above her normal fears. In her whole life, she might never see a night like this again, and she was determined to make it memorable.

"I cannot say I have much experience," she heard herself saying. "But I wouldn't mind giving it a try."

Immediately she thought about taking back the words, but clamped her lips tight. Handing their goblets to a passing serving maid, Ford led her closer to the music.

The tune ended and another began. A minuet. Taking her by both hands, he swept her onto the makeshift dance floor.

She knew the steps, and for the first time in her memory, she didn't worry about tripping. He danced with an uncommon grace for a man, and her feet seemed to know what to do. The music matched the staccato beat of her heart. She could scarcely believe she was here at Gresham College, dancing with the most handsome member of the Royal Society.

Cool night air brushed along the skin that he'd heated in the carriage. She met his eyes, and her cheeks flushed at the boldness of his gaze. Here beneath the stars, he seemed different, in his element. Not that he was shy and retiring in any circumstances, but she'd expect a man of science to be more like her, preferring solitude to social occasions. Which just went to show how little she could trust her preconceived notions.

They turned, and when his heady scent wafted to her nose, she found herself enjoying this particular social occasion more than she'd thought possible. For once, she had no desire to hide out, no wish to stay safely at home.

They rose on their toes, and he pulled her closer. Closer than the dance required, close enough to make butterflies flutter in her stomach.

He was touching her. Just his hands, but he was touching her. Even though this sort of touch wasn't as intimate as his caresses in the carriage, she still felt that lurch of excitement. That frisson of awareness. That building heat in her middle that seemed to illogically weaken her knees.

From just a touch. The *Master-piece* hadn't prepared her for that.

Men outnumbered women by double or more, and the dance floor was surrounded by clusters of them absorbed in conversation. More than a few glances were aimed her way. Violet suspected people were wondering what she was doing here with Ford.

And wondering about her spectacles. No sooner had she and Ford made their way off the dance floor than they found themselves approached by curious men.

"Trentingham's eldest, are you not?" One of them offered her a courtly bow. "I'm pleased to meet you," he added. "Christopher Wren."

Christopher Wren. Mathematician, scientist, architect...the man currently engaged in rebuilding all of the City's churches that had burned in the Great Fire. She was surprised to find him no taller than she.

"Violet Ashcroft," she returned. "I'm glad to make your acquaintance."

"Are those a new sort of spectacles?" he asked without further preliminaries. Not at all the serious, dour man she had imagined him to be, he seemed cheerful and open. She guessed him at a decade older than Ford. "May I see them?" Before she gave permission, he reached toward her eagerly.

She slipped them off and handed them to him. "Lord Lakefield made them for me."

"I'm not surprised." Wren turned them in his hands, then raised them to his own sparkling brown eyes and blinked. "Do they help you to see?"

"Very much. They've changed my life."

Wren nodded thoughtfully, his wavy brown periwig moving along with his head. Beneath a patrician nose his mouth curved pleasantly, as though he smiled often.

He turned to Ford. "This frame to hold them on the face, it's brilliant. Why didn't I think of it myself?"

Ford laughed. "You've thought of plenty. Give another man a turn."

Someone else walked up. "What have you there?"

"Spectacles," Wren told him. "Designed by Lakefield here, with a clever frame to hold them on the face." Leaning forward, he gently slid the eyeglasses back on Violet.

"Lovely," the newcomer said. "Both the spectacles and the lady." A few years younger than Wren, the man topped him by but a couple of inches. His physique somehow looked crooked, his face twisted and much less than beautiful. But his large, pale head was crowned with a wig of dark brown curls so delicate they made Violet jealous.

"Robert Hooke," Ford introduced him. "May I present Lady Violet Ashcroft?"

"I've read your book *Micrographia*," Violet gushed, over-whelmed to find herself chatting with such a great intellect. "It's marvelous."

"I'm pleased to make your acquaintance." Hooke's gray eyes smiled along with his thin mouth, but in contrast to Wren's, his face crinkled in a way that made Violet think he rarely grinned. "The gardener's eldest, are you not?"

She couldn't remember ever meeting these people, but they seemed to know her. That was what came of hiding in corners, she supposed. "Is my father's hobby so well known, then?" she wondered aloud.

"Legendary." Hooke shifted his awkward form, looking loath to say more. "Charming man, though," he finally added.

"Mr. Hooke is Gresham's Professor of Geometry," Ford told her. "He lives here, right under that new observatory they're building." He indicated a corner of the quadrangle, where a small, square tower poked up from the roofline, surrounded by scaffolding.

"Convenient," Hooke said. "If I fall down stumbling drunk, I'm close to my bed."

They all laughed.

"How go the plans for St. Paul's?" Ford asked.

Hooke and Wren exchanged a glance, the kind shared by friends with secrets between them. Odd to think that a curmudgeonly man and such a cheerful one would be close.

"I'm working on a model," Wren said carefully.

Hooke let out a snort. "Twelve carpenters are working on it, and he's sunk five hundred pounds into it already. We can only pray the king likes it and the clergy give their approval."

"Approval for what?" someone asked in a voice with an Irish lilt. And before she knew it, Violet was introduced to Robert Boyle, a tall, thin man who also wanted a look at her spectacles.

No sooner had he finished exclaiming over them than another man walked up. Boyle handed him the lenses, and without them on her face, all Violet could tell about the newcomer was he was short and a bit stout.

"They belong to you, my lady?" he asked after examining them closely. He returned them with a bow. "Isaac Newton, at your service."

"Lady Violet Ashcroft," Ford introduced her. "The Earl of Trentingham's daughter."

With the spectacles safely back in place, Mr. Newton looked to be Ford's age, or perhaps a year or two older. Although prematurely gray hair peeked out from beneath his wig, he was a handsome man. Beneath his broad forehead, brown eyes were set in a sharp-featured face with a square lower jaw.

"We're pleased you remembered to attend," Boyle teased him.

The men's laughter confused her, and her expression must have shown it. "Mr. Newton is known to be a bit absentminded," Ford explained.

"That," Hooke said, "is an understatement of the greatest magnitude." More laughter rang through the quadrangle as the assembled men evidently agreed. "He once entertained me for supper and went off to fetch more wine. An hour later I found him in his study, working out a geometrical problem. He'd completely forgotten I was there."

"It was an important problem," Newton protested good-naturedly. Violet couldn't help noticing that, compared to the other men, he looked rather slovenly. His suit was finely made, but so wrinkled she wondered if he'd slept in it.

Wren rubbed his chin. "Tell her about that time you rode home from Grantham."

"That could happen to anyone."

"I think not." Wren turned to Violet. "He dismounted to lead his horse up a steep hill, and at the top, when he went to remount, he found an empty bridle in his hand. His horse had slipped it and wandered away unnoticed."

Even Violet had to laugh at that.

And so an hour passed while it seemed she met most every man connected with modern-day science. Between examining her spectacles and regaling her with stories, they talked casually of their various projects.

The king's most favored architect, Wren had recently written a paper explaining how to apply engineering principles in order to strengthen buildings. He'd also patented a device for writing with two pens at once, and invented a language for the deaf and dumb, using hands and fingers to "talk."

Besides Hooke's improvements on the microscope that had allowed him to research and write *Micrographia*, he'd developed astronomical instruments that revealed new stars in Orion's belt. Ford whispered that he'd show her them one night. Hooke had also formulated a new law of physics, asserting that the extension of a spring is proportional to the force applied to it. A lively discussion broke out over his proposal to introduce the freezing point of water as zero on the thermometer.

Since Hooke often assisted Robert Boyle, the two talked about their experiments with the new air pump Hooke had built. Using it to create a vacuum, Boyle had proven that the pressure of a gas is inversely proportionate to its volume.

"That is now called Boyle's Law," Ford told her.

Violet drank it all in, thrilled to be in their company. Although some of the men were aristocrats, many were not. Here, dukes rubbed elbows with commoners. The Royal Society was open to men of every rank and religion, so long as the proposed member held an interest in promoting discovery and science.

As each new arrival exclaimed over the genius of Violet's new spectacles, Ford basked in celebrity. And she didn't feel uncomfortable wearing them at all. Being the center of attention wasn't nearly as bad as she'd thought.

But as more eminent scientists gathered to praise Ford, she began to wonder if showing off his brilliant invention had been his real motivation for bringing her here. Disappointment took her by surprise, making the canary wine seem to sour in the pit of her stomach. While it was true Ford had never implied they were attending as a romantic couple—he'd invited her as a kindness so she could meet John Locke—she suddenly realized that, somewhere deep inside, she'd begun to hope he really liked her.

Ford's offer to introduce her to Locke had been no more than an excuse to put her spectacles on display for his celebrated friends, she finally decided. She was a fool for falling for his meaningless advances, for forgetting that if he wanted her at all, it could only be for her inheritance. The realization was an ache, a heaviness in her chest. It didn't matter that she should have known the truth all along. No amount of telling herself so worked to allay the hurt.

"Is Locke here yet?" Ford asked the ever-growing assembly.

"Inside," Boyle said, waving to a chamber off the quadrangle. "Holding court."

"Excuse us, gentlemen."

Now that she was actually about to meet the esteemed John Locke, a knot formed in Violet's middle. "I was enjoying that conversation," she said as Ford drew her away. If this was her only chance to ever mingle in such company, she was determined to make the most of it.

"And they were enjoying you." He smiled down at her, appearing as warm and sincere as ever. "We'll talk to them again later."

Her head spun with confusion.

The chamber Boyle had indicated turned out to be the refreshment room. Along one wall, long tables were laden with bottles of canary, Rhenish wine, and claret. Guests filled their plates from platters piled with fine cakes, macaroons, and marchpanes. Splendidly dressed men and women chatted while they ate, seated at small round tables. At one of these, a man stood with one foot perched on a chair, talking to a large group that had gathered around him.

"John Locke," Ford said, nodding in the man's direction. Tall and slim, there was little in his appearance to suggest greatness. Although his speech was animated, his eyes looked melancholy, set in a long face with a large nose and full lips. Like Ford, he wore no wig, but his hair was straight and pale. His hands moved when he talked, his long fingers waving from the ruffled cuffs at his wrists.

As they drew close, she could hear his words. "Government," he said, "has no other end but the preservation of property."

A squat, balding man crossed his arms. "How can you speak such blasphemy? I've never heard such a thing."

"New opinions are always suspected, and usually opposed, without any other reason but because they are not already common."

"He's quite busy now," Ford whispered. "An introduction must probably wait for later."

"Oh, but may I stay and just listen?" She waved an arm toward the tables bulging with refreshments. "Go get yourself something to eat and drink. I'll be right here."

# THIRTY-THREE

**F**ORD SMILED as he moved toward the refreshment tables. He appreciated a woman who understood a man's stomach came before a philosophy debate, although he had to admit Locke's ideas were more intriguing than most.

However, not nearly as intriguing as what he was bound to learn from *Secrets of the Emerald Tablet*.

"Why the grin?" Newton asked while filling a plate at the bountiful buffet.

Gresham College was certainly welcoming the Royal Society back in style. Deliberately nonchalant, Ford picked up a plate for himself. "No reason."

"I'm not *that* oblivious." Newton studied a strawberry before adding it to his selections. "It's that woman, I'd wager. Lady Violet? Lovely, isn't she?"

"No. I mean, yes, of course she's lovely." Violet *did* look lovely tonight, and it wasn't only the spectacular gown. The excitement in her eyes lit her whole face. He'd never thought to meet a woman excited by science, or anything much academic. Tabitha certainly hadn't been.

Thinking about that, Ford chose radishes and slices of musk melon. "But I wasn't smiling about Lady Violet."

Newton bit into a macaroon. "What, then?"

"I..." Dying to share his good fortune with someone who would truly understand, Ford leaned close and whispered, "I've found *Secrets of the Emerald Tablet.*"

"You found *Secrets of the Emerald Tablet?*" Newton fairly bellowed.

"Hush! It's yet to be translated. I'm not ready to announce—"

But it was too late. Heads had turned, and a speculative murmur ran through the room.

Hooke rushed over. "Is it true? *Secrets of the Emerald Tablet* exists? You have it in your possession?"

"Not at the moment," Ford hedged. But at the sight of Wren and Boyle approaching, he gave up. They'd find out soon enough, anyway. "I've given it to an expert to translate. But yes, I found it, and I own it."

More men pressed close to hear the incredible news. "How much did it cost you?" someone asked.

"A shilling." As a stunned silence filled the room, he felt a grin stretch his face. "The bookseller thought it was worthless," he added.

"I'll buy it for fifty pounds," a man offered.

Hooke raised a hand. "A hundred."

Normally the most polite man Ford knew, Wren elbowed his good friend out of the way. "I'll pay you five hundred."

"I'll double what anyone else offers."

Silence reigned again as they all turned to look at Newton. His wrinkled suit notwithstanding, the man could well afford to honor the bid. He was wifeless, childless, and his father had died three months before his birth, leaving a tidy estate to his only son. Newton had inherited land from a subsequent stepfather as well.

He sounded sincere, and no one moved to say he wasn't; the man was known to sometimes take offense when none was intended.

"It's not for sale," Ford said at last. "Not at any price."

"Well." Newton held his cup of Rhenish aloft in a toast. "I trust you'll let me know if ever you change your mind."

Conversation broke out in a deafening babble as people exclaimed over the find and maneuvered toward Ford to pump his hand and offer congratulations. The room turned hot and close as more guests made their way inside to join the crowd. Spirits were passed hand to hand from the tables to the back of the chamber, and soon everyone was clinking goblets to celebrate the discovery of the decade.

An hour flew by before Ford managed to work his way through the throng and into the corner where he'd left Violet. Along with the rest of Locke's audience, she was gone. The area had been overtaken by people marveling over *Secrets of the Emerald Tablet*.

Light-headed with success—and more wine than he customarily drank—Ford hurried outdoors to the improvised ballroom. But the colonnaded courtyard was sparsely populated, and only a few couples graced the dance floor. It seemed every member of the Royal Society was in the refreshment room.

Though another chamber blazed with light, a peek into it nearly had him backing away. It was crammed with chattering ladies—all those deserted, he supposed, by the men in the other room. He pushed his way in, not really expecting to find Violet. She didn't strike him as the social, gossipy type.

He was correct.

Stopping three times to acknowledge congratulations, he crossed the quadrangle and walked through a building, finding the door to a small, deserted piazza.

The little courtyard looked dark and peaceful, especially after the excitement elsewhere in the college. He stepped outdoors, breathing deep of the fresh night air. Then, suddenly struck by an idea—perhaps not as brilliant as the spectacles, but clever nonetheless—he headed back inside to talk to one of the serving maids.

# THIRTY-FOUR

*H*ALF AN HOUR later, Violet entered the quadrangle and nearly bumped into Ford. She smiled when his hands went to her shoulders to steady her, although it hadn't been necessary—these days, with her spectacles, she hardly ever tripped.

"Fancy meeting you here," she quipped, feeling a loss when he let go.

He failed to return her smile. "I've been looking all over for you."

"We had to escape that room."

"We?" he asked, looking a bit vexed as he eyed her low bodice.

She yanked up on it. "Mr. Locke and I. Whatever was happening in there drew everyone's attention, and suddenly I found myself alone with him."

His eyes filled with an odd mixture of relief and concern. "But I hadn't made an introduction."

"None was needed." Locke had introduced himself without even making mention of her spectacles, simply accepting her as she was. "It seems he recognized a kindred soul. We wandered off and talked and talked..." She frowned suddenly. "Where were you all that time?"

"Word got out about me finding *Secrets*—"

A bewigged gentleman came toward him with an outstretched hand. "Heard of your astounding luck, Lakefield. Congratulations. If ever you want to sell it—"

"I don't." Ford pumped his hand. "But I thank you."

"Just let me know."

As the two of them watched the man walk off, Ford sighed. "It seems everyone has to congratulate me—or make an offer to buy it. And Newton has offered to double anyone's bid. Can you imagine?"

What she couldn't imagine was him passing that up when he so obviously needed money. She measured his clear blue eyes. "You were serious, then, when you claimed you wouldn't sell at any price."

"I meant it. Considering the book went missing for so many years, it seems magical that it should end up in my hands. No matter that I don't believe in such things, it feels like fate."

She did understand how he felt. If ever she should find an ancient philosophy book, handwritten by one of the masters, she'd be reluctant to sell it as well. And she supposed it would feel like fate, too.

"Maybe it *was* fate," she said softly. "Do you believe that sometimes things are meant to be ours?"

He only smiled, a mysterious smile that for some reason made her uneasy.

She reached up to adjust her spectacles. "Well, I'm happy your announcement provided a distraction," she said by way of changing the subject. "I expect without that I'd never have spoken privately with Mr. Locke, and oh, we had the most lovely conversation."

"Tell me about it." When another well-wisher approached, Ford impatiently took Violet's arm. "I know a place where I can listen without interruption."

He led her across the quadrangle, where the dance floor seemed to be filling now that men and women were filtering out of the buildings and meeting up with one another. She noticed Wren with an apple-cheeked, brown-haired lady. Hooke, ungainly and awkward, danced with a beautiful, willowy woman quite a bit taller than himself.

Ford took Violet through a building and pushed open a door. And they stepped into a veritable wonderland.

Candles sparkled everywhere—perched on the sills of the windows surrounding them, sitting on the benches around the perimeter, scattered on the patterned brick paving. Their flickering flames warded off the night, bathing the small piazza in a romantic glow. In the center sat two chairs and one of the small round tables from the refreshment room, offering a selection of sweets and savories. A pair of goblets rested side by side, an open wine bottle nearby.

Gasping, she turned to Ford. "How did you know all this was here?"

"It wasn't." The door shut behind them with a soft thud. "I arranged it."

Though there were buildings all around, their windows were completely black. They were alone. She and her brilliant country neighbor were alone in a piazza in London. A piazza he'd had prepared especially for her.

Stunned, she shifted her gaze to meet his. "This isn't like you."

He gestured at her gown. "This isn't like you, either."

Heat rose into her cheeks as he reached to gently remove her spectacles. He curved an arm around her waist, drawing her close. "Perhaps," he continued, "we bring out the best in each other." And she felt the length of him pressed against her as he bent his head to meet her lips.

This wasn't a stolen kiss, impulsive and rushed while the children's heads were momentarily turned. This was sweet and unhurried. The lightest brush of his mouth, first on her bottom lip, then the top. Over her cheek and across her forehead and down to her chin. He cupped her face in his hands and ran a thumb over her lips before he finally covered her mouth with his own.

She felt...cherished. Her eyes closed. Her breath caught. Her heart seemed to stop, then began pounding in her chest. She hadn't known it could feel like this, hadn't thought she wanted a man. But suddenly she did, with every fiber of her being.

Oh my, the *Master-piece* had been right. Her mind was definitely stirred to venery.

Still gentle and slow, he deepened the kiss, coaxing her lips to part. She was floating, whirling. His tongue slipped inside to mingle with hers, and it was shocking, but glorious, too. Soft, sweet, tasting of the wine of celebration. His hair smelled lightly of soap and fresh air, his skin emitted that exotic, spicy scent. It felt so good to be held. Her head spun with the wonder of it all.

When he pulled away, she just stood there, swaying for a moment, and then she opened her eyes. All around them, the candles flickered, gilding his features in a pale, golden light.

"Thank you," she whispered.

As he slid the spectacles back on her face, the beginnings of a smile curved his lips. "You're entirely welcome," he said.

He sounded sincere. Was she wrong, then, about his intentions? He'd claimed to have invited her expressly to introduce her to a man who could help make her dream come true. Then he'd gone to great trouble to whisk her off to this romantic hideaway when they could be with his friends instead, showing off her spectacles and celebrating his miraculous book discovery.

His kiss had transported her to another world, a place where she'd felt cared for and wanted. Could he actually want *her*, plain Violet...for herself?

No. She couldn't allow herself to forget his words in the heat of a kiss. To forget his beliefs about women and money. To forget why he'd really brought her here.

She shook her head to clear it, but it didn't quite work. And why should it, really? For this one magical night, a night of dreams come true, she would let herself live a fantasy. For just this night...

She fluffed her satin overskirts, gazing at him while she willed herself to believe she was a fair lady in the company of a man in love with her.

"I'm famished," he said, and she laughed, breaking the tension. He led her to the table and seated her, then poured two goblets of wine. While she sipped, he moved the other chair close to hers and sat.

He lifted a strawberry and raised it to her mouth.

Oh my, he was feeding her.

"What did he talk about?" Ford asked.

"Who?" A berry had never tasted so delicious.

"King Charles."

For a moment, she looked around in confusion.

Then he laughed. "I meant John Locke, of course."

"Oh." A little giggle threatened to escape, so she sipped more wine. "He's brilliant."

He swiped a spear of asparagus off a plate piled high. "More brilliant than I?"

She cocked her head, making a show of considering. "In a different way." Sipping again, she warmed to her subject. "Do you know what he told me? He said all mankind should be equal and independent, and no one should have the right to harm another in his life, health, liberty, or possessions."

He bit the end off his third asparagus. "Not even the king?"

"No one." It was so radical a thought as to be startling, but so clear the way Locke had explained it. "There should be a standing rule to live by, common to everyone, and made by legislative power—a liberty to follow one's own will in all things where one does not harm another, and not to be subject to the arbitrary will of another. Arbitrary power, he said, becomes tyranny, whether those that use it are one or many."

"I wouldn't discuss this with Charles," Ford said, handing her a marchpane.

She bit into the sweet almond confection. "I've never discussed anything with the king, but if I ever get a chance, I just might."

"Damnation, what have I started?" he said with a good-natured roll of his eyes.

"Locke says every man has property in his own person, and no one has any right to that but himself. The labor of his body, the work of his hands, are his, and the only reason for men to unite and put themselves under government is the preservation of their property."

"You're excited by these ideas." He'd finished the asparagus. From yet another plate, he spooned up a bite of cheesecake blanketed in rich puff pastry. "I can hear it in your voice," he said, holding out the spoon.

Enjoying the traces of nutmeg and mace, she allowed the creamy cheese, somehow both sweet and tart, to melt on her tongue. "I *am* excited. These are new things to think about. A new way to look at our world." She drained her goblet, feeling woozy from both the wine and the ideas spinning in her brain. "Thank you so much for inviting me."

"Thank you for accepting." He reached to refill her cup, then leaned even closer, brushing her mouth with a feather-light kiss. "You enjoyed hearing about the scientific discoveries, too, if I'm not mistaken?"

"Very much." Her lips tingled. "I surprised myself."

"I'm surprised to find the philosophy interesting as well. So we're even this night."

"This night." Just this one night. She sighed, taking pleasure in the wine and the company, the candlelight, the music that drifted through the air, the stars in the clear summer sky. Knowing it had to end. "Can you hear the laughter from the quadrangle? I think everyone must be out there now." But she didn't want to join them. She didn't want to leave this magical, private place.

Afraid he might assume she wished to rejoin the party, she changed the subject. "Is Hooke really a drunkard?"

His brow furrowed in confusion. "Whatever makes you think that?"

"He said living here is convenient, because when he falls down stumbling drunk, he's close to his bed."

His face cleared. "Don't let his dry humor fool you. Far from being a drunkard, I think he and Wren are addicted to coffee, if anything at all. Best of friends they are, too."

The faint music from the quadrangle stopped. Another burst of laughter sounded. "Their wives must be proud of them," Violet said.

"Wren's wife is very kind." With one finger, he traced little circles on the back of her hand where it rested on the table. "Hooke has yet to marry, though."

She hid a delicious shiver. "Well, then, whom was he dancing with?"

"Why did you assume she was his spouse? You're here with me, and we aren't husband and wife."

"Of course we aren't," she said quickly, and if the tone of his voice implied he wanted them to be, she had to remind herself why she didn't. Still, her face heated at the thought, and she was thankful for the concealment of the night.

"The Gresham professors are required to be bachelors," he explained, still lazily teasing her hand. "Hooke calls that woman his housekeeper."

"She lives with him?"

"Mm-hmm."

She grinned. "You don't dance with Hilda."

"Hilda doesn't look like that." He raised his hand and ran a warm fingertip alongside her face. "And she's a *real* housekeeper."

"Oh." Her skin tingled wherever he touched. "Oh. You mean she's really a—oh."

"Yes. Oh," he repeated with a devilish lift of one brow.

All at once, the door was flung open and the sounds of laughter grew louder. A few couples spilled out into the piazza.

"We've been found," Ford said with a groan.

"There he is," one of the women said, drawing a man to where Violet sat with Ford.

"Ah, yes." The middle-aged man shot the woman a rather impatient look before he addressed Ford more neutrally. "We've heard you found *Secrets of the Emerald Tablet.*"

"I have." Ford reluctantly rose, bringing Violet up with him and curling an arm around her waist. "John Evelyn," he said by way of introduction. "May I present Lady Violet Ashcroft."

"I'm pleased to make your acquaintance." Evelyn had a lean, thoughtful face, shadowed by his graying hair. "My wife, Mary."

Mary was much younger, a pretty woman with a round face and curly hair that brushed shoulders left bare by a neckline even lower than Violet's. She smiled and bobbed a curtsy, her large pearl earbobs bobbing along with her. "It's a pleasure to meet you, my lady."

"The pleasure is mine," Violet said.

Introductions concluded, the woman turned to Ford. "Would *Secrets of the Emerald Tablet* be for sale, my lord?"

"I'm afraid not." His words sounded genial enough, but Violet felt him tense. "And you'd have to fight Mr. Newton for it, anyway."

"It's just as well, my dear," Evelyn said.

The tone of his voice confused Violet. She turned to look up at Ford.

"I think," he said, "that we'd best be on our way." And he drew her out of the lovely piazza he'd created, leaving the others to enjoy it.

"What was *that* all about?" Violet asked as they walked back through the building. "I would think he'd be pleased she wanted to buy him the book."

He dropped his hand from her waist, linking his fingers with hers instead. "She wants it for herself. Her husband calls her a 'kitchen scientist.' Not fondly, I might add."

"I could tell." The quadrangle was quickly emptying, the musicians packing up. "Does he not approve of her interests, then?"

"He believes housekeeping should be her priority. His wedding gift to her was a calligraphy copy of his own treatise on marital duties. The ladies at court think his wife must be the unhappiest woman in the world."

"I cannot blame her," Violet said, stepping carefully in her heeled shoes as they crossed the dew-damp grass.

"Her husband would say she has her children to console her."

"And you would say?"

He shrugged, squeezing her hand. "I know only that were I to be deprived of my scientific interests, I would be unhappy, too."

"Then let us hope your wife will be more indulgent than Mary Evelyn's husband," she heard herself say.

Egad, how could she speak of his future wife?

But he only laughed, drawing her through the passage that led back to the Reading Hall and entrance. In the arched tunnel, he stopped and turned to face her. "I'm hoping my wife will be very indulgent, indeed," he said in a husky drawl.

"She'd have to be." A nervous giggle escaped her lips. "Are we leaving now?"

"In a minute." He stepped closer, backing her against the stone wall. "There will be a long line for the carriage this late."

The evening had flown. "What time is it?" she asked.

"Does it matter? Your mother mentioned no curfew. I think she must approve of me." Her heart raced as he slowly drew off her spectacles and slipped them into his pocket. "The church bells rang one o'clock quite a while ago."

"Oh. I wasn't listening."

"I wonder why," he mused with a smile, skimming his hands up and down her sides. She was finding it hard to listen now. Everywhere he touched felt so warm, so tingly, so aware.

He lowered his head, his mouth inching toward hers, and she waited, waited, her breath catching when he finally found his target. His lips were gentle but insistent, and despite all her reservations, she returned his kiss with reckless abandon.

"Violet," he murmured, his mouth turning urgent, the caress deepening until his tongue mingled with hers. His hands continued their explorations, stroking her shoulders, gliding around to her back, trailing down to cup her bottom and pull her close.

Though she was shocked, her body arched toward him instinctively. Buffeted by new sensations, she moaned, a soft sound of capitulation. Pleasure streaked through her, sweeping her from the tunnel to another place where only he and she existed...

...and all the while he still kissed her.

He tasted of berries and wine, and she wanted more. Her hands reached beneath his coat to explore his body the way he was touching hers. Firmness against her softness, warmth against her palms. She pressed closer, molding herself to him, feeling a hardness down below, that, according to the *Masterpiece,* meant he wanted her.

Right or wrong, whatever his reasons, he wanted her. *Her,* Violet Ashcroft. The realization stole her breath, robbed her of thought—

Laughter burst through her pleasurable haze as two other couples entered the passageway, clearly in their cups.

"'Night, Lakefield," one of the men called facetiously. "Sweet dreams."

Ford pulled back with a groan, snatching his hands from

Violet's posterior. "'Night, Hartwell," he mumbled. His labored breath seemed to echo in the tunnel as he waited for the intruders to clear the other end.

When Ford and Violet were alone again, he smiled at her, a rather dazed smile that made her heart lurch. He leaned close, angling his head. His lips trailed her forehead, her cheek, her throat. In the sensitive area afforded him by her scandalous neckline, he nibbled and kissed, his tongue tracing a shivery line to her cleavage. Her hands clenched his shoulders; she sagged back against the wall—

And three more men stumbled into the tunnel.

"'Night, Lakefield," they called in drunken unison.

"Let's line up for the carriage," Ford said with a sigh. "At least there we'll be able to find some privacy."

# THIRTY-FIVE

*V*IOLET RODE IN a carriage, crossing London on roads so impossibly smooth it felt as though she floated. The sidelight illuminated a crimson velvet interior, rich, plush, decadent. And upon this upholstery she reclined...while Ford kissed her senseless.

Knock-knock-knock.

A soft moan escaped her lips, half passion, half annoyance. Some very rude person was rapping on the carriage door.

Knock-knock-*knock*!

"Don't answer," she whispered to Ford. To be sure he complied, she threaded her fingers through his hair and held his mouth captive to hers. He responded with a violent passion, his lips devouring...

*Knock-knock-knock!*

With a growl born of frustration, she bolted upright, wrenched unwillingly from the dream. Her eyes popped open, but everything looked pitch black.

"Who is it?" she forced through gritted teeth.

*Knock-knock-KNOCK!*

"Who *is* it?" She swung her legs off the bed and pushed open the hangings, reaching for the floor with her bare feet. Feeling blindly for her spectacles, she managed to locate them and shove them on, but of course they didn't help. Black was black.

*KNOCK-KNOCK-KNOCK!*

*"Who is it?"* she yelled, padding toward her door and fumbling in the darkness for the latch. When her fingers finally closed on it, she jerked it open.

It didn't open very far.

*Bang!* Like a gunshot, the noise came across the corridor, accompanied by a feminine shriek. Then the latch was yanked from Violet's hand, as—

SLAM! her own door flew closed.

Her frustration mounting, she opened it again.

*Bang!*

SLAM!

*Bang!*

SLAM!

She paused for a moment, shaking the last dregs of sleep from her head. After drawing a deep breath, she gingerly opened her door again, just a crack.

And heard the sound of a young boy's giggles.

"Rowan!" she admonished, but her own laughter bubbled up, neutralizing the sternness she'd intended.

Her hand was still on the latch, and something pulled on the door, though it didn't slam this time. A steady pull.

"Rowan?" Rose's voice called.

From down the corridor came the sound of another door opening, then Lily's sleepy voice. "What's all this noise?" she said through a yawn.

"I got you!" Rowan crowed. "I got you both. It worked!"

"What worked?" Violet asked suspiciously. A soft flare of light illuminated the corridor as someone—Lily, she guessed—approached with a candle.

"Rowan, I cannot believe what you did!" Lily exclaimed. Instead of disapproval, admiration tinged her voice. "You clever boy!"

"What?" Rose snapped, apparently still trapped behind her door and as mystified as Violet. "What did he do?"

Lily's laughter echoed in the corridor. "Wait a minute." Violet heard the small *clink* of the silver candlestick landing on a table, then a rustling, scratching sound as Lily did something with her door.

A moment later, it opened wide. "He t-tied your doors together with r-rope," Lily said, the words tumbling out between giggles. "So you were slamming each other's open and shut."

Directly across the corridor, Rose opened her now-free door and glowered at their brother. "You're lucky you didn't wake Mum."

Rowan shrugged. "Mum's room is too far away in this house. Besides, she'd find it funny, don't you think?"

"I ought to murder you, you rapscallion."

His little chest puffed out proudly. "I had to knock forever to wake you. But it was worth it. Jewel said it would work. Too bad she wasn't here to see it."

Violet's heart squeezed at the melancholy look that stole across his face. "You miss her, don't you?"

"I do. And I don't know if I'll ever see her again." A sheen of tears brightened his eyes. "I didn't think I'd like a girl, but she's not like any girl I ever knew. She's more like a boy."

Violet suspected pretty Jewel wouldn't remind him of a boy a few years down the road. "You'll see her again, I'm sure. And in the meantime, don't forget we're going home tomorrow, and Benjamin should be home by now, too."

"Benjamin!" Benjamin and he had grown up together, close as two neighbors could be. With a boy's short attention span, Rowan forgot Jewel immediately. "I'm going to sleep now, so tomorrow will come faster." And with that, he took off down the corridor, to his own room across from Lily's.

"What a rude awakening," Rose said.

Violet sighed. "He yanked me from the most wondrous dream."

"Did he?" Lily picked up the candle and swept past Violet into her room, Rose right on her heels. She lit Violet's bedside candle from her own and set them both on the night table. "What was your dream about?"

When Violet didn't answer immediately, her sisters exchanged a look, then sat in unison on the edge of her bed. "Tell us," Rose said.

Violet's cheeks flushed hot. She shut the door, cocooning the three girls together. "It was nothing, really."

Rose crossed her arms. "You said it was wondrous."

"Oh, all right." She dragged the stool over from her dressing table and sat facing them, setting her hands on her knees. "We were coming home—"

"We?" Lily interrupted.

"Ford and myself. From the Royal Society reception."

"How did that go?" Rose asked. "I tried to stay up to hear, but you returned home so late—"

"Hush," Lily said. "The dream first."

With all this squabbling, the dream was fading fast. In an effort to recover the mood, Violet shut her eyes. "We were riding home in his carriage, but it seemed to be floating—"

"Floating," Rose echoed, and though Violet's lids were closed, she could swear she saw her sister's head nod knowingly. "Floating in a dream is supposed to be carnal in nature."

"Rose!" Violet's eyes flew open. "You are only seventeen. You're not supposed to think about that."

"Oh, rubbish. Father and Mum have been hanging all over each other since the day I was born. And *you're* the one who showed me that book. *Aristotle's Master-piece.*"

"I didn't show it to you. You barged in on me reading it."

Rose raised a brow. "Let's read it some more."

"Not now," Lily said, giving Rose a little shove. "I want to hear the rest of the dream."

"All right." Violet swallowed and rubbed her suddenly damp palms against her nightgown-clad knees. "Ford's carriage is rather ancient, as you know, but instead of the hard leather, the interior was all plush red velvet. And I was leaning back against it, and he was kissing me—"

A romantic sigh came from Lily. "Did he kiss you really?"

"He already kissed her," Rose said. "In the library."

Lily turned on the bed to face her. "That doesn't count. You described it to me in detail, and it was a quick kiss, not a real kiss." She shifted back to Violet. "Did he give you a real kiss in the carriage?"

"Well," Violet hedged. "Not then. Not on the way home. Lord and Lady Ailesbury begged a ride home, and since they only live around the corner, we had no time alone together."

"But after you dropped them off?" Rose pressed.

"The street out front is very rutted, you know—the springs in that old carriage might as well be nonexistent."

"But he tried." Rose's gaze was much too piercing for Violet's comfort. "Or he kissed you earlier, didn't he? At the ball. Or later, when he saw you to the door."

Violet looked away.

"Or both!" Rose concluded. "I knew it!"

Lily laid a graceful hand on the white cotton that covered her chest. "Goodness." A theatrical sigh escaped her lips. "How did it feel?"

"I never said he kissed me."

Her two very different sisters fixed her with matching, demanding glares. Rose spoke for both. "Let's hear it, Violet."

"Oh, all right." Violet crossed her legs and leaned forward conspiratorially. "It was very nice."

"Nice?" Rose folded her arms.

"It was more than nice. It was wonderful." Warming to her subject, Violet's voice gentled. "The most amazing feeling. It made my knees weak, and my head seem to spin, and when he touched his tongue to—"

"Violet!" her sisters interrupted together.

Even Rose looked scandalized.

"Well, you did ask." Violet swallowed hard, wondering how she could have shared such a thing.

"Gemini." Rose fanned herself with a hand. "I must find someone to kiss. Tomorrow."

Violet reached out and caught her wrist. "No, you won't. You must care for someone before you kiss him."

Lily's eyes softened to a hazy blue. "Oh, Violet, that's so romantic."

That was taking things a bit too far. "It's over now. We're going home tomorrow, and he's staying here to meet with his solicitor. And even after he returns to Lakefield, Jewel has gone home, so there's no longer any reason for me to visit."

"But you care for him. You just said as much. And since he kissed you, he'll be asking you to wed him, will he not?"

"It doesn't work like that, Lily. Men don't put such store behind a kiss. The *Master-piece* says a woman is truly more moist than a man."

Lily frowned. "What's that supposed to mean?"

"I'm not sure. But he won't be asking me to marry him."

"But if he did?" Rose pressed. "That would be wonderful, wouldn't it?"

"No," Violet said flatly. "If he's making a show of courting me, you can be certain it's because of my inheritance. And I won't marry for anything less than true love."

"But Violet." Concern filled Lily's earnest gaze. "You must care. Or you wouldn't have kissed him. You said a woman must care for a man before she—"

"I'm not looking for one-sided love, Lily. If I cannot have a love like Mum's, then I'd rather live life on my own." She turned to Rose. "And you can stop worrying—I don't care if you marry before me. I don't care if I marry at all." And because that suddenly wasn't true, she made a big show of yawning. "It's very late. I have much to tell you both about the ball, and especially Mr. Locke, but it will have to wait until morning."

Lily rose and kissed her softly on the cheek. "I would love to hear it all, Violet."

Rose's kiss wasn't nearly as sweet. "I don't care about Mr. Locke," she said, "but you should marry Lord Lakefield."

Long after her sisters had left, Violet lay awake, her mind and heart in turmoil.

# THIRTY-SIX

*L*AKEFIELD HOUSE was quiet. Too quiet.

Hilda and Harry knew better than to disturb Ford when he was working, but Jewel had never quite mastered that bit of etiquette. Now Ford found his gaze straying toward the door, waiting for his niece to burst through, a grin on her heart-shaped face and a ribbon clenched in her fist.

Or an insect. One never quite knew what to expect from Lady Jewel.

But the one thing he hadn't expected was to feel this sudden loneliness. Emptiness. Bloody hell, he missed her.

Ford Chase missed a child.

Whoever would have thought? Mere weeks ago he'd been sure that having a family was the last item on his list of priorities. Though he'd known he'd have children eventually, he'd never really envisioned them in his life. But now, instead of finishing his watch, he found himself daydreaming. A girl and a boy, like Jewel and Rowan. And a mother for them, of course.

Violet would be perfect.

Gears fell from his hands as that thought took root in his brain. He dropped to his knees to reach one that rolled beneath his workbench, then bumped his head as he came back up.

Rubbing where it hurt, he sat on the floor to analyze when and how he had fallen in love with Violet Ashcroft.

He'd always thought he wanted someone like Tabitha. Effervescent, confident, sophisticated, a lady whose looks stopped men in the street. Violet was none of those things. But she listened to his ideas and challenged him with her own.

He'd never imagined a woman like Violet existed.

Perhaps it was logical, after all, for a man like him to find himself attracted to a lady with Violet's odd qualities.

But it was illogical for him to pursue the matter. He couldn't ask for Violet's hand when his estate and finances were in such sad shape. The meeting with his solicitor had not gone well. There were bills to be paid and no funds to settle them.

The man had presented two options. One, turn Lakefield into a working estate and see that it prospered. Two, sell the damned place. Only a small portion of the land was entailed. Selling the rest—including the house—would raise enough money to support Ford for years to come, allowing him to pursue his scientific interests.

As a third son, Ford should never have had a title, and while he enjoyed that part of it well enough, he wasn't cut out to be a landowner. True, he'd assisted his brother Jason with Cainewood's never-ending responsibilities—he knew the ins and outs of running an estate. But that wasn't the life he wanted.

Working the land, caring for tenants, collecting rents. It was all so tedious and nonproductive. At the end of a typical peer's life, one's legacy was naught but more of the same passed down to an heir. Nothing new to contribute to knowledge and mankind.

His life had always been in London with his experiments and the Royal Society.

But now his heart was here.

Agitated, he rose to his feet and tossed the gear into the mess on the table. What did it matter where his heart was? Regardless of how much Violet's parents might seem to like him personally, they were unlikely to bless their daughter's marriage to an impoverished viscount. Under normal circumstances, the fact that Violet came with a sizable inheritance as well as a dowry might mitigate the situation, but nothing about Violet was normal. Knowing her feelings about men marrying for money, he was sure he'd have a hell of a time convincing her he wasn't after her fortune.

He closed his eyes and rubbed them. It was hopeless. He might as well put her out of his mind. And he knew just how to go about that, too.

For once he was happy that he seemed unable to concentrate on more than one thing at a time.

He wanted to invent a watch with two hands. That was why he had come to Lakefield in the first place. Without Jewel to distract him, he ought to be able to achieve his goal at last.

It was a good thing he'd taken time to analyze the situation, because these lofty romantic aspirations had nothing to do with his life. Nothing to do with his plans.

He took a deep breath, opened his eyes, and got to work.

## THIRTY-SEVEN

*T*HE ASHCROFT girls rushed into the summerhouse and shut the door behind them. "Now," Rose said, "where did we leave off?"

Violet sat in their now customary spot with her sisters on either side. She opened the book, flipping pages. "We were reading about what should be eaten to induce erection."

Lily's hands went to her cheeks. "I cannot believe we're reading this."

"You can leave," Rose said pointedly.

Lily didn't.

Having found the correct passage, Violet cleared her throat. "'The desire of coition, which fires the imagination with unusual fancies, may soon inflame the appetite. Eat such meats as are of good juice, that nourish well, making the body lively and full of sap, to cause erection, as hens eggs, pheasants, wood-cocks, young pigeons, partridges, capons, almonds—'"

"Almonds aren't meat," Lily interrupted.

"Hush." Rose leaned across Violet, narrowing her eyes at their hapless younger sister. "Do you want to learn what to feed your husband or not?"

"Go on," Lily said with a sigh.

"All right, then." Violet resumed reading. "'Almonds, pine-nuts, raisins, currants, all strong wines, especially those made of the grapes of Italy. But erection is chiefly caused by parsnips, artichokes, asparagus...'"

She paused, thinking of a plate piled high with asparagus in a piazza twinkling with lights. And later in the passage, when Ford had pressed against her, and she'd felt—

Faith, the *Master-piece* was right.

"Violet." Looking concerned, Lily touched her hand. "Why did you stop?"

Violet blinked. "No reason," she said, her cheeks burning. "Sometimes my mind just wanders."

"Let me read instead." Rose grabbed for the book.

Violet held tight. "No." To focus better on the words, she slipped off her spectacles and set them on her lap. "'Asparagus, candied ginger—'"

"Enough with the food," Rose said. "We will never remember this long list, anyway. What comes after that?"

Violet turned to the next chapter and read the title. "'Of the Genitals of Women.'"

Rose nodded. "That sounds good."

"Lily?" Violet looked to her youngest sister.

Though Lily was red-faced, she nodded, too. "It sounds like something we should know."

"All right, then." Having read this section already in the privacy of her room, she took a deep breath before sharing with her sisters. "'Those parts that offer themselves to view at the bottom of the belly, the fissura magnaor with its labia or lips, the mons veneris, and the hair, are called by the general name pudenda.'"

A frown creased Lily's smooth young forehead. "These parts have names?"

"Of course they do, you goose." Rose leaned in closer. "Go on."

"'The clitoris is a substance in the upper part of the division

where the two wings concur, and is the seat of womanly pleasure, being like a yard—'"

"A yard?" Lily asked.

"That's what they call a man's..."

"Oh. That." Her blue eyes widened. "It's not actually a *yard*,
is it? I mean, when it's—"

"Erect?" Judging from the single breathy word, Rose seemed
to be lacking her customary aplomb. "Good God, I hope not. It
couldn't be. It's not really a yard, Violet, is it?"

"Why do you think I would know?" But her face heated as
she remembered feeling that hardness. "No, of course it isn't,"
she said as matter-of-factly as she could manage. "It wouldn't fit
if it were, would it? And it would show, don't you think? When
men just walked around? I'm certain it's not a yard."

"Probably men call it that because they *wish* it were a yard,"
Rose said dryly.

Even Lily giggled at that.

Violet blinked hard and continued reading. "'The clitoris...
being like a yard in situation, substance, composition and erection, growing sometimes out of the body an inch, but that never
happens except through extreme lust.'"

Rose harrumphed. "So a man gets a yard and we get an
inch."

"Oh, Rose," Violet groaned.

"Keep reading," Lily said.

"All right." Violet flashed Rose a look of warning. "'By the
neck of the womb is the channel which receives the yard like a
sheath, and that it may be better dilated for the pleasure of
procreation, in this concavity are diverse folds, wrinkled like an
expanded rose.'"

"A rose?" Rose harrumphed again. "That 'concavity' looks
nothing like Father's flowers." When her sisters gaped at her, she
bristled. "Well, it doesn't. I've looked. With a mirror." She
narrowed her gaze. "Don't tell me you haven't."

Violet just cleared her throat. "'The hymen, or claustrum

virginale, is that which closes the neck of the womb relating to virginity, broken in the first copulation. And commonly, when broken in copulation, or by any other accident, a small quantity of blood flows from it, attended with some little pain.'"

Silence descended on the summerhouse.

"Little pain," Lily whispered finally. "That doesn't sound too bad, does it?"

"I'm sure it's not," Violet said firmly.

But they all took a deep breath in unison.

"All right, then." Violet turned the page. "Listen to this." She swallowed. "'There are many veins and arteries passing into the womb, dilated for its better taking hold of the yard, there being great heat required in such motions, which become more intense in the act of friction, and consumes a considerable quantity of moisture, which being expunged in the time of copulation, greatly delights the woman.'"

"Greatly delights the woman," Rose breathed. "Gemini. We *have* to get married. Soon."

Suddenly they heard a jaunty tune being hummed outside. "Oh, God!" Lily exclaimed. "It's Mum!"

Leaping up, she ran for the door and jerked it open, Rose at her heels. The two of them pushed through at the same time, all but stumbling over each other.

"Good afternoon, Mum," Rose said. "Come along, Lily. Father is waiting."

"For what?" Mum asked, frowning at Violet as her younger daughters practically trampled her and ran for the gardens.

Shrugging, Violet snapped the book closed and set it face down on the bench. "What are you doing out here?"

Unlike Father, Mum avoided the outdoors, especially on a nice, sunny day like this one. She worried for her creamy complexion. Now she was wearing a big straw hat and carrying a basket over her arm, filled with stale bread. "I thought I'd just take some air," she said. "And feed the swans."

When Violet stood, her spectacles tumbled from her lap to

the red-brick floor. She bent to retrieve them, hoping her mother wouldn't notice the book on the bench. "Shall I come with you?"

"That would be lovely."

She slipped the frames on her face as they crossed the wide, green lawn to the river. A multitude of daisies sprouted among the blades of grass; heaven forbid Joseph Ashcroft leave any part of his land free of flowers.

Mum bent to pick one as they went. She twirled the white and yellow posy in her fingers. "Is the book you were reading interesting?"

Egad, she'd noticed.

"It's philosophy." Well, it was. In a sense.

"What is it called?"

"Um..." Violet felt her face heat, but the title certainly wasn't a giveaway. "*Aristotle's Master-piece.*"

Stepping onto the bridge, her mother threw her an arch look. "And is it?"

Her heart stuttered. "Is it what?"

"A masterpiece."

"Oh." Halfway across the bridge, Violet stopped and turned to the rail. She focused out over the river. "It's Aristotle, you know. I'm sure you've heard me jabber enough about him." She reached into her mother's basket and broke off a bit of bread, tossing it out to the lone swan nearby. "I don't expect you'd find it very interesting."

"You might be surprised."

Violet wondered what her mother meant, especially considering the tone of her voice, but she didn't want to ask. She had a feeling she was better off not knowing.

More swans glided near, and Mum tossed a few crumbs. "You miss him, don't you?"

*Him.* Mum had to mean Ford. But Violet had never admitted to any interest in him, so how could Mum know?

"Miss whom?" she asked.

"Lord Lakefield, of course. Don't be coy, Violet. For weeks

you saw him every day, but now that Jewel is gone, you have no excuse to visit. I know you're fond of him."

"He's a nice man," Violet said carefully.

"You don't allow a man to kiss you just because he's nice."

Violet's jaw dropped open. She closed it, along with her eyes, then opened them and turned to her mother. "Wherever did you get the idea he kissed me?"

"One of your sisters." Mum held up a hand. "No, I won't tell you which one, because it doesn't matter."

"It matters to me! It was Rose, wasn't it?"

"I won't be saying. Because it *doesn't* matter. It's acceptable to experiment. Do you imagine I never kissed your father before we married?"

Despite her outrage, Violet had to bite back a smile. Mum had done more than kiss Father. Violet knew she'd been born impossibly "early"—the girls had calculated the dates years ago.

But that was beside the point. "I'm not marrying him, Mum."

Below them, the swans squawked, and Mum broke off more bread. "Why not?"

"Well, for one thing, he hasn't asked me. And for another, I wouldn't agree if he did."

"Can you explain why?"

"Why?" To avoid meeting her mother's eyes, Violet took a hunk of bread and faced the graceful white birds. "Why should I? With or without my spectacles, I'm not blind. I know I'm no beauty. If he asked for my hand, it would only be to get my ten thousand pounds—God knows he needs it, as Rose has pointed out countless times. And I won't marry for less than true love, Mum. I...I suspect marriage isn't all it's purported to be, anyway."

She wished she could still believe that with the fervor she once had. But she wasn't quite so sure any longer, not since reading the *Master-piece*. Now, late at night, she lay in bed alone, wishing the feel of the sheets on her body were the feel of a man's hands instead. Wondering if the sensations were as wonderful as the *Master-piece* claimed.

And Ford's kisses had done nothing to convince her differently.

*Great heat...in the act of friction...greatly delights the woman.* Her very limited experience notwithstanding, she could believe it.

Her mother threw the last of her crumbs to the swans. "I see."

Violet didn't care for the way Mum had said that. Tossing the rest of her own crumbs, she turned to face her. "You're not going to try to match me up with him, are you? Because—"

"Heavens, no! I want you to be happy, Violet. Married or not —whatever makes you happy."

Mum sounded sincere. But on the way back to the house, Violet couldn't help but wonder.

# THIRTY-EIGHT

*C*HRYSTABEL LOVED the nighttimes.

In the quiet of the master chamber, her dear Joseph could always hear her. It didn't quite make sense, which was why she sometimes teasingly accused him of selective listening. But he said it had to do with competing sounds. That during the daytime, there were noises, always noises: the servants going about their work, the animals in the fields, birds in the skies, dishes and silverware at mealtimes, and children talking all at once. He claimed that with more than one sound, he couldn't distinguish any of them.

But within the thick, solid walls of their room, the nighttimes were blessedly quiet. And he also claimed that her voice was the one he could hear most easily, especially when there were no competing sounds. The perfect pitch.

That *did* make sense to her. Because they'd always, always been perfect together.

But now he had nodded off, though she'd expressly asked him not to. She leaned over the bed and poked him. "I told you to stay awake."

Rolling over, he yawned and forced open his eyes. "Has Violet fallen asleep yet?"

"Yes. Finally." She tapped the book she'd just placed on her night table. "I got it."

"What?" He rubbed his face, then struggled up onto his elbows to see better. "What in blazes is this all about?"

Before answering, she lifted the covers and slid languidly between the sheets. When she spoke, her voice was low and seductive. "*Aristotle's Master-piece.*"

"Holy Hades. The marriage manual?" Both his face and tone radiated his shock. "Where the hell would Violet get such a thing?"

"I haven't the slightest idea, but I'm glad."

"Glad?"

"Don't be such a prude, Joseph. I know this book is supposed to be scandalous, but frankly, I hope she reads it from cover to cover."

She saw no need to mention their other daughters were reading it as well. Dear Joseph wasn't always as open-minded as she. Often he needed some time and guidance to come around to her way of thinking.

She brushed a stray lock of hair from his forehead. "If Violet finds the book stimulating enough, perhaps it will make her give up this ridiculous notion that she doesn't want to marry." Deliberately, she wiggled closer to her husband. When he put an arm around her, drawing her against his warm body, she looked up at him coquettishly. "Marriage has its benefits, darling, wouldn't you agree?"

He gave her a long, slow kiss before he answered, the sort of kiss that had been making her senses spin from the very day they met. "Perhaps," he allowed huskily, "if you put it that way."

She nodded her woozy head. "It's not as though we were saints before we wed. Violet is about to turn one-and-twenty, a woman grown." At only one-and-forty herself, Chrystabel could well remember a young woman's naïveté. "It will do her good to know a bit of something before she lands in her marriage bed. And this book might be our only hope of ever getting her there."

"Hmmph." Narrowing those green eyes that always made her melt, he rubbed his chin. "As Violet's father, I believe it's my responsibility to approve her reading matter." He reached across her body toward the book. "Let me see it."

"I was hoping we could read it together. It could be…what did I call it?" She licked her lips. "Stimulating."

"Stimulating." A slow grin spread on his face. "Now, Chrysanthemum, we've never needed outside stimulation. But I suppose it wouldn't hurt to have a look. For curiosity's sake."

As he opened the book, she snuggled happily under his arm. "For curiosity's sake, of course."

$\mathcal{A}$N IMPATIENT KNOCK came at the laboratory door before Hilda's voice called through it. "Will you be wanting breakfast, milord?"

Ford blinked and then carefully, reverently, set aside his watch. Still in somewhat of a daze, he rose and went to admit her. "Is it morning already?"

His housekeeper's hands fisted on her hips. "Have you not bothered to look out a window lately?"

He turned to the one right over where he'd been working. The sky was blue. Birds were chirping, the perfect accompaniment for a beautiful, sunny day.

"Did you stay up all night again?" Hilda demanded.

"What is it with the questions?" Ford shook his head, refusing to let her disapproval ruin his ebullient mood. "Come, I have something to show you."

She followed him to his workbench, weaving around a water bath and flicking her dust rag as she went. "If you'd let me in here to clean once in a while, this wouldn't be such a skimble-skamble mess."

Accustomed to her lectures, he ignored this one and reached

for his watch. "Here it is," he said with a broad smile. "I'm finished."

"It's very nice." She raised a glass funnel and wiped it off.

Nonplussed, he stared at her. "I know it's not fancy, but do you see here? It's different from other watches. It has a minute hand, like a clock. So you won't have to guess how far into the hour it is by looking at only the single hand."

"Well, that is very nice, my lord." She smiled, but her faded blue eyes didn't sparkle with the enthusiasm he was seeking. "Although you have clocks enough around here for me to tell the time, I expect for some this will be quite convenient." She set down the funnel and glanced around the attic, sighing at the clutter and dust. "Will you be wanting breakfast now, then?"

He was silent a minute before mutely ordering himself to shrug off the disappointment. "Breakfast would be nice. I'll be down shortly."

He watched her calico-clad back as she picked her way through the maze that was his sanctuary. *Convenient.* She'd called his watch convenient. Although he supposed it was, that hadn't been the reaction he was hoping for.

After years of planning and experimenting, he'd finally managed to come up with something that could benefit mankind. He wanted excitement, appreciation. A bit of hero worship wouldn't be amiss, either. Suspecting Jewel would have reacted more to his liking, he found himself missing her all over again.

Luckily, another enthusiastic female lived not so far away.

# FORTY

*A*N HOUR LATER, having bathed, shaved, and gulped down some breakfast, Ford found himself in the galleried entry of Trentingham Manor, proudly holding up his watch for Violet's inspection.

"Oh my," she said, her brandy-colored eyes wide with unabashed admiration. "It's amazing. I cannot believe it! Can I just stand here a while and watch it work?"

Ford laughed, finally feeling that flush of success, wanting to hug and kiss her for giving it to him. "If you'd like. But if you'd care to invite me into a room with chairs, you can sit and watch it instead. That would be more comfortable, don't you think?"

"Oh. I'm so sorry." Holding the book he'd given her, she turned and started down the corridor. "I've forgotten my manners."

He walked beside her. "I'd forgotten how lovely you are."

In his single-minded focus on his watch, he *had* forgotten. Intentionally forgotten. But she blushed prettily at the compliment.

"Besides," he added, "I'm the one who's socially inept. I should have exchanged pleasantries before shoving my invention in your face. Your manners, by contrast, are impeccable."

She flashed him a smile that might as well have been a stab to his heart. Damnation, he shouldn't have come. Neither she nor her parents would ever agree to a match, and here he was, falling in love all over again.

It was akin to torture.

She was wearing a yellow gown today, and her matching heels clicked on the corridor's polished oak floor. "Would you show my family the watch? I'm certain they will be just as impressed as I."

Remembering Hilda's reaction—or rather, lack of one—Ford wasn't so sure.

"Mum is in her perfumery," Violet told him, and he shrugged and followed her to the left, through a study he hadn't seen before. Unlike the pretty feminine desks in the library upstairs, this room's desk was heavy and utilitarian. There were papers all over it, and a pile of ledgers that looked ready to topple. He figured this was where Joseph Ashcroft ran his estate. It was obviously hard work—an onerous job Ford had no desire to tackle for Lakefield.

But that's exactly what he'd have to do if he were to have a prayer of winning Violet.

He looked away from the desk, preferring instead to gaze at her back as he followed her through the house. The yellow silk flared over shapely hips and nipped in at her waist above. Even as his hands itched to span that waist, he sighed to himself.

The entire Church of England could pray on his behalf, and it would make no difference at all. He'd never win Violet.

His watch was finished. He really should go back to London.

Like many old houses, Trentingham had few corridors, most of the rooms simply opening on to the next. The adjacent chamber was tiny, more or less a closet. But it would do as the storeroom for a laboratory. The walls were lined with row upon row of shelves, upon which rested vials of liquid. Chemicals.

He stopped dead, looking around.

"Mum is through here."

He blinked. Violet was gazing at him, the red-covered book he'd given her clutched to her chest. "I'm coming," he said.

The next room *was* a laboratory.

True, it was nothing like his. While his had but a single small window over his work space, Lady Trentingham's large windows afforded glorious views of the gardens and the river. While his had only one wooden chair for him to sit and work, hers had six upholstered ones, arranged in pairs with elegant inlaid tables between them. Clearly this room was used for socializing as well as work. But it was a laboratory nonetheless.

Forgetting the watch in his hand, he found himself drawn to the center of the chamber, where Lady Trentingham stood at a large, rectangular table, plucking flower petals and tossing them into some sort of contraption.

"Good morning, Lord Lakefield," she said, beaming at him as though he were her long-lost son.

He wished.

"A pleasure to see you again," he told her.

"Yes, it's been a while, hasn't it?" If he wasn't mistaken, her tone was slightly critical. "What is it you've brought us?"

"He hasn't brought it for us, Mum, not exactly. Just to show." Violet shoved her spectacles up on her nose, looking a bit flustered, and Ford wondered if that was due to her mother's attitude. It certainly surprised him.

Perhaps the Ashcrofts would be more amenable to a match than he'd thought.

Violet set the book on a table. "Give me a moment to fetch the rest of the family."

The room seemed immeasurably emptier after she left. Listening to her fading footsteps, Ford set his watch on another of the small marquetry tables. "What is *that*?" he asked Lady Trentingham, indicating the odd device.

Favoring him with a smile, she tossed a final few petals into the bowl. "Joseph has given me the last of this year's roses. I'm about to make essential rose oil. Would you care to help?"

"Certainly." He wiped his palms on his breeches, approaching the crude apparatus. "What is it you'd like me to do?"

"Just hold the bowl while I pour boiling water, then quickly set this other bowl on top. Upside down." She demonstrated. "Ready?"

"Pour away," he told her, gripping the bowl while she turned to take a kettle from the fire. He watched while she poured, noting how much steam escaped before she finished and he was able to place the second bowl over the rising vapors.

"It's called distillation." Replacing the kettle, she swiped the back of a graceful hand across her brow. "When the drippings cool, they separate into water—rosewater, in this case—and essential oil." She indicated the tray below.

"I see," he told her. It was a still. But although he could tell it would work, it was like no other still he'd ever laid eyes on. Her process would be more efficient with the heat supply directly beneath, the water and petals contained in a flask so the vapors couldn't escape. And with tubing and a water-cooling method, the oil—

"Violet said you invented a new watch," Rose said, walking into the room with her two sisters in her wake. Rowan came close behind, making a beeline for the table where Ford's invention waited.

"Uh-uh-uh," Violet said before he could touch it. She reached to clasp his wrist. "Wait until Father arrives."

"But, Violet—"

"Here." She fetched the book Ford had given her. "Lord Lakefield brought you this from London."

"*Micrographia*," he breathed, opening it to the middle. "Look at this." He shoved a picture in Rose's face.

"Ewww." She wrinkled her nose. "What is that?"

"A blue fly up close."

Violet smiled. "I met the author at Gresham College."

The sudden blush on her cheeks made Ford wonder if she

was remembering their kisses that night. He hoped so, which was positively absurd.

"That was *very* nice of Lord Lakefield," Lady Trentingham said. She was beaming in Ford's direction again. "What do you say to him, Rowan?"

Before Rowan could offer his thanks, Violet's father barged in, his hands full of colorful flowers.

Lilies? Violets? Ford recognized only roses, and there were none of those.

"What's this all about?" Lord Trentingham asked.

"Lord Lakefield has designed a new watch," Violet said.

"Lord Lakefield has resigned? Resigned from what?"

The three sisters giggled.

"Quiet, everyone." Lady Trentingham set down the bottle she was holding and walked over to her husband. "Thank you, darling." She took the flowers and stuffed them into a vase she took off a shelf, one of many. "Lord Lakefield has an invention to show us. Would you care to see?"

"A new sort of watch." As Ford lifted it, everyone else moved to huddle around.

"Look," Violet said. "There's an extra hand to mark the minutes, so you no longer have to guess. Isn't it amazing?"

"Very impressive," Lord Trentingham said.

"Brilliant." His wife's smile looked so genuine that Ford once again had the impression she might really approve of him.

"I want one," Rowan said.

"Let me see," Rose demanded, and Lily chimed in more softly with "Me, too."

Ford handed over the timepiece, watching to make sure they'd be careful with it. But then his gaze was drawn to Violet. He hadn't seen her in a week. Hadn't touched her in a week.

Damnation, he still wanted her.

Their eyes searched, met, locked. Sparkling behind the lenses he'd made, hers were the most beautiful thing he'd ever seen. An unspoken message passed between them.

"If you've no objections," he said slowly, "I would like to take your daughter for a walk."

"Go ahead, dears," Lady Trentingham said. "We're watching the time pass!"

## FORTY-ONE

ATCHING TIME. How much time, Violet wondered as they strolled toward the river, until Ford returned to London?

This last week had been so monotonous while he'd been holed up working on his watch. She could hardly remember what she used to do with her days before he'd arrived with Jewel in tow. But now the girl had gone home, and he was finished with what he'd come to do. Soon, he'd be leaving. He'd probably asked her out here to tell her that.

She crossed her arms and hugged herself.

"Cold?" he asked.

"Not really." The August day was breezy yet warm, and the grass felt springy beneath her shoes. As they approached the bridge, she bent to pick one of the daisies that dotted the green. Idly she plucked the white petals.

*He loves me, he loves me not.*

But of course he didn't. The new yellow gown she was wearing might be fancier than her old ones, but a dress couldn't make her pretty. Since the reception at Gresham College, she may have been allowing Margaret to coax her hair into fashionable ringlets, but the curls didn't hide the overly intellectual brain hiding beneath.

The only thing she had that a man would be attracted to was her money.

She tossed the daisy at the foot of the bridge as they started across. "Have you missed Jewel this past week?"

He gave her a melancholy smile. "I've surprised myself by missing her something fierce. I've written her two letters already. She loves getting mail."

In the middle of the bridge, she stopped and turned to face him. "How thoughtful."

He shrugged. "It's partly selfish, to be honest. I'm hoping for letters in return." Water flowed under the boards beneath their feet, and two swans glided near, but she had no food to toss to them. "I missed you this past week as well," he said quietly.

Had he? She searched his brilliant blue eyes. "It felt odd not to be heading for Lakefield in the afternoons."

"Then you missed me, too?"

She couldn't deny it. But what good would it do to confirm? Admitting her feelings would change nothing.

Reaching to raise her chin, he looked deeply into her eyes. Without closing his own, he moved in to kiss her. Tender and sweet, no more than a fleeting touch of lips. "I care for you, Violet. I've been trying to analyze why. But I think—no matter how much it pains me to admit this—there are some things one cannot analyze."

She didn't know how to respond, but her lips tingled. His fingers felt warm on her skin. When he moved toward her again, her gaze darted up to the perfumery's windows. Her family lurked behind the glass, probably still exclaiming over Ford's invention. A pale oval appeared behind a pane, then disappeared. She'd bet the *Master-piece* it was Rose, spying.

He raised that devilish brow. "Afraid we're being watched?"

"I wouldn't put it past my sisters."

He nodded, and they strolled across the bridge and along the far bank of the river. Cattle grazed in the fields beyond, and a hawk circled lazily overhead. As Ford slipped his hand into hers, her gaze flicked once more to the window, and he chuckled beside her.

They walked in silence, listening to the whinnies of the horses in the field and the songs of two lovebirds in a tree. Violet focused on the feel of their joined hands, startling when he slipped his thumb inside to play upon her palm. The sensation sent a little thrill through her.

If only she could believe it was the same for him.

A small wooden gate marked the entry to the woods, and they paused only long enough to open it.

Here were new sounds: twigs crackling beneath their feet, leaves rustling overhead. Still playing with her hand, Ford led her to a tree stump and sat upon it, drawing her down to his lap.

It was most improper, but she didn't want to move. Though they weren't actually far from the house, the canopy of trees made this place feel secluded and private. She shifted sideways to face him, noting the faint circles under his eyes. "Looks like someone's not sleeping," she said quietly.

"I was up all night finishing the watch." He raised their joined hands to brush his lips over her knuckles. "Didn't even realize it was morning until Hilda offered me breakfast."

"You should have slept, then, after you were done."

"I couldn't. I was too excited. I wanted to show it to someone." He paused, pressing a slow kiss to the back of her hand while slanting a glance up at her. "I wanted to show it to you. Only you, Violet."

Her breathing shallowed at the thought. Faith, she wanted to believe him. "I'm sorry, then, that I brought my family—"

"No. I enjoyed showing it to them, too." Still holding her hand, he used his free hand to sweep the hair off her neck. "But you were the one I truly wanted to share it with." He bent his head, his warm lips grazing her nape.

Pleasure rippled through her.

She wanted this. Whenever he touched her, especially like this, she wanted *him*. It was as though she had no control over her own body.

His mouth trailed the back of her neck, her collarbone, her shoulders revealed in the wide neckline of her new gown. She felt his breath, the heat of it sending a shiver down her spine. He drew off her spectacles and set them on her lap, then placed his hands on her cheeks. His mouth met hers, his thumbs gently stroking as he kissed her.

She was undone. Resistance fled, and she twisted to more fully face him, slipping her hands beneath his coat. His mouth turned wild and demanding, his tongue fencing with hers, an impassioned bid for possession.

And oh my, she thought with what little ability to think she had left, she wanted to be possessed. She strained closer to him, wanting. That curious warmth was spreading in her middle.

*Great heat…greatly delights the woman.*

He threaded his fingers into her hair, cupping her face in his hands as he tilted it back. His lips traced a path down her chin, her neck, a hot, damp swath of sensation. Then his tongue crept out, licking, stroking, dipping into the valley between her breasts. A bolt of excitement streaked through her, straight to a place she hadn't had a name for until last week.

Her seat of womanly pleasure.

"Ford," she breathed, her hands tightening where they gripped his sides. "What are you doing to me?"

Although she hadn't meant him to answer, he stilled and raised his head to meet her eyes, a dazed expression in his own. "It's you, Violet. You make me lose my head. I know I shouldn't be doing this."

He drew a long breath and slowly let it out. With a small, wry smile, he reached beneath his coat to remove her hands from his body. He set the first in her lap and lifted the second to his mouth, kissing her fingertips before he placed it atop the other.

"I think I may have fallen in love," he confessed in a husky whisper.

Her world skidded, then righted itself. It wasn't quite "I love you," but close. He was saying all the right things, in just the right way to make her question all her old insecurities. When he looked at her like that, with those incredible blue eyes, she wanted to believe him more than she'd wanted anything, ever.

She just didn't know whether she could.

She slipped her spectacles back on, determined to regain her control, to focus her mind on other, more practical things. "Where will you sell it?" she asked quietly.

His eyes cleared, a concern stealing into them, a disappointment in her lack of response. "Sell what?"

"Your watch."

"My watch?" He sighed, then bent his head, his hair flopping forward like a young boy's.

A hot stab of love sliced through her.

"I'm not planning to sell my watch," he said. "I'm not equipped to manufacture watches."

Stunned, she sat up straight and felt him tense in response. "Well, then," she asked, "what do you plan to do with it?"

He straightened, too. "I'll take it to the next Royal Society meeting. I'm certain it will be a sensation."

"And then..."

"That's it. I have other projects I'm working on—"

"You're serious, then?" She couldn't believe it. "You have no plans for the watch?"

"I invented it. That was my plan." When she tried to rise, his arms tightened around her. "I'm not a businessman," he said softly. "I have no knowledge of that world. The creation was a satisfying end in itself."

"I don't understand you," she said. True, the aristocracy in general saw trade as beneath them, but only a rich man had the luxury of doing what he pleased without thought to profit.

Or a man who planned to rely on his wife for income.

She didn't want to think that of him. His words to her had sounded too sincere, his admission about the watch too uncalculated. She'd seen how much he cared for Jewel; she knew his heart was a good one. His steady gaze looked honest, not deceitful, and she no longer believed all his kisses were only a ruse.

But she couldn't help wondering.

He stared at her for a long, silent moment. A bird fluttered from one tree to another. A cow lowed in the fields beyond the woods. She heard her blood pounding in her ears.

"I don't understand me, either," he agreed, and finally let her rise.

## FORTY-TWO

"HAVE YOU AND Ford had a fight?" Sitting cross-legged on Violet's bed that night, Lily patted Maydew on her face from a bottle she'd purchased in London. "He didn't seem very happy when he came back for his watch."

Violet paced her bedchamber, restlessly touching things at random. "No, we didn't fight."

She had no idea how to explain what had happened in the woods, because she hadn't yet figured it out. The two of them had walked back in silence, as though they had nothing left to say to each other. But Ford hadn't seemed cross. Before they'd reentered the house, he'd even brushed a kiss across her forehead at the door. And then sighed before he opened it.

She sighed now. "I still cannot believe he isn't going to do anything with the watch."

Rose played with her hair, examining herself in the mirror at Violet's dressing table. "Not everyone is as ambitious as you are, Violet." She turned from her reflection, her tresses twisted up high. "Do you prefer it up or down?"

"Up," Lily said at the same time Violet said, "Down."

"Some help you two are." Rose stood, fluffing her white nightgown. Violet was struck anew by her younger sister's stunning beauty, but quickly suppressed the stab of envy. "It's not like you can change him," Rose told her. "And why would you want to, anyway? You keep insisting you're not interested in him."

Violet plopped on her bed so hard the ropes creaked a protest beneath the mattress. "I just find it hard to believe he can invent something so important and not be interested in selling it. Or patenting it, at least. At the Royal Society event, I heard that Christopher Wren patented a device for writing with two pens. If anyone uses his idea, they have to pay for it."

Lily scooted nearer and wrapped an arm around her shoulders. "Why is this bothering you so, Violet? It's not your invention."

"I just hate to see such brilliance go to waste."

Blinking, Lily shifted to face her. "Perhaps Ford isn't motivated by money, but it's not as though he's lazy. It's only that he does things for other reasons than you would. He might invent something to make someone happy, or create something he hopes will be a benefit to mankind. His values may be different than yours, but that doesn't mean they're inferior."

Violet wondered when young Lily had become so wise. "I never thought of it that way," she murmured, more confused than ever.

Her two sisters exchanged a glance. "Did he kiss you again?" Rose asked.

"Maybe." Violet stood and resumed pacing. She could feel her sisters' gazes following her as she trod back and forth. Facing away from them, she stopped. "All right, he did."

"And was it as wondrous as before?" When Violet failed to answer, Lily rose and came up behind her, settling her hands on her shoulders. "If you love him," she said softly, "why won't you consider marriage?"

"He hasn't asked me." Violet twisted out of her sister's grasp. And because Ford had as much as said he loved her, something in her middle twisted as well. "And even if he did ask me, I would wonder if it were only for my inheritance. I'm not a woman who inspires love."

Compassion flooded Lily's deep blue eyes. "*We* love you, Violet!"

"You're my sisters. That's different."

"Now I see why you're so upset," Rose said. "You wish he would sell watches and make a lot of money. Because if he still seduced you then, you'd know it was for yourself."

That could be so, Violet realized, though she hadn't thought of it in that way before. Rose was entirely too shrewd for her comfort.

Lily stepped closer. "Or is it your dream of publishing you don't want to give up? Are you afraid that if you marry, your money will go to your husband instead of your dream?"

"No. Not that." Maybe she would have agreed with Lily last month. But although she still wanted to write a philosophy book, she had new dreams now.

Yet she was sure, deep down, that if Ford were suddenly showered with gold, those new dreams still wouldn't come true. And it irritated her that she'd even begun dreaming. She used to be content with her lot, and that had been much easier.

"My own money has nothing to do with it," she said. "I just hate to see wasted potential. It disagrees with the practical in me."

"But Violet," Lily said quietly, "what is it you really want?"

Good question, Violet thought. She didn't know anymore. "Maybe we should talk of something else."

Rose shrugged, then grinned. "We could read more of the *Master-piece*." She snatched the book off Violet's bedside table. "Where did we leave off?"

"Here, give it to me." With a sigh, Violet took the book and climbed into bed.

Lily ran around to the other side, and the three of them huddled together beneath the covers. "Just like old times," Lily said. "Do you remember when we couldn't read yet, Violet, and you used to read to us at night?"

"Read to us again, big sister." Rose smiled with scarcely a trace of the innocence from their childhood. "We were learning about women's parts. Is there a chapter on men's parts, too? That's what I want to hear about."

"There is, but we need to finish this first." Violet opened the book to Chapter Fourteen, "A Description of the Womb's Fabric." "'In the lower part, where the lips are widest and broadest, for which reason women have likewise broader buttocks than men—'"

"We do not," Rose interrupted.

"Some of us do." Picturing Ford's slim hips compared to her own, Violet cleared her throat. "'The womb's figure is in a manner round and not unlike a gourd. There are diverse little nerves, placed chiefly for sense and pleasure. As for the neck of the womb, it is of an exquisite feeling.'"

"Goodness." Using a hand, Lily fanned herself.

Rose reached over to turn the page, showing no surprise or discomfort. "We're learning so much, aren't we?"

"Absolutely," Violet said dryly. She looked back down at the book. "'The externals are designed to receive the yard, and by their swelling up, cause titillation and delight in those parts. The action of the clitoris in women is like that of the yard in men, and the seat of the greatest pleasure in conception.'"

"Goodness," Lily repeated.

"It sounds wonderful," Rose said, "but what about the men's parts?"

"Oh, very well. I think that's Chapter Sixteen." Violet flipped ahead. "'Of the Organs of Generation of Man.'"

"That sounds like the chapter I want to hear."

"You would," Lily said.

"Hey—" Rose started.

"Just listen," Violet interrupted. She couldn't face an argument. Not tonight. "'The instrument of generation in man,'" she rushed on, "'commonly called the yard, and in Latin, *penis a pedendo*, is long and round. When the nerves are filled with animal spirits, and the arteries with hot and spiritous blood, then the yard is distended and becomes erect.'"

"Have you seen one erect?" Lily asked nobody in particular.

"No." Violet was fairly sure she'd felt one pressed against her, but that wasn't the same as seeing it.

"I've seen more than one," Rose said.

Both Violet and Lily swung to stare at her.

"Covered by breeches," she added, "but I could still tell."

"You shouldn't be looking there." Violet snapped the book shut. "It's not polite."

"Well, I cannot help it. And I cannot help it if men get like that around me, either."

Her two sisters groaned in unison.

With a sigh, Violet reopened the book. "'At the end of the yard is the glans covered with a very thin membrane, by means of which and its nervous substance, it becomes more exquisitely sensitive, and is the principle seat of pleasure in copulation.'"

"Do you think it's as pleasurable for men?" Lily asked.

"More," Rose said. "Else why would they always be after it?"

Her sisters gasped.

"Well, they are," she said defensively. "No sense glossing over the matter."

Lily yawned. "Is there more?"

"The hour grows late," Violet hedged, thinking that Rose didn't need a book and Lily had heard enough.

"Let me see." Rose grabbed the *Master-piece*. "There *is* more on men's parts." She scanned the page. "About testiculi and something called a scrotum. And the next chapter is..." She paused to turn the page. "'A Word of Advice to Both Sexes, Being Several Directions Respecting Copulation.'"

"We must read that," Lily said.

"Not tonight." Violet had already read it several times. There were sections she didn't understand, but she suspected they weren't fit for the tender ears of her younger sisters. Or at least one of her sisters. "We're finished for tonight," she said.

Lily yawned again. "All right."

Rose threw back the covers. "I suppose we should all get our beauty sleep so we can catch men and try what we've learned."

Lily groaned and whacked her on the shoulder as the two of them padded off to bed, closing the door behind them.

Violet removed her spectacles and leaned to blow out her candle, then lay beneath her sheets, staring into the darkness.

Every word of the *Master-piece* seemed to make her think of Ford in new and delicious ways.

And every word made not having him hurt even more.

# FORTY-THREE

OR THE DOZENTH time, Ford turned over in his lonely bed. His project was finished, but for some odd, annoying reason, he still found himself sleepless in the wee hours of the morning. Or perhaps it was *because* his project was finished.

It was time to leave Lakefield.

Tabitha's elopement was behind him. Far behind him. So far behind him, he wondered what he'd ever seen in the woman—on the rare occasions he thought of her at all.

His watch was done, and although he had another idea to add a chime to wake the watch's owner at a certain time of the day, he could work on that at Cainewood, or even in London. With the Royal Society settled back in its old home, the meetings would be more regular. He wanted to attend them.

But even though he knew Violet would never be his—even though he'd cursed himself a hundred times since this afternoon for not just leaving her the hell alone—he still found himself oddly reluctant to leave.

He levered up on an elbow and stared into the darkness at nothing in particular. When he grew bored with that—which was more or less immediately—he climbed from the bed and wrapped himself in a robe. As long as he couldn't sleep, he might as well start designing the wake-up bell.

On his way up to the laboratory, he bumped into Harry coming down. "Pardon, my lord." Holding a candle in one hand, Harry rubbed his bald head with the other. "I was just sneaking down for a midnight raid. I wouldn't be averse to some company."

"Midnight raid?"

"On the kitchen." The houseman patted his round belly. "Hilda is always nagging me not to eat, so I don't much. Not so she can see it." He grinned. "She baked bread before retiring."

As usual, Hilda's offerings this evening had been less than enticing. Feeling his own stomach rumble, Ford followed Harry downstairs and drew a stool up to the big table in the cavernous kitchen.

Harry swiped a fresh loaf off the counter and reached for a knife. "Quiet around here since Lady Jewel left, if I may say so."

"It is." Ford watched him slice the coarse brown bread. "She's a charmer."

Scooping butter from a crock, Harry slathered it onto a piece. "She is that. And Lady Violet, too."

"Lady Violet?"

"Don't tell me you haven't any interest."

Ford accepted the buttered bread. "Bloody hell, you're as meddling as your wife." But unlike Hilda, the man managed to probe without asking a single question. "What business is that of yours?"

The man didn't so much as bristle. "Just wondering how long you'll stick around here is all, my lord."

"As I've no excuse not to leave, most likely I'll be heading to London soon." He bit into the chewy bread. "Or not," he added around the mouthful.

"Just," Harry said, buttering his own hunk of loaf, "as I thought." He took a hearty bite. "Those Ashcrofts have made you feel right welcome."

"They have," Ford admitted. In a few short weeks, he'd begun to feel like Violet's family belonged in his life. Even her parents, which surprised him.

His oldest brother had been fairly simple to manipulate, and he'd always imagined real parents would be a nuisance. But Violet's were rather amusing.

He swallowed and nodded. "I find myself shouting at Lord Trentingham with the rest of them now. And earlier today, I helped Lady Trentingham make essential oil."

Harry drew a pitcher of ale and grabbed two goblets off a shelf. "Sounds like a messy business."

"Not particularly, although she has a disaster of a distillery." Ford watched while the man poured. "Perhaps I could make her a new one," he mused. After all, Lady Trentingham had been the soul of kindness and had even allowed his attentions to Violet, regardless that he was unworthy. He owed her a world of thanks —and a new, sophisticated distillery would be just the thing.

"Sounds like a good enough excuse to stick around," Harry observed.

Ford raked back his hair. "It has nothing to do with that. Lady Trentingham deserves it, as a token of my thanks for her hospitality."

"Of course." Harry's brown eyes twinkled as he raised his cup. "Drink up, my lord."

Ford did, his mind already occupied by how to best arrange the copper tubing.

# FORTY-FOUR

$O$THER THAN THE odd squeaks and groans emitted by any old house, Trentingham was deathly quiet. By candlelight, Violet sat at her desk in the library, chewing on the end of a quill.

Nodding to herself, she dipped it into the ink and began writing.

*Dear Mr. Wren,*

*It was a pleasure meeting you at the Royal Society function last month, and it is my hope that we renew our acquaintance sometime in the future.*

The quill's scratch sounded loud in the empty room.

*In the meantime, I am requesting your assistance with some information. You had mentioned patenting an invention, and I would be grateful to know how to go about doing so. A few lines of instruction would be most appreciated.*

*Yours truly,*

*Violet Ashcroft*

Simple and straightforward. She read it over twice before folding it, then added a seal and addressed it to the Royal Society for delivery. Surely someone there would see it reached Christopher Wren's hands.

Now to the more important letter. She had already addressed the backside of the paper to *Daniel Quare, Watchmaker, Fleet Street, London*. She'd found the information engraved on the backs of two of her father's watches.

*Dear Mr. Quare,*

*I have invented a new watch with an additional hand to mark the progress of the minutes. I am querying your interest in producing and selling the design, a vast improvement on all current watches. I am certain you can envision the profits as patrons must replace their old watches with this newer one, which could very well allow you to domi-nate the market. I have patented the design—*

She removed her spectacles and rubbed her eyes. That wasn't quite a lie—she *did* intend to see it patented.

*—so there is no sense in your own craftsmen attempting to duplicate my idea. I am asking—*

She hesitated again, then took a deep breath.

*—twenty-five thousand pounds for my sketches and the working sample, plus a royalty percentage to be negotiated. You have two weeks in which to answer, after which time I will offer my invention to Mr. Thomas Tompion. I hope to hear from you in the affirmative, with a contract ready to be signed.*

*Yours truly,*

For a third time she stopped and closed her eyes. Then she opened them, redipped her quill, and etched the name.

*Ford Chase, Viscount Lakefield*

If he had no ambition for trade, she figured she had enough for them both.

# FORTY-FIVE

"MOVE ASIDE, if you will. Please. This is heavy."

At the sound of Ford Chase's voice, which she hadn't heard for far too many days, Chrystabel looked up to see Violet scurry into her perfumery. Ford and a footman followed close behind, an enormous machine held between them.

At least, she *thought* it was a machine.

"What *is* that?" she asked.

With some effort, the men maneuvered it to her worktable and set it down. "My thanks," Ford said to the footman, who bowed and took his leave. "It's a distillery, my lady."

"A distillery?" The machine wasn't like any distillery Chrystabel had ever seen. Well, besides her own, she hadn't seen any distilleries other than the one her aunt Idonea had used to teach her how to make perfume. Which had looked very much like the one she owned now. Two wooden bowls, a wooden block, a wooden tray beneath it all.

But *this...this* was all metal and glass and copper tubing. It positively gleamed.

And she hadn't a clue how it would work.

"You're sure that's a distillery?" she couldn't help asking.

He stroked the thing, very much like Lily petted her beloved stray animals. "I'm certain. I assure you there's nothing radical about the design."

"He has a much bigger one in his laboratory," Violet said.

Ford nodded. "And at Cainewood, yet another that dwarfs that one. But they all work on the same principles." He smiled at Chrystabel. "I hope you'll enjoy using it."

"Enjoy using it?" Her head swam with confusion, an unusual state of mind for Chrystabel. "Do you mean...can you mean to give it to me?"

He blinked. "Of course. I made it for you. Why else would I bring it here?"

"Why..." She felt speechless, another atypical condition. "That's so generous, I...I don't know how to thank you."

"No thanks are necessary. I saw a need, I filled it. One does that for friends."

Unsure which she appreciated more, his declaration or his gift, she came forward to take both his hands. "Then I'm fortunate to be counted among your friends," she said warmly, her gaze drifting to Violet.

Chrystabel hoped to be more than Ford's friend; she hoped to be his mother-in-law. But she was clever enough to keep her mouth shut lest she thwart her plans. One wrong word from her lips, and her skittish daughter would go running the other direction.

Her best bet was to keep throwing the two of them together until Mother Nature did her work. Chemistry—she'd wager that was how Ford thought of it. And she knew it was only a matter of time before those natural urges got the better of these two, the same way they had with herself and her dear Joseph.

Very few mothers would plot to compromise their own daughters, but Chrystabel feared it was her only hope. Violet was too particular and too stubborn for her own good.

She squeezed the viscount's hands before dropping them. "I do thank you, whether you feel that's required or not."

Her daughter circled the large table, ostensibly examining the distillery. "Will you show us how to use it?"

"Of course," he said, following Violet. A mating dance, Chrystabel thought with an inward smile.

"This container down here is for oil." He lifted a lid. "Not your essential oils, but fuel, if you will. I've filled it for now, but you'll need to add more as you use the still."

"That makes sense," Chrystabel said, watching her daughter move away again.

He shifted closer to replace the lid, which had a hole in the middle. "Make sure the wick is thick and long at the top," he instructed, inserting one he pulled from his pocket. "You'll want the flame high enough to boil the water. At home, this part of my still is brick—a proper oven. But for your purposes, this should do fine."

For the next step of the dance, Violet crossed back to Chrystabel's side of the table. "It looks very complicated."

A large glass bulb sat in a frame, and a second glass bulb was attached by a tube. Smaller, it was designed to rest on the tabletop.

"Put your petals in here," Ford said, coming halfway around again to indicate the larger bulb. "Then fill it with water. There's room here beneath the cover for the steam to collect, you see, but not too much room. Soon it will be forced down the tube, and on the long way down, away from the heat, the essential oil will condense and collect in this second receptacle." He showed them how to remove it. "Does that make sense?"

Still amazed that he'd gifted her with this, Chrystabel nodded. "It does!"

"It will take a bit longer than your original method, but you won't be losing any steam. Your oil will be purer and stronger."

"It will," Violet said with a smile. "It's quite obvious, and quite brilliant."

Overjoyed, Chrystabel rounded the table to impulsively wrap

Lord Lakefield in a hug. "You're a genius!" she exclaimed. "And so generous."

And so perfect for her Violet.

His face was flushed when he pulled back. "It's nothing, really."

"It's everything," Violet disagreed from across the table, leaning forward on both hands. "Few men would take a woman's hobby seriously, let alone devise ways to improve it. Most would be like John Evelyn with his 'kitchen scientist' wife Mary."

Chrystabel hadn't the slightest idea who John Evelyn was, but Violet's eyes were filled with admiration. Her daughter was falling for Ford, she was sure of it. However, things weren't progressing as quickly as she'd like. The man had a disconcerting habit of disappearing for days at a time while he invented one thing or another.

"Violet's birthday is tomorrow," she told him. "We're having a family celebration. I'd be pleased if you would join us."

"Mum—"

"I'm delighted to accept," he interrupted smoothly. "But I was planning to ask if Violet might take supper in my company tonight."

A little gasp came across the table. "Alone?" Violet asked.

"Well, Harry will be there, and—"

Violet opened her mouth.

"I'm sure she'd be pleased," Chrystabel rushed to say before her daughter could decline the invitation. She just managed to suppress a grin.

"Shall I come for her at six, then?"

"Wait." Violet raised both hands, palms forward, looking altogether defensive. "Have I no say in this?"

"Of course you do, dear." Chrystabel fixed her with a steady gaze. "I just couldn't imagine you refusing such a request after Lord Lakefield went out of his way to make this new distillery."

Ford walked around the table, stopping nose to nose with her daughter. Or they would have been nose to nose, if he wasn't so much taller. The dance had ended. As Chrystabel watched him capture Violet's gaze with his own, her heart sang to see her daughter's eyes soften.

Surrender.

"Would you rather not come?" he asked quietly.

"I..."

"Please say you will."

Silence for a heartbeat. "All right."

A less than enthusiastic response, but Ford looked as happy to receive it as Chrystabel was to hear it. This was exactly the sort of opportunity she'd been hoping would come along.

"I'm looking forward to it." He bowed to both ladies. "Until six, then."

## FORTY-SIX

*N*O SOONER had Ford cleared the door than Violet's sisters rushed in to see what he'd brought.

"He made this?" Rose dumped an armful of flowers on the table. "He really and truly made this without you even asking?"

Mum laughed. "How could I ask? I had no idea such a thing even existed."

"That was nice." Lily ran a finger down the gleaming copper tube. "*Very* nice." She turned to Violet. "You should marry him."

Violet's mouth gaped. Though she'd discussed the subject with her sisters, she had trusted them to be more discreet. Especially in front of Mum. They had their pact to maintain a united front against any matchmaking.

"Has he asked you to marry him?" her mother asked with widened eyes.

"No," she said shortly. That, at least, was true.

Lily bit her lip, looking to Violet in apology. "I was just teasing her, Mum. But it was very nice of him to make this. I cannot wait to see you use it."

"And she should marry him," Rose put in.

"Oh, do hush up," Violet said, dropping onto a chair. She raised her spectacles and rubbed her eyes, then pushed them back into place to focus on her mother. "Why did you invite him to my birthday celebration? It was supposed to be a private party. Family." The day would be disconcerting enough without celebrating it in public. "You're not trying to match me up with him, are you?"

"Of course not." Mum waved a dismissive hand. "He'd just brought me a gift. I felt it necessary to reciprocate in what little way I could."

That made sense. Maybe. "Then what is your explanation for encouraging me to join him for supper? Alone, Mum? Harry and Hilda don't count."

"You're twenty-one years old now, a woman grown. I'm sure I can trust you."

Violet wasn't sure she could trust herself.

"Besides, it was very much like I said, dear. He'd just done me an enormous favor, and I didn't feel it would be right to refuse him a boon. It's naught but a couple of hours in his company—surely you cannot find that too onerous."

"But you really should marry him," Rose said again.

Violet turned on her. "Why? So you can start your own husband hunt?"

"No." Rose actually looked hurt, which made Violet feel terrible for lashing out. "You just seem perfect together. Mum, don't you agree?"

Their mother's fingers played over the flowers scattered on the table, picking out the white jasmines. "I promised you girls I would allow you to find your own husbands."

"That doesn't mean we don't want your opinion," Lily said.

"Yes, Mum," Rose agreed. "What's your opinion?"

Violet didn't want to hear anyone else's opinion. If she thought she could get away with it, she'd slink from the room.

Mum lifted the lid off the new still and began plucking jasmine petals, tossing them in as she talked. "I think he is brilliant."

Rose began collecting carnations, doubtless planning another floral arrangement. "Which makes him perfect for our Violet, doesn't it?"

"I didn't say that, Rose."

"But you thought it."

Violet gritted her teeth. "Rose, would you hush up?"

"Girls. Stop bickering. It's up to Violet to choose her own husband. I said from the first I thought Lord Lakefield was too much of an intellectual, and I haven't changed my opinion."

"But he's so nice," Lily said.

Violet's fingers clenched on the chair's arms. "You think so? Then would *you* marry him?"

"I'm not looking for a man like him," Lily protested. "I'm looking for a man who shares my love for animals."

"You're too young to be looking at all," Mum said.

Rose rubbed a pink bloom across her lips. "I like looking."

"We all know that by now," Violet said, rolling her eyes.

"Viscount Lakefield is very nice to look at."

"You think so?" Violet repeated. "Then why don't *you* marry him?"

Rose tossed her gleaming chestnut ringlets. "I'm looking for a man who appreciates my femininity. Your Ford looks right through me."

"Not too difficult, since you're so shallow."

"Violet!" Her eyes wide, Mum stopped plucking.

"I'm sorry," Violet muttered. She hadn't meant to be mean; she was just tired of being pressured. "It's only that Rose is so intelligent, yet she tries so hard to hide it."

Rose turned to pull a vase from the shelf. "I've told you, men aren't interested in intelligence."

"Lord Lakefield is," Lily said.

"And that," Rose declared, plopping the carnations into the vase, "is why he's so perfect for Violet."

A sigh escaped Violet in a rush. *How long will you abuse my patience?* she paraphrased Cicero in her head, but the familiar quotation did nothing to help her regain her own.

266 | LAUREN ROYAL

This discussion was going nowhere at all, and if she heard one more time that she should marry Ford—from her mother, her sisters, *anybody*—she feared she would scream.

She rose and headed for the door. "I need to go get ready."

Lily came to block her way, her blue eyes concerned. "Don't you want to see the distillery work?"

"Perhaps tomorrow," she said, skirting around her sister. "Today I have no time."

Thanks to Mum's meddling, she had a supper date in less than three hours.

# FORTY-SEVEN

"*V*IOLET!" HER father called from over by a border of pink candytuft. "Where are you going?"

Walking through the garden with Ford, she cast him an apologetic glance. "I'm off to Lakefield House for supper!" she shouted. "Did Mum not tell you?"

As they drew close, Ford took her hand. Father's gaze focused on their linked fingers, and a smile flirted on his lips. Apparently *he* wanted her to marry Ford, too.

Egad, just what she needed. More family pressure.

"Have a pleasant time, dear." Father leaned to kiss her on the cheek. "Be back by supper."

"Supper?" Ford repeated. "Lord Trentingham—"

"Forget it," Violet told him. "We could stand here all night. Mum will explain when I'm not at the table." She gave her father's arm a squeeze, knowing he hadn't heard her low comments. "I'll see you later, Father."

"What?"

"I'll see you later!" she shouted with a smile. "Sorry about that," she said to Ford as they walked away. "We yell a lot in this family, but we never mean anything by it."

"If you're thinking that will put me off, you're wrong. My

family yells, too. And none of us are deaf." Still holding her hand, Ford led her around the corner.

And there was that silly, old-fashioned barge.

She stopped in her tracks. "Where is your carriage?"

"It's a beautiful evening," he said, pulling her along. "I thought to spend it on the river."

His sudden smile was disarming. She was speechless as they crossed the lawn, and although she hadn't tripped in weeks, she nearly did as she stepped onto the barge. Nodding to Harry and the stable hands to cast off, Ford drew her into the unsuitable cabin that had nothing but a bed.

Only it wasn't quite so unsuitable now. A little table and two chairs were also crammed into the cozy space. And the whole of it was lit by dozens of flickering candles.

He'd made a wonderland for her again, this time on his elegantly decrepit barge. The table was covered by a soft pink cloth, and silver domes hid various dishes. While she stood gaping, he leaned forward and swept one off.

"Supper," he said. "Since Hilda's culinary skills are a mite lacking, I had Harry fetch it from the cookshop in the village. I only hope it hasn't all gone cold."

Butterflies erupted in Violet's middle. She laid a hand on her blue moiré stomacher. At this moment, more than any other, she wished she were a conventional beauty. Sure of herself, confident the man in front of her could have feelings for her that were real.

Because what she was feeling now was becoming rather overwhelming.

"Are you all right?" he asked, looking concerned.

"I'm fine."

This was ridiculous. She'd been alone with him on the way to Gresham College, not to mention in the piazza while they were there, and nothing much had happened. Kisses, that was all.

But there had also been that moment in the passageway at Gresham. And that day in the woods. And snatches of the *Master-piece* kept running through her head.

And her entire family wanted her to marry him.

Two goblets sat on the table, the red wine in them gently swaying in rhythm with the barge's movements. She reached to raise one to her lips and took a gulp for courage. "I...I thought we were dining at Lakefield."

He drew out a chair and waited for her to sit, then pulled the door shut. "I never said that. I only asked if you might take supper in my company tonight." He seated himself across from her. The table was so small their knees touched, yet it and the chairs filled every inch of available space. "Don't you think this is more romantic?"

She wasn't certain she wanted romantic. His knees felt warm against hers, even through her skirts. Her gaze kept straying to the bed, so close she could easily touch it.

"Where are we going?" she asked. They were moving at a good clip already.

He shrugged one blue-velvet-clad shoulder. "Nowhere. Up, then back. We scientists call that perpetual motion," he added with a grin.

She shifted uneasily. "Nowhere?"

"Just you and me and the river, food, heady drink, candle-light...is it not enough?" In the flickering light, his eyes looked dark and earnest. He leaned across the table and took her hands, white lace falling away from his wrists. "I love you, Violet. I'm out to persuade you to love me back."

There it was. *I love you.*

"Violet, did you hear me?"

Of course she'd heard him, and she wanted so much to believe him. She'd dreamed of someday hearing those three words—especially from someone as handsome and intelligent as Ford Chase.

But she remembered too many balls where she'd hid in corners and no man had ever tried to coax her out. And before that, when she was younger, those torturous Sundays after church, when boys would huddle around her little sisters while she sat nearby with a book, pretending not to care. Faith, even when she was just five, and Rose and Lily still babies, strangers would coo over them while she stood by unnoticed.

When she failed to respond, Ford rose and turned to stick his head out the window. "Johnnie, my lady is not yet persuaded. We need music."

Almost at once, the strains of a violin reached her ears.

Despite her distress, a laugh bubbled out of her. "You've thought of everything, haven't you?"

"Almost everything. I forgot about the cold night air. Wouldn't want you to be chilled." He closed the window's shutters and reseated himself with a smile.

He was smooth, too smooth for her to handle. Her senses were spinning already, and he hadn't even really touched her. And she knew what would happen the moment he did that.

She would want him. Her mind would be stirred up to venery.

No, more than that. Because she loved him. Because she so desperately wanted to be loved in return.

He was a study in contradictions. Part logical scientist, part romantic rake, part responsible uncle, part irresponsible boy. And she loved every confusing facet.

He dressed like a prince and lived like a pauper. He was the most generous man she'd ever known. He'd made her spectacles; he'd made her mother a distillery.

He was out to persuade her to love him back, but God help her, she already did.

And yet...before he'd managed to close the shutters, she'd glimpsed Lakefield House as they glided by. In the shadows of the waning day, it had looked even more shabby than she remembered, reinforcing her fears. She couldn't help but wonder if his ever-more-frequent kisses—and his declarations of love—were only because of...

She didn't want to think about that now. Thanks to her mother's meddling, she was alone in a cabin with a man who claimed to love her. A man who could make the heat pool deep inside her with no more than a look.

Tomorrow she would turn twenty-one. Tomorrow she'd become a spinster. Tonight she intended to enjoy herself.

"Will you eat?" he asked, uncovering the rest of the platters.

As she'd expect from a country cookshop, the supper was simple. A lamb pie and a sweet potato pudding. And parsnips and asparagus.

*Erection is chiefly caused by parsnips, artichokes, asparagus...*

Violet thanked her lucky stars that artichokes, at least, weren't on the table. Enjoyment was one thing, unbridled lust quite another. She piled parsnips and asparagus on her plate, determined to make sure Ford didn't eat more than his share.

She raised her cup to her lips, then froze.

*...all strong wines, especially those made of the grapes of Italy.*

"Is this wine Italian?"

He blinked. "No. It's French."

"Oh, good," she said, gulping a swallow. Flowing down her throat, it felt warm and seemed to relax her.

The sweet potato pudding was smooth and tasty, swimming in butter with eggs, nutmeg, and dark sugar. The lamb pie was flaky and delicious. As they dined, they discussed the books they'd recently read—excluding the *Master-piece*—and the latest discoveries in science.

No other man had really listened to her, or spoken to her as though she were his mental equal. Violet slowly came to realize that those weeks when Ford was gone, working on one project or another, it wasn't just his kisses she'd missed. Even more so, she'd missed their conversations.

He didn't touch her during supper, didn't so much as nudge her foot with his. But all the time he talked, he gazed into her eyes in a way that had her heart beating erratically, a way that said he'd rather be kissing her than making pleasant conversation.

In the face of that banked passion, she found it hard to eat, but she finished all her parsnips and asparagus.

When his plate was empty and she was only picking at hers, he refilled her wine cup. "Violet?" He reached across the tiny table and gently pulled off her spectacles. "May I kiss you now?"

He'd never asked before, and she didn't know what to say. In the flickering candlelight, he looked blurry. But he must have seen her answer in her eyes, because he rose from his chair, taking her hands to bring her up with him. He leaned across the table, and she caught her breath as his lips met hers—

And a pewter platter crashed to the floor.

"Everything all right in there?" came Harry's voice through the shutters.

Violet jerked back.

"We're fine," Ford called to Harry, looking a bit shaken as he bent to retrieve the platter. He set it back on the table, then ran a hand through his hair. Raggedly.

"This won't work," he told her, softly enough that Harry couldn't hear. "Do you suppose I can coax you into joining me on the bed?"

She gasped.

"On it, not in it." She couldn't see him very well, but she thought he raised a devilish brow. "There's a difference."

"Of course there is." And there was nothing for it, really. There were men outside on the deck and no room in the cabin save for that broad expanse of bed. If she didn't join him there, they might as well sail for home.

And she did want another kiss. She'd been waiting all through supper for a kiss, and the one he'd just pressed to her lips hadn't been satisfying in the least.

Her gaze locked on his, and they moved as one toward the bed. The table was shoved up against it. She sat primly on one side of it, he sat heavily on the other.

The barge rocked gently, a soothing motion. Violin music drifted through the shutters. Ford's gaze trailed over the bodice of her new blue moiré gown, which she suddenly realized was cut much lower than it had seemed at her last fitting. Again. She made a mental note to have a talk with that seamstress.

All at once there was a flurry of movement, and the next thing she knew, she was flat on her back.

Shocked, she tried to struggle up, but Ford hovered over her, his hands gently pressing her shoulders to the mattress. The look in his eyes made her heart leap. "I just want to kiss you, Violet. May I?"

Swallowing hard, she nodded.

And when his mouth met hers, everything changed.

He had kissed her before, but never like this. This was wild, primal, a meeting of lips and teeth and tongue the likes of which she'd never even imagined. And she'd never imagined the effect such a kiss would have on her, either.

Desire shot through her, stole her breath, her thoughts, her will to resist. Her spirits became brisk and inflamed, and her blood was most surely stirred to venery.

She threw her arms around him, her hands frantically wandering his back, and he broke the kiss long enough to rise and tear off his surcoat. And then his cravat. He leaned closer, his fingers working at the laces at his collar until they loosened, exposing a neat V of bare chest.

Skin. Her heart racing, she reached to touch it. Her fingertips first, and then her whole hand flat against him. Warm, impossibly warm. Her thumb felt the pulse in his neck. Strong and fast.

His blue gaze darkened. With a groan, he lowered himself, his lips meeting the sensitive hollow of her throat. She tilted her head to allow him access. Deprived again of his skin, her hands moved to tug at his shirt, pulling and pulling until the whole long thing finally slipped free of his breeches and she was able to slide her hands up underneath.

He gasped at her touch, as though he'd been unaware of what she'd been doing. Her fingers skimmed his back, his sides, his shoulders, feeling his strength, the softness of his skin over the hardness of sinew and bone. He smelled of soap and patchouli, the warmth of his flesh emitting a fragrance uniquely his. His muscles twitched beneath her questing hands, and his mouth trailed lower, tracing a warm, damp pattern down to her cleavage.

Thank goodness scandalous necklines were in fashion. She revised her mental note about talking to the seamstress—the lower the better.

"Violet," he breathed, one of his hands following his lips. He slipped a finger beneath her bodice and rubbed the tip of her breast, and she gasped so loud she was sure Harry had heard it.

"Faith." She'd never dreamed her body was so sensitive. She was feeling those short breathings she'd read of, and tremblings of the heart, and—

Suddenly his fingers were fumbling with the tabs on her stomacher.

She knew she should stop him. But oh, she burned to feel the things the *Master-piece* had promised. She burned to feel them with Ford. Before she could even think it through, he'd dropped her stomacher to the floor and loosened her laces. He spread her bodice wide.

Instinctively, she arched, as though she were a wanton offering herself for plunder. But she felt no shame. And when he fastened his lips on one peak, tasting her through the gossamer fabric of her chemise, her short breath got even shorter, her heart trembled even more, and—

He tugged down on the chemise, and suddenly his mouth was on her bare breast. Hot, wild, wonderful, he licked and nibbled and suckled until she was certain she'd go out of her mind. Her arms clenched around him, her body straining for something she couldn't put a name to.

*Pleasure, delight...extreme lust.*

Even the *Master-piece*'s words failed to describe it.

Thrilling at the new sensations, she shifted restlessly against him. Oh my, she could feel…well, apparently when she hadn't been watching he'd eaten quite a lot of parsnips and asparagus.

And part of her—that part of her that would receive him like a sheath—wanted him. There. Now.

"I want you," she whispered.

His head shot up, his eyes hazy and disbelieving. "Are you sure?" he asked in a broken whisper.

She was sure. She was breaking through her modesty to satisfy herself in unlawful embraces, but she couldn't have cared less. Tomorrow she'd become a spinster, but at least she wouldn't be a lifelong virgin. She'd experience the *Master-piece*'s mysteries before she resigned herself to lonely years studying philosophy.

Oh, forget all those rationalizations. She wanted him.

"I'm sure," she said. "I want you."

# FORTY-EIGHT

*I WANT YOU.* The one phrase Ford had despaired of ever hearing from Violet's lips, whispered in a tone so fierce, he had no doubt she meant it with every fiber of her being.

He thought—he hoped—her parents approved, regardless of his dismal financial situation. He was positive her mother liked him, at least, and her father had smiled when he'd seen them holding hands. He knew he was taking an enormous chance, but if Violet herself wanted him...

His heart soared as though it glided above the Earth on da Vinci's flying machine. He'd brought Violet here hoping to convince her he loved her, but this was more, much more than he'd dared hope for. She would be his. His wife. Mother of his children. And if they joined together tonight in anticipation of their wedding, it couldn't be wrong. Nothing that felt as perfect as this could be wrong. She was already his wife in his heart.

When had that happened? He didn't know. He knew only that, slowly but surely, she'd woven her way into his life, until she was as much a part of him as his hands and his feet and his analytic brain. Until he found himself building distilleries as an excuse not to leave her side.

He gazed into her brandy-wine eyes, which were glazed with passion. For him. The thought made something squeeze painfully in his chest.

"My love, are you very, very sure?" Though the ladies at court thought nothing of sharing their bodies for sport, he knew Violet had been raised differently. And he knew, too, that was one of the things he loved about her. Her differences.

Besides, this wasn't sport. Not even close. This was something that transcended sport to a degree he'd never imagined back in the days he'd considered bedding women a pleasant diversion.

This was a melding of hearts.

He buried his nose in her hair. She smelled of flowers, sweet Violet flowers...

"Are you sure?"

She arched toward him. "Oh, yes!"

He crushed his mouth to hers as his hand made its way down to her shoes. He wanted to make this first time slow and special for her.

He feared he couldn't.

Like in her dream, Violet seemed to be floating. But this was so much better than the dream. Slowly, slowly, Ford drew off her shoes and rolled down her stockings, his fingers leaving fiery trails along the length of her legs. She clenched his shoulders to keep from crying out.

He raised her skirts, and his hand skimmed her calves, her knees, her thighs, raising goose bumps in its wake. She slid her fingers into his hair, kissing his temple, his cheek, his nose. Frantic. And then his mouth covered hers, and his fingers were *there*.

At her seat of womanly pleasure.

They teased her, so gently she wondered she could even feel it. But feel it she did. The most exquisite sensation ever. The rocking of the barge added to her dizziness as he stroked her until a whimper escaped her throat and her hips shot off the bed.

"Has no one touched you here?" he asked in a whisper tinged with amusement.

Was he *jesting*? She shook her head wildly, incapable of forming words at the moment.

"Good," he grated out and jerked away, rising on his knees to struggle out of his clothes.

Yes, it was good. Even better when his elegant clothing had hit the floor.

He was magnificent. And it wasn't a yard. Plenty long, but—thank goodness—nowhere near a yard. She didn't have much time to muse on that, because he hurried to help her rise, wiggled her out of her gown, and pulled her chemise over her head.

"You're beautiful," he breathed, his hands reaching out to skim her sides, her hips, her legs. In the glimmer of the candles his eyes looked the deepest blue, and for that moment, she believed him. And then they were together on the bed, skin to skin.

She'd never imagined such perfect bliss. His hands went everywhere, tantalizing and teasing while he kissed her so thoroughly she thought her head might spin off and fly away. Near her seat of womanly pleasure, an ache was building, and a heat, an exquisite heat.

He stroked where she ached, kissing her, kissing her, kissing her until she didn't know where she ended and he began. The violin music grew faint as the blood rushed through her ears. Her hazy mind seemed to remember the *Master-piece* saying a man was exquisitely sensitive, which meant she should be able to give him the same incredible pleasure he was giving her.

She reached down. His gasp made her pulse leap as her fingers closed around hardness encased in soft velvet. Warm velvet. She stroked experimentally—

"No," he forced out through gritted teeth. "This time is for you. I cannot—*No*—"

Alarmed, she let go. And he slipped a finger inside her body.

Her world tilted.

She opened her mouth to say something, anything, to tell him how he was making her feel. But no words came out.

*The externals are designed to receive, and by their swelling, cause titillation and delight in those parts.*

*Unbearable* delight, the book should have said.

Her desire to carnal embraces was absolutely, positively insuperable.

"I need you," she whispered.

"I know. I need you, too." He still seemed to be gritting his teeth. "Are you sure?" he asked again

When she nodded, he raised her knees and moved over her, settling himself between her thighs. She felt him there, at the neck of her womb, and it was indeed of an exquisite feeling. And then she felt him slowly pressing, herself stretching, opening…

*Attended with some little pain…*

She sucked in a breath, but the *Master-piece* had been right. The little pain was fading already. Her sisters would be relieved to hear it, except she would never, ever tell them.

Then he moved in her, and her sisters were the last thing on her mind. Her entire world was filled with him. He moved again, and she moved with him, learning the rhythm of love. It built and built, until she was certain she couldn't stand more. The great heat, the friction, and yes, the considerable quantity of moisture, which being expunged in the time of copulation—

She cried out, lost in the wonder. Then suddenly she felt herself convulsing around him, wave after wave of spectacular pleasure. She'd thought it would be a momentary thing, but it went on, intensifying when he groaned and shuddered and she felt him spill inside her.

He collapsed against her, and she held his dark head, stroking his hair while she struggled to catch her breath. The barge was still rocking, and the violin was still playing, a lazy, lilting tune that matched the utterly exhausted bliss she was feeling. The *Master-piece* hadn't prepared her. Or maybe she hadn't quite believed it. But "greatly delights the woman" struck her as an abysmally weak description for what she'd just felt.

It had been so much more than that. She actually felt tears of emotion prick behind her eyes.

"Is it like this for everyone?" she wondered.

"No." Not knowing how to explain, Ford shook his head, feeling her fingers slide in his hair. "It's hardly ever like this. At least it's never been like this for me."

He kissed her eyes, her nose, her forehead. She was everything he hadn't known he wanted in a woman. And she wanted him. He was the luckiest man in the world.

"Violet?"

"Hmm?" She stretched beneath him, warm and languid.

He kissed her chin, her cheek, brought his lips close to her ear. "I cannot wait to get married."

He felt her stiffen and lifted his head to meet her gaze.

"I never said I would marry you," she said, her brandy eyes filled with confusion. "Why...you haven't even asked me."

"Oh." Of course. She wanted to be romanced. He rose to his elbows, brushing fingers alongside her face, fingers that had brought her such pleasure minutes earlier. Then he gave her his famous smile. "Will you do me the greatest honor I can imagine and become my wife, Violet Ashcroft?"

Her eyes looking bare without her spectacles, she blinked. "No."

"What?" It had never occurred to him that she wouldn't wed him after surrendering her virginity. She was no courtier, but a sheltered country miss. And the only woman he'd ever met who didn't make him feel thickheaded.

Until now.

He must have heard her wrong. "I...I thought you said you wanted me."

"I didn't mean it like that." He saw her jaw set and felt a pit opening somewhere in his gut. "Did you do it on purpose, then?" she asked. "To secure me as your bride?"

"No!" He sat up on the edge of the bed, rubbing his face. "I didn't intend for this to happen. You said you wanted me, Violet, and I couldn't resist you—because I love you. That's what tonight was all about."

"Seduction," she said.

"Well, yes. But not this far. Just supper, candlelight, music… and then I meant to propose."

"I'm not upset, Ford."

The words were said much too calmly. After what they'd just shared, there ought to be passion in her voice.

He turned to face her, his gaze sweeping her lush body, still aglow from their lovemaking. "How could you not be upset? I misunderstood you, and I…I've ruined you. And now you won't let me make you an honest woman."

"I'm a bit more enlightened than to believe that. Honesty has nothing to do with this. I honestly wanted you. And I don't regret what we did. But I'm not prepared to say I'll marry you."

At least *I'm not prepared to say I'll marry you* wasn't an outright refusal. But he couldn't understand, would never understand, how she could not regret their lovemaking and yet not want to marry him now.

Even though he'd felt that way with other women.

This had been different. This had been more than mere lovemaking. And with every fiber of his being, he was sure it had been as special for her as it had been for him.

"Question Convention," he quoted woodenly.

He was beginning to understand what she'd meant when she said the Ashcrofts weren't a conventional family…but he wasn't at all sure anymore that he liked it.

# FORTY-NINE

ORD WAS SITTING at his desk the next morning, struggling to make sense out of a mound of Lakefield's neglected paperwork, when his family showed up.

And showed up, and showed up—three carriages worth of them.

He'd known, of course, when he'd ordered Colin and Amy not to visit or bring the rest of the family, they were going to ignore him. But that didn't mean he had to be happy about it. Especially on a day like this.

Lucky for him, most of them stayed outside while his twin, Kendra, came into the study, wearing an all-too-cheerful yellow gown.

"We're here!" she announced, as though they'd sent notice ahead.

"I deduced as much when I heard the children shrieking." All seven of the precious angels. For the first time in weeks, he was pleased with the sorry state of his garden—at least there was little they could do to harm it.

Kendra stopped beside his chair, her dark red hair glimmering in the too-bright sun that streamed through the window at his back.

He scowled up at her. "Who invited you?"

She leaned down to give him a hug. "I've missed you, too."

"Right," he grunted without rising.

Backing off, she went to find a seat. He'd piled ledgers on the only extra chair, so she perched on the old iron chest he'd never managed to open.

"How was Scotland?" he asked her grudgingly.

"Beautiful. Hamish is in good health, and Niall has done wonders with Duncraven." He'd never met these people—her husband's family—but felt he knew them from her lively descriptions over the years. "And Cait's family is well, too. Cameron and Clarice had another baby."

"That's good." And no surprise. Everyone connected to the Chases seemed to have plenty of babies. Assuming it would be the same for him, he thought amidst another round of shrieks that perhaps Violet's refusal had been for the best.

"Well." Kendra crossed her legs, the foot on top swinging up and down with its red-heeled shoe. "We've come to meet Violet, so enough of the pleasantries."

"Have I been pleasant?" Ford wondered.

Her green eyes flashed with all-too-familiar annoyance. "What's wrong with you, anyway?"

"Besides the fact that the woman I love won't agree to marry me?"

"Colin said you were over Tabitha," she said, frowning, and then, "Oh. Oh! It's this Violet, then, isn't it? Oh, my God. I cannot believe you admitted that. Ford Chase in love, wanting marriage." The annoyance faded from her eyes as they flooded with compassion instead. "Why on earth won't she have you?"

"Look around," he said, gesturing toward the peeling walls. "I believe you'll begin to get the picture."

"Well." Now her eyes filled with outrage. "If she values gold above love, then she doesn't deserve you, anyway."

"It's not like that," he said with a long-suffering sigh. "She's more interested in books than material comforts. But she has money of her own, and she's convinced herself no man would want her save to have it. I'm afraid the condition of this place has done nothing to reassure her my motives are otherwise."

When Kendra came to hug him this time, he rose and let her wrap him in her arms.

"Poor Ford. You've always managed to get everything you've wanted before, haven't you?"

Everything but Violet. Torn between taking comfort and bristling at his sister's patronizing view of him, he opted for the comfort. "I guess so," he mumbled into her lavender-scented hair.

"Where is she?" Kendra demanded, pulling back. "I'll talk to her and explain that your intentions are sterling. The sort of man you are—"

"Violet is busy today," he said quickly. The last thing he needed was his family poking their noses in—which was exactly why he hadn't wanted them here. Violet's family might be unconventional, but his was mad as a cell full of Bedlam inmates.

The words Violet had left him with were *I'm not prepared to say I'll marry you.* One glimpse of the family she'd be marrying into, and her answer would be an unequivocal *no.*

"Are you sure?" Kendra asked. "We've come all this way—"

"I'm positive." He plopped back onto his chair, willing to discuss anything to get off the subject of Violet. "Sit down and catch me up on the gossip."

She wandered back to sit on the chest. "Cait is with child again."

"What took her so long?" he asked dryly. "It's been nearly two years since their last." Jason and Caithren had two boys already. "And you?"

"Oh, two girls are enough."

"Trick isn't wanting an heir?"

"If one comes along, he wouldn't mind, I suppose..." The

faint blush on her cheeks told him she and her husband, Patrick, were trying to conceive. She looked down, her fingers tracing the decorative metal strips on the chest. "You know," she said, also a master at changing the subject, "this chest has always reminded me of the treasure chest Trick and I found and brought to King Charles. Every time I see this one, I wonder what might be in it."

"I've always wondered that myself."

Her head whipped up. "You don't know?"

He shrugged. "It came with the place, and there's no key for the lock, and—"

"I'll have Trick open it, you fool. Let me go get the others." Before he could respond, she'd shot out the door.

While he waited for the invasion, he leaned his elbows on the desk and dropped his head into his hands, shutting his eyes against all the paper. Bills, letters, a notice from his mortgage holder that a payment was overdue. If only he had enough money to settle it all, get a fresh start...

He would have to see how Rand was coming along with the translation. But even if *Secrets of the Emerald Tablet* did hold the key to making gold, it could take months or possibly years to get the formula to work...

He jerked upright, staring at the chest across the room. He'd always assumed it wouldn't have been left here if it contained anything valuable, but what if Kendra were on to something? The chest she and her husband had found for King Charles had been filled with precious metal and jewels, and for all Ford knew, this one could be stuffed to the brim with gold.

The solution to his problems might have been sitting here all along: the means to pay the debts, the proof to convince Violet he didn't need her for her inheritance.

His heart was racing by the time the family trooped in. Colin led the regiment with Amy, who was holding their baby son Aidan in her arms. Ford's oldest brother, Jason, followed behind with his wife, Caithren. Kendra brought up the rear, her husband, Patrick—or Trick, as they all called him—by her side with their one-year-old girl.

Their remaining collective five offspring burst in after them, racing around Ford's desk, hanging on his back, climbing on the chairs and the iron chest.

Whatever had made him think he wanted a couple of these wild creatures? Then Jewel climbed up on his lap in greeting, and as she pressed a damp kiss to his cheek, he suddenly remembered why.

"Here it is," Kendra said, leading her tall, golden-haired husband to the chest. She plucked her nephew Hugh off of it and plopped him on his feet.

The boy looked up. "Can you open it, Uncle Trick?"

Trick grinned, displaying a front tooth with a slightly chipped corner. "I wasn't a smuggler in my prior life for nothing, you know." Handing his baby daughter to his wife, he pulled out his knife and dropped to one knee to get to work.

While his brother-in-law probed the heavy lock, Ford rose and set Jewel down, taking her hand as he walked closer. As though the chest were a magnet attracting metal shavings, everyone else drifted near and gathered around, until they were all hanging over it in anticipation. An expectant quiet descended on the room. Even the children stopped playing.

Ford's heart hammered against his ribs. This could be the answer—

A rusty *click* shattered the silence. Trick twisted the old padlock from the hasp. Ford held his breath as the man's hands went to the heavy lid and lifted it.

As one, the family exhaled.

Jewel tugged on Ford's breeches. "It's empty, Uncle Ford."

"I can see that." Concealing a sigh, he lifted his niece and buried his nose in her fragrant little-girl hair.

It would have been such a nice, neat solution. But he'd always known there was nothing of value in that chest. Other-wise, he'd have hacked off the lock years ago.

He might be slightly desperate, but he'd never been stupid.

Kendra reached to touch his arm. "I'm sorry."

At that, Colin sighed. "Were you expecting this to solve all your problems?"

Ford's jaw tensed. "Who says I have problems?"

Giggling nephews and nieces were clambering into the empty chest. Jason moved closer to hold the lid safely open. "You're always looking for the easy way out." The compassion in his brother's voice didn't cut the sting of his words for Ford. "One of these days, you're going to have to face life and learn to deal with it."

Ford's arms tightened around Jewel. Would his family forever see him this way? He'd made several important scientific discoveries, and he'd changed, hadn't he? He'd fallen in love and wanted to get married.

"Who invited you here to pick on me?"

"We need no invitation. We're family. Do you ask for an invitation before coming to Cainewood?"

"That's different. I live there."

"Do you?" Jason raised a brow. Maybe he sensed the changes in Ford, after all.

And Ford wondered: where *did* he live? At the Chase town house in London? Or the big castle at Cainewood? Or here?

He wanted to live here, he realized. Not in bustling London near the Royal Society and all his friends, not at his brother's castle with his family. Here, in the staid countryside. With Violet.

Bloody hell, love changed a man more than he'd thought possible.

Amy and Cait exchanged a sympathetic glance. "Ford—" they started together.

"Milord, do you not think you should have left for Lady Violet's celebration already?" Hilda bustled into the room, a steaming pie in her hands. "I've made a tart for you to take. Cherry, the young viscount's favorite."

"A celebration?" Kendra's eyes lit. "What is it for?"

"Her birthday," Ford said shortly. "And none of you are invited."

"But Uncle Ford." Jewel turned her little face up, her eyes pleading. "Mama promised I can see Rowan."

In the face of an argument like that, there was no hope in fighting this battle. Already, he had lost.

# FIFTY

*T*WENTY-ONE. It felt no different than twenty, which Violet found amazing, especially considering she'd also graduated from girlhood to womanhood last night.

Standing before her dressing table, she peered into the mirror and straightened one of the bright green ribbons that Margaret had woven through her hair. She squinted and moved closer, removing her spectacles. Shouldn't there be fresh lines around her eyes? A new sophistication in her features? As she thought about the bed on the barge, a melting heat spread from her middle down her legs, making her sit suddenly on the tufted velvet stool.

When a knock came at her door, she shoved the spectacles back on. "Come in."

The door opened a crack. "Violet?"

"Yes, Mum." She swiveled on the stool to face her. "Is it already time for the celebration?" A glance at the clock on her mantel—an old one with just a single hand—told her only in the vaguest terms. "It would be nice to have one of Ford's new watches, wouldn't it?"

"It would. And yes, it's time." Mum came in, closing the door behind her. "I've come to tell you that your father spotted Ford's barge heading down the river."

"That silly barge again?" Memories flashed of last night on that barge, and her face heated.

"Are you quite all right, dear?" Oh, no. Could Mum tell? Just by the blush on her cheeks? "You've been hiding up here all day," she added, much to Violet's relief.

Violet forced a laugh. "You know we older women take longer to get ready. To create the illusion of youth." She rose and wandered to the window, nervous about seeing Ford, half surprised he was still coming after she'd refused his proposal last night.

The barge hadn't arrived yet. "I'm fine, Mum. It's only that these fancier gowns take forever to get on properly."

Clearly not falling for those excuses, her mother joined her at the window. "Did something happen last night? I waited up for you, but you went straight to bed without saying goodnight."

"Well..."

Violet had never hidden things from her mother—at least not anything that counted. But there were some things one didn't share. She could come clean with part of it, though.

She paced back to the center of her room, more comfortable with some distance. "Ford asked me to marry him."

Mum turned to face her, hope in her eyes. "And what did you say?"

"I told him no," Violet said, and watched that hope fade.

Regret filled her heart. Faith, she wished she'd said yes. At the moment she'd refused him, she'd been feeling closer to him than she'd imagined possible. Closer to him than she'd felt to any other person ever. She'd wanted to believe his offer was from the heart, that he loved her as he claimed, unreservedly.

More than anything, she'd wanted to say *yes*. A loud, enthusiastic *yes*.

But he'd just finished seducing her, after all. Having taken her maidenhead, only a bounder would fail to offer a wedding in return. So all she could think at the time was that his offer hadn't come from the heart—that it had come from duty instead. That she would be foolish to believe their lovemaking had changed anything.

"I told him no, Mum," she repeated. "Don't you see? I want a marriage like you and Father have, or none at all."

"What makes you think you wouldn't have that with him?"

She wished she could explain it, but it was all too confused in her head. Maybe she *could* have that with him. She just didn't know for sure, and until she did...

Mum was gazing at her, waiting for an answer. An answer she didn't have. "You and Father won't make me marry him, will you?"

"I'm a good judge of people," Mum said quietly, "which is why I'm so good at arranging marriages. I believe Ford is a good man. I also believe that he truly loves you. I've seen it in his actions and on his face. However, your father and I would never make you marry anyone. I thought you knew that."

Tears sprang to Violet's eyes. She felt relieved and frustrated all at once. A tiny part of her *wished* her parents would make her marry Ford, but that wasn't the thinking part, the part of herself she trusted.

"Your father and I raised you girls to think for yourselves," Mum continued. "A folly for which we've suffered ridicule all our days. But the Lord knows, after all these years, we'd be fools to make you do anything now. You're not likely to put up with it, and your sisters would stand beside you."

Despite Violet's mood, a crooked smile curved her lips. No matter their constant bickering, her sisters would always be there for her. It was comforting to know some things never changed.

Tomorrow all this fuss over turning twenty-one would be finished. And now that she'd refused his proposal, soon enough Ford would leave for London, probably not to return for months or years.

Everything would go back to the way it had been—except for Violet herself.

Mum turned back to the window. "He's here. No, *they're* here."

"Who?" she demanded. "Mum, have you invited someone without telling me?" She didn't even want to see Ford today, and not only because she was sure she'd feel awkward with him after last night. She didn't want to face anyone but her family on this, the official first day of her spinsterhood.

"I would never have invited anyone else without asking you first. But there are others on the barge, too."

"Harry," Violet said with not a little relief. "And the stable hands." She headed for the window. "He uses them as crew—"

She broke off, staring toward the river.

"Egad," she breathed. Horror struck her heart. "Who *are* all those people?"

$\mathcal{B}$Y THE TIME she made it downstairs and into the gardens, Violet was shaking—from frustration, anger, fear, or maybe a combination. She wasn't sure. But when she saw Ford, she stopped and stared.

A little girl rode on his shoulders, a little boy hung on his leg, and a baby lay cradled in his arms.

Her heart suddenly hurt. He would make such a good father. And God knew—*she* knew after last night, she mentally amended with a blush—she would certainly enjoy making babies with him.

Her mother was right. She should have said yes.

The shaking stopped, replaced by trembling of another sort. If only he would still have her, she *would* say yes. And she wanted to tell him that now. Whoever they were, she wanted all of these people gone. Despite her fears of awkwardness with Ford, she wanted to talk to him. She needed to know if she'd ruined her chances last night—

"Violet!" Spotting her, Ford came closer with an apologetic smile, dragging the clinging little boy behind him. "This is my family."

His family. If she'd been thinking clearly at all, she would have realized that, of course. He proceeded to introduce everyone, and she smiled and exchanged pleasantries, trying to memorize names and faces.

The two dark-haired men were his older brothers, the redhead his twin sister. Although Ford was the only one of the four siblings blessed with those incredible blue eyes—the rest had eyes of green—they all bore a marked resemblance to one another, and she thought she might be able to keep them straight.

Their spouses and all those children, however, were another matter altogether.

And she wanted to make a good impression. Suddenly that seemed very important.

"Are those spectacles?" one of the women asked. The raven-haired one. Egad, who was she?

Disgusted with herself, Violet removed the eyeglasses and forced a smile. "They are. Ford made them for me and designed these frames to hold them on my face." She handed them to the lovely amethyst-eyed lady. "The members of the Royal Society were all very impressed."

As had happened at Gresham College, they passed the spectacles around, exclaiming over them and trying them on and praising Ford for his brilliance. Watching with a plastered-on smile and a sinking heart, Violet realized she couldn't remember who anyone was except Jewel. Too many names, too many faces. Too many people at a party that was supposed to have been private.

She wasn't happy about that, but she was happy to be by Ford's side. Belying her expectations, he was treating her with the same mix of teasing respect he always had. Perhaps he did still want her.

She needed to know. She wanted nothing more than to slip away and lose herself in his arms. She wanted to tell him she would be honored to become his wife. But his family was here. And hers.

The sun was hurting her eyes, or maybe it was all these people making her head ache. Her blurred gaze wandered to the summerhouse. One of the doors stood open, and it looked blessedly dim and peaceful inside. Maybe...

Her mother rang a bell, and everyone looked to her. "My husband wishes to speak," she called.

Egad, Violet thought, Father was going to embarrass her in front of Ford and all his family.

One of Ford's sisters-in-law returned her spectacles, and she shoved them back on her face. Everyone began moving to where her father stood by a table covered with a bright white cloth. As they walked, Ford slipped an arm around her waist, and she glanced around to see who might have noticed, catching the eye of one of his brothers. Jason or Colin? Whoever he was, he winked at her, and despite everything, a smile burst free on her face.

With all her heart, she wanted Ford's family to like her.

When her father cleared his throat, she turned.

"Due to the terms of my own father's will, the age of one-and-twenty holds unusual significance in our family. And I've two special surprises," he announced, "to celebrate our Violet's birthday."

Theatrically he whipped off the cloth, revealing a table covered in an artistic arrangement of fruits and fancy sweets, plus one homely cherry tart set off to the side.

"A pineapple?" Lily gasped, staring at the centerpiece, a prickly brown fruit raised on a pedestal. "Is it real? Wherever did you get a pineapple?" Pineapples were so rare in this part of the world, King Charles had had himself painted with one.

"May I try it?" Rowan yelled. "Oh, please, please!"

"Please, please!" four other children echoed, taking up the chant. "Please!"

"There isn't enough for everyone," Ford said loudly, sweeping his siblings with an accusatory glance before looking back to the young ones. "You weren't invited here, remember?"

"Nonsense," Father said. "Yes, it is real, and yes, everyone may try it. A bite, at least. But first"—he paused and looked toward the door—"here comes the second surprise." Four house-maids and two footmen approached, each holding a thick green bottle in one hand and stemmed glasses in the other. "The new French champagne. Who will have a taste?"

"Me!" Rowan yelled. "Me! Me!"

"Me! Me!" Ford's nephews and nieces joined in.

"You're too young," Rose told Rowan. "Champagne is too costly to water down."

Father looked to Mum. "Wash her gown in champagne?"

"Water down the champagne, darling. But we won't be doing that." Mum scanned the gathering. "Rowan may certainly have a taste," she announced, "as may any other children whose parents agree."

The maids poured while the footmen bore the esteemed pineapple back to the kitchen to be sliced.

Father handed the glasses around and raised his in a toast. "To our Violet, on the anniversary of her birth." The center of attention, Violet felt her face burn. "May she live in health and happiness another one-and-twenty years times four."

"Hear, hear," everyone said, smiling in her direction.

Whoever they all were.

She looked down and took a cautious sip. "It's like drinking stars," she breathed. She'd never tasted anything like it. It tickled the back of her throat.

Rowan spewed his mouthful onto the grass. "Zounds, I've got bubbles up my nose. Ick." Violet cringed at her brother's lack of manners, but at least no one had to worry about him drinking too much, since he immediately set down his glass.

"It's an acquired taste," a man told him. The golden-haired one. Trick, Violet remembered, congratulating herself.

Well, that was one memorable name.

Lily looked awed. "Have you tried it before?"

He nodded. "It's all the rage at court."

"Have you been to court, then?" Rowan asked.

Jewel elbowed him. "Of course he has, you goose. He's a duke!"

Rose sighed. "I've never been to court. Father won't allow it. He says it isn't a place for nice, unmarried girls."

"A wise decision," Ford said dryly. He dropped his voice to whisper in Violet's ear. "The bucks there would have an innocent like her for supper."

Though she suspected Rose could handle herself, her eyes widened at this news.

"Have you never been, either?" he asked.

Sipping the sparkly drink, she shook her head. "Is it beautiful?"

"Whitehall is magnificent. Court itself can be amusing or boring, depending on who deigns to show up that particular day. But I was raised with the court in exile...I imagine you would find it exciting."

She'd felt more at home among the Royal Society than she'd expected. "Maybe now that I'm twenty-one, Father will take me someday."

"I was thinking *I* could take you," he said with that devilish smile. "After we're wed."

He sounded terribly confident, which normally would have irked her. But this time, her heart sang instead. Despite her refusal last night, he hadn't given up on her. Held captive by his gaze, she remembered how it had felt to lie with him, skin to skin, heart to heart. A rush of warmth shuddered through her.

She wanted to tell him yes. Here. Now. Her gaze went wistfully to the summerhouse again, but this was no time to sneak away, not while she was the center of attention.

Yet she was dying to tell him, and if he had whispered a private message to her, she could do the same...

She leaned up on her toes. "Ford—" she began quietly.

"The pineapple!" Rowan squealed, and the moment was lost. They all turned to see a footman approaching, bearing a silver bowl filled with small cubes of yellow fruit. "I hope I like it better than the champagne," Rowan said as the man put it down.

"Have you tried *this* already?" Rose asked Trick.

He shook his head. "Never."

"I've seen pineapples before at parties, but only as a decorative centerpiece," Ford's sister said. "I suspect someone is making a fortune renting the things so people can impress their friends."

Mum laughed at the idea. "Do you expect they actually spoil before anyone eats them?"

"I imagine so," said one of those dark-haired brothers. Jason, Violet thought as he curved his arm around the waist of the sister-in-law that had long tawny hair. "From what I understand, most of them rot on the way from the islands. But this one looks perfect."

"I hope it is," Father said. "I've heard it said that if I dry the crown for a couple of days, I may be able to plant it and grow pineapples, providing I can keep the bush warm during the winter. They're supposed to have pink flowers that look like a pine cone." He lifted the bowl and held a spoon out to Ford. "As our guest, will you honor us by trying it first?"

"But this is Violet's day." Ford took the spoon, scooped up a cube, and moved it toward her lips.

He'd fed her in the piazza at Gresham, and now, as then, it seemed a most intimate act. Her gaze darted around to see how their families were reacting, but everyone just looked expectant. And the moment the fruit touched her tongue, she forgot to be self-conscious. Flavor burst in her mouth.

"Oh my," she said, chewing slowly. "It's the sweetest thing I've ever tasted!"

Everyone else scrambled to try it.

"Do you like it?" Violet asked Rowan.

He grinned, yellow pulp in his teeth. "It's much better than champagne."

"Now, that I'm not so sure of." Lily daintily sipped from her glass. "The champagne is light and delicious, while the pineapple is sweet but…"

"Acidic?" Ford suggested.

"Well, I'm not exactly certain what that means, but it sounds about right."

He smiled and grabbed a bottle to refill her glass. "Acids react with a base to form a salt."

Jewel looked up to the sister-in-law with the beautiful raven hair. "Uncle Ford is clever, isn't he, Mama?"

"I assume your Uncle Ford is *very* clever," the woman said with a smile, "since I understand only half of what he says."

Jewel's mother. Violet committed that to memory, trying to figure out which man was her husband. Probably the one who laughed now, then leaned down and pressed a kiss to the top of her head. Colin. She remembered Ford telling her Colin played pranks, so of course he would be Jewel's father. It was all coming together.

Rowan grinned at Jewel. "I'm glad Violet had such an important birthday."

"Me, too," Lily said, sipping more champagne.

"Me three," Rose added, all but gulping hers.

If Violet didn't miss her guess, her sisters were getting a bit tipsy.

Striving to relax, she looked around at everyone drinking champagne and chatting amiably. The sister-in-law with the straight tawny hair caught her eye and smiled. Jason's wife, she thought happily, glad she was finally figuring out who was who. She liked them. They seemed friendly.

Then once again, Father cleared his throat. When nobody took heed, he raised Mum's bell and gave it a shake. Violet winced, sure something else embarrassing was about to come out of his mouth.

"This is quite a momentous occasion. As the oldest, our Violet is now the first to come into her inheritance. I hope you will save it and spend wisely, my dear daughter."

Violet sighed. She'd been right. Sometimes Father could be so—

"She can use it to buy a husband!" Rose announced with a tipsy giggle.

Violet wished the earth would open up and swallow her.

"Now, Rose," Mum chided, reaching to brush a bit of pineapple off Father's surcoat.

"It was but a jest!" Rose poured herself more champagne. "Can you people not take a jest?"

But Rose was absolutely right; most women would use a large inheritance to buy into a highly ranked family, and most men would be happy to accept that bargain. Violet took a gulp of her own champagne, but she wasn't feeling tipsy, just sick.

To think, mere minutes ago, she'd nearly told Ford yes. Now doubts niggled at her again. She tilted her head back, letting the rest of the bubbly drink run down her throat, wishing it could restore her world to balance.

She was so confused. If she could just spirit Ford away from this crowd and talk to him, maybe she could tell whether he was sincere. After sharing her body with a man, a woman ought to be able to tell, oughtn't she?

With a sigh, she reached to pour herself more champagne.

"I think you may have had enough," Father said, gently prying the glass from her clenched fingers. "Come with me to the summerhouse for a moment."

"Not now, Father."

"Always arguing." He shook his head. "Chrysanthemum, Violet, Rose, and Lily...my lovely flowers always argue. Except for the ones in my garden. No wonder I like them so much."

Violet couldn't help but smile. He grabbed a bunch of grapes off the table and started toward the summerhouse, leaving her to follow.

After shutting the door, he gazed at her fondly and wrapped her into a hug. It was quiet in the summerhouse—quiet enough that he could hear without her yelling. Quiet enough that she could hear her own heartbeat as she felt herself calming in his arms.

"How's my eldest flower?" he asked, pulling back. "You looked upset there, for a bit."

She couldn't stay vexed with him. His speeches might have been embarrassing, but they were well intended, after all. To outsiders, he might seem rather addlepated, but that was only because he couldn't hear well enough to participate in many conversations. Those close to him knew he was wise.

She gave him a crooked smile. "I'm well, Father. Sort of like fine, old wine, aged but better for it."

"You're not so old," he said, sitting down on one of the benches that lined the curved red-brick wall. "Don't go consigning yourself to spinsterhood yet."

She saw the truth in his face. "Mum told you Ford proposed."

"You know we share everything." He pulled four grapes off the bunch. "That's what I want for you, Violet. Someone to share your life with."

"I was sure I'd never have that. But now…"

"Yes?" He popped one of the grapes into his mouth.

"I don't know. I'm confused. Socrates said the unexamined life isn't worth living. But I'm driving myself mad examining and reexamining."

Chewing on the grapes, he rose and wandered back to the door. "Sometimes," he said quietly, "we just have to take a leap of faith. When the time comes, you'll know."

Would she? She felt inadequate to make such a decision. Philosophy, after all, taught one to question everything. And the single thing she'd been sure of all her life—that she would never find true love—she'd now caught herself rethinking.

She felt like she didn't know anything anymore.

He handed her a grape. "Now go back out there and smile at your guests."

They weren't *her* guests, but as he opened the door, she decided that, for once, she'd be the flower that didn't argue.

Besides, she really wanted to get Ford alone here in the summerhouse.

She stepped outside, blinking in the bright sunshine. Everyone had scattered. The children had organized themselves into a game of duck-duck-goose, and Jewel was "it." On the far side of the garden, Ford was picnicking beneath the giant oak with his brothers and their wives, both of the women with babies on their laps. He looked over and waved, and she waved back, noting the others watching. They were discussing her, she was sure of it. She'd give up *Aristotle's Master-piece* to hear what they were saying.

Fairly certain one of the two babies belonged to Ford's sister, Violet looked around, then blushed to see the fiery redhead in the shadows of a tree-lined path, passionately kissing her husband.

Once upon a time, she would have averted her eyes, but now the sight made her warm inside. She wanted that for herself, and she wouldn't allow Rose's thoughtless remark to change her mind. She wouldn't let her old insecurities haunt her. No matter what her sister said, she wasn't buying a husband. Ford had told her he loved her, and she believed him.

She was ready to take that leap of faith.

With a new determination, she headed past the children toward Ford.

"Duck, duck, duck—" Rounding the circle, Jewel broke off. "Rowan, why do you keep scratching?"

He scraped his fingernails on his shirt. "I don't know," he said, raking his leg, then the back of one hand.

Jewel stepped into the circle and gasped. "Gads, you have red spots all over your face! Measles!"

Violet detoured into the circle, knowing her brother was entirely too lively to have measles. "Let me see." She bent and peered into his face, wiping the remnants of cherry tart from the corner of his mouth. "Rowan, did you drink chocolate?"

"Just a little," he squeaked. "The champagne was icky."

"Oh, Rowan!" Exasperated, she hauled him to his feet. "You know chocolate gives you hives. Now you'll be scratching for days."

"He looks funny," a little girl said with a giggle.

"Funny, funny!" The other children took up the chant.

Jewel stepped closer and poked him on the chest. "You goose!" She burst out laughing.

Clearly mortified, Rowan ran for the house. All the adults rushed over to see what had happened, except for Mum, who followed Rowan.

This birthday was turning out every bit as miserable as Violet had feared.

She just wanted to be alone with Ford. Over the giggling children's heads, she met his gaze, and a silent communication passed between them. She inclined her head toward the summerhouse, signaling him to meet her there.

Seeming to appear out of nowhere, his sister touched her arm. "May we have a word with you, Violet?" Her two sisters-in-law stood behind her. "Do you mind if we call you Violet?"

"I...of course not. Not at all." She sent Ford a questioning glance, but he just shrugged apologetically.

There was nothing for it, she thought with an inward sigh. She couldn't rebuff his family. Her answer to his proposal would have to wait a bit longer.

She tried to muster a smile. "Shall we talk in the summerhouse? It's quiet in there."

As they followed her silently, she braced for what she was sure would be an unpleasant barrage of questions as they assessed her worthiness for their brother.

When the door closed behind them, Ford's sister returned her tentative smile. "I'm Kendra, in case you don't remember. And this is Amy and Cait."

Violet nodded, feeling rather outnumbered as she mentally noted who was who, hopefully once and for all.

She didn't want to make any mistakes.

Dark-haired Amy was Jewel's mother and Colin's wife. And she was a jeweler, Ford had said. Colin had rescued her after her father's London shop burned in the Great Fire.

Cait, Jason's wife, had friendly hazel eyes. Her straight wheaten hair, while less than fashionable, seemed to suit her perfectly. She stood with a hand on her middle, and although her stomach looked flat, Violet wondered if she might be with child.

She wondered if she and Ford would ever have a child.

"My brother is a good man," Kendra announced without further ado.

"A very good man," Amy added.

"A very, very good man," Cait echoed in a distinct Scots accent.

Ford had told Violet that Cait was Scottish, so she was sure she had the right names with the right faces now. But she was stunned. She backed up and sat on a bench. "I know he's good," she said slowly.

This wasn't the grilling she'd been expecting. Instead, were they trying to talk her into marrying him?

It seemed so.

"He loves you," Kendra said.

"Very much."

"Very, very much."

She didn't know whether to laugh or just hug them for caring so deeply for Ford's happiness. "He's told me he loves me," she assured them.

Kendra crossed her arms. "But you don't believe him." It was a statement, not a question. "Look," she said, dropping to sit beside her. "Let me tell you something. If Ford were looking for money, he could have married Lady Tabitha ages ago. She had pots full of it."

"Lady Tabitha?"

"He courted her for years. But he never asked her to marry him. And do you know why?" Kendra didn't wait for an answer. "He didn't love her," she finished with a decisive nod.

Violet shoved her spectacles higher on her nose. What his family was doing here was sweet. Very sweet. Very, very sweet, she thought with an inward smile. And she liked them very much. But she couldn't figure out what Lady Tabitha had to do with anything. "What happened to her?"

"Right before he moved home to Lakefield, she surprised the hell out of him by marrying someone else," Kendra said, surprising the hell out of Violet with that language.

But it fit her, somehow. Kendra was the most outspoken woman Violet had ever met. More outspoken than Rose, even.

"Was he upset?" she asked carefully.

"Of course he was. He'd expected to marry her someday, and his pride was wounded. But not his heart, because he'd never really cared. Which was why he'd never asked her to wed him, and why she eventually ran off and wed another. But he asked *you* to marry him, Violet. *You* he cares for. *You* he loves."

"Very much," Amy added.

"Very, very much," Violet said together with Cait, and they all laughed.

Twenty minutes later they spilled out of the summerhouse, best of friends, and she went in search of Ford, wanting more than ever to get him off alone.

But he was nowhere to be found.

# FIFTY-TWO

$\mathcal{A}$T LADY TRENTINGHAM'S invitation, Ford walked with her in companionable silence along a path that took a meandering route to the river. All day, her speculative looks had been convincing him Violet had told her something.

He just wondered *what*.

"She told you, didn't she?" he finally asked.

In the dappled light that came through the trees, she stopped on the path and nodded. "Yes, she told me you proposed. We're a close family. Some think us a bit odd."

They shared an easy smile, Ford relieved that apparently Violet hadn't told her mother he'd stolen her virginity. He wasn't looking forward to dueling Lord Trentingham.

"Your family seems close, too," she said.

"We are," he agreed, knowing it was true, no matter how irritating they could be sometimes. "We lost our parents long ago at Worcester, so we've always leaned on one another." By tacit agreement, they resumed walking, the gravel crunching beneath their shoes. "I'm hoping to have a close family of my own soon," he said carefully.

Still strolling, she met his gaze. "Violet fears you're only pursuing her in order to get your hands on her inheritance."

Lady Trentingham was direct—in that way, she reminded him of his twin sister. But the news hurt, even though he'd suspected as much from the start.

"How can she think that?" he wondered aloud. "I've told her I love her." Despite everything, hearing those words from his mouth prompted an embarrassed half-smile. "I never thought I'd be sharing that with her mother."

"And I'd suggest you not tell her you did. If Violet knew I was doing anything to encourage this marriage, she'd run the other way. I've something of a reputation as a matchmaker, and my daughters are all dead set against becoming one of my statistics."

"I won't breathe a word." *Encourage this marriage* still rang in his ears, making his heart soar with premature glee. He'd hoped Violet's parents weren't an obstacle, but now he knew for sure. That left only the lady herself. "What can I do to persuade her?"

"It won't be easy," Lady Trentingham warned. "My daughter decided she was unmarriageable long before she met you. Old convictions are difficult to overcome." She discreetly cleared her throat. "And I'm afraid the condition of your estate is doing little to convince her you're not in need of her funds."

He'd known that, too. "What if I told you I *am* short of funds, but that's not the reason I want to marry her?"

They reached the river and turned, her brown eyes reminding him of Violet's as she met his gaze for a long, silent moment. "I'll give you points for honesty," she said at last with a nod of approval. "But I fear it will make your task even harder. Lakefield's sad state isn't only due to neglect, then?"

"Mostly. I am not in dire straits." Heading back toward the house, he sighed. "The place was unoccupied long before it was deeded to me, and...well..."

He supposed since she was giving him points for honesty, he might as well follow through. If his situation would make him unacceptable as a son-in-law, he'd as soon learn that now rather than later.

But that didn't mean he was obliged to make things sound worse than they were.

He raked his fingers through his hair. "I'll admit I've never made Lakefield a priority. But although I understand the estate was prime horse-breeding property before the Civil War, nothing remains of that now save a few ramshackle stables. And I imagine you're aware there have been several disastrous agricultural years since I obtained it in '61. However," he rushed to add, "I assure you I've always made certain no one dependent on the property has suffered as a result." Indeed, in order to see that none of the tenant farmers went hungry a few years ago, he'd been forced to mortgage the estate. Those payments were proving to be his downfall now.

"I'm sure you have," Lady Trentingham said soothingly. A touch of understanding infused her voice, making his blood rush with hope. Apparently he still passed muster. "But I understand there were few tenants left by the time you took over."

"True enough. If the estate is to produce a decent income, I must attract more people to move here." And repair the housing meant to shelter them. Dozens of crumbling cottages—more costs he was too strapped to bear. But perhaps Rand was finished with the translation by now, and regardless, somehow he would work it out.

He just hadn't cared enough before this. Loving Violet made all the difference.

He smiled at her mother, thinking having parents of this sort mightn't be such a bad thing. "I just need to put my mind to it."

"And you've got a brilliant mind there." She smiled back. "Perhaps Violet's dowry will ease your way. You do know it's three thousand pounds?"

"No, I didn't. It's very generous." More than he'd been expecting.

But it wasn't enough. No amount of money would be enough. Oh, he supposed there was some number of thousands that would dig him out of debt—to his chagrin, he didn't know how much—but he was coming to realize that without his ongoing efforts to ensure that Lakefield produced sufficient income to support all the people who depended on it, it would soon sink back into the morass.

He was ready to take on that responsibility.

Lady Trentingham was waiting for more of a reaction. "I'd have to win Violet first, and even then her marriage portion wouldn't be enough," he admitted, then realized she could take that the wrong way. "I mean, my own hard work—"

"I understand." She touched him on the arm. "My husband is an expert estate manager. I'm sure he'd be happy to consult with you."

Ford wasn't too proud to accept help. "I'd be pleased to listen to any advice he'd be willing to give me."

"You may have to shout a bit in the process." Her smile this time was the same warm smile she'd given him the first day in his garden. "I have faith in you, Ford. And despite what she may think, I know my daughter well, so I'll tell you this: She wouldn't mind that you need her inheritance, as long as she were convinced you weren't marrying her for it."

He wasn't sure he believed that, and in any case, he didn't want to take Violet's money. Her dowry was one thing, her inheritance quite another. Having aspirations of his own, he'd think twice before stealing her dream of publishing.

No, he'd think ten times. Twenty. Surely there was another way to solve his problems.

Lady Trentingham peered through the trees. "I think your family may be ready to leave."

Indeed, they were all gathered by the barge, shifting from foot to foot. A quick glance at the sun told him if they didn't get back to Lakefield and their carriages soon, they wouldn't make it to their homes by nightfall.

But ahead of him, at the end of the path, stood Violet. Looking distressed.

Ignoring his siblings' shouts, he hurried to meet her.

## FIFTY-THREE

*W*ATCHING FORD approach, Violet took a deep breath.

Since the conversation with his sisters, niggling doubts had begun to attack her again, but she wasn't going to jump to conclusions. She'd had enough of that today—enough of indecision. She would talk to Ford calmly...and she wouldn't let him touch her until afterward, because if he put his hands on her, she knew she'd surely lose her head.

But before she managed to say a word, he took her hand. And the next thing she knew they were in the summerhouse, and he was pulling off her spectacles and dragging her into his arms. And lose her head, she did.

When his mouth met hers, her knees weakened so, she feared she would tumble to the bricks beneath her feet. He kissed her for a long, heady minute before finally drawing back.

"I want you," he said.

She searched his eyes, still close enough to see. "You've had me."

"But that isn't enough." He set her away, backing up until he looked blurry, until the backs of his knees hit the bench. "I love you, Violet," he said, rushing on as though he'd prepared a speech. "Everything will get much easier after Rand completes the translation. I'm going to Oxford to see him tomorrow. I know my home isn't good enough for you, but I'm going to fix it up. Either way, whether Rand is done or not. I never did before, because...well, I'd never planned to live here. But now I want to."

"Just like that?" she asked, still feeling dizzy, still suffering the effects of that kiss. And God help her, still wanting another one.

"Just like that," he said.

She stared at him, longing to believe him, struggling to regain her equilibrium. Faith, how she wished she'd never heard Lady Tabitha's name! Yet she knew the three women had been well-intentioned. Good people, loving sisters. They hadn't meant for her to think on their words and suddenly fear that perhaps after being jilted by an heiress—an heiress he'd intended to marry even though he hadn't loved her—Ford had come here hoping to find another.

An irrational fear, she was sure.

Almost.

"I like your family," she said at last, walking closer until he came back into focus.

"I like your family, too. I want to live here, near your family."

"Ford—" She paused, drawing breath. "Tell me about Lady Tabitha."

"What?" The shock on his face confused her. "Where did you hear about *her*?"

"Your sister. And Amy and Cait—"

"Bloody hell." He stepped closer still, so close the scent of patchouli overwhelmed her. "She meant nothing to me, Violet. *Nothing.*" His eyes burned into hers, willing her to believe.

And perhaps she did. But she'd been too buffeted by emotions today to think straight.

*He loved her, he loved her not.*

She felt like she'd been through a war.

He switched tactics, running a hand down her arm, and, predictably, she weakened all over. It was uncanny, this effect he had on her body. And not only was her body weak, her heart was weak as well. Slowly but surely, Ford was conquering it, conquering her, robbing her of her ability to reason.

"Marry me, Violet," he said in a harsh, pained whisper.

Because too much of her wanted to blurt out yes, she took a step back and searched his eyes. After what they'd shared, she should be able to find the truth there, shouldn't she?

She loved him—of that she was certain. But as for the rest, she was only confused.

"Marry me, Violet," he repeated. "Please."

And before she could answer, she was back in his arms.

When he kissed her this time, she forgot why she wasn't sure she could marry him. She forgot she'd decided not to touch him. She forgot her own name.

And when he finally let go of her, she ran.

Out the door, through the garden, across the wide lawn to the portico and front door.

"Violet!" Mum called. "Dear heavens, what has happened?"

"He asked me to marry him again, the wretch!" she screamed before slamming the door.

## FIFTY-FOUR

"*T*HE LAST OF the champagne." Joseph handed Chrystabel half a glass before climbing into bed beside her. "How is our dear eldest doing?"

"She'll survive. She didn't want to talk at first, but she was glad I returned her spectacles." Chrystabel sipped, letting the sparkling liquid slide down her throat and soothe her frayed nerves. "He shouldn't have proposed again so quickly. His timing couldn't have been worse."

Joseph took the glass from her and drained it. "What do you mean?"

She sighed. "Following *your* ill-timed announcement of her inheritance, and Rose's subsequent comment—"

"Ouch."

"Yes, but it wasn't only that. His sister also spilled past history, confusing Violet. It reinforced her fears that no man would ever want her save for her money."

"She has a point." He grinned, clearly not understanding the gravity of this situation. "You married me for *my* money."

Well, he was just a man, so she shouldn't expect him to understand. Giving in to his playfulness, she punched him lightly on the shoulder. "I did not. I married you for your flowers. How else would I make my perfume? And without my perfume, I'd have no excuse to visit and chat with all the neighbors—and find out Nancy Philpot's son has left the army and is living with a Parisian whore."

"Ah, I see where that could be much more important than money." He set down the empty glass and turned to gather her in his arms. "But are you certain that was the only reason you married me?"

It was a long moment before she answered. "Well, I suppose I craved your yard too, you rascal. But it definitely wasn't the money."

"It won't come down to money for Violet, either," he told her. He turned momentarily to blow out the candle, plunging the room into darkness. "Violet wants that man as much as you wanted me. As much as we *still* want each other." His voice came husky in her ear, his breath warm on her skin. "I know when a woman wants a man, and I've seen that look in our daughter's eyes."

"Are you going to tell me not to worry again?" she asked breathlessly.

"Absolutely not. Because I'm finished talking."

"Thank God," she said, and pressed her mouth to his.

# FIFTY-FIVE

*S*OME PLACES never changed. The King's Arms, a tavern in Oxford where Ford and Rand had whiled away many a night during their university years, was one of them.

They sat at one of the familiar long tables, sipping ale and ignoring a nearby argument about radical politics. That was nothing new, either. John Locke's basic ideals had germinated here in Oxford as an undergraduate at Christ Church College, after all.

Ford twisted his tankard on the table, trying to be patient while Rand complained about his father's latest insults. The two had never done well together, which explained why a marquess's son was still at Oxford more than ten years after arriving to study.

Not that Rand wasn't happy here. In this insulated, academic world, he'd managed to work his way up from student to fellow to his current position, esteemed Professor of Linguistics, all in record time. And with no help from his family.

Finally, Rand wound down. He drained the rest of his ale and stared pensively into the empty tankard. "If you've come to ask about the translation, I'm afraid I have no good news for you."

Ford's heart sank. "What seems to be the problem?"

"It's more difficult than I had anticipated. There are words—and symbols—that seem unrelated to any language I've ever encountered."

"Symbols?" Ford frowned. "I saw a few formulas, which was one of the reasons I thought it might be *Secrets of the Emerald Tablet*. But those were just numbers, mathematics—"

"Not that. There were a few pages stuck together—"

"I opened a couple and saw nothing special, and I was afraid I might tear the paper."

"I steamed the rest open. Most were stuck from age, I imagine. But one...one, I believe, was on purpose."

"On purpose." Ford sipped, swallowed, tried to tamp down his rising hopes. "Are you thinking it might be the page that reveals—"

"No, nothing like that. I see no indication the secret you're searching for will be found on a single page. It's not going to be that simple." Rand's words reminded Ford of his family telling him something similar. "But this page is at the end, and it seems to be a legend for part of the code—perhaps for the author's own use. There are words—most of which I cannot read—with other words beside them, like a list, you understand?"

Ford nodded. "Go on."

"Well, that's the page that has some odd symbols." Rand tipped his tankard, letting the dregs of his ale run onto the table. "One of them, I think, looked like this." He used a finger to scribble in the wet, a design like a triangle with a three-branched candelabra perched on top.

"Air," Ford said.

"What?"

"That's the alchemical symbol for air. Or one of them. There are hundreds of similar symbols, some common, some not. Many whose meanings have been lost, but I can identify a number of them."

Excitement lit Rand's gray eyes. "So even though I cannot

read the word beside that symbol—which is gibberish, I suspect —when I find it in the text, I'll know it means air." He smeared the puddle, then used a finger to draw another mark. "How about this one?"

Ford frowned at the squiggle. "I don't recognize that."

"And this?"

A circle with three dots that suggested eyes and a nose. "That's a human skull."

Rand grimaced. "You mean a dead person?"

"Yes. A skull can be powdered and—"

"Never mind. I'd rather not know." He smoothed the liquid and sketched another design. "What's this?"

It looked like the letter *I* with an arrow curving up through it. "That's an instruction, not an ingredient. It means to filter."

After four more tries, one of which Ford could identify and three which he couldn't, Rand gave up. "I cannot remember any more. We'll fetch the book later, and you can write down the ones you know. But, Ford..."

His friend's gaze looked serious. "Tell it straight, Rand."

"Don't get your hopes up, will you? It's a single page of clues, and the symbols are few compared to all the other things I find undecipherable. Even with this help, the rest of it could take years."

Something fisted in Ford's middle. Or rather, the fist tightened—it had been there for days already. "I don't have years. Not if I want Violet."

"Ah. It's like that, is it?" Rand signaled for another round. "Tell me about it."

Though Ford normally wouldn't, his tongue was loosened by ale—and something akin to desperation. "My family approves. Her parents approve. But Violet refuses to marry for anything other than true love—"

"Odd woman, that. Most folk would be thrilled to wed a Chase, given your family's connections to King Charles. And most fathers would insist on it."

A comely serving maid plunked two more ales before them, fixing Ford with a leering grin. But he wasn't interested. He flipped her a coin. "The Ashcrofts are different from 'most folk.' They've raised their daughters to make their own decisions. They have the most absurd family motto: *Interroga Conformationem.*"

"Question Convention," Rand translated, looking amused. "Regardless, she should choose you. For security." He took a long swallow. "Even without the Philosopher's Stone, you're hardly a pauper. Take her to Cainewood if she wishes to live in luxury."

"I don't want to live at Cainewood." He was tired of living under his brother's scrutiny. He wanted to be self-sufficient. "Anyway, it's not luxury, per se, that concerns Violet. She's not a frilly female, and she has her own money."

"Ah. I remember. Given to her by that eccentric grandfather. To 'leave her mark on the world.'"

"Yes. And having seen the state of Lakefield, she's convinced herself I want her only for her inheritance. She won't believe I love her."

Rand shrugged. "It would be a good start to tell her."

"Bloody hell, I have. Repeatedly. In every way I know how." Closing his eyes, Ford lowered his head and raked both hands through his hair.

When he looked up, his friend's features expressed sympathy. Or disbelief. Or maybe both.

"Man, you've got it bad." Rand drained the ale and signaled for yet another. "I've never told a woman that."

Ford cocked a doubting brow. "Never?"

"Not when I meant it, anyway."

# FIFTY-SIX

*S*O HE WASN'T going to be making gold anytime soon. Their minds numbed by several more ales, Ford and Rand had concluded that didn't mean he had to give up on marrying Violet. All he had to do was convince her he loved *her*, not her money, which should be a simple enough task.

First, they decided, he had to keep *showing* her how much he loved her. He'd made a good start there, Ford explained to Rand in a drunken boast. Continued sensual assaults ought to eventually wear her down. It was only a matter of time before he became part of her the same way she had become part of him.

Rand groaned at that sentimental slop and ordered another round.

Second, Ford would change his priorities, put managing the estate first and relegate his science to a hobby. He'd already decided he was willing to do that and told both Violet and her mother as much. And it was infinitely more palatable than the alternative, which was losing Violet.

Love changed a man.

Of course, it would be a good while before the estate earned an income sufficient to pay all the debts, but in the meantime, Ford and Rand had reasoned, if he fixed up Lakefield, it wouldn't keep reminding Violet of his temporary lack of finances.

Which was why he was now outside, hacking away at his garden.

Hilda approached, bearing a tankard of fresh lemonade.

"A gift from heaven." He thunked his ax into the ground and held the cold drink against his forehead.

Hilda settled her hands on her wide hips. "Just what do you think you're doing out here?"

"Cleaning up." He gulped greedily. "Then I'll plant."

"Plant what?"

"I'm not sure. I'll think about that when I get there." He knew zero about plants, other than what some of them looked like extremely close up, thanks to *Micrographia.*

She eyed a ladder propped against the wall. "Are you planning to plant vines?"

"Excellent idea." He sipped again, letting the sweet coolness flow down his throat. "That would save me from painting, wouldn't it?"

"You're going to paint, too?"

"That's the plan. I sent Harry off for paint. Didn't he tell you?"

"Since when does Harry tell me anything?" She took the empty tankard from his hand. "What was the ladder for, then?"

"I tried to fix the roof." Turning away, he lifted the ax. "If you wouldn't mind going into the laboratory—"

"Into your private domain?" She laid a hand on her pillowy bosom. "Be still my heart."

"—you may find some foreign matter has fallen from above."

He whacked at an overgrown bush. Or vine. He wasn't sure which, but he was fairly certain the thing wouldn't be termed a tree. "I'm going to have to ask Harry to find a roofer." He whacked again, then turned sharply when he heard her snort. "Are you laughing at me?"

"Of course not, milord. That would be terribly disrespectful, wouldn't it?" She cleared her throat. "You know, some of that may be salvageable if you prune it instead of killing it."

He ran a grubby hand back through his hair. "Is that so? I had no idea you were knowledgeable about vegetation. I'm thinking perhaps you—"

"Think again." She drew herself up to her full height of five feet. "I'm a housekeeper, not a gardener. It's dirty work, that is."

It certainly was, if the state of his clothing was any indication. Deciding he'd done as much to destroy that plant as possible, he moved to the next one.

"Why are you limping?" Hilda's eyes narrowed. "Your breeches are torn."

He started to wave the ax in a dismissive gesture, then thought better of it. He was reasonably proficient with a sword, but the ax was another matter. "It's nothing," he said. "Just scratched myself a bit up on the roof."

"Fell through, you mean, do you not?"

On second thought, if the woman failed to curb her tongue, the ax could come in handy. His hand tightened on the hilt. Or the grip. Or whatever one called the wooden part of an ax. "Perhaps my foot did slip. I told you there might be foreign matter in the laboratory that needs to be cleared away."

"Well, I hope your blood isn't mixed with it." Shaking her head, she walked away, leaving him in peace at last.

As soon as she disappeared around the corner, he plopped onto a stone bench, groaning when a tangle of twigs poked into his anatomy. He swiped a hand across his brow and eyed his handiwork.

He'd been chopping away for nigh on four hours, and the job looked bigger than when he'd started.

# FIFTY-SEVEN

"*V*ERY INTERESTING," Violet said, staring at the dried top of a pineapple.

Lily smiled sweetly at their father. "What an exciting project."

"It's an ugly thing," Rose said.

Father gave her an indulgent smile—or perhaps he hadn't quite heard her. All plants were beautiful to him, and he'd been known to take offense on their behalf. "I'm going to plant it in a big pot and keep it here in the Stone Gallery at nights and all winter."

Violet didn't find the plan surprising, since he was already trying to grow oranges indoors. The long, narrow chamber, which was lined with windows and occupied the entire ground floor of the west wing, had been used in Tudor times to take exercise in inclement weather. But now one could hardly walk two steps without bumping into a plant.

Rowan's foot tapped on the black-and-white marble floor. "How many pineapples will it grow?"

"I'm not sure." Father frowned. "Maybe only one."

"One? We'll eat it in a trice!"

"But then I'll have another top, and I can grow more—"

"And by the time Rowan is married with children," Rose

finished for him, "we ought to have a decent crop. Anyone want to go riding?"

It seemed a long time since Violet had exercised anything but her heart. "I'm game," she said.

"Me, too," Lily added.

"Me three." Rowan scratched his head. "No, make that four."

They all laughed as they trooped outside.

A few minutes later they were mounted on their horses and riding along the river. Violet took the lead and automatically headed toward Lakefield, hoping Ford was back from Oxford. She wanted to see him. She wanted to look into his eyes and decide if she was prepared to take the next step.

The sun felt warm on her skin, and Socrates's white hide was tickly against her legs. She leaned into a turn, loving the wind in her hair, the fluid movements of the animal beneath her. Suddenly she felt like she'd been cooped up in the house entirely too long. The fresh air felt marvelous. She decided she should leave her books behind and get out more often.

"We should ride the other way," Rowan said.

Lily pulled up alongside him. "Why is that?"

He shook his head ruefully. "I don't want to see Jewel."

Three days had passed since he'd drunk the chocolate, and he was still scratching. And doubtless still hearing Jewel's laughter in his ears.

Rose laughed now. "Jewel went home with her parents, you goose."

"Oh."

"And anyway," Violet soothed, "I'm sure she won't…"

Her words trailed off as Lakefield House came within sight.

"Oh my," she said, staring at the decimated garden. "What do you think happened?"

"A storm," Rowan guessed. "With lots of blowing."

Lily's eyes sparkled with amusement. "I expect we would have felt the effects of that at Trentingham."

Rose shaded her eyes with a hand. "Is that a hole in the roof?"

They drew nearer. "Oh my," Violet said. "Is that—oh my."

"On the ladder there." Lily cocked her head. "Is it Ford?"

Rose drew breath and let out a very unladylike shout. "Lord Lakefield! Is that you?"

Her voice carried so well, even their father would have turned his head. Which the man on the ladder did, to reveal a face splattered with paint. His clothing wasn't faring any better. As they rode closer and came to a stop near the house, Violet watched a white blob roll down his hair and land on one of his boots.

She burst out laughing.

Ford backed awkwardly down the ladder and limped over to look up at her on her horse. He crossed his arms, then dropped them, grimacing at the white handprints he'd just made on his clothes. "What's so funny?"

At that, her sisters burst out laughing, too.

With a supreme effort, Violet controlled herself. "What," she asked, "do you think you're doing?"

"I told you I was going to fix this place up."

Another little giggle escaped. "I didn't think you meant to do it yourself."

Rose snorted. "It looks worse than when you started."

He glared at her a moment, then his lips twitched before he broke into a full-fledged grin. "My lady, I reckon you're right." He turned to address Violet. "May I speak with you for a moment? In private?"

She looked to her sisters, but this, after all, was what she had come for. So she shrugged and handed her reins to Lily, slid off Socrates, and followed Ford around the corner of the house.

The moment they were out of sight, he dragged her into his arms.

Her gasp of surprise was covered by his mouth. The familiar weakness stole over her, and her body went limp as her whole being focused on his kiss. His lips opened hers, and his tongue swept her mouth, gentle and demanding at the same time. He smelled of Ford and paint, of forbidden lust. She ached for the pleasure she now knew he could give her.

Breathless, nearly senseless, she pulled back, then looked down at her gown and gasped again.

"Sorry," he said. "I'll buy you another."

"I'm more concerned with what my family will think."

He ran a paint-stained finger down her arm. "They'll think I couldn't help myself, because I'm in love with you. Which is true."

She shivered. "Ford—"

"Will you come over tonight? Will you let me show you how much I love you?"

"I cannot do that!" It was one thing to go to supper and inadvertently end up in a bed. It was quite another to plan such an assignation from the outset.

This wasn't what she had come for. She'd come to look into his eyes.

But she did that now, and all she saw was temptation.

He grinned, his teeth as white as the paint. "How about if I scrub up first?"

"That—that has nothing to do with it. I cannot come here at night, Ford." She brushed at her hopelessly stained skirts. "What would my family think?" she added, knowing well what they would think. They would most likely think it was perfectly all right. And they would definitely think she should marry him.

"You came once for supper with your mother's blessing," he reminded her—as though she hadn't spent half her waking hours replaying that night in her head. "Besides, your family has no need to know."

She was shocked speechless for a moment. "You mean I should...sneak out? I couldn't!"

"Why not?" While she stood there with her mouth open, he elaborated, reaching to twirl a lock of her hair. "I'll come and get you—I'd never ask you to make your way here alone." Her scalp tingled. "Or if you'd prefer, I'll sneak into *your* chamber instead."

"No!" She'd be mortified if they were caught. "For one thing, from what I've seen here today, you can barely climb a ladder."

"Too true." Dropping the curl, he gestured at the house. "I think this project is finished. At least until I can hire some competent laborers."

"That's the first sane thing you've said this afternoon."

He curved an arm around her waist and pulled her close again, nipping softly at her bottom lip with his teeth. "Wait until you hear what I have to say to you this evening…"

"Ford…"

"I'll be there, waiting, at eleven o'clock." He kissed the corner of her mouth. "Below your window."

Greedy for a real kiss, she turned her head until her lips met his. And took what she wanted. And wanted still more.

"I am *not* climbing out a window," she whispered when she finally came up for air.

# FIFTY-EIGHT

*D*UE TO THE state of her gown, Violet's sisters had teased her mercilessly all the way home. Never mind that she had a reputation for tripping, they'd refused to believe she'd stumbled and fallen against the paint.

When they arrived at Trentingham, she'd endured more teasing from Father and Mum.

And now, hours later, after a bath and supper and many feigned yawns as she took herself off to bed, she was *not* climbing out a window.

She was sneaking out the back door instead.

The faintest sound of a pebble hitting her window had sent her racing downstairs. She simply couldn't help herself. Before sending her off to face her sisters in her paint-stained gown, Ford had given her one last kiss that had buckled her knees. She'd known then and there that she would find a way to meet him.

One night. A few precious hours. She was hopelessly in love —and equally determined not to let that influence her decision.

And the truth was, she was more confused than ever.

Had she not seen, just this afternoon, the very proof he wanted her for her money? Ford Chase, the man who'd refused to manufacture his watch because aristocrats didn't go into trade, was reduced to painting his own house, tending his own gardens. If that wasn't proof he was desperate, she didn't know what was.

Yet his eyes, when they'd met hers at the end of that final kiss, had looked so honest, so straightforward, so sincere...pools of deep blue she'd have sworn reflected a true passion in his heart.

Confusion. It should have made her refuse to meet him.

But now that she knew the bliss she could find in his arms, she seemed helpless to resist. There were also practical reasons for agreeing to this night—she was a practical woman, after all. Perhaps by sharing herself with him again, she would uncover his genuine motives. And if those motives weren't the ones she so desperately hoped for, well, then at least she would've grabbed her happiness while she could, knowing it might have to last the rest of her life.

Besides all that, she had questions and wanted answers, and he was the only person she felt she could ask.

She'd only just slipped out the door when she found herself caught up and swung in a wide circle. "I knew you'd come out!"

"Hush!" she admonished in a harsh whisper. "We'll be caught."

"Then you'll be forced to marry me." Sounding not at all displeased with that possibility, he set her on her feet. "Come here, my darling Violet."

"I'm here," she whispered, searching his eyes, which looked black in the moonlit night.

Something in them changed as he murmured, "No, come here." And he pulled her close, crushing her against his body.

She barely had time to rip off her spectacles before his mouth descended on hers, hot and needy. For a long, heady moment she almost wished they *would* be forced to marry. What a relief it might be to have the decision taken out of her hands. Then she ceased to think at all, just feeling instead. Feeling the things only Ford Chase had ever made her feel.

When he finally let her go, the book dropped to the grass between them. He bent to pick it up. "What's this?"

She turned hot, thankful for the cover of darkness. "*Aristotle's Master-piece*," she mumbled, fumbling her spectacles back on.

He tugged her close again, running a hand down her back to her bottom. She felt all melty inside. "Hmm?" he asked. "Why'd you bring a book?"

"I...well...there are things I don't understand." She licked her lips. "I was hoping you could explain them."

"*Me?* Explain philosophy to *you?*"

"It's not philosophy, Ford."

❧

*U*PSTAIRS, CHRYSTABEL let the curtain drop closed. "She's not alone, Joseph. Ford was waiting."

"I told you Violet was too clever a girl to go wandering off by herself. Even if she wasn't bright enough to realize we'd notice. Now come back to bed."

"Should we go after her?" She perched herself on the mattress, wrapping her arms around one raised knee as she faced her husband. "Are we doing the right thing?"

"He's a good man. She'll be safe."

"She'll be *ruined.*"

"Oh, Chrysanthemum, this was your idea in the first place. After you took such pains to explain it to me, I cannot believe you're having second thoughts. Besides..." His hand sneaked under her nightgown and up her thigh. "Were *you* ruined?"

She tingled. "Of course not. But that was different." She met his eyes, that emerald green she'd sunk into from the first time they met. "We'd already decided to marry."

"So has Violet. She just hasn't figured it out yet."

When his hand brushed her hip, she sighed. "I suppose

you're right. I expect she needs this to push her over the edge. I know they're perfect for each other, I just think—"

"Stop thinking, Chrysanthemum. Our Violet is in trustworthy hands." With fingers made agile by long years of practice, he swept the nightgown up and off. "Stop thinking now. It's time to feel instead."

## FIFTY-NINE

*S*EATED ON THE faded red couch in Ford's drawing room, Violet watched him flip pages.

"You're right," he said, his eyes widening. "This is *not* philosophy."

She sipped the wine he'd poured upon their arrival—white Rhenish, not red Italian. "It was supposedly by Aristotle. I thought it was philosophy when I bought it."

"When *I* bought it, you mean. I cannot believe I bought you a bloody marriage manual!"

"Hush!" Violet kept picturing Hilda lurking in the corridor, and just her luck, Mum was planning to deliver more Spiced Rosewater perfume tomorrow. She could imagine the tell-all that would ensue if she and Ford failed to modulate their voices. "I just need an explanation." She opened to a page where a bit of paper stuck up; she'd marked the confusing spot before leaving to meet him. "This chapter. 'A Word of Advice to Both Sexes: Being Several Directions Respecting...'"

"'Copulation,'" he finished for her, turning redder than the draperies. "Shouldn't you be asking your mother these things? Why the devil are you bringing this to *me*?"

She would die before asking her mother. "You're a scientist. This is physiology, isn't it?"

"Not of the sort I learned at Wadham College."

"Well, can you help me or not?"

"Let me see what it says." Blowing out a breath, he focused on the book. "'Since nature has implanted in every creature a mutual desire of copulation—'"

"Wait." There was that word again. Egad. "This room has no door. What if Hilda overhears? Or Harry?"

He grinned. "Perhaps they'll get an education."

"Ford—"

"I was fooling, my love. They sought their beds hours before I left for Trentingham. Relax, will you?" He reached to refill her cup. "They don't even know you're here."

"But they could come downstairs."

He seemed to consider that a moment. "Then shall we go up? The rooms upstairs have doors." Even as the words came out of his mouth, he rose and tucked the book beneath one arm. Handing her both cups, he took the bottle and a candle to light the way. She followed him up the worn steps, wincing at every crack and creak.

Thank heavens Hilda and Harry were old and hard of hearing.

On the landing, he turned right and walked her into a chamber.

A bedchamber.

"D-do you sleep here?" she asked. No matter that she'd come here expecting to share his bed, actually seeing it was a shock.

"Yes, I sleep here." Setting the wine on a small table, he took the candle around the room, lighting others. "I'm sorry it's not more elegant. It will all be repaired, though, Violet. I hired some laborers today after you left."

She sipped, staring at the bed, a four-poster so enormous it couldn't possibly fit through a door—it had to have been built in the room. It was fashioned of heavy oak, darkened with age and smoke from the blackened brick fireplace. Grayish bed-hangings draped from a wooden canopy overhead, looking as though they might once have been rich and possibly blue.

A very long time ago.

The walls were paneled with plain smoke-stained oak, divided into squares with simple molding. She looked up to find a beamed ceiling coated in peeling white paint.

"It's very...interesting," she said, for lack of a better description.

"I believe it's the roof of the original great hall, retained when the floor and fireplace were added some years later. Soon, it will all look good as new."

"That will take a lot of money," she said dubiously.

"Not so much," he assured her. "The building itself is sound. And I'm going to live here and manage the estate, see that it earns a profit."

She was listening with half an ear, avoiding looking back to the bed. With some relief, she noticed an open door across the chamber. In the way of older houses, a room lay beyond with no corridor to divide them. "What's that?"

"A sitting room of sorts." His half-smile told her he was aware of her nervousness. "Come, I'll show you."

A short, unpadded settle, a single armless chair, and a small, low table filled the tiny room. Although it was less than beautiful, like the rest of the house it was clean. And there was no bed.

"Lovely," she said, setting down the wine cups and settling herself on the low-backed oak bench.

He'd carried the candle in with him, and he set that on the table, too. Instead of taking the chair as she'd expected, he squeezed onto the settle beside her. "Would you mind if I get comfortable?"

Without waiting for an answer, he tugged off his boots. And peeled off his stockings.

Her mouth went dry. She moistened her lips. "Will you explain *Aristotle's Master-piece* now?"

"Of course," he said, wiggling his toes. With a flourish, he opened the book to her marked spot and tilted it to catch the candlelight. "'Since nature has implanted in every creature a mutual desire of copulation, I thought it necessary to give directions to both sexes for the performing of that act.'" Frowning, he glanced up. "Did you feel directions were necessary?"

His warmth wedged next to her made it difficult to focus on the words, but she already knew what the book said. She kept staring at his toes. He had very nice toes. "Just keep reading," she told him. "Please."

Before he did so, he shrugged out of his surcoat and laid it over the settle's arm. "Very well, then," he said. "'It would be very proper to cherish the body with generous restoratives, so that it may be brisk and vigorous, and if their imaginations were charmed with sweet and melodious airs, and cares and thoughts of business drowned in a glass of racy wine, that their spirits may be raised to the highest pitch of ardor and joy, it would not be amiss.'" Leaving the book open on his lap, he worked the knot in his cravat. "'For inspiration, creativity, and resourcefulness enrich the delights of Venus.'"

"See?" she broke in, alarmed to find he wasn't just removing his shoes—he looked to be undressing. "This is what I don't understand."

He twisted on the settle to face her. "Generous restoratives, sweet and melodious airs, and a glass of racy wine—did I not provide those for you, my love?"

Her face flushed hot. Yes, he'd provided food, music, and wine, and although she wasn't sure what was meant by *racy*, the word seemed to fit the mood of that night. "It's the other that makes no sense. Imagination. Inspiration, creativity, and resourcefulness."

"Doesn't it?" He drew off his cravat, setting the froth of white on the table.

"Read the rest."

"As you wish." He shifted even closer to her, if that were

possible. "'It is also highly necessary, that in their natural embraces, they meet each other with an equal ardor and an eye to ingenuity.'" As he read, he loosened the laces at his neck. "'I do advise them, before they begin their conjugal embraces, to invigorate their mutual desires with much daring and inventiveness. Freshness and originality will make their flame burn with a fierce ardor, by those endearing ways that love can better teach than I can write.'"

"See?"

Apparently finished "getting comfortable" for now, he reached for his wine. "See what? The author is rather enamored of the word *ardor*, isn't he? Three ardors in two paragraphs. And it would enhance readability if he broke up all those long sentences...who wrote this, do you know?" Sipping, he flipped back to the title page single-handedly.

"It's anonymous."

"I can see why." He shut the book and set it on the table, looking relieved to be finished with the reading. "Now, what is it you don't understand?"

"All of it! What ways can love teach better than he can write?"

"Almost anything is better than he can write."

She ignored his sarcasm. "What does he mean by giving these directions to invigorate mutual desires with ingenuity and daring and inventiveness?" Although she'd never shared this chapter with her sisters, she'd read it so many times the words were burned into her brain. "And freshness and originality?"

"What do you mean, what does he mean?"

"I mean, how can one be creative in copulation?" She blushed at her use of the word, but went on. "I've seen the animals in the fields, and each species has only one way to go about it."

A grin spread on his face.

Suddenly, she felt very, very stupid.

"What?" she asked suspiciously, trying to scoot farther away on the settle but only managing to smash herself against the hard wooden arm.

Very slowly, he ran a finger down her nose. "Let me tell you, darling, there are many, many ways to go about it."

"Oh." The finger continued down to her lips, tracing them lightly. "Oh," she repeated against it. "In that case, never mind."

"No, no." Smiling, he handed her his cup. "You came to me for physiology instruction, did you not? Let me explain the many ways." His eyes sparkled with devilment, and she couldn't quite decide whether to be irked or intrigued. "First, there is the disrobing. Many ways to be creative with that."

Intrigued, she decided, gulping a mouthful of wine. "Are there?"

"Absolutely. For example, you could dance for me while you remove your clothing."

"Dance?" she gasped.

"Oh, yes. You could hum a tune or sing a song while you did that, and I would enjoy it very much. Or I could dance for you."

Although he'd proven himself a good dancer at the Royal Society event, she couldn't quite wrap her mind around that picture.

"No?" he continued, obviously reading her face. "Well, then, of course, we could remove each other's clothing instead." She looked down to see him doing just that, his fingers detaching the tabs of her stomacher. "Inventively."

She drained the rest of the wine. "Inventively?"

"Mm-hmm." The stomacher dropped to the floor. "For example, I could use my teeth."

"Your *teeth*?"

"My teeth," he murmured, inclining his head. He bit one of her laces and drew back to untie the bow. Her heart slammed against her ribs. With his head down there, she was sure he could hear it.

He knelt at her feet and pulled off her shoes, then eased his hands beneath her skirts to raise and drape them over her thighs.

It was a good thing she'd finished the wine, because the cup dropped from her fingers and rolled across the planked floor. It stopped against the wall with a *clink*.

"My teeth," he repeated, using them to capture one of the ribbon garters she'd tied below her knees. In a trice, both were gone, and he used his teeth—his teeth!—to draw off her stockings after that.

He used his tongue, too, tracing hot, wet trails down her legs.

When a shiver rippled through her, he raised his head. "Are you, by any chance, feeling ardor right now?"

A nod was all she could manage.

With a grin of pure masculine pride, he rose to his feet, taking her hands to bring her up with him. "Now, before we begin our conjugal embraces, we are instructed to invigorate our mutual desires with much daring and inventiveness."

How could he speak so matter-of-factly, she wondered, after undressing her with his teeth?

"I think..." She licked her lips. "I think I can see now, there are indeed many ways, so—"

"But I would be remiss if I failed to demonstrate the wide range of options in invigorating our mutual desires." As he talked, he pulled his shirt off over his head. The resulting ripple of muscles invigorated her desires quite effectively. "For example," he continued conversationally, his long fingers working the laces that secured his breeches, "one can employ *things* in an invigorating manner."

"Things?" she asked breathlessly.

"Yes, things." Pausing, the breeches still hanging on his hips, he scanned the Spartan room. "There's nothing much in here, though, is there? In the way of things, I mean."

"No," she agreed, drifting slowly down toward the settle. Her knees felt inordinately weak.

He seized her around the ribs and held her up, his hands feeling hot through her bodice. She blinked. "What sorts of things are you looking for?" she asked, half afraid to hear the answer. Or maybe only one-quarter afraid, because truth be told, she was also intrigued beyond bearing.

"Oh, any number of things," he said blithely, raising his hands to her shoulders. He eased her gown and chemise down to her waist. "A feather, for instance," he elaborated as he plucked her limp arms from her sleeves, "can engender many pleasant sensations."

Her jaw went slack, and her gaze dropped down to her bared torso.

"Yes, there."

The thought of that made her pulse leap. Then it raced when he brushed her breasts with his fingertips. Lightly, lightly.

"Feather-light," he whispered as she watched herself tighten in response. "But not nearly as effective as an actual feather."

She closed her eyes, swaying, imagining that feather, thinking it was very difficult, actually, to imagine anything feeling better than what he was doing now.

Then she felt her gown pool at her feet, and her eyes flew open to find his gaze riveted *there*.

"Yes, there," he repeated. "A feather can be very effective there."

He had no feather. Yet she imagined herself sprawled wantonly on that enormous bed in the next room while he teased her with one.

Faith, she could feel it. He wasn't even touching her now, and she could feel it. Her face was getting hot—no, her whole body was getting hot. She sank back onto the settle.

"Are you perhaps feeling ardor?" he inquired, fetching the chair and dragging it over to face her. His breeches were the last of his clothing, and those looked as though they might slide off his slim hips.

She half wished they would.

He sat and scooted the chair closer, so close their knees touched. Then closer still, until one of his legs slipped between both of hers.

She stared at his bare chest, thinking she must be dreaming. She was stark naked, and a man's knee was between her legs. Her open legs, exposing where he wanted to tease her with a feather.

Reaching out, he raised her chin. "Violet? Are you paying attention?"

His muscles flexed with his movements. She wanted him. Now. She couldn't take any more of this lesson. "Ford, I—"

"I'm remembering," he interrupted smoothly, "that the book gave directions to be resourceful. Therefore, since the only *thing* we have here is wine, I should use it to demonstrate creativity." He raised his cup and swirled the liquid with two fingers. "For example, we can use it as paint."

Holding her gaze, he anointed the crest of one breast with a sweeping, circular motion.

Shocked, she looked down. A droplet of wine seemed poised to fall, and she gasped when he bent his head and caught it on his tongue. Then his lips closed over her, and he suckled the rest of it off.

Her breath caught as a dizzying wave of excitement rolled through her, matching the rhythm of his mouth.

"Ford—"

"Hmm?" His eyes looking glazed, he dipped his fingers again and painted her other breast. "Mmm," he murmured, not a question this time, but a sound of satisfaction. "Red wine would be most flattering on this rosy little confection, but white looks fetching as well."

How could he *talk* like that while he was doing this to her? The wine felt cool on her skin, and his tongue felt hot as he licked it off, ever so slowly and thoroughly. She forgot whatever it was she had meant to say. If she'd even known in the first place.

Finally he sat back, giving her a lazy, seductive smile. "Now," he announced, the instructor again, "there is the finale, otherwise known as 'conjugal embraces.' There are many ways—"

"I am sure there are many ways," she cut in. She ached, an ache that was becoming unbearable. "I liked the first way we tried perfectly well."

As though he hadn't heard her at all, he cocked his head and eyed the settle. "That looks damned narrow and uncomfortable, but if we move to the bed, we could try it on our sides. Either face to face, or me behind you. Or I could lie back and let you ride me—"

She gasped, but he only grinned.

"Not ready for that? Or is it that you wish to stay in this chamber? I suppose we could try it standing against the wall, or...I know, right here on this chair." And before she could react to that astounding barrage of ideas, he'd grabbed her by the waist and hauled her, facing him, to straddle his lap.

Somehow he'd maneuvered his breeches down, because she could feel him, right there where she ached. "Oh my," she breathed, closing her eyes to revel in the sensation. Amazed at her own boldness, she wiggled closer.

She was dying to have him inside her.

She ran her hands up his chest and felt him gently tug off her spectacles. Her eyes flew open as she realized he'd brought her this far, to the brink of completion, without so much as a single kiss.

He made up for that lack now.

His lips slanted over hers, his tongue invading her mouth, stroking hers, gentle and tender at first, almost exquisitely so. Then more insistent, more emphatic, angling his head, nipping her bottom lip, coming back to settle on her mouth and stay there, working his magic until she felt nothing but heat and a wild dance of tongues and lips and teeth.

For a long time, he just kissed her, until, wanting more, needing more, she rocked against him and her hands began roaming his body. And then, still kissing her, he began to touch her, too.

In this position, his hands were free. They teased her breasts, sending the blood in a rush through her veins. They cradled her face, making her heart melt with tenderness. They threaded into her hair, making her feel sweetly possessed. They wandered down her back, warm and swift, all the way to her bottom. He pulled her closer. A moan escaped her lips as she felt him pressing, pressing against where she ached. Until he finally slid inside.

And then deeper, still kissing her, kissing her until she wondered if she'd ever catch her breath. But she didn't want him to stop. Deeper still, and he shifted, tilting his hips, and she moved with him. That feeling she remembered was building, an excitement so urgent she could barely keep from crying out. She was spiraling up, up—

And then suddenly he stopped, holding her hips in place with his hands. His lips clung to hers, one more sweet, lingering caress before he drew back.

Still straining against him, she opened her eyes.

"Sometimes," he said softly, "one can find 'freshness' in an encounter by temporarily reversing the process."

Her fingers clenched his shoulders. "Wh-what?"

"Although we are here in a conjugal embrace, there is nothing to say we cannot resume invigorating our mutual desires."

Her squeak was one of distress, but he smiled as he eased her away, and the smile widened when she moaned at his withdrawal. Standing, he swept her up, cradling her with an arm beneath her knees and another around her shoulders, as she imagined he would carry Jewel were she asleep.

But Violet wasn't asleep. Every fiber of her body was alarmingly awake. Wanting him back inside her.

He walked into the other chamber, kicking his breeches off as he went, and deposited her flat on her back in the middle of the bed. She gazed up at him. She could see he was still ready for her. Magnificently ready.

Faith, she wanted him more than she'd wanted anything in

her life. Beseechingly, she held up her arms, waiting for his warm, welcome weight.

"We're going back, remember? To invigorating our mutual desires." Instead of joining her, he sat beside her and reached for the bottle of wine. It seemed like hours since he'd left it on the night table.

"Hmm," he said speculatively. Her heart beat faster. She was beginning to anticipate that speculative "hmm"—and with good reason, as it turned out. He raised the green bottle so the candle-light shone through it. Then he spilled a bit into her navel and immediately leaned to lap it up.

His hot tongue in that little indentation made her belly quiver and sent a jolt of passion streaking through her. The ache between her legs intensified, an almost unbearable wanting. She called his name in a breathy cry.

"Hmm?" he murmured, a hum against her skin. His dark head moved lower, his tongue licking, his teeth nipping, down her pelvis and over the tender insides of her thighs.

And then he hovered there, where she ached.

She waited, feeling his warm breath washing over her, and when nothing happened, she grabbed his shoulders, his hair.

He lifted his head, meeting her gaze.

"Ford?" she whispered, wondering what she was asking. Would he touch her there with his mouth? She'd never imagined such a thing, but the thought of it sent such a hot stab of lust coursing through her, it completely stole her breath.

"No," he decided with a reluctant shake of his head. "I'm going to save that for our wedding night."

Air rushed between her parted lips. She wanted him there so badly, touching her, stroking her, filling her...

"Are you feeling ardor now?" he asked.

"Oh, please," she breathed in reply, unsure whether she was asking for his mouth or his body, but needing something.

Some part of him, completing her.

At long last he came over her, warm along her length,

groaning as his lips met hers above while down below he slid inside. Her blood sang at the sheer perfection of the way their bodies fit together. He thrust once, twice, and—

She exploded. That was all it took, and there was no other word to describe it. Lost to sensation, she barely felt him draw out of her before he shuddered and collapsed, burying his face in the crook of her neck.

"Violet," he choked out, "I love you."

Struggling to catch her breath, she missed him inside her already. But she hadn't missed the fervor in his voice, the force behind his words. And when he finally lifted his head, she saw it there.

Love, true and honest.

She searched his eyes, learning this gaze by heart. And then she smiled, a tentative smile, wanting to tell him she loved him, too, but unable to find the words. After all she'd put him through, she wanted her declaration to be perfect—

A different light entered his eyes as he rolled off her, still holding her in his arms. A glint of humor. "You see, my sweet," he said, a playful grin curving his lips, "there are many, many ways."

"There are," she breathed, knowing now there must be so much more. That reminded her. "You didn't do that the last time. Leave me at the end."

She felt him tense. "Last time," he said, all the playfulness suddenly gone, "I thought we would soon be married."

"Oh." She knew he was waiting for her to say they would. But she was shocked beyond any more speech. A simple "Oh" was all she could muster.

How could she, levelheaded Violet Ashcroft, have done such an irresponsible thing?

He'd pulled out this time but, faith, they could have conceived a child that night on the barge. She'd been so carried away, she hadn't thought about the consequences, never mind that the *Master-piece* had been quite clear in that regard. Thinking about it now brought a chill to her heated flesh.

She lay a while beside him, waiting for her heart to calm and her head to focus. Thank heavens he loved her; thank heavens she'd seen it in his eyes. The Ashcrofts might be unconventional, but a child born out of wedlock would strain their family motto a bit too far.

"Ford?" she called softly, but there was no answer.

He'd collapsed for real this time. He was sound asleep.

Her arms tightened around him, and her heart squeezed to match. She pressed a kiss to his warm, dear temple. She'd let him sleep a few minutes before she woke him and told him she'd be honored to become his wife.

# SIXTY

"J OSEPH?" CHRYSTABEL called softly.

"Hmm?"

"Do you think our baby is still an innocent now?"

He rolled to face her. "She's been alone with him before, my love."

"You don't think...no..."

"Yes." He struggled up on his elbows, peering at her through the darkness. "Who, after all, brought home *Aristotle's Master-piece*?"

"I'm sure she thought it was a philosophy book."

He snorted and fell back to the pillows. "You just go on believing that, Chrysanthemum. Whatever makes you happy."

No matter that she'd plotted to allow Ford to seduce her daughter, she would have known had it actually happened. She was sure of it. "If she'd been with him before, I would have seen it in her face."

This snort was even louder than the first. "One cannot tell from a woman's face whether she's made love. If so, you'd be going about wearing a veil all your days." She blushed, and he touched her cheek, then his eyes drifted closed. "But you believe whatever makes you happy, Chrysanthemum my love, so long as you let me sleep."

~

"FORD, WAKE UP!" Sitting beside him on the bed, Violet shook his shoulder. "I must get home!"

With a groan, he rolled against her, and for a moment all she could think was she wanted to crawl back into bed with him. Even through her skirts he felt impossibly warm and wonderful.

But *impossible* was the operative word. She finished attaching her stomacher and shook him again. "It's morning already!"

He cracked an eye open and, seeing nothing but the single flame of a candle to break the darkness, promptly closed it. "It's not morning."

"Well, it will be soon. I cannot believe I fell asleep!"

Grabbing the candle, she hurried next door to fetch her spectacles. When the tiny chamber came into focus, her gaze fell on the single chair. Last night, she'd been entwined with Ford on that chair in a shockingly wanton conjugal embrace.

Her blood heated at the memory.

In the soft glow of the candlelight, the room didn't appear nearly as shabby as she'd thought. Besides, he'd told her he was fixing up Lakefield. He hadn't done it before because he hadn't planned to live here, but now he was going to fix it up. He'd hired laborers already. *Just like that*, he'd said in the summerhouse. And last night he'd said he was determined to see the estate earned a profit. It was going to be his home.

*Their* home.

Home. She had to get home. She streaked back into the bedchamber. "Get up, will you? Or should I go home alone?"

"No." He struggled to sit and ran a hand through his hair, leaving parts of it sticking straight up. Sleepy like this, he looked charmingly boyish, and the thought made her smile. Especially now that she knew he was so very much a man.

"I'll get dressed," he muttered. "Just give me a moment." He blinked, shook his head, and began to rise from the bed. Stark naked.

She wasn't ready for this. This morning-after business was more than she could take. "I'll wait for you downstairs," she told him. "Hurry." But she sneaked him a sideways glance while she lit a second candle before rushing out the door.

My, he was magnificent.

She wanted him. God help her, she wanted him for good.

On her way down the stairs, she smiled at the worn boards that creaked under her feet, at the paneling on the walls that so badly needed refinishing, at the peeling paint on the beams overhead. None of it bothered her. The truth was, the condition of her home didn't overly concern her. She just needed to know, deep in her bones, that the man she wed truly loved her. *Her*, Violet, not the monetary bounty that would come along with her.

And now she did know that, all the way down to her marrow. Love, true and honest—she'd seen it in Ford's eyes. And though he hadn't said it in so many words, he'd made it clear he didn't need her inheritance. She could marry him now, knowing it was for all the right reasons. Knowing it was for love, not money.

Her entire body seemed to sing with happiness. As soon as Ford came downstairs, she would tell him she would be honored —no, thrilled—to become his wife.

It wasn't as late as she'd feared. To her great relief, Hilda and Harry were nowhere in sight. She set the candle on a small marble table that could use a serious buffing, then paced Lakefield's entrance hall while she waited for Ford and thought about her new life—the wonderful new life the two of them would have together.

Her dowry should cover the costs of renovation, leaving more of his funds available to improve the estate, which in turn would allow it to run more profitably. She was anxious to go over his plans. Since she wouldn't be publishing her book for many years, perhaps she should suggest they use her inheritance to accelerate the improvements. The investment would surely come back to her long before she needed it.

Now that she knew Ford wasn't marrying her for her inheritance, she wouldn't mind him making use of it. In fact, it made little sense to let all that money sit idle for years.

Her gaze went up the empty staircase. What was taking him so long? Wondering if the sun were rising already, she jerked open the front door.

A shocked face was on the other side. Violet squealed, and the young boy turned tail and began running.

"Wait!" she called.

He stopped and pivoted back. "I have a letter, madam."

*Madam.* Was her loss of innocence so obvious to a stranger, then? Or was it only that she'd reached the advanced old age of one-and-twenty?

Rather cautiously, he approached the door, holding forth a rectangle of sealed parchment. "Will you give this to the lord?"

"Of course. Let me just…wait." She'd noticed a bowl with a few coins on the table in the entrance, and she went inside to fetch one, pressing it into the boy's hand on her return. "Thank you."

He touched his cap and took off.

She slowly closed the door, turning the letter in her hands. It looked long and very official. There was no return address, but she hoped…could it be from Daniel Quare, the watchmaker?

Her heart pounded at the thought.

She sent a furtive glance up the stairs before slipping her fingernail under the seal.

*My dearest Lord Lakefield,* she read. *It is my sad duty to inform you that I have received a foreclosure notice on your estate. You have thirty days…*

The letter fluttered to the floor, her heart sinking along with it.

It wasn't in response to her query, and she had no business

reading Ford's private mail. But the parchment mocked her from where it sat on the dull wood planks. She took a deep breath before stooping to retrieve it, then set it on the table beside the bowl of coins. Ford would find it later. After he'd taken her home, after she'd told him she saw no reason to see each other anymore.

*Foreclosure.*

She would have to pray she wasn't with child. Because he'd tried to fool her, and she'd done her best to fool herself...but she no longer had any illusions about why Ford Chase had been pursuing her so avidly.

## SIXTY-ONE

WO MEN WERE working on Lakefield's roof. Three were painting the exterior of the house, two the interior. Another man was busy stripping the dark Tudor paneling for refinishing, and in the gardens, two more toiled, making order out of the disarray Ford had left.

In the meantime, he paced his laboratory, the letter in his hand.

*Foreclosure.*

The single word was like a fist to his gut. He'd had no idea his situation was this bad. Never again would he allow himself to stay ignorant of his finances.

He'd thought if he put his mind to the task—and the funds he usually spent on his science into the estate—he could make Lakefield profitable and dig himself out of debt. And he could, according to his solicitor. But it would be much more difficult than he'd imagined.

*Foreclosure.*

All these people he'd hired yesterday he'd have to dismiss this afternoon. In lieu of selling the estate, his solicitor had outlined an emergency plan to save it, but it certainly didn't include funds for cosmetic restorations. His income would have to go into the fields, purchasing livestock, fixing the stables, and repairing crofters' cottages so new tenants would have a place to live.

But that wasn't the worst of his troubles.

He'd been sure the tactics he'd plotted with Rand were working, but for some reason he couldn't fathom, after what he'd considered a night of shared bliss, Violet had awakened this morning and seen him in a different light. A light so dim and dreary, she'd made it clear she had no interest in seeing him ever again.

And now his dreams of repairing Lakefield so she'd view him in a brighter light were finished. Gone. His hopes of winning her were gone as well. Along with his spirits.

The disappointment was a physical ache. Empty years yawned ahead. He knew, with a sureness that crushed him, that he'd never find satisfaction in his scientific accomplishments again. Not without Violet here to share them.

Unless...

The letter fluttered to the floor as, determined, he set his jaw. He had one last chance to win her, one final opportunity to convince her, once and for all, that he loved her, not her inheritance. One way to fill his coffers with the kind of money that would make hers superfluous.

It would be the hardest thing he'd ever done...but with his only other option losing Violet, he had no choice.

No other choice he could live with.

## SIXTY-TWO

*V*IOLET LOOKED UP from her philosophy book, muttering under her breath. She'd read the same page four times and still didn't understand it. It had been three days since she'd seen Ford—three days during which she couldn't concentrate on anything and snapped at everyone within earshot.

"Violet?"

Exasperated, she swung toward the door. "Yes?" she bit out, then bit her lip. Her mother didn't deserve her misplaced ire. It wasn't Mum's fault that Violet was too plain and odd for any man to love except for her money.

She closed her eyes momentarily, then opened them, drawing on her last reserve of patience. "What is it, Mum?"

"There's a man here to see you. Not Ford," she added in a rush, and Violet was chagrined, knowing the leap of hope must have shown in her eyes. "His friend," Mum said gently. "Lord Randal Nesbitt."

Rand? Why would Rand want to see *her*? "Are you sure he isn't here to see Rose, Mum? She's the one who likes languages."

"He asked for you. He's waiting in the drawing room."

Sighing, she reached for her spectacles. In a fit of melancholy that terrible morning, she'd tried to put them away in a drawer, because they'd reminded her too much of Ford. Of her dreams, dashed and broken. But after three or four hours of walking around half blind, she'd decided that was ridiculous. She wasn't going to forget him anyway, and there was no point in bumping into things for the rest of her life.

She slid them on and made her way downstairs to the drawing room.

When Violet entered the chamber, Rand stood. "Ford doesn't know that I'm here, my lady, and I'd prefer to keep it that way."

"As you wish." She waved him back to the cream-colored chair and took the matching one for herself. "What's this all about?"

Mum had served him tea, and he raised the cup and sipped. "Ford wrote to me two days ago, and I thought you should know."

"Know what?" Taking a biscuit from a tray, she nervously broke off a piece. "You're confusing me, my lord."

"Rand," he reminded her. "And my apologies. I'm just so shocked, I wasn't sure how to...well...he asked me to sell *Secrets of the Emerald Tablet*. To take bids on it and then contact Mr. Isaac Newton."

"Sell *Secrets of the Emerald Tablet*?" Unheeded, the crumbs dropped to her lap. She remembered Ford clutching the book the day he found it. His declaration that he'd never sell it. His eyes glittering with excitement every time another bit was deciphered. "It's his favorite thing in the world, his chance to discover the Philosopher's Stone and deliver it to all of humanity. You must be mistaken."

"I assure you, I'm not. According to Ford, Newton has offered to pay double the highest bid, and he wishes to collect." Rand sipped again, watching her over the rim. "It's the only path he can see clear to winning your heart."

That heart skipped a beat. Involuntarily, Violet raised a hand to her chest. "I don't understand..."

He set down the cup and leaned forward, bracing his hands on his knees. "I've known Ford since we were lads together at Oxford, but never have I known him in love. Until now."

She shook her head. "You're mistaken, my lord—"

"Rand."

"Rand, then. You're mistaken. Look at me, Rand. Really look. I'm not a woman who inspires love—"

"What are you *talking* about?" he interrupted.

She sat straighter in her chair. "I have a mirror, and two good eyes." Her hands went to her beloved spectacles. "Well, bad eyes, actually, until Ford made me these, but—"

"Two good eyes and half a brain," he interrupted again.

She must warn Rose he had terrible manners, she thought absurdly.

Then his intense gray gaze pierced hers, demanding her attention. "Ford loves you, Violet. And no matter what you think, you're a fine-looking woman, but that's not the reason why. He loves your spirit and your intelligence and the way you listen to his ideas. And the way you have ideas of your own."

"And he loves my money."

"No. That he hates. Because it's the reason you won't take his declaration at face value." He waited a moment for her to digest that. "Ford is a third son, the third son of a man who squandered the family fortune fighting the king's war. Under the circumstances, he's doing all right for himself. He's in a bit of financial trouble now, but nothing he cannot handle if he moves carefully, except—"

"His estate is being foreclosed upon."

"No. I mean, yes, but...how do you know that?"

She raised her own cup to her lips, hiding her hot cheeks behind it. "My mother is a terrible gossip."

"Oh. I see." He didn't look like he saw at all, but he continued anyway. "The foreclosure is a fact, but beside the point. He's working with his solicitor to resolve that."

She looked down at her cup, held between trembling hands.

Could that be possible? She hadn't read the balance of that long letter.

"Ford's problem, Violet"—he waited for her to look up—"is he's lacking enough funds to both rescue his estate and remodel it in a way that would please you."

"Which is the reason he wants my money."

"No. He's convinced you won't wed him unless he has enough money that you'll believe he doesn't need yours, which is why he's selling the book." He paused to let that sink in. "He's trading the book for *you*, Violet."

"Oh, God." Her cup clattered to the table, and she dropped her head in her hands.

Ford loved her.

He'd told her so, over and over, and she'd never believed him. Nothing he could say would overcome her stubborn failure to accept his honest declarations. Not even his tender hands on her body had convinced her to admit what she knew in her heart...

Ashamed, she felt hot tears prick her eyes. That he would go to the point of selling his most cherished possession...

"I cannot let him do it."

Rand stood and, pulling her from the chair, wrapped his arms around her shuddering frame. "I was hoping you'd say that," he whispered.

❧

"*F*ATHER," VIOLET said loudly, "I'd like the use of my inheritance."

Seated across from her at the library's round table, Joseph glanced at Chrystabel before looking back to their daughter. "Have you an investment in mind?"

"No. Well, yes." She lifted her chin. "An investment in my future."

Chrystabel barely suppressed a smile. "Can you explain yourself, dear? This is very confusing."

"Ford is planning to sell *Secrets of the Emerald Tablet*. I wish to buy it."

Joseph frowned. "You hardly need your inheritance to buy a book."

"This book costs ten thousand pounds."

Watching her husband's jaw drop open, Chrystabel reached beneath the table to take his hand. "Why do you want to buy it?" she asked Violet calmly.

She thought she knew the answer. She *hoped* she knew the answer. And when tears sprang to her daughter's eyes, she knew she knew the answer.

"He's s-selling it," Violet stuttered out, "so he can fix up his house and win *me*."

"Then let him do it," Joseph said. "You don't need to spend your—" He broke off when Chrystabel kicked him under the table. "What the—"

"What your father means to ask," she interrupted, laying her free hand on Violet's arm, "is what you intend to do with the book once you have it?"

Her daughter's eyes cleared, and she drew a deep breath. "Why, give it back to him, of course. As a wedding present."

"Oh, dear." Chrystabel's own eyes glazed over. Her eldest was getting married. "I was hoping you'd say that."

## SIXTY-THREE

*H*ER PARENTS watched while Rand handed Violet the book. She clutched it to her chest, wishing she were clutching its owner instead. But she hoped to be clutching Ford soon enough.

"Father's solicitor will send the money tomorrow. You won't tell Ford who really bought it, will you? Even though he's your friend?"

"My best friend. But I wouldn't dream of it. Your secret is safe with me."

"You're a good friend, Rand."

He nodded toward the book. "So are you."

She sent him a tremulous smile. Ford would have her inheritance now, but if she felt a tiny pang at the loss of her own dream to publish a book, it was completely eclipsed by the joy of finding love. True love. A lifetime of love was so much more precious than any academic goal she might reach as a lonely old lady.

"Thank you, Rand. For everything."

"You're more than welcome." He turned to leave, then swiveled back. "Where's your sister Lily?"

"Outside, I believe. Tending to her poor, bedraggled menagerie."

His eyes lit, and he looked to her father. "May I have your permission to stop and visit with her?"

Father blinked. "What?"

"Joseph," Mum explained loudly, "Lord Randal is asking if he might visit with Lily."

"I have lilies in the garden."

"Of course you do, darling." She smiled at Rand. "Go ahead. I expect Lily will be pleased. But she's young, Lord Randal. So visiting is all that will happen."

Wide-eyed, he nodded and left.

Slack-jawed, Violet turned to her mother. "Lily?" she asked. "What about Rose? If she hears of this, she'll be furious."

"I'm not telling her," Mum said. "Are you?"

"Absolutely not."

"Tell who what?" asked Father.

$\sim$

*T*WO WEEKS LATER, Ford paced Lakefield House, satisfied with the progress of the renovations. Not that everything was complete—even with an army of skilled laborers, there was only so much one could accomplish in two weeks. But the roof was sound, and the exterior was a gleaming white. The garden had been cleared, and if it had a way to go before one could call it beautiful, even Ford's untrained eye could see promise in all the new plants and flowers.

And he could easily find his sundial now. A quick glance told him it was nearly noon—nearly time for Violet to arrive from Trentingham.

He felt as though he'd waited his entire life for this moment. Thanks to the sale of *Secrets of the Emerald Tablet*, Lakefield shone not only in ways that showed, but behind the scenes. The latest farming implements were on order, and tenants were moving into the newly refinished cottages. The estate hummed with productivity and the promise of more to come. The threat of foreclosure was behind him, and despite spending a prodigious amount of money to accomplish his goals, he had enough funds remaining to live well for a few months until Lakefield started producing the tidy income it should.

He'd been surprised to find he didn't mind the labors of a landowner, either. Although it would never replace the scientific work that claimed his heart, it was satisfying to use one's brains and brawn to improve a place of one's own. He wasn't facing the months and years ahead with dread, but rather with anticipation of watching his efforts pay off.

No matter how painful it had been to sell the book, he knew he'd done the right thing—and, for perhaps the first time in his life, the *responsible* thing.

While he wouldn't be the one to bring the Philosopher's Stone to the world, Violet meant the world to him, anyway. If he could only see that long-sought-after acceptance in her eyes, it would all have been worth it.

His stomach knotted at the sight of an approaching carriage.

Here was his moment of truth.

He'd done right by Lakefield and all its people. He'd secured a future for his children, and his own future along with it.

But if Violet refused to share it with him, it would be a bleak future indeed.

## SIXTY-FOUR

*A*FTER WAITING what seemed an eternity while she wondered if Ford had taken her goodbye to heart, Violet had been confused when a note arrived inviting her entire family to dine at Lakefield House this afternoon.

Now on their way, she twisted her hands in her lap, not really listening to her sisters and Rowan chatter in the carriage. As they approached Lakefield, she leaned to part the carriage curtains. A trickle of relief stole through her when she saw Ford pacing by the door, apparently as impatient as she.

Mum placed her gentle fingers over Violet's busy ones. "Are you ready?"

"For what?" Rose asked.

Violet exchanged a glance with her mother. "Just to visit," she said in as offhand a manner as she could. "You needn't read something into every sentence."

"What are you reading?" Father asked.

"Egad." Violet took a deep breath as the carriage rolled to a stop. They were here. Whatever was going to happen would happen now. She'd never considered herself much of an actress, but she had a role to play today, and she intended to do it well.

Ford greeted them outdoors with a formal reserve that did

nothing to relieve her fears, inviting them all for a tour of the house before dinner. Violet followed him, wondering what her parents would think, whether they would still bless this possible marriage when they saw how poorly he lived.

But then she stepped inside.

The old dark paneling in the entrance hall was now a honeyed tone, and their first tour stop was the drawing room, where the floor had been stripped and polished, the walls painted a soft turquoise in place of the faded red.

"This is lovely," Rose said in awe.

Had Rose seen the place last week, Violet thought, she'd be making one of her saucebox remarks instead.

But the room *was* lovely. Unbelievably lovely.

"I still need to order furniture," Ford explained, "and draperies." He looked to Violet. "I've no eye for decor, so I'm hoping for help with that."

She nodded, hoping he was hoping for *her* help. Hoping she hadn't spoiled her chances by refusing him one time too many.

His study was similarly refurbished, done in shades of cinnamon and olive green. Gone was the ugly brown decor in the dining room, replaced with walls of deep burgundy to set off the refinished cabinetry.

Hilda was setting the table. "It will be half an hour or more before dinner," she told Ford, "but I've set out some victuals in the garden."

"We're going there straight after our tour," he assured her.

"The garden?" asked Father.

Hilda smiled and raised her voice. "If you'll but wait a moment, Lord Trentingham, I'll show you outside."

The rest of them headed upstairs. The staircase had new, polished balusters, and the steps didn't creak. "I've hired a cook," Ford told Violet as they climbed, "so Hilda is just a house-keeper now."

In Ford's bedchamber, the peeling ceiling had been stripped, revealing dark beams with colorful painted designs from some fanciful former owner. "It's changed so much," Violet breathed.

Lily's eyes were round blue orbs. "You've been in here before?"

Violet's face burned. "Not *here*. I meant the house in general."

The chamber looked entirely different. The massive oak canopy bed had been refinished to a warm tone, and the old bed-hangings were gone. The room next door had been opened to combine with this one, providing a sitting and dressing area, currently furnished with the same settle, chair, and table that had been in the space when it was separate.

"I thought it would be nice to have more furniture in the room," Ford said, capturing Violet's gaze. "I envision changing it to something more comfortable. Except for that chair. For some odd reason, I'm rather attached to that plain oak chair."

"Why?" Lily asked, clearly confused.

Ford only shrugged, while Violet focused on the shiny wood floor.

"'You cannot conceal love or a cough,'" Rowan read slowly, and she turned gratefully to see an inscription above the door.

"That was there already," Ford rushed to explain, looking a little uneasy at hearing the romantic sentiment aloud. "We found it beneath layers of paint."

Mum smiled. "It's a clever turn of phrase."

He nodded, shooting Violet a significant glance. "I suppose I agree with it, too."

"You should marry him," Rose whispered to Violet as they left the room. "He even has a nice house."

For once, Violet wasn't tempted to slap her middle sister. And if she was reading Ford's silent messages correctly, this wedding was going to happen.

Buoyed by that thought, she practically floated into the next room, a small one painted pale green.

Ford told them it was "Jewel's room."

"Will Jewel come to visit and sleep here?" Rowan asked.

"I hope so."

"Me, too." Apparently, now that he was no longer scratching, he'd forgotten that Jewel had laughed at him.

"There are two other chambers off the corridor," Rose pointed out. "Why did we walk past those?"

"I haven't done anything with them yet. I'm hoping to fix one up as a nursery."

Another unspoken message, one that made all the eyes in the chamber seem to converge on Violet. She was finding it hard to breathe.

When Rowan yelled, "Come see the laboratory!" she could have kissed him. They all trooped up to the attic. Nothing had changed in that room, but she wouldn't have wanted it to. It was Ford, plain and simple.

She didn't remember drifting down the stairs, but a few minutes later they'd joined her father in the garden, where he was in the middle of explaining the newest pruning techniques to poor old Harry.

Leaving her family to the refreshments Hilda had set out, Ford drew Violet aside. "Come with me," he whispered. "I've something else to show you." And he walked her around the corner of the house.

There, hanging from three oaks, were three swings: two regular swings and one wider version that was more than just ropes and a board. It had a back and armrests as well.

A swing for two.

"For us," Ford said softly, taking her hand to lead her toward it. "I remembered how you like to swing."

"Not too high," she reminded him, suddenly nervous. "I notice you didn't hang them on trees near the river. Are the other two for Jewel and Rowan?"

"For now." His hand squeezed hers. "But I hope different children will use them someday. Our children."

"Ford…" Faith, how did one tell a man she wanted to live

with him all of her life? She had no experience with this sort of thing.

But he didn't seem to be expecting an answer now. Reaching the double swing, he smiled and said, "Sit," just like that day on the riverside.

Slanting him a glance, she did so, and he stepped behind her. She waited for him to push, but instead he tilted her back, just like the day on the riverside. And when he drew off her spectacles and lowered his mouth to meet hers, it was just like that day, too.

Except it wasn't, because they hadn't really known each other then. Their upside-down kiss that day had been shocking and exciting, where today's was tender and heartfelt. They were once again kissing each other's bottom lip, but this time her heart turned upside down in the process.

It was a good thing she was seated, she thought as he drew away and the swing bobbed upright. Because her knees were so weak, she doubted they would support her.

He gave her a gentle push. "What do you think of the house?"

"I think…" Here came the acting. She wouldn't dream of ruining the surprises—either his to her now, or hers to him later —by revealing she'd been the one to buy the book. Even though the white lie weighed a bit on her conscience, that wouldn't be fair to either of them.

"I think I'm confused," she said, thankful he couldn't see her face. Without her spectacles, the river looked blurry in the distance.

He pushed her again. "Confused about what, sweetheart?"

The endearment filled her with a cautious thrill. "About everything. Why was this place so run down if you could afford to fix it up? Just because you never lived here?"

"No," he said without hesitation. He wasn't going to try to hide anything from her, and she loved him all the more for it. "I thought I could afford to fix it up, but that turned out not to be true. Until I asked Rand to sell *Secrets of the Emerald Tablet* for me." He walked around to face her. "He got ten thousand pounds."

She gasped. "Ten thousand pounds! Why...that's as much as my inheritance!"

"I know." Grabbing one rope, he stopped the swing and slid onto it. "It's amazing, isn't it? I suspect the buyer was Isaac Newton, since he'd pledged to double any other bid, but Rand told me the purchase was made on condition of anonymity."

"I wouldn't want anyone knowing I owned such a valuable thing, either." That much, at least, was the truth. "I expect it would make him a target for robbery."

"Perhaps." Raking a hand through his hair, Ford scooted closer, close enough to be in focus. He captured her gaze with those incredible blue eyes. "I hope this will change your mind."

"Ford, I'd already—"

"In a matter of months, Lakefield will be earning a goodly profit." He pushed off with both feet, setting the swing to swaying. "You can marry me now without fear that I'll spend your inheritance and rob you of your dream to publish."

As though battered by the back-and-forth motion, her heart hurt. "Is that what you thought? That I valued a philosophy book over you?"

Suddenly she could see where he could have inferred as much, and her shame escalated beyond bearing. Her throat tightened painfully.

"I would never put a book before you," she choked out. He hadn't valued a book over her, either. He'd sold his precious alchemy book to win her. "*Never*. It's just...well, I couldn't bring myself to believe anyone would want me for myself. It was my failing, not yours. I'm sorry."

Tears welled, and one rolled down her cheek.

She wasn't acting now.

He reached to wipe away the moisture, his fingers a warm

promise on her skin. "Don't cry," he said as the swing slowed to a halt. "Just say yes. Please. Marry me."

"I'd be honored," she whispered.

He caught her up in a hug so tight it threatened to crack her ribs. "I love you," he said. "Have I told you I love you?"

"Only about a million times." She laughed through her tears. "But I've neglected to tell you the same."

His eyes looked anxious. "I'm waiting."

She kissed him on the lips. "I love you, Ford Chase." His mouth felt warm and dear on hers, and she kissed him again, thrilled when he pulled her closer and deepened it.

She sank into the embrace. The blood thrummed through her veins as his kiss convinced her she was his—and his alone. She hadn't known it, but she'd been waiting for this all her life. This love, this trust, this acceptance of her as a woman.

There was that weakness again, those languid waves of pleasure flowing through her. That heat was building inside, that ache to take him into her and make him a part of her forever.

She wanted him. Here, now, today, tomorrow, for all time.

"I love you," she said again breathlessly when he finally pulled back. "And faith," she added with a shaky laugh, "I think I would've let you take me right here on this swing."

That devilish brow lifted. "We'll have to experiment with that sometime."

Not only would she not put it past him, she looked forward to it.

A smile curved his lips as he toyed with a lock of her hair. "Before you change your mind, I expect I should ask your father for your hand."

"Is that why you invited my whole family? Planning ahead?" she teased, reaching to his pocket for her spectacles. "All right, then. Just don't forget to shout."

## SIXTY-FIVE

"SIX MONTHS," Mum said after the congratulations and the hugs and the kisses. "It will take that long to arrange everything and allow people time to make plans to attend."

"Tomorrow," Ford countered loudly, evidently remembering Violet's instructions to shout.

"Tomorrow!" Rose snorted. "Madame Beaumont cannot make a wedding gown by tomorrow."

He turned to Violet. "Tell me you're not going to London to order a gown."

She shrugged. She was a newcomer to caring about fashion and knew nothing about planning events. "Three months?"

"One week."

At that point, Father pulled Mum aside for a whispered conversation. Mum's mouth fell open, and she nodded violently before turning back.

"Two weeks," she said, "and that's final."

~

*T*WO WEEKS LATER, Violet's wedding day had arrived, and she still wondered about her parents' whispered discussion in Lakefield's garden. She couldn't be sure, but she thought she'd heard the words "with child."

She'd been mortified at the time to find they suspected she'd shared Ford's bed, although between then and now she'd found herself a bit sad to learn she hadn't conceived.

Maybe this month, she thought with a secret smile as Margaret finished threading a pale blue ribbon in her hair. Truth be told, she couldn't wait to get back in his arms.

The two weeks since her betrothal had been excruciating. Odd how her parents had become so vigilant all of a sudden, when earlier they'd seemed so lax. She hadn't found more than five minutes alone with Ford at any one time. Barely time to steal a kiss, and she ached for so much more than that.

"Why are you smiling?" Rose asked, watching Violet's face in her dressing table mirror. "Brides are supposed to be nervous."

"I'm not," Violet told her. She wasn't nervous in the least. This marriage was so *right*. Her mother had been wrong to think Ford was too intellectual for her—so wrong she wondered if Mum might be losing her matchmaking touch.

When her maid left, she stood and turned to face her sisters.

"You look beautiful," Lily breathed.

Today, in her pale blue satin wedding gown, Violet *felt* beautiful. Still smiling to herself, she absently traced the pearls embroidered in scrolling designs on her stomacher. It no longer mattered that she would never be as pretty as either of her sisters. The man she loved wanted her, and that was all that counted.

"You should leave off your spectacles," Rose said. "At least for the ceremony."

"No." She wanted to see everything clearly, especially Ford's eyes when they exchanged vows. "Ford said I look fine in them. And I believe him."

"I told you that you should marry him." Though Rose's voice sounded gloating, Violet didn't care. "Just think, Violet," she continued, her tone changing to one of half awe, half envy. "Tonight you're going to learn the secrets of the *Master-piece*."

"Oh, Rose," Lily started, but then a knock came at the door and she went to answer it.

"A delivery," the majordomo said, holding out a long, flat box. "From Lord Lakefield to Lady Violet."

"Thank you, Parkinson." Lily shut the door and carried the small wooden box over to Violet. "What do you suppose it could be?"

"Jewelry, I'm sure," Rose said. "It's a wedding present, after all. A necklace, I'd wager, from the shape of the box. Maybe diamonds."

"I think not." Generous though he might be, Ford was focused on the estate these days, and Violet doubted he had enough of her ten thousand pounds left to feel comfortable spending money on diamonds.

The box was tied—very crookedly—with a purple ribbon Violet thought she remembered seeing in Jewel's hair. "Open it," Rose said, reaching for it. "I'm dying to see what he gave you."

Violet pushed her sister's hand away and untied the bow herself, then lifted the box's lid.

"A feather!" Lily exclaimed. A question lit her gorgeous blue eyes.

"A feather?" Rose's lovely brow creased in a puzzled frown. "What kind of wedding present is that?"

Her heart suddenly racing, Violet shrugged and hid another smile. She already knew the secrets of the *Master-piece*, but it was obvious her sisters didn't.

## SIXTY-SIX

*A*S EVENING FELL, it began raining. Violet stood with Ford and her family within Trentingham's covered portico, watching the last of the guests sprint to their carriages while she waited to say goodbye to her father.

"It was a nice wedding," Mum said, "wasn't it?"

Violet sighed. "I can hardly remember it."

"Perhaps you've had too much champagne?" That hint of the devil was in Ford's eyes. "I remember it perfectly. A rather solemn ceremony, right here in Trentingham's chapel." It hadn't been solemn at all. Violet's lips twitched as he continued. "I have lingering impressions of much Tudor woodwork and jewel-toned stained glass, with my beautiful bride a glorious vision in blue."

Lily giggled. She'd definitely had too much champagne. "I cannot believe so many people showed up with only two weeks' notice! All of Father's friends from Parliament, and your friends from the Royal Society—"

"And everyone Mum knows," Rose cut in. She was *still* drinking champagne. "Which means everyone who lives within a twenty-mile radius."

Ignoring her middle daughter, Mum smiled at Ford. "You have very nice friends."

Although Violet would swear her mother had once referred to Ford's friends as "that odd group of scientists," today she'd seemed to hang on their every word. "I saw you chatting with Mr. Hooke's 'housekeeper,'" she teased her.

"I enjoyed chatting with Rand," Rose said dreamily, taking another sip. "And dancing with him."

Rand had danced with Lily more often, but apparently Rose hadn't noticed. Meeting Lily's guilty gaze, Violet decided to hold her tongue on that subject. "I think at least two hundred people tried on my spectacles. My face hurts from smiling."

Making sympathetic noises, Ford pulled her close. "My poor wife," he said, kissing her softly.

"Ewww." Rowan made a face. "More kisses."

Everyone laughed. Earlier, Jewel had informed Rowan her Aunty Cait said kissing was encouraged at weddings, then planted one smack on his lips. Violet had never seen anyone turn quite so red as her brother.

"Here we are," Father announced, coming out with a footman bearing the last of Violet's trunks. He kissed her on the cheek. "I hope we'll still see you around here."

"Oh, it's time," Mum said with a sniffle, and wrapped her in a hug.

Rose drained the last of her champagne. "I want a full report on your wedding night. Tomorrow."

"Oh, Rose," Violet said with a groan. But she kissed her anyway. Tearing up, she gathered Lily and Rowan close.

"Enough," Ford said. "Any more of this, and you'll all turn to mush and be washed away by the rain."

He grabbed Violet's hand, and they made a dash for the carriage. She barely had time to lift her skirts before he grabbed her by the waist to swing her up and inside.

"I thought we'd never get out of there," he complained as the door shut behind them and he dragged her into his arms. She'd been dying to be alone with him, too, and when he crushed his lips to hers, his kiss was hot and wild and wonderful. That delicious heat started spiraling through her.

But when the carriage lurched to begin the short, jarring journey to her new home, they bumped noses and then teeth. She laughed, smiling up at him as she snuggled closer.

Rain beat on the carriage's roof, a soothing tattoo that made her feel even more warm and cozy and protected by her new husband.

"I've decided," Ford said, "that rain brings me luck."

"Because it sent everyone home early?"

"That, too," he said cryptically.

She felt entirely too drained to figure out what he meant. For a woman who preferred not to be the center of attention, the day had proved both exhilarating and exhausting. "Mum was right. It was a nice wedding."

"You can thank me for that. I extracted Colin's vow, under pain of death, there would be no pranks."

"He wouldn't," she protested. "Not at a wedding."

"I can see you don't yet know my brother. Ask Kendra and Caithren about *their* weddings sometime."

"I will," she said, very much looking forward to that. "I like your family."

"I was sure they'd scare you away. They're loud, and meddlesome—"

"And they love you."

"I know," he said. "And now that I've married you, I'm hoping they'll approve of me, too."

She didn't quite understand what he meant by that either, but it sounded like something better discussed another time.

A few minutes passed in companionable silence. Then his arm tightened around her shoulders, and his voice turned low and velvet-edged. "Have you brought the feather?"

She'd spent the entire day thinking about that feather. Her heart suddenly pounding, she reached into her bodice and pulled it out, its satiny edges tickling between her breasts as the length of it slid free.

His eyes widened, and a grin spread on his face. He took the plume and tickled her nose, then pressed a slow kiss to the top of her head. A kiss so cherishing, she felt tears spring to her eyes.

"Oh, Ford," she whispered, holding him closer, breathing in his heady patchouli scent. He trailed the feather across her lips and down the length of her neck, swirling it on the skin exposed by her wedding gown's low décolletage.

She shivered, remembering his words. *I'm going to save that for our wedding night.* And then she shuddered, a luxurious shudder she felt clear down to her toes.

His smile now was pure male as he used the feather to tilt up her chin. "Darling, is that ardor I'm detecting?"

Later, she wouldn't remember how she made it into the house. She wouldn't remember how she came to be unclothed. She wouldn't remember how she ended up on that towering four-poster bed now hung with new blue brocade.

But she would never, in her entire life, forget the feel of the feather she'd been anticipating all the long day of her wedding.

He had that feather dancing over every inch of her body, brushing, grazing, skimming, raising gooseflesh, and igniting delicious shivers. Her sensitized skin prickled with pleasure, yet the physical sensations paled compared to the love that swelled in her heart. Captured in his intimate gaze, she felt a sense of belonging she'd never imagined possible.

That ache was building, that hot ache that made her yearn for him to complete her. When the feather had kissed every part of her but there where the ache was centered, Ford dropped it and closed his eyes, lowering his mouth to meet hers.

This kiss was a promise, a vow, more binding than any words they'd recited in the chapel. She sank into its velvet warmth, savoring its wordless pledge. And when it turned demanding and hungry, the thrill of it sang through her veins, making her breath catch and her heart stutter and restart, then race in response to his fervor.

When he broke the kiss, she released a long, languid sigh. He kissed the corner of her mouth. He kissed her chin and her cheeks. He kissed his way lower. Rain pattered against the window as his mouth worshipped her body, a damp trail of kisses that touched every place the feather had touched earlier.

Every place but where she most wanted him.

He kissed her shoulders, her breasts, her rib cage, rolling her over to make certain no inch of flesh went unadored. His lips traced her spine, moving lower. He nipped her toes, his tongue flicking at her arches.

Her fingers clutched at the sheets, and she heard little moans and realized they were hers. Rolling her to her back once again, he kissed his way up her calves, her knees, urging her thighs apart to rain their delicate skin with more kisses. So close to where she ached to have him join her.

When he paused, her eyes flew open. She looked down to find his head was raised, and he was measuring her with that deep blue gaze. In the sudden stillness, her breath sounded harsh, her heartbeat unnaturally loud. He reached once more for the feather…

And then slowly, slowly traced it down the cleft where she ached.

And again.

The strokes were gossamer, the sensations ethereal, tantalizingly exquisite. She bit her lip to keep from crying out, squirming under the assault, throwing her head back in wild abandon. Again and again, and the heat was spreading, every nerve in her body alive, tingling, aroused nearly beyond bearing.

The storm intensified, both outdoors and within her. Rain slashed against the windows as he tossed the plume and replaced it with his tongue—a shocking caress, so hot and slick and intimate she thought she might die, might simply expire from a surfeit of sensation. It was building, that urgent sweetness, that raging desire. It seemed to be lifting her up toward the heavens.

A flash of lightning was followed by a rumble that matched the thundering of her pulse. Her entire world centered on where he was licking and suckling, and then, when she was certain her heart would burst from pleasure, he slipped a finger inside her, too, and she rocketed into the clouds.

It was a long, long fall back down. Plunging, spinning, tumbling, until at last she found herself grounded and back in his arms. For long moments she lay there, waiting for her heart to slow, her breathing to calm.

And then, starting over with the feather, she did to him all the things he'd done to her.

Ford inhaled her sweet scent, the essence of Violet. She smelled of flowers and desire, and every touch of the plume, every brush of her fingers and lips made him more certain of the rightness of them together. Her brandy-wine eyes were glazed, flooded with passion, and an answering passion flooded his heart. A depth of wanting he'd never even imagined.

It was the difference between mere lust and true love. The difference that made his blood pump when before it had only flowed. The difference that aroused him nearly to the point of pain.

The difference that made her his.

Her mouth on him was sweet and hot, and he shuddered beneath her, her tender onslaught robbing him of his wits and his breath. And when at last he couldn't stand any more, and he drew away and covered her with his body and slid into her welcoming warmth, he knew he was home. Home was wherever Violet was, and Violet was right here.

He shifted slowly within her, forcing himself to hold back, wanting to give her all the pleasure she was giving him. But her hands on his hips urged him on. And when he felt her peak for a second time, his heart gloried as he went with her.

For a very long time, he held her in his arms, kissing her hair and drawing in its sweet scent. He didn't want to let go, didn't want to move, didn't want to break the spell. Usually one to turn over and go to sleep, he decided she must have enchanted him.

"I have a wedding present for you," she said softly.

"Damnation." The moment lost, he kissed her again, then sat up against the headboard. "I have nothing for *you*."

"You sent me the feather, remember? And the ring is more than enough." She smiled at it in the candlelight. Like Violet, it was simple: one large, rectangular amethyst with a row of small diamonds flanking each side. "It sparkles so," she said. "It's the prettiest ring I've ever seen."

"A violet-colored gem for Violet. Amy made it. Especially for you."

"But she'd only met me the once!"

"I think she captured you perfectly, though."

"She did." Still smiling, she dropped her hand. "Let me get your gift."

When she slid from the bed and walked across the room, all he could think was that Violet undressed was the most beautiful thing he'd ever seen. Gorgeous breasts rose above a curvy waist his hands itched to span. Flared hips led to long, shapely legs. Who'd ever have guessed all that was hidden beneath her plain gowns?

"Stop," he said. "Right there."

"What?" Her eyes darted furtively around. "Is there another hairy spider?"

"No." He laughed. "I just wanted to look at you. You're perfect."

"I am not." Self-consciously she folded her arms across her breasts. "I'm neither tall like Rose, nor petite like Lily. Neither plump nor slender."

"Exactly. You're perfect. Now, what have you brought me?"

"Just this." Slipping back into the bed, she handed him a package wrapped in fabric, gathered and tied with ribbons on both ends.

He felt its shape. "A book? For a wedding present?"

"Just open it." She grinned, looking so excited he thought if he didn't hurry, his beautiful, naked wife might actually bounce on the bed.

He pulled off the ribbons, letting the fabric fall open.

And the breath left his body.

He stared down at it a moment, then raised his gaze to meet hers. "*Secrets of the Emerald Tablet.* How—how did you get this?"

"I bought it. With my inheritance."

"From Newton?"

"From you."

He pushed it into her hands. "Give it back. I won't have you sacrificing your own dreams for this book. I've already given it up, and I'm not sorry for the bargain." His voice sounded rough to his own ears, and he forced himself to gentle it. "It's not that I'm ungrateful, my love. It's just that—"

"No. You're not understanding. *I* bought it, Ford. In the first place. Rand told me you'd instructed him to sell it, and I couldn't allow that to happen. I couldn't let you sacrifice your prized possession just to convince me of your love."

His heart squeezed painfully in his chest. It was a moment before words would come, and when they finally did, he had only three.

"I love you."

## SIXTY-SEVEN

$\mathcal{I}$T WASN'T THE first morning Ford had awakened with a woman in his bed, but it was the first time with Violet. The first time that really counted.

At first he just lay there a while, watching the rise and fall of her breathing, enjoying the color he'd put in her cheeks, her lips still rosy from their middle-of-the-night encounters. Finally, unable to help himself, he reached out, brushing the side of her face with the backs of his fingers.

"Ford?"

"Hush, my sweet. Sleep."

With a sigh, he rose so she could do so. Quietly he padded to the washbasin and splashed his face, then reached for a towel.

He stared at himself in the mirror.

What kind of a man was he? He'd thought he was doing the right thing, the responsible thing, when he'd sold the book to save Lakefield. He'd been so pleased with himself when he'd managed to make his home livable and still have money left to last for a while until the estate could turn a profit. It was the first time in his life he hadn't spent every shilling the moment he laid hands on it.

Last night, when Violet returned the book, he'd been stunned and thrilled to discover the depth of her love and generosity. But as he studied himself this morning, reality set in.

Bloody hell, her money had paid for everything. And would continue to pay their expenses for the next few months, at least.

He closed his eyes, guilt battering his newfound happiness. Never mind that he was accustomed to living hand to mouth, he was now a married man. Shouldn't he be the provider?

Society said not necessarily, but his heart told him yes. Especially because he'd been telling Violet that all along.

Straightening, he looked in the mirror again and ordered himself to come to terms with it. Like it or not, his new wife had been his anonymous benefactor. At this point, all he could do was resolve to work hard, and not in his laboratory. Instead, on his land and in his study—he would do whatever it took to make sure his renovated estate proved successful.

As he tossed the towel to the washstand, his gaze fell on *Secrets of the Emerald Tablet*. He would ask Rand—the scheming bastard—to resume the translation, too. But he would no longer depend on an ancient book to rescue him. Gold wasn't waiting at the end of rainbows. Or in an alchemy crucible, either.

Someday, somehow, he would provide Violet with the funds to publish her book. But the way it looked now, he thought with a resigned sigh, "someday" was far in the future.

A knock came at the bedroom door. He hurried into his breeches and went to answer it.

"Will you be wanting breakfast, milord?"

He looked from Hilda to Violet. "In an hour," he whispered. "My wife is still abed."

*My wife.* His heart swelled at hearing his own words.

"She'll wake, will she not? It's hot and ready now. Eggs and cheese. This new French cook certainly is fancy." Hilda shoved a heavy tray into his hands. "Your mail is there, too."

Openmouthed, he watched her sway down the corridor before he shut the door. "If I cannot control my servants," he muttered, "how will I deal with my children?"

"You never did manage to control Jewel."

"Too true." He turned and put the tray on the bed. "You're awake."

"And famished." Violet struggled to sit and spooned up a bite of the rich dish, puffed from oven baking and redolent with the scent of sharp Italian cheese.

He sat beside her and sipped coffee from a steaming cup. Setting it down, he took the first letter and snapped open the seal.

"'Dear Lord Lakefield,'" he read aloud, thinking it might be a congratulatory note on their wedding. "'I am writing on behalf of my client, Daniel Quare, Watchmaker, who is very interested in buying the rights to produce your patented watch. Please find enclosed a contract—'" He looked up. "What the devil…?"

Violet's face was pure white. "Oh my. They've responded. I gave them two weeks, and it's been way over that, so—"

"You gave them two weeks to what?"

"To agree to buy your watch before I took my offer else-where. Your offer, I mean." Some color rushed back into her cheeks. "I signed your name."

His wife was obviously confused from lack of sleep. "I haven't patented my watch, darling. I haven't even shown it to the Royal Society yet—"

"*I* patented it. I wrote to Christopher Wren and asked for instructions. I remembered him saying he'd patented a device for writing with two pens at once."

"You sold my watch?" It was all beginning to click into place. Shaking his head in disbelief, he scanned farther down the page. His heart stopped. "You sold my watch for twenty thousand pounds? *Twenty* thousand pounds!"

His heart had started again, but it was about to hammer right through his ribs.

"Twenty thousand?" She grabbed the letter from him. "Is that all they've offered?" she said, sounding disgusted.

"All? All! Violet, it's twice the amount of your inheritance!"

She looked up from the page. "But I asked for twenty-five. What makes them think they can get away with a contract for twenty?"

He started laughing. And laughing. "T-t-t-twenty-five," he forced out. "You asked for twenty-five."

"And royalties. Was it not enough?" she asked. "I know your design is revolutionary, but I thought twenty-five thousand pounds was…well, you're worth more than that, of course. You're priceless."

"*You're* priceless," he said. "Give me back that contract."

"You're not going to sign it, are you? I hope not. They didn't offer enough. We need to negotiate."

"Oh, I'm signing it, Violet." To make certain she wouldn't stop him, he rolled the paper and stuck it in his breeches. "I wasn't planning to do anything with the watch, remember? Thanks to you, I'm about to be a wealthy man."

Thanks to his ambitious, practical, intelligent wife—a woman who embodied all the things he'd once thought unimportant in a female—"someday" had just come a lot sooner than he'd ever dreamed.

His mind raced with plans. "I can sink more money into Lakefield or buy a second estate. Or both." He grinned. "I can finance the publication of my brilliant wife's book."

She cracked a small smile, a smile that stole his heart. "Do you suppose that can wait a while?" she asked. "I'm hoping to raise some children first, with your help."

She made him happy. Damn, he was happy. Happy with his wife, happy with his life.

"Hmm," he said, watching her speculatively. "I believe we'll have to *make* those children first."

And lowering his lips to hers, he poured all his love into a kiss.

# EPILOGUE

*Seven months later*

*V*IOLET WAS READING in bed when Ford burst into the chamber. "I've just had a message from Jason. Cait is delivering their babe, and the family is gathering at Cainewood to celebrate. If we leave soon enough, you may even witness the birthing."

"That would be nice," she said dreamily, toying absently with the cover of her book.

"What's that?" He walked closer. "*Aristotle's Master-piece* again? Surely there's nothing in there you still don't understand." His lips curved in a suggestive half-smile. "If so, I'd be willing to give you more lessons."

She sat up against the headboard and grinned. "I'm thinking I could give *you* lessons by now. But I'm suddenly interested in this particular chapter. Listen." She patted the bed beside her and waited for him to sit. "'Signs taken from the woman are these. The first day she feels a light quivering or chillness running through the whole body; a tickling in the womb, a little pain in the lower part of the belly—'"

"What the devil?"

"Just listen." She turned the page. "'Ten or twelve days after, the head is affected with giddiness, the eyes with dimness of sight—'"

"Violet—"

"'—the breasts swell and grow hard, with some pain and prickling in them'"—smiling to herself, she pulled off her spectacles—"'the belly soon sinketh, and riseth again by degrees, with a hardness about the navel.'" Though her husband's breathing was sounding a bit ragged, she kept reading. "'The nipples of the breast grow red, the heart beats inordinately, the natural appetite is dejected, yet she has a longing desire for—'"

Ford's hand clenched her arm. "What's the title of this chapter?"

She turned back to the previous page. "'Of the Signs of Conception.'"

When she looked up, his heart was in his shining blue eyes. "Does this mean…?"

"Yes," she whispered. "I hope you're pleased."

And a heartbeat later, he gathered her into his arms, telling her without words just how very pleased he was.

Apparently being with child had some effect on her responses. When his mouth met hers, her head was affected with giddiness, and a delicious heat started spiraling through her, making her heart beat inordinately. His hands went to her breasts, and she felt some swelling and prickling…

*Wait*, she thought, with what little sense she had left. He always made her feel those things.

*Always.*

They were going to be late to Cainewood.

~

**DEAR READER,**

It goes without saying that Ford didn't invent frames to hold spectacles on the face—credit for that goes to a London optician named Edward Scarlett, who came up with the idea in 1730. The first spectacles for reading were made in the late 13th century (and the first ones for distance about 300 years later), but before Scarlett's innovation they were simply held to the face or balanced on the nose—momentarily helpful, but not something one could wear all day long. I like to think that if Ford Chase had really lived, he'd have been brilliant enough to invent eyeglass frames half a century earlier.

Although the minute hand began appearing on watches around 1675, it's not clear who managed it first. Obviously someone missed a chance at a profitable patent! Everyone agrees the two-handed watch was developed in England, but some historians claim that Daniel Quare was the first to sell such a timepiece, while some say it was Thomas Tompion or others. But what *does* seem to be clear is that the minute hand was made possible by Robert Hooke's 1660 invention of the spiral spring, which brought watches from a totally unpredictable performance to within two or three minutes' accuracy a day.

A true genius, Robert Hooke did much more than revolutionize timekeeping; he also made important contributions in chemistry, meteorology, astronomy, and physics. Other scientists of the time are much revered today, including Isaac Newton, Christopher Wren, and Robert Boyle. Yet Hooke has been largely forgotten. Newton and Wren were both knighted, so why not

Hooke, arguably a greater scientist? In 2003, Gresham College marked the 300th year of Hooke's death by a series of lectures designed to resurrect his reputation.

Gresham College has provided free public lectures in London for over 400 years. Over time, it's occupied several different locations. The lectures currently take place at Barnard's Inn Hall, in a building that dates from the late 14th century. To see the upcoming schedule, visit the college's website at www.gresham. ac.uk.

The Royal Society really was welcomed back to Gresham College in 1673, "with six quarts of each of canary, of Rhenish wine and of claret, and with fine cakes, macaroons and marchpanes," as the City Archives describe an account of their entertainment. But the actual date of the celebration was Monday, December 1. I took the liberty of tweaking history a bit in moving the event to the warm summertime, so Ford could decorate the piazza. All of the people I mentioned at the ball were members at the time, including John Evelyn, best known for his diary that has given us a window into the Restoration period, and John Locke, whose ideas were a powerful influence on the subsequent history of the Western world. Thomas Jefferson called Locke one of "the three greatest men that have ever lived, without any exception," and drew heavily on his writings in drafting the Declaration of Independence.

Along with these men of note, I enjoyed bringing Hooke and the other scientists—and yes, alchemists—to life. Although the mere idea of making gold from base metals is a laughable one today, up until the mid-18th century it was considered a serious science. During the 1600s, most of the luminaries of the day practiced alchemy, King Charles included. Ironically, it was his chartering of the Royal Society that eventually led to alchemy's decline. In that ordered environment, modern chemistry and the new scientific methods taught men to free themselves from the old traditions and question theories that had prevailed for centuries.

Although I invented the title *Secrets of the Emerald Tablet*, Alexander the Great did claim to have discovered the Emerald Tablet in the tomb of the legendary Hermes, and medieval alchemist Raymond Lully was said to have written a treatise about it that subsequently disappeared. No one knows the title, however, and although other writings attributed to Lully survive, that particular one was never found.

A combination sex manual and advice to midwives, *Aristotle's Master-piece* first appeared in the late 1600s and by the turn of the century was a veritable bestseller—likely to be found in any newlywed couple's home. All of the words Violet and Ford read were actual passages from the book. Reflecting the attitudes of the time, this book presented sex as an act of pleasure without sin or guilt. In later years, of course, society became much more strait-laced about such matters, yet the *Master-piece* saw count-less reprintings up until about 1900.

As usual, the homes I used in this story were based on real ones that you can visit. Though I moved it to the Thames, Lake-field House was loosely modeled on Snowshill Manor in Gloucestershire. Snowshill was owned by Winchcombe Abbey from the year 821 until the reign of Henry VIII in the 16th century, when, with the dissolution of the monasteries, it passed to the Crown. Thereafter it had many owners and tenants until 1919, when a man named Charles Paget Wade returned from the First World War and found it for sale. The house was derelict, the garden an overgrown jumble of weeds, including—of course!—a sundial. Wade bought Snowshill and restored it, removing the plaster ceilings, moving partitions back to their original places, unblocking fireplaces, and fitting Tudor paneling to many of the rooms to recapture the original atmosphere. He scorned the use of electricity and modern conveniences, so the house appears today much as it would have during Ford's time. Wade never lived in the house, instead using it to showcase his amazing collection of everyday and curious objects, literally thousands of items including musical instruments, clocks, toys, bicycles, weavers' and spinners' tools, and Japanese armor. The home is now owned by the National Trust and open April through October to view the house and collection.

Trentingham Manor was inspired by another National Trust property, The Vyne in Hampshire (which I also relocated to sit on the banks of the Thames). Built in the early 16th century for Lord Sandys, Henry VIII's Lord Chamberlain, the house acquired a classical portico in the mid-17th century (the first of its kind in England) and contains a grand Palladian staircase, a wealth of old paneling and fine furniture, and a fascinating Tudor chapel with Renaissance glass. The Vyne and its extensive gardens are also open for visits April through October.

I hope you enjoyed *Never Doubt a Viscount!* For a chance to revisit Ford and Violet, look for *The Scandal of Lord Randal,* the next book in my *Chase Family Series.* Please read on for an excerpt!

Always,

Lauren Royal

Read on for an excerpt from

# The *Scandal* of *Lord Randal*

Book 6 of the
*Chase Family Series*
by Lauren Royal

**Lily Ashcroft fell for dashing Oxford professor Lord Randal Nesbitt at sixteen. Four years later, her older sister Rose wants him—and with two sisters locked in a tempestuous love triangle, scandal can only be around the corner...**

~

*Trentingham Manor, the South of England*
*August 1677*

**HE'D FORGOTTEN** about her.

Well, maybe he hadn't quite forgotten about her, but he'd certainly put her out of his mind.

Well, maybe he hadn't quite put her out of his mind, but he'd known she was only sixteen. And sixteen was too young, so, being the sort of man he was—an honorable one, or so he liked to think—he'd made a conscious decision not to pursue her.

For the four long years since their last meeting, whenever thoughts of Lily Ashcroft had sneaked into Lord Randal Nesbitt's head, he'd reminded himself she was only sixteen.

But now, Rand realized with a start, she must be twenty.

Focused as Rand was, the priest's voice, reciting the baptism service, barely penetrated his thoughts. Nor did the wiggling month-old child in Rand's arms. Instead of looking at the altar, he gazed at Lily standing beside him in her family's oak-paneled chapel, her sister's other twin baby held close.

Twenty. A lovely dark-haired, blue-eyed twenty. A marriageable twenty.

In all of Rand's twenty-eight years, he'd never really considered marriage, so the notion was jarring.

"Having now," the priest continued, "in the name of these children, made these promises, wilt thou also on thy part take heed that these children learn the Creed, the Lord's Prayer, and the Ten Commandments, and all other things which a Christian ought to know and believe to his soul's health?"

"I will, by God's help," Lily replied softly. Gently, gazing down at the babe in her arms.

Rand was unsurprised. In four years she had changed, of course. But her gentleness, that innate sweetness, hadn't changed. Couldn't have changed. It was what made her Lily.

Ford Chase, Rand's friend—and father of the children in question—elbowed him in the ribs.

"Hmm?" Startled, Rand looked down to the lad he was holding, its bald little head patterned with colors made by sun streaming through the chapel's stained-glass windows. Ford's child, he thought, surprised by a rush of tenderness. Rand's godchild...or at least the tiny babe and his twin sister would be his godchildren once they managed to get through this interminable service.

"I will," he answered, echoing Lily's words and vaguely wondering what he'd just agreed to.

"By God's help," the priest prompted.

"By God's help."

God help him get through this ritual. Mass, and then a lesson, and now this ceremony at the font—Rand felt like he'd been standing on his feet forever. Delivering a two-hour lecture at Oxford wasn't nearly this exhausting. He feared his knees were locked permanently.

He wanted this to be over. He wanted to talk to Lily. Never mind that she'd barely noticed him. He'd arrived at the last minute and had no chance to greet her before this rigmarole all began.

The priest turned a page in his *Book of Common Prayer*. "Wilt thou take heed that these children, so soon as sufficiently instructed, be brought to the bishop to be confirmed by him?"

"I will." Rand and Lily said the words together this time. Their voices, he thought, sounded good together.

"Name these children."

The child squirmed in Rand's arms, choosing then to begin wailing. "Marcus Cicero Chase," Rand bellowed over the cries.

"Rebecca Ashcroft Chase," Lily said more softly and with a smile, even though the girl's cry had joined her twin brother's, seeming to fill the chapel all the way up to its sculpted Tudor ceiling.

Whoever would have thought such small infants could make such a huge racket?

The priest rushed to finish, scooping water into his hand. It trickled through his fingers, running in rivulets down the backs of the two babies' heads and landing on the colorful glazed tile floor. "I baptize thee in the name of the Father, and of the Son, and of the Holy Ghost." He muttered some more words and made crosses on the children's foreheads. "Amen."

Amen. It was over. Well-wishers crowded close. Still holding his squalling godson, Rand turned to Lily.

She was gone.

How could she have disappeared so quickly? Using his height to advantage, he peered over heads. But she'd vanished.

Nearby, Ford held tiny Rebecca and was chatting with an older man. Lily's father, if Rand remembered right. Or rather, Ford was shouting at the man, since the Earl of Trentingham was hard of hearing.

Marveling that his tall, masculine friend looked so comfortable holding an infant, Rand shifted little Marc uneasily. Rebecca had stopped crying, apparently content in Ford's arms, but in Rand's arms, her twin brother still howled.

Glancing around for help, Rand was relieved to see Ford's wife, Violet, moving close. When she reached for her son, Rand gave her a grateful smile. But then he found himself oddly reluctant to hand Marc over. The babe might be loud, but he smelled sweet and had a pleasant, warm weight.

When Violet took him, Marc quieted immediately. Resisting the urge to run his fingers over that fuzzy little head, Rand leaned a hand on one of the intricate carved oak stalls. "I assume you chose his name, Marcus Cicero, for the philosopher."

Violet bounced the lad in her arms, her brown curls bouncing along with him. She looked more motherly than Rand usually pictured her. Did children change people so much? "It was only fair," she said. "Ford had the naming of our firstborn."

"Nicky? Ah, Nicolas Copernicus," Rand remembered. "Well, I suppose it's a better name than Galileo Galilei."

"Ford's other scientific hero?" She laughed, her brown eyes sparkling with humor behind the spectacles Ford had made for her. "Even *he* wouldn't saddle a good English child with Galileo for a name."

"And Rebecca? Who is she named after?"

"No one. I just like it. And there's never been a major female philosopher."

"Yet," Rand added, knowing Violet hoped to publish a philosophy book of her own someday.

"Yet," she confirmed with a nod, clearly appreciating his support. She touched her husband's arm, claiming his attention. "We'd best be heading home," she said when he turned, "or our guests will arrive there before us."

When Ford smiled at her, Violet's return smile transformed her face. Perhaps she wasn't as beautiful as her sisters, Lily and Rose, but she was attractive in her own, unique way, and it had nothing to do with the magnificent purple gown she'd donned for the baptism.

Moreover, it was obvious she made Ford happy. A sort of happiness that glowed from his eyes whenever he looked at her. A sort of happiness neither Rand nor Ford had dreamed of back in the days they attended university together.

It was frightening how much the man had changed.

Ford still held his new daughter, her tiny fist tangled in his long brown hair. Unable to resist this time, Rand skimmed his fingers over Rebecca's dark curls. "So soft," he murmured.

Violet nodded. "All babies are soft."

"I haven't touched a baby since I was a very small child myself."

"Really?" She looked surprised to hear that. "Well, someday you'll have children of your own."

"Perhaps," he allowed. "My favorite truism is 'never say never.' But God willing, should it happen, it won't be too soon."

Her laugh tinkled through the nearly empty chapel. "We really must be going."

"Come along, Rand," Ford said. "I want to show you the water closet I built. It's much better than the ones imported from France."

A smile curved Rand's lips as he followed them out the door. It seemed his friend hadn't changed that much, after all.

**"WHAT?"** LILY laughed as her friend Judith Carrington pulled her toward a carriage. "What's so important you couldn't wait until we got to Violet's house to tell me? So important you made me almost drop my niece, not to mention nearly dislocated my arm dragging me out of there?"

Before climbing inside, Lily waved at her parents and sister Rose, lest they think she'd abandoned them. Hers was a handsome family, she thought suddenly. Her father was tall and trim, his eyes a deep green, his real hair still as jet-black as the periwig he wore for his grandchildren's baptism. Her mother and Rose were both dark-haired and statuesque. They looked elegant in their best satin gowns, Mum's a gleaming gold and Rose's a rich, shimmering blue.

Looking at them, one would never guess they were so eccentric.

Her mother waved back distractedly, holding her two-year-old grandson, Nicky, as she busily ushered guests out the door to their waiting transportation.

Feeling Judith's hand on her back, Lily laughed again and

lifted her peach silk skirts to duck inside the carriage. "What?" she repeated.

"Oh, just this." Even though they weren't ready to leave, Judith pulled the door shut. Then she settled herself with a flounce. "I'm betrothed."

"Betrothed?" Lily blinked at her friend. "As in you're planning to wed?"

"Well, Mama is doing the planning. But it's ever so exciting. Come October, I'm going to be a married woman. Can you believe it, Lily?"

"No, I cannot believe it." The third of her friends to marry this year. Yesterday they'd been children; now suddenly they were supposed to be all grown-up. "Who will be your groom?" Lily asked.

"Lord Grenville. Didn't your mother tell you she'd suggested he offer for my hand? Father says it's a brilliant match."

Grenville was wealthy, but thirty-five years old to Judith's twenty. "Do you love him?" Lily wondered aloud. She hoped so. Judith was plump and pretty, but even more important, she was genuinely nice. A good friend who deserved happiness.

"I barely know him. But Mama assures me we'll grow to love each other—or get along tolerably, at least." The excitement faded from Judith's blue eyes, replaced with a tinge of anxiety. Her fingers worried the embroidery on her aqua underskirt. "It will all work out fine, I'm sure of it."

"I'm sure of it, too," Lily soothed, reaching across to take her friend's cold, pale hand. She squeezed, wishing she were as certain as she sounded. Lily's parents had promised their daughters they could choose their own husbands, but she knew it didn't work that way for most young women.

Her family was different. The Ashcroft motto—*Interroga Conformationem*, translated as Question Convention—said it all.

The Carringtons, on the other hand, were as conventional as roast goose on Christmas Day. Judith forced a smile and pushed back a lock of bright yellow hair that had escaped her careful coiffure. "Who was that handsome man who stood as godfather?"

Lily sat back. "One of Ford's old friends. Lord Randal Nesbitt."

"Wouldn't it be fun to be newly wedded together, have babies together?" Some of the color returned to Judith's cheeks. "You should marry *him*."

"Wherever did you get that idea?" Lily crossed her arms over the long, stiff stomacher that covered the laces on the front of her gown. "I barely know Rand."

"Rand," Judith repeated significantly, making it clear she'd noticed Lily's familiar use of the name. "What does that matter? I hardly know Lord Grenville, either. And believe me, he doesn't look at me the way *Rand* was looking at you."

"Looking at me?" Lily echoed weakly. She'd hardly looked at him at all. She'd been focused on the cooing baby in her arms, her sister's first daughter. Her first niece. Nicky was great fun, of course, but now she'd have a little girl to play house with, to fix her hair, to—

"Lord, he didn't take his eyes off you the entire time." Judith's lips curved in an impish grin. "Watching him was certainly more entertaining than the baptism."

Lily felt her face heat and wondered if Judith could be right— if instead of watching the ceremony, everyone had been watching Rand watch her.

But surely that hadn't been the case. Why would Rand be interested in *her*? The two of them had nothing in common. Her friend had seen something that wasn't there. "You just have the wedding fever," she said lightly, rubbing the faint scars on the back of her hand. "Besides, if he's interested in anyone, I'm sure it's Rose. They share a passion for languages."

"Ah," Judith said with a smug tilt of her pert nose. "You know more about the man than you're willing to admit."

Ignoring that, Lily leaned to look out the window. But there was a long queue of carriages. They were going nowhere.

"Who's that?" her friend asked, following her line of sight. "The girl in pink, coming out of the barn with your brother?"

"That's Jewel, Ford's niece. Rowan and she have been friends forever."

"What sort of friends? And what do you suppose they were doing alone together in a barn?"

"Goodness, Rowan is only eleven and Jewel ten. Your mind is too much on romance these days. Knowing the two, they were probably planning a prank."

"In a *barn?*"

Lily laughed at the expression on her friend's face. "Over the years, there's hardly a building on either property they haven't used to stage a prank."

Judith looked likely to say more, but the door popped open and her mother poked her head in. "Were you leaving without me, dear?"

"Of course not, Mama." Judith scooted over to make room. "We just came inside to talk."

A large, jolly woman, Lady Carrington wedged herself beside her daughter and tucked in her voluminous coral skirts. Before her footman could shut the door, Lily's striped cat nimbly leapt inside.

Lady Carrington sneezed. "Shoo!" she exclaimed, waving a manicured hand at the hapless feline.

"Beatrix," Lily said softly, "you cannot ride in this carriage."

The cat gave her a hurt look but leapt out.

"Much better," Judith's mother said as the door shut. She turned to Lily. "This afternoon, I'm hoping your father will advise me about flowers for Judith's wedding."

The Earl of Trentingham was nothing if not an expert on flowers. "I'm certain Father will fancy being consulted," Lily assured her.

The carriage began moving at last. "I've my heart set on yellow flowers," Lady Carrington told Lily, "because Judith looks best in yellow. But she wants to be married in blue. What color will you wear for your wedding?"

"Blue is nice," Lily said with a vague smile.

She wasn't ready to think about weddings, and most certainly not her own.

Rose was a year older—her wedding should come first.

∼

**AVAILABLE NOW!**
**Learn more about *The Scandal of Lord Randal* at**
**www.LaurenRoyal.com**

# ENTER FOR A CHANCE TO WIN
## a sterling silver filigree heart pendant like the one Ford gives Jewel in this book!*

Visit the Contest page on Lauren's website
at www.LaurenRoyal.com
and answer a question to be
entered in the monthly drawing.

No purchase necessary. See complete rules on the site.

*Please note: Depending on when you enter, the prize may be another piece of jewelry associated with one of Lauren's books. The author reserves the right to discontinue this promotion at any time.

# ABOUT LAUREN ROYAL

**LAUREN ROYAL** is a *New York Times* and *USA Today* bestselling author of humorous historical romance. Her "truly enchanting" novels have won many awards including *Booklist*'s "Top 10 Romance of the Year" and earned raves from reviewers including *Publishers Weekly*, who calls her "an impressive talent."

All of Lauren's books are complete, stand-alone stories, and yet they are also all connected—because they all feature her beloved "outrageously funny, loyal, compassionate, and unconventional" Chase family.

Lauren writes steamy historical romance on her own and sweet/clean historical romance with her daughter, Devon Royal. She lives in Southern California with her family, their constantly shedding cat, and a stupendous collection of fuzzy socks. When she's not busy writing, she enjoys singing along (off-key) to Hamilton, dancing (badly), and (wasting time) watching HGTV.

# ACKNOWLEDGMENTS

~

**MY HEARTFELT THANKS:**

To Al Stewart, for writing "House of Clocks," a song that sounded so eerily like Ford Chase that it inspired me to rewrite the beginning of his story to make it start on St. Swithin's Day (check out Mr. Stewart's album *Down in the Cellar* if you'd like to hear it).

To Geoff Pavitt, Facilities Manager at Gresham College, for finding an incredible amount of information for me, including stuff I didn't even know I needed until he sent it.

To librarian Claire Andrews, at the Heritage Park Library in Irvine, California, for all her hard work finding obscure 300-year-old books and arranging inter-library loans for me.

To Peter Do and Martha Altieri, for the Latin translation.

To my dad, Herb Royal, for *attempting* the Latin translation.

To all the honorary Chase cousins in my Chase Family Readers Group, for their enthusiastic support.

And, as always, to all my readers.

Thank you, one and all!

# CONTACT INFORMATION

**Lauren's Newsletter**

littl.ink/LaurensNews

**Facebook Readers Group**

facebook.com/groups/ChaseFamilyReaders

**Facebook Page**

facebook.com/LaurenRoyal

**Website**

www.LaurenRoyal.com